Also by Jane Heller

Cha Cha Cha

The Club

Infernal Affairs

Princess Charming

Crystal Clear

Jane Heller

Sis Boom Bah

St. Martin's Press ● New York

BOOK DESIGN BY JUDITH STAGNITTO ABBATE

Library of Congress Cataloging-in-Publication Data

Heller, Jane.
Sis boom bah : a novel / by Jane Heller.—1st U.S. ed.
p.   cm.
ISBN 0-312-20312-8
I. Title.
PS3558.E4757S57   1999
813'.54—dc21   99-18057
CIP

First Edition: June 1999

10   9   8   7   6   5   4   3   2   1

For my sister, Susan Alexander

Acknowledgments

*S*is *Boom Bah* is a work of fiction and, therefore, its characters and the situations in which they find themselves are entirely my creations. Its setting, on the other hand, is in and around Stuart, Florida, where I live, and many of the places mentioned in the novel are those which I have frequented and enjoyed.

Several "locals" were extremely generous with their time as I was writing the book, offering their ideas and expertise. Thanks to: Patricia Austin; Ginger Smith Baldwin; Steve Bernardi; Eden Cross; Marc "Answer Man" Cross; David Delmas, R. PH.; Kathy Erickson, R.N.C.; Paul Hartnett; Beverly Bevis Jones; Ruth Ross; Cindy

Rybovich; James Sospko, Esq.; Mary Anne Tonnacliff, R.N.C.; and John Ziegler.

Thanks, too, to the following law enforcement professionals: Lt. Sarah Marich, Criminal Investigations Division, Martin County Sheriff's Office; Lt. Glen Lockwood, Warrants & Extraditions Division, Martin County Sheriff's Department; and Wilbur C. Kirchner, Chief of Police, Sewall's Point. (Forgive me for taking liberties with the facts for the sake of the story!)

Enormous thanks to Allison Seifer Poole, who handled every research question with efficiency and humor. Allison: I can't imagine writing another one without you. More thanks to Jeri Butler, whose piece about me in the *Palm Beach Post* inspired Allison to contact me.

Others who were tremendously helpful: Henry Spector, M.D., who advised me on medical matters; and Laurence Caso, the smartest (and nicest) man ever to work in daytime television.

Special thanks to Ellen Levine, who is everything a writer could hope for in a literary agent; Louise Quayle, who makes the complicated business of selling foreign rights look easy; my editor and champion, Jennifer Enderlin, whose enthusiasm for my work continues to be a revelation to me; and Ruth Harris, who is not only my friend and sounding board but the undisputed Title Queen.

Oh, and thanks to all the sisters who shared their tales of woe with me. (You know who you are.)

Last but hardly least, thanks to Michael Forester, my husband, who critiques my books before the "professionals" do and is my partner in every sense of the word.

Part
One

Chapter One

If my sister were my husband, I'd divorce her."

"You don't have a husband, Deborah," my mother reminded me. "Forty-three years old and still no husband." I could feel her disappointment coursing through the telephone wires.

"I was talking about my relationship with Sharon, Mom," I said. "About the fact that when you're incompatible with your spouse, you can divorce him, yet when you're incompatible with your sister, you're stuck with her for life. It doesn't seem fair somehow."

"What doesn't, dear?"

My mother wasn't senile, just in denial when it came to her two daughters and their lifelong bickering. She spoke of her "girls" as if

Sharon and I were the chummiest of chums, as if she didn't realize that my sister and I had nothing in common except the accident of our births. She ignored our snits, our spats, our she-did-its; made light of the potshots we regularly took at each other; pretended there weren't months, even years, during which we were estranged.

"Never mind," I said. "About divorcing Sharon, I mean. Divorcing her would be a non-event at this point. Everybody's already done it."

Well, not *everybody*. The truth was, three men had divorced my sister. Husband number one was a TWA pilot who fell in love with a flight attendant during a long layover in Paris and never came home. Husband number two was a polygamist who was married to four other women in four other states and is presently serving a long prison sentence. Husband number three, a dashing fellow, decided that he no longer wanted to *be* a fellow, announcing on his forty-fifth birthday that he intended to undergo a "sexual reallignment." Now I ask you: Is it any wonder that Norman, Sharon's eighteen-year-old son by the polygamist, chose military school over Syracuse, becoming one of the only Jewish cadets ever to attend the Citadel?

Not that *my* track record was so hot. Sharon may have been a compulsive marrier who'd waltz down the aisle with just about any man who asked her, but I too had involved myself with an embarrassing cast of characters. Like the bond trader who spent the last six months of our relationship bonding with my best friend on her waterbed. Like the computer programmer who bought me a diamond ring from Cartier that was really a cubic zirconium knockoff he'd hondled from a street vendor. Like the traveling salesman who shouted out the names of other women whenever we had sex and expected me to believe it was because he had Tourette's syndrome. As I said, my judgment wasn't exactly unerring when it came to men, but at least I didn't *marry* the bozos.

"About the party," said my mother, pulling me back into the conversation, "you *will* fly down for it, won't you, dear? It isn't every day that I turn seventy-five."

The purpose of her long-distance phone call that Sunday afternoon in January had been to inform me that Sharon, the dreaded sibling, was hosting a birthday luncheon for her the following month and that I was expected to drop everything and be there. Never mind that I lived a thousand miles away in Manhattan. Never mind that I had an extremely demanding job as a writer for the venerable *From This Day Forward*, the longest-running daytime drama on television. Never mind that I was about to enter into a thrilling affair with one of the show's hunkiest actors and that the last thing I wanted to do at such a crucial stage in the romance was leave town. (Yes, I'd been unlucky in love in the past, but hope springs eternal.) Apparently, Sharon had decided—without consulting me, of course—that the party was to be held in Florida, where she and my mother resided.

"Please, Deborah. I would love it if both my girls were there," my mother persisted.

"But your girls haven't spoken to each other in two years, ever since we had that squabble over Lester."

"Who?"

"Lester. Sharon's third husband. The one who looked better in her lingerie than she did."

"Oh, that one."

"Yes. After she and Lester broke up, I merely suggested—because I *cared*—that she shouldn't rush into marriage, that it was important to get to know the man first. And what was her response? 'You're just jealous, Deborah, because you couldn't get a man to marry you if you paid him.' Then I said something equally childish, and she slammed down the phone. In a way, it's been a relief not to have spoken to her in two years, sort of like having an illness and being in remission."

"Nonsense. You and Sharon are sisters, and sisters should communicate with each other. At their *mother's* birthday party, for instance."

"If I show up at the party we'll communicate all right, but it'll be the same old nastiness. I'll say, 'Hello, Sharon, you're looking well.' Then she'll say, 'So are you, Deborah, although I thought shoulder pads went out with Joan Crawford.' Then I'll be forced to retaliate with, 'Yes, but fortunately for you, Sharon, padded bras have made a comeback.' It'll be ugly, Mom. I'm telling you."

"And I'm telling *you* that you'd be pleasantly surprised if you came. I think Sharon would *appreciate* it if you were there."

"Oh, Mom." I sighed, wishing she would get it. "Sharon would *appreciate* it if I were in Mogadishu."

"Deborah."

"What I'm trying to say is that she likes me far away, and the feeling's mutual."

It was sad, really. Sharon was two years older than I was, my contemporary. We should have been pals, buddies, confidantes. But for some reason she resented me, had always resented me, and I honestly didn't know what I had done to inspire her ill will. Yes, she was the firstborn, and yes, firstborns often resent the little squirts with whom they're made to share their toys, their friends, their parents. Like many older siblings, Sharon was told she couldn't go to the movies or the hamburger place or the school picnic unless she dragged her baby sister along, only to have me act up and ruin her fun. But I had loved her so when we were kids, loved tagging along on her adventures. I had idolized her, revered her, tried to imitate the way she talked, walked, dressed. I was grateful to her for looking out for me and sorry for the burden I must have been, and I'd said so on numerous occasions. Why didn't any of that count? Why did she have to drag her bitterness toward me into adulthood? Why did she have to give me a dig, a zinger, a putdown every time we saw each other? And worse, why did I have to react the way I did, allowing her to push my buttons, as they say? Why did I have to fire a zinger right back at her and then retreat, withdraw, wither under the weight of her simmering rage? Wasn't it time to let it all go?

"Where is Sharon having the luncheon?" I asked my mother, knowing I would probably give in and attend the party, in spite of my protests.

"At her house. She insisted."

Insisting came as naturally to my sister as breathing. "So she's put herself in *charge* of your birthday, just like she puts herself in charge of everything."

"Well, she *is* a professional party-giver, Deborah."

I couldn't argue with my mother there. Sharon was a wedding planner. ("Wedding architect" was what it said on her business card.) For those who could afford her services, she coordinated virtually every aspect of her clients' nuptials—the florist, the caterer, the photographer, et cetera. She even pumped the bride and groom for information about their guests and then drew up seating plans in an effort to avoid the sort of petty slights that were the hallmark of her relationship with me. Though she had clients up and down south Florida's east coast, the bulk of her business came from Boca Raton, aka "Boca," a sort of Great Neck with palm trees. Sharon was a big success in Boca, not only because she lived there (in a gated golf community where the houses are enormous and right on top of each other—"McMansions," I call them), but because the kind of wedding that was her signature—ostentatious, glitzy, unrestrained—was so, well, *Boca*. In Boca, where even the maids wear Rolexes, you either had a Sharon Peltz wedding or you didn't get married at all.

"You could fly down for the weekend and stay with me," my mother suggested. "It's awfully cold up there in New York, isn't it?"

"Very," I said, peering down at the ratty flannel nightgown and wool socks I was wearing. Even though there was plenty of heat in my apartment—that awful, dry heat that makes your skin crack, not to mention your scalp flake—I couldn't get warm, couldn't thaw out. Maybe a trip to Florida wasn't a bad idea after all. "You're right, Mom," I said finally. "Your seventy-fifth birthday *is* special and I wouldn't miss it for the world. I'll make plane reservations as soon as we hang up."

Okay, I told myself. So you'll have to put up with Sharon for an afternoon. You're a big girl. You'll live.

I brightened at the thought of seeing my mother and of being able to mellow out at her house in Sewall's Point, a lush, tropical peninsula linked by a causeway to the city of Stuart, about an hour north of Palm Beach.

She and my father had bought the place, a rustic, two-story, wood-frame house overlooking the St. Lucie River, as a winter escape for the family when Sharon and I were in high school. My father, a doctor in Westport, Connecticut, had dreamed of living in Florida full-time once he retired, but he died of cancer just before his sixty-second birthday and never realized his dream. A year-to-the-day after his funeral, my mother realized it for him: she sold our house in Westport, packed up her belongings, and moved them and herself to Sewall's Point. Before long, she made friends in the quiet, close-knit community, did volunteer work for the Council on Aging, the Historical Society, and other nonprofit agencies, and eventually took a more challenging volunteer job, becoming a mediator in small-claims court, of all things. Her mission was to get people who were suing each other to settle their differences without having to go to trial.

I found it pretty ironic that she spent several days a month en-couraging plaintiffs and defendants to come to a compromise, yet she couldn't get her own children to agree on much of anything. We couldn't even agree on Stuart versus Boca. While I thought Stuart was uniquely charming in its low-key, unhurried lifestyle, Sharon found the place deadly dull, provincial, a cultural wasteland. (This from a woman whose idea of "culture" was watching brides and grooms do the Macarena.) As a result, Sharon settled in Boca after college, which was fine and dandy with me; whenever I visited my mother, I felt secure in the knowledge that my sister was an hour and a half away.

I said goodbye to my mother, booked the flights, and hurried into the shower. Philip Wiley, the hunky actor I mentioned earlier, was picking me up at seven, and while I still had an hour before he arrived, I wanted to take my time getting ready.

You see, in the six years I'd worked for *From This Day Forward,* I had never dated an actor from the show, never even had a brief dalliance with one. As a result, I was giddy with the novelty of the situation, giddy with the idea that a catch like Philip Wiley, who had worked with—done love scenes with—the most beautiful women in the world, was interested in *me.*

Not that I'm a dog or anything. I will never be mistaken for one of those stunning creatures who appears on soap operas, but I have what my mother calls a "sweet face," which I take to mean that I am neither beautiful nor homely but winsome, perhaps because I smile a lot, as opposed to my sister, who does not. (Not at me, anyway.) What's more, while my hair isn't worn in a particular *style,* other than it's shoulder-length and parted on the right, it's thick and glossy and a rather lustrous reddish-brown, and no matter how humid the conditions, it doesn't go limp on me. As for my figure, it's about what you'd expect for a forty-three-year-old woman with a sedentary job and a fondness for moo shu pork. In other words, I still get the occasional wolf whistles from construction workers, but I could stand to lose a few pounds.

When my doorbell rang at just after seven o'clock, I practically leapt across the apartment to answer it.

"Hey, don't you look super," Philip observed as I opened the door. A tall, fortyish, sandy-haired ex-model who'd been raised in London and spoke with a clipped, veddy veddy British accent, Philip played the role of Holden Halsey on our show. His character was the long-lost brother of Jenny Halsey Slater Peters Dyer Ruzetsky, a woman who'd been married even more times than my sister.

"Thanks for the compliment," I said. "Please. Come in."

"Love to," he said. Then he turned suddenly, grabbed me by the shoulders, and kissed me.

Gee, this guy doesn't waste any time, I thought as the kissing went on for several seconds, several very stirring seconds.

"So this is where you live, Deborah," he said, finally coming up for air. He surveyed my living room, a generic rectangular space that I had furnished from a Pottery Barn catalog. Buckingham Palace it wasn't.

"Yes, this is home. Let me take your coat," I said, and offered him a drink.

"Scotch would be lovely. With a splash of soda and a wedge of lemon, if you've got it." Philip removed his coat and handed it to me, flashing me his Holden Halsey grin, a veritable spectacle of perfectly aligned white teeth. I was tempted to ask if they'd been bleached and/or bonded, but I already knew the answer. There wasn't a cast member on the show whose body parts hadn't been enhanced in some way.

I prepared his scotch and poured myself a glass of wine, placed both drinks on a tray along with cocktail napkins and a bowl of salted peanuts, and hurried back into the living room.

Philip wasn't there.

"Philip?" I said, wondering if he had changed his mind about our date. "Hello?"

When I got no response, I set the tray down on the coffee table and went to look for him, eventually finding him in the guest room that doubled as my office. He was standing beside my desk, his head buried in a file folder marked "From This Day Forward #12,136."

"Philip?" I said. He jumped. I had startled him. "What are you doing?"

He slid the folder back onto my desk and smiled sheepishly, a kid caught with his hand in the cookie jar.

"I came upon the file quite by accident," he said, batting his long golden lashes at me. "I hope you're not angry, Deborah."

"Actors aren't supposed to read our breakdowns," I reminded him, a "breakdown" being a scene-by-scene outline of each episode. "Woody's adamant about that."

Woody Davenport, the head writer of *From This Day Forward,* was my boss, responsible for creating the overall "bibles" of the show, the long-term storylines covering up to a year's worth of plots, characters, cliffhangers, and resolutions.

"You wanted to find out what's going to happen with Holden. Is that why you read the breakdown?" I asked.

"Well, I *was* curious to see where Woody's taking the character," he admitted.

"He would have a fit if I told him," I said. "He really does have a cardinal rule about this."

It's a given in the business: Let actors in on the future of their characters and the next thing you know they're demanding rewrites, calling their agents, whining, and the show becomes a cesspool of battling egos.

"Then don't tell him," said Philip. "It won't happen again, so why raise his blood pressure?"

I wasn't sure what to do. I didn't want to lose my job, but I didn't want to lose Philip, either.

"You know, I'd never seen a breakdown before," Philip mused. "I had no idea how hard you must work. All those pages and pages you've got to come up with every week, the carefully laid-out scenes, the dramatic moments, the continuity from show to show. You're very good, Deborah. Very talented."

"Oh. Well. Do you think so?"

"I do indeed. *I* certainly couldn't write a breakdown. It takes a special kind of skill that I don't have. You, on the other hand, have it—to the max."

I felt my expression soften. "It's nice to have the positive feedback, Philip. Thanks."

Sensing that he had melted my anger, that his flattery had melted it, he walked toward me and took me in his arms. "I meant what I said about poking my nose where it doesn't belong. It won't happen again, Deborah. Forgive me."

He drew my face close to his and kissed me, more insistently this time. I forgave him. Who wouldn't?

We returned to the living room, arm in arm, sipped our drinks, and went to dinner. At the restaurant, Philip was extremely attentive to me—reverential, almost—even while signing autographs. He held my hand, then brought it to his lips and kissed it—palm, fingers, knuckles, you name it. By the time dessert and coffee were served, I had forgotten about the incident in my apartment involving the breakdown.

Seconds after bringing me home, Philip was all over me, murmuring terms of endearment to me as he nibbled away at my lips. I cut things short, though, reminding him that I had to get up early for Woody's Monday meeting, an exhausting, day-long event that was held at his extravagantly decorated Park Avenue apartment and was mandatory for breakdown writers.

"When can I see you again?" Philip asked as we stood by the door. "Next weekend? Friday night? The sooner the better."

"Friday night would be wonderful," I said, flushed with the intensity of his ardor and my own.

We kissed goodnight and then he left.

I leaned against the door for several minutes, eyes closed, heart racing, reliving Philip's every word and gesture. It seemed to me that I had finally managed to snare a good one. I congratulated myself.

Chapter Two

Woody Davenport was a legend in the field of daytime television, a larger-than-life figure whose flair for the dramatic was evident in his appearance as well as his work. At six-feet-six inches tall, he literally towered over us, his blue-black toupee combed into a great pompadour that added another two or three inches to his height. He wore flamboyant neckties, drank copious amounts of alcohol, bedded women of all ages. He was a character in an industry of characters, but most significantly he was a survivor; while a parade of executive producers had come and gone during his seventeen years with *From This Day Forward,* Woody remained. No one could even contemplate the show without him. I certainly couldn't, and neither could the other four writers who convened in his living room, an enormous high-ceilinged space decorated in a classic Greek motif. (I found his affinity for columns, arches, and moldings amusing since he grew up on a farm in Kansas, not the Parthenon.)

It was business as usual that particular Monday until we broke for lunch. Helen Mincer, a tart-tongued fifty-something who had joined our writing staff after stints at *The Bold and the Beautiful*, *The Young and the Restless*, and *General Hospital*, approached me at the buffet table and said she'd heard I was seeing Philip. As Helen is an incredible busybody, I was not surprised that she knew about Philip and me. What surprised me—floored me—was what came next.

"Stay away from the guy," she warned. "He hits on writers so he can sneak into their offices to read their breakdowns. He figures if he gets a look at the episodes in advance, he'll have more control over his storylines and grab more air time."

I felt my cheeks flame, remembering the night before, when I had found Philip in my office reading *my* breakdown.

"I heard this from three different writers on *General Hospital*," she added for good measure. "Your boyfriend pulled his crap on all of them."

I was stunned, but I refused to believe Helen. Not right away.

"If Philip 'hits on writers,' as you put it, why hasn't he hit on Nancy or Kiki or Faith?" I asked, referring to the show's other three breakdown writers.

"Because Nancy's married. Kiki's Woody's girl. And Faith's a lesbian."

"Faith's a lesbian?"

"Boy. You *are* out of the loop."

Obviously. "What about you, Helen? Why hasn't Philip gone after you and *your* breakdowns?"

"He knows I'm on to him," she replied. "He wouldn't dare try his shit with me."

"But he'd try it with *me,* is that it?"

Helen shrugged. "You're the one he's romancing."

I was tortured by Helen's bombshell, couldn't decide whether to trust her or Philip. But as I sat at my computer the next day, trying in vain to crank out my weekly writing assignment, I knew I had to put myself out of my misery, knew I had to find out if Philip Wiley was a prize or a prick.

And so I came up with a plan. When he telephoned about our getting together Friday night, I suggested that we have dinner at my place. I was going to write a bogus breakdown in which his character, Holden Halsey, would be killed off the show—an outline that I would leave in a folder on my desk, right where he could see it if he happened to wander into my office while I was busy cooking.

One way or another, I'll have my answer, I vowed.

Not the answer I wanted, unfortunately. I was whisking up a nifty vinaigrette Friday night, while Philip was supposedly in the living room relaxing, when he stormed into the kitchen, waving the counterfeit outline in the air, his pretty-boy face contorted with anger.

"Woody's killed me off!" he shouted. "He's bloody well gone and killed me off! He won't get away with it, do you hear me? Do you?"

"The whole building can hear you, Philip." So he took the bait, I thought, my heart sinking. The guy actually slithered into my office the minute my back was turned and read the breakdown, the slimeball.

I was disappointed but not devastated, I realized, as Philip ranted and raved about his contract, his agent, his fans. Maybe it was because Helen had prepared me for this outcome. Maybe it was because I'd only had one real date with Philip and hadn't invested that much time and energy in our relationship. Or maybe it was because my romances regularly ended badly and so what else was new? Still, I didn't appreciate being had.

"You haven't been written out of the show, Philip," I told him as I poured the vinaigrette down the drain, along with the beef stew I'd prepared. "The breakdown you read was a decoy. I left it on my desk purposely. To see if you were as big a rat as Helen Mincer said you were. If you'd read the real breakdown, the one I handed in this morning, you'd have learned that you've got a juicy storyline coming up. Holden is going to be a hero, Philip, and you're going to be a star."

He stared at me. "A star?"

"A big star."

"A big star." His eyes widened and the Holden Halsey grin reappeared. Then came the laugh. Ha ha ha ha ha. As if his loathsome behavior toward me had merely been a practical joke. It occurred to me that of all the creeps I'd dated over the years, Philip Wiley was the creepiest.

I pushed him out the door and locked it.

I was about to run off into the living room, fling myself onto the sofa, and have a good cry when the phone rang. It was Helen.

"You were right about Philip, if that's why you're calling," I said.

"It isn't," she said. "Woody's been fired. The network's gonna announce it tomorrow."

I was dumbstruck. Woody canned? *The* Woody Davenport? After nearly twenty years at *From This Day Forward*? How would the show survive without him? How would I survive without him? Why would the network want to get rid of him?

Helen explained that he was taking the fall because our ratings were down—and because he was fifty-seven.

"They're bringing in a team of head writers to replace Woody, all of them in their thirties," she said. "Their mandate is to attract a younger audience to the show."

"Oh, great. We'll be writing about teenagers now."

"If we're still writing."

"You don't think—"

"You know what happens when there's a shakeup. Nobody's job is safe. I've already got a call in to a producer-friend of mine at *Another World*. If you want, I'll put in a good word for you, Deborah."

I thanked Helen, but at that moment, writing for a soap opera seemed redundant.

The new head writers were three women who had never watched daytime television, let alone worked in it. One came to our show straight from the editorial department of Harlequin Romances. Another had produced and directed an episode of *Baywatch*. And the third had written the copy for that series of television commercials in which a man and a woman fall in love after discovering their shared affection for a particular brand of coffee. I mean, what was the network thinking?

Not that I wasn't a good soldier. I went to my new bosses' weekly story meetings, never mentioning Woody unless they mentioned him first, never appearing disdainful of their lack of experience, never even rolling my eyes when one of them (the advertising genius) suggested we conduct focus groups to determine whether the show was resonating with younger viewers. I played the game, handed in my breakdowns, deposited my checks in the bank. I steeled myself to the turmoil that was going on around me, to the politicking, the backstabbing, the bitching. I did not even flinch when Helen informed me that the ex-Harlequin editor was dating Philip.

I felt lucky to have a job—a well-paying job at that—but, deep down, I was miserable. I yearned for the old days, when the very idea of working with actors and actresses was a thrill. I had loved my job then, loved seeing my episodes broadcast on millions of TV sets, even loved the pressure of meeting deadlines. It hadn't mattered a bit that I wasn't writing for *Masterpiece Theatre*, that my characters regularly developed amnesia, returned from the dead, and ran off with mysterious monarchs of tiny foreign countries. I'd gotten a kick out of the melodrama that defines soap operas, the zany plot twists, the overheated love scenes. But times had changed. I was no longer the wide-eyed ingenue, seduced by what I perceived to be the glamour of show business. I was tired and jaded and bored. I was a breakdown writer heading for a breakdown.

Of course, what finally broke me down wasn't the job or missing Woody or even the aborted fling with Philip. It was the burglary.

It happened on the first Monday in February, the week I was leaving for Florida for my mother's birthday party. I'd gone to the head writers' story meeting and when I'd returned to my apartment at about eight o'clock that night, I inserted my key in the lock only to find that the door was already open. Assuming I'd simply forgotten to lock it, I stepped inside, expecting to find everything just as it had been earlier in the day. I was wrong.

I guess I'd been naive about crime up to that point. Yes, I'd lived in Manhattan for nearly twenty years and was hardly unaware that the Big Apple had its share of Bad Apples. But I had never been victimized by crime, never even had my purse snatched, and so I'd been lulled into the conceit that bad things happen to *other* people.

And then I walked into my apartment that night and saw that the place had been ransacked, my Pottery Barn furnishings trashed. Gone was my computer. Gone was my TV. Gone was my jewelry, including the gold cufflinks that had belonged to my father and meant more to me than everything I owned. Gone was my sense of security.

"Looks like an inside job," said the police officer in charge, a world-weary veteran of the force, judging by his craggy face and air of resignation. "Someone in the building. One of the doormen, maybe."

"Should I speak to the super about it?" I asked.

"You want my advice?" said the cop. "Move. Once these people see your place is vulnerable, they'll wait for you to replace all the stuff they took, then they'll break in and clean you out again."

"Not if you catch them first."

He shrugged.

"So the chances are, you won't catch them?"

"Like I said, if I was you, I'd move."

The rest of the week was a blur. There was my wreck of an apartment to tidy up, as well as new locks to be installed. There were calls to my insurance company to ensure that my claim would be processed quickly. There were trips back and forth to the production office so I could borrow one of the computers. There were hours and hours of work on my breakdown, in order to finish it by Friday. And there was packing to be done, as my flight to Florida was leaving LaGuardia at five P.M. the same day.

I accomplished it all, though, and by seven-thirty on Friday night, the plane had landed at Palm Beach International Airport and my mother was waiting at the gate to greet me.

"Yoo-hoo! Here I am, Deborah!" she called out when she spotted me entering the terminal. She waved her handbag in the air to catch my attention and inadvertently hit a ticket agent upside the head.

I waved back, careful not to hit anyone, and before I knew it I was rushing into my mother's arms like a six-year-old with a boo-boo.

"Deborah," she said soothingly as she patted my back. "My little girl."

She was the one who was little, I was startled to see. She had shrunk considerably over the past few years, but she seemed especially frail this time, breakable almost. Nevertheless, Lenore Peltz was an attractive woman who looked younger than seventy-five, I thought. She had a trim figure and wavy, silvery hair and an expressiveness that automatically drew people to her. But it was her eyes that were showstoppers. "Tiffany blue," my sister, the shopper, had labeled their color. They were exquisite and spectacular and the first thing you noticed about my mother when you were introduced to her; the only negative about them was that neither Sharon nor I had inherited them.

"I'm so glad I came for your birthday, Mom," I said, still clinging to her. "I really needed a break."

"Work getting you down, dear?" she asked. She stroked my cheek in a way that only a mother can stroke a cheek.

"Among other things," I said. "I'll explain it all when we get to the house, okay?"

She regarded me. "This isn't about Sharon, is it? Please tell me it isn't."

"No, Mom. It has nothing to do with Sharon."

She breathed a sigh of relief. "Then whatever it is, we'll just put our heads together and figure out what to do about it, like we've done since you were a child."

I smiled. My mother, the mediator. My mother, the problem-solver. My mother, the sweetheart. How could such a nice, even-tempered woman have produced such quarrelsome offspring? I wondered. And then I reminded myself that I'd had two parents.

———

We headed north from the airport on I-95, passing the exits for Riviera Beach, Palm Beach Gardens, Jupiter, and Hobe Sound before getting off in Stuart. The drive took a little over an hour. It would have taken less time but my mother had to stop for gas. She always had to stop for gas. Her Oldsmobile Delta 88 was the size of the *QE2* and only got ten miles to the gallon. The other problem with the car was that she could barely see over its steering wheel unless she sat on a telephone book. I used to wonder why she didn't get a newer, more compact car, but then I realized that many of her contemporaries in Florida also drove big old boats and that it must be a generational thing.

It was close to nine-thirty when we finally crossed the Evans Crary Bridge, over the St. Lucie River and onto the peninsula of Sewall's Point.

My mother had updated the house over the years—fresh coat of paint, new carpet, new kitchen appliances—but it was still the rustic 1970s vacation home I remembered, the tropical getaway my father had adored. Set on three acres amid what was almost junglelike foliage, the house was perched on stilts and overlooked the St. Lucie River and, beyond, the estates along Stuart's St. Lucie Boulevard.

There were two staircases leading up to the house plus another stairway inside, and as I mounted them I wondered how much longer my mother would be able to. No, being seventy-five didn't make her an invalid, but I knew there would come a time when the house would be a handful for her, a time when climbing stairs would be an exertion, if not an impossibility.

After I put my things away in one of the two guest bedrooms, I joined my mother in the kitchen. While I told her my troubles, we feasted on the chicken she'd roasted earlier.

"Maybe it's time to move out of the city," she said when I had come to the end of the sorry saga.

"That's what the cop said," I remarked. "But where would I go?"

"How about right here? You could bunk in with me. You've always loved this house."

"I know, but at forty-three I shouldn't be freeloading off my mother."

"Then you'll find your own place nearby, settle down, meet a nice man."

"No offense, Mom, but all the men around here are your age."

"Yes, and the women they're interested in are *your* age."

I laughed. "Men aren't a priority at the moment. It's my lifestyle I'm rethinking. I'm looking for less stress, more fulfillment."

"I'll say it again, dear. Move to Stuart. And forget that crack of mine about the old men. You'd be surprised how many young people live here now."

"Actually, I wouldn't be surprised. I've been reading these magazine articles about people my age who are fleeing the cities for small towns like Stuart. They're giving up big careers so they can become chefs, run B&Bs, learn how to paint."

"You used to paint when you were in high school, dear. Self-portraits, wasn't it?"

"No. Sharon was the one who painted self-portraits, although they all came out looking like Natalie Wood." (The only characteristic Sharon shared with Natalie Wood was an attachment to Robert Wagner.) "I painted bowls of fruit, vases of flowers, that sort of thing."

"Well, you could pick it up again, couldn't you? Get a job and paint in your spare time."

"Possibly. But what kind of jobs do they have in this area? Stuart isn't exactly a bustling industrial center."

"No, but it just dawned on me that Melinda Carr, the director of the Historical Society, mentioned at lunch the other day that she's got a job opening. I used to be a volunteer for the society, remember, dear? When I worked at the Elliot Museum out on Hutchinson Island?"

I nodded. Hutchinson Island is a barrier island famous for its ocean beaches. Accessed from Sewall's Point by a bridge spanning the Indian River, it's Stuart's answer to Miami Beach, its wall-to-wall condos rising high over the Atlantic, its population of five thousand doubling during the winter months. I spent many a holiday weekend there when I was in college, walking on the beach, picking up shells, wondering what I would be when I grew up. Little did I know I'd still be wondering at age forty-three.

"Anyway," my mother went on, "Melinda said they need a keeper."

"Don't we all."

"That's what she called the position, Deborah. A keeper. Like a lighthouse keeper. I guess she means a caretaker, you know?"

"Did she say what, exactly, needs caretaking?"

"Yes. The House of Refuge over on MacArthur Boulevard."

I perked up. Gilbert's Bar House of Refuge, as it's more formally known, is a pea-green, wood-frame building that was erected on a rocky stretch of Hutchinson Island coastline over a hundred years ago as a safe haven for shipwrecked sailors. Restored by the county and listed in the National Register of Historic Places, it's open to the public as a museum, offering crusty old nautical charm and a view to die for. "So the Historical Society wants someone to run the House of Refuge?" I asked.

My mother shook her head. "No, just to live in the keeper's cottage next door. To make sure the House of Refuge doesn't fall down, probably. I've never been inside the cottage, but Melinda said it has a bedroom, living room, kitchen, office, and, best of all, a porch facing the ocean. You wouldn't make close to the kind of money your soap opera pays you, but you'd make something and you'd be able to live right on the water, rent-free. You could paint, read, decide what you want to do with the rest of your life. It could be a good temporary solution, don't you think?"

"Absolutely." The idea of spending six months or even a year living on the ocean, all by myself, with no thieving doormen to tip, no weekly breakdowns to write, no self-absorbed actors to dump, practically had me drooling. "But there's got to be a catch. The job sounds too good to be true."

"Well, you might not be qualified for it."

I laughed. "You mean, I might be *over*qualified for it, don't you?"

"No. I mean, they might want someone with experience in building maintenance, someone who can get things fixed."

"I can get things fixed," I told my mother. "I just pick up the phone and call someone to fix them. I did it all the time in my apartment. I was on very good terms with the super."

Lenore Peltz smiled. "Think about it over the weekend. If you're really serious about moving out of the city, I'll call Melinda and try to arrange an interview for you. Meanwhile, it's late and I've got a big day tomorrow. The luncheon's at noon, but Sharon wants us down in Boca at eleven."

"Why, so she can have an extra hour to vilify me?"

"Deborah."

I hugged my mother. "You go to bed. I'll clean up the kitchen."

She nodded. "Tomorrow will turn out better than you think. I have a feeling that you and your sister will finally bury the hachet."

Yeah. In each other, I thought, as I kissed my mother goodnight.

Chapter Three

After my mother and I pulled into Broken Sound, the golf community where Sharon lived (I joked that it should be called "Broken Record," because she was one), we made our way through the maze of streets into her brick-paved, circular driveway. There, we were greeted by a man wearing a double-breasted suit, slicked-back dark hair, and a fake handlebar mustache. As he helped us out of the car, he flashed us the gun that was wedged inside his waistband. I have some pretty scary relatives, but this guy wasn't one of them.

"Who's he?" I whispered to my mother. "He looks like a gangster."

"He's supposed to," she whispered back. "He goes with Sharon's theme for my party."

"Her theme?"

"Yes, dear. You know, the way she has themes for her weddings? Since I was born in 1924, she decided to have a Roaring Twenties birthday party for me. This man's the valet parking attendant."

I smiled weakly and helped my mother to the front door.

She rang the bell. Seconds later, a flapper let us in—a young redhead in a black satin dress and matching feather boa. No, she wasn't a family member, either.

"You must be Mrs. Peltz," she said, shaking my mother's hand. "I'm Paula, Sharon's assistant. I've heard so much about you."

"Nice things, I hope," said my mother. She turned to me. "And this is Deborah, my other daughter."

Paula did not shake my hand. "I've heard a lot about you too," she said instead.

Paula guided us inside her boss's palace with its requisite vaulted ceilings, marble floors, and faux-finished painted walls. For the special occasion, it had been schmaltzed up with little touches from the '20s—music from the period, models of antique cars, magazine articles about Douglas Fairbanks and Mary Pickford. Most touchingly, Sharon had blown up a dozen grainy, sepia-toned photographs of my mother when she was a child, framed the pictures, and displayed them in the living room, where she had also hung a huge banner, proclaiming:

HAPPY SEVENTY-FIFTH BIRTHDAY TO LENORE!
AND HERE'S TO ANOTHER SEVENTY-FIVE MORE!

A regular Emily Dickinson, my sister.

My mother seemed genuinely moved by the to-do in her honor. "I can't believe the trouble Sharon went to," she marveled, shaking her head. "She really outdid herself, don't you think, Deborah?"

"Oh, yes," I said, feeling desperately inadequate suddenly. All I'd done for my mother's seventy-fifth birthday was to show up. Sure, I'd gotten her a gift—a cashmere sweater from Saks—but I still felt like a slug, compared to you-know-who. It wasn't so much that I hadn't helped with the party—Sharon hadn't even called to invite me, let alone included me in the planning. It was that it hadn't occurred to me that my mother needed or wanted such a flashy display to mark her seventy-fifth year. She'd always seemed content to celebrate her birthdays quietly, with little fanfare, particularly after my father died. But there she was, obviously thrilled by Sharon's effort and creativity and extravagance, and the whole thing made me want to wrap Paula's feather boa around my neck and strangle myself.

"If only you *could* live another seventy-five years," I told my mother. "Forever would be okay too." It was important that she knew I loved her, banner or no banner. And not just because I was feeling competitive with Sharon. I really did think she was a wonderful mother. Aside from her inability to face her daughters' antipathy toward each other, aside from her often too-stiff upper lip when it came to sharing her own problems, aside from her unwillingness to acknowledge that she ever *had* any problems, Lenore Peltz was the type of mom you could be proud of. She was affectionate, fair-minded, supportive without being possessive. She offered advice but didn't nag, for the most part. She even told jokes every now and then, although in recent years she couldn't remember the punch lines. When I was growing up, it was my father who was God (it's impossible to upstage a kindly general practitioner who makes house calls), but it was my mother who was *there.* She made sure that we were fed and clothed, helped us with our homework, and meted out our punishments. She was a '50s wife, but she was no June Cleaver leaving it to big Ward to make the tough decisions. While my father was out saving the good people of Westport from ailments of varying degrees of severity, she rolled up her sleeves and raised two children.

The fact that her two children still behaved like children wasn't her fault. As I said before, we had a father.

I was pondering the impact he had on my relationship with Sharon when she entered the room on a dead run, breathless, harried, focused on her responsibilities as the hostess, firing instructions at Paula, the flapper-assistant.

So she's a blonde now, I mused, noticing that her once-brown, chin-length hair was a rather loud reddish-gold.

Otherwise she looked just as she had the last time I'd seen her—

petite like my mother, pretty in a calculated, heavily made-up way, and pinched, really tight, as if there were too many tasks for even a little dynamo like her to complete. That was another thing about my sister: she was so capable yet so joyless; superwoman and supervictim, simultaneously.

"Here you are, Mom," she said, hugging my mother, chatting with her about party decorations, pretending I wasn't standing there. I cleared my throat. She turned, unable to avoid me without seeming totally out of it. "Oh, and here's Deborah. It's been so long I hardly recognized you." She hesitated, then stepped forward and air-kissed me, with the affection of a python.

"It's good to see you, Sharon," I said, determined to at least start things off on a positive note, knowing how quickly they could deteriorate. "I love your dress." She was not attired in Roaring '20s garb—that was for the hired help, apparently. She was wearing a turquoise linen dress adorned with large gold buttons that were nearly the same color as her newly golden hair. Very Boca.

She thanked me and then appraised my outfit, a loose-fitting cotton dress with a floral pattern. I braced myself.

"Your dress is lovely, too," she said. "I had an old tablecloth just like it."

Off we go, I thought. Fasten your seatbelts, everybody.

"How's Norman?" I asked, referring to her son, the freshman at the Citadel. "Is he happy at school?"

"Reasonably," said Sharon. "He told me he got a letter from you. He was surprised."

"Surprised? Why? He *is* my nephew," I reminded her.

"Yes, but after you skipped his high school graduation—"

"I was sick that day, Sharon. I had a one-hundred-three-degree fever. Norman knows I would have come to the graduation if I could have."

"What Norman knows is that his aunt is very busy in New York, writing for a"—she smirked—"*soap opera.*"

"Do you have a problem with my show, Sharon? Is that what this is about?"

"God, no. I've never even seen it. I don't have time to watch that kind of trash."

I glanced at my mother and said, "Don't say I didn't try, okay?" And then I stormed outside, to the patio, and sat by the pool, hyperventilating.

A few minutes later, my mother joined me. I apologized for Sharon and myself. "I'm ruining your birthday because I can't get along with my own sister."

"You're not ruining my birthday," she assured me. "I'm going to have a wonderful time in spite of you and Sharon. She just took me into the kitchen to see all the food. My goodness! What a spread!"

I regarded her. Was it possible that her daughters' sniping didn't bother her as much as I thought? Or was she doing what she always did when it came to my relationship with Sharon—keeping her emotions in check, swallowing her hurt and disappointment, putting on a smily face when inside she was boiling?

"You're going to have a wonderful time too," she added.

"Come on, Mom. You were a witness to that." I pointed inside the house. "My first exchange with Sharon in two years, and it was a beauty, huh?"

"Yes, but it's over now," she said cheerfully. "You girls have broken the ice. Everything should be fine from here on."

The guests started arriving at noon—about forty people, more than half of them relatives. Like me, they had flown down to south Florida especially for the party. Unlike me, they were spending an entire week in the area, making a vacation of it, heading up to Orlando the next morning so they could go to Disney World.

There were my mother's three brothers, Uncle Bill, Uncle Bob, and Uncle Bernie (the Killer B's, they called themselves), along with their wives, Aunt Gloria, Aunt Jean, and Aunt Harriet, as well as their children, *their* children, and an au pair or two. Members of my father's family showed up too, among them his brother, Uncle Stanley, and his wife, Aunt Lydia, his divorced sister, Aunt Shirley, and her unmarried daughter, Jill.

During the first hour of the party, I mingled.

Uncle Stanley told me stories about my father, the same stories he told me every time we got together—the one about their sandlot baseball team, the one about their first car, the one about the day my father met my mother and decided right then and there that he was going to marry her. I listened attentively, as I always did, because they were nice stories and Uncle Stanley recounted them well and I missed my father so talking about him made me happy.

I had my usual, bizarre conversation with my cousin Keith, Uncle Bob and Aunt Jean's fifty-year-old son. Keith was a travel agent who lived alone in Philadelphia. His claim to fame was that he was once a contestant on *Jeopardy* and would have beaten the other two contestants if not for a question concerning the Yangtze River. Keith was a major trivia buff who was also a major bore. He tried to dazzle you with his knowledge of impossibly obscure facts and never asked you anything about your personal life or gave away anything about his own. I had a hunch that all the minutia he spouted was a cover; that he was probably with the CIA or FBI or KGB and didn't want his family to know about it.

Keith's polar opposite, personality-wise, was his younger sister, Marcy, who'd had a lifetime of adventures in psychotherapy and was interested exclusively in delving into personal issues, largely her own. She was incapable of making superficial chitchat, as I was reminded when she struck up a conversation with me at the party. The question "How've you been, Marcy" triggered a long, rambling response involving eating disorders, self-mutilation, and sexual encounters with cable TV repairmen.

I was escaping from Marcy when I was cornered by Uncle Bill's wife, Aunt Gloria, an avid watcher of *From This Day Forward*. Whenever we got together, she loved quizzing me about the show, loved getting the inside scoop on the plot so she could tell her friends in Parsippany.

"You *have* to fill me in about Holden Halsey," she begged, referring to the character played by my old pal Philip. "The actor is exquisite, Deborah. Absolutely exquisite."

"Not in person," I told her. "He has acne scars."

"Really? You can't see them at all," she marveled. "On TV, he looks like an angel."

"It's the makeup," I said. "Up close, he's grotesque. Trust me."

After bursting Aunt Gloria's bubble, I wound up talking to Aunt Harriet, Uncle Bernie's wife. She took me aside to register her disapproval of my cousin Jill, Aunt Shirley's daughter. Jill was my age but not my weight; while I had a little excess baggage around my hips and butt, Jill had genuine thunder thighs, made even more thunderous by the revealing, skin-tight clothes she wore.

"That girl's skirt is so short she should wear a hair net," Aunt Harriet whispered, as we observed Jill sitting on the sofa and crossing and uncrossing her legs. "Men don't appreciate that sort of advertising. That's why she's never found a husband, if you ask me."

"Then what's *my* excuse?" I kidded, pointing at my billowy, ankle-length dress, which was about as revealing as a nun's habit.

"That's easy," said Aunt Harriet. "You've never found a husband because of your sister."

I laughed. "You mean, because I'm afraid she'll scare him off?" I assumed Aunt Harriet had seen Sharon at her witchiest.

"No," she said. "Because you're afraid you'll piss her off."

"I'm not sure I understand what you're—"

"Look, Deborah. You're a sweet girl so I'm going to speak plainly to you." Aunt Harriet was an extremely opinionated woman. I had never known her not to speak plainly to anyone. "Sharon's had nothing but bastards for husbands. Three of them, right?"

"Right."

"Imagine how mad she'd be if you brought home a husband who wasn't a bastard, a good man who really loved you. That's the problem, isn't it?"

"Well, I—"

"I'm telling you, honey. That's why you're not married. Because you don't want to outshine Sharon. I had a similar situation with *my* older sister, may she rest in peace."

"You did?"

"Oh, yes. Whenever Lottie got a B on a test in school, I made sure I got a C or worse. For the longest time I let everybody think I was dumber than Lottie, but I was only hiding my light under a bushel. So I wouldn't outshine her. You think about what I'm saying, okay?"

"Okay. Thanks, Aunt Harriet."

She hugged me, then refocused her attention on cousin Jill. "It's a pity," she *tsk*ed-*tsk*ed. "The girl's got a pretty face. She should get rid of all that weight and start dressing like a normal person."

"Maybe she's hiding her light under a bushel too," I offered, "although she's an only child; no older sister to outshine."

"Yes, but she's got a mother." Aunt Harriet nodded toward Aunt Shirley, who was thin and beautiful and tastefully outfitted, everything her daughter wasn't. "Sometimes that's worse."

At one-thirty, Sharon, from whom I had successfully kept my distance until then, announced that lunch was served. I went into the dining room where I spotted my mother, admiring the sumptuous offerings Sharon had not only arranged attractively but prepared herself, with her own two hands. Yes, she had put the entire meal together without a caterer. She did it all, my sister.

"Deborah. There you are, dear," said my mother, motioning for me to join her.

We sampled the buffet together. She *ooh*ed and *aah*ed at the overabundance of food (while I kept thinking about the starving people in China), and then *ooh*ed and *aah*ed at the spectacularly decorated chocolate cake that Sharon and Paula carried in from the kitchen. They set it down on the table and everybody sang "Happy Birthday."

"Okay, Mom," said Sharon. "Time to blow out the candles— seventy-five of them."

My mother demured, said she couldn't believe she was old enough for seventy-five candles, and asked her "two girls" to help her blow them out. I peeked over at Sharon. I could tell she hated the idea of being lumped together with her no-good younger sister, who was too busy writing for a soap opera to attend her son's graduation. Still, she forced a smile and the three of us blew. It was a beautiful thing.

The party lasted for another couple of hours or so. By four-thirty, my mother and I were standing outside, in front of Sharon's McMansion, waiting for the gangster-valet parking attendant to bring the car around. Sharon was there too, checking my mother's shopping bags to make sure she hadn't forgotten any of the presents people had brought her. I watched my sister as she kept busying herself, anything so as not to have to interact with me.

"Sharon," I said when I couldn't take it anymore. "The party was a big success. And to think you pulled it off by yourself."

She glared at me. "What choice did I have? You were too consumed with your life in New York to pitch in."

I sighed. "I didn't even know about the party until Mom told me about it."

We both looked over at our mother, who was chatting animatedly with Sharon's assistant and paying no attention to us.

"And what happened after she told you about it?" my sister demanded. "Did you pick up the phone and call me? Did you offer to *help?*"

"How could I call you?" I said, immediately on the defensive. "You weren't speaking to me."

"I wasn't speaking to *you?* You were the one who wasn't speaking to *me*," she insisted. "Two years ago you made a remark that was incredibly demeaning to me and then you slammed down the phone in my ear."

"No, Sharon. That wasn't the way it was at all. *You* made a remark that was incredibly demeaning to *me* and then *you* slammed down the phone in *my* ear. I remember it very clearly. Every word. I've been replaying the incident in my mind ever since."

"Every word? Gee, Deborah. It sounds like you should get a life."

"*I* should get a life?" I said hotly. "I'm not the one who can't go fifteen minutes without marrying somebody."

"No. You're the one who's gone fifteen *years* without marrying somebody."

"There. That's the same demeaning remark you made two years ago. Maybe you need new material, Sharon."

She flared her nostrils and tossed back her brassy head. I could tell she was gearing up for the Big insult, the Knock-out Punch, the Grand Finale. I didn't want to hear it.

"Timeout," I said before she could utter another word. "The party may be over, but it's still Mom's birthday. We should at least make an *attempt* to get along. For her sake. It doesn't matter which of us was wrong two years ago, it really doesn't. What matters is that we're adults and, regardless of who did what to whom, we should move on, forget the past. How about it, Sharon?"

Just then, I caught a glimpse of my mother's Delta 88 lumbering into the driveway. I looked expectantly at my sister, hoping she would grab the olive branch I'd extended to her in time to show my mother that all was well between us, but she turned away in a huff.

I shrugged and walked toward the car. I waited while my mother kissed Sharon goodbye. When she was ready to leave, I offered to drive us back to Stuart. She said she wasn't tired and wanted to take the wheel herself. We got into the car.

As she was positioning herself atop her telephone book, I stuck my head out the window, waved to Sharon, and thanked her again for having the party. She responded by mouthing the words "Fuck you."

"Can I ask you something, Mom?" I said as she was releasing the emergency brake and placing her foot on the accelerator.

"Of course, dear."

"Was Sharon a colicky baby?"

Chapter Four

As soon as we got back to the house, my mother toddled off to her bedroom to take a nap. When I tiptoed in an hour later, she was still out cold and slept straight through until the next morning.

"I don't know what hit me," she said when I came down for breakfast. "I didn't persuade you to spend the weekend with me so I could poop out on you."

"Are you feeling okay?" I asked. My mother had never been one for naps, especially those that lasted twelve hours.

"I'm fine," she said, waving off my concern. "It must have been the excitement of the party. What's bothering me is that I wasn't very good company for you last night. I left you all by yourself."

"I'm used to being by myself," I assured her. "When I saw you were sound asleep, I went out on the deck, read a book, looked at the water, listened to the breeze. It was the first relaxing evening I've had in ages."

"You remind me so much of your father," she laughed ruefully. "He used to call this spot his Shangri-la, remember?"

"I do," I said, picturing my father outside the house, down by the river, nestled in the hammock he had strung between two palms and announcing to nobody in particular, "*This* is my Shangri-la." Back in Connecticut, he was the very important Dr. Henry Peltz, always working late, always getting up in the middle of the night to rescue a patient, always on the run—a dedicated physician who was worshiped by the sick and the infirm and hardly ever home. But when he was in Florida, he was just plain laid-back Dad, swimming in the ocean, picking bananas and mangos and avocados from the trees on the property, going fishing with the man who lived next door, snoozing in the hammock. In Sewall's Point, his rhythm slowed to a nice, easy crawl. In Sewall's Point, Sharon and I finally had a crack at getting his attention.

"Would you like it if I moved here, Mom?" I asked, wondering if she was lonely without my father around, even though she rarely spoke of her true feelings.

"The important thing is whether moving here would make you happy. Would it?"

"I honestly don't know. I've been going on and on about all the stress I'm under in New York. But what if my problems have nothing to do with geography? Sharon lives down here and she's not happy."

"Sure she is, dear."

"How can you tell with her?"

"Deborah. You can see that she's made a full life for herself here. She has a loving son, lots of friends, a beautiful home, a successful business. She's so competent, such a go-getter."

So competent. Such a go-getter. As opposed to *me*, did she mean? I wasn't exactly an underachiever by anyone's standards. I had a career in the glamorous world of daytime television, with a six-figure income to match. And yet, if I was such a go-getter, why wasn't I going or getting anywhere? I'd spent over ten years working for *From This Day*

Forward—the first four in the production department, the last six as a breakdown writer. Why then, with my vast experience, hadn't I even been considered as Woody's replacement after the network decided to dump him? Why was it assumed that Deborah Peltz was fine where she was? Why did I have the sense that my star wasn't on the rise anymore, that my life was stalled, that my arrow wasn't pointing up?

Maybe I've been hiding my light under a bushel both professionally and personally, I thought, recalling my conversation with Aunt Harriet. Maybe I really was afraid of outshining Sharon. And maybe it was time to snap out of it.

"If you like, dear, I could try to reach Melinda Carr at home today, about the job with the Historical Society," said my mother. "Talking to her now would give you a head start if you decide you do want to relocate here at some point."

"Why not? It would be great if you could call her, Mom."

She patted my shoulder. "You eat your breakfast and I'll go into the bedroom and find Melinda's number. This will all work out, you'll see."

I smiled at my mother. "You are definitely the most positive person I know," I told her. "Doesn't anything ever depress you?"

She was about to respond when she stopped herself, almost as if an invisible hand had reached out and clamped her mouth shut.

"Mom? Were you going to say something?" I asked.

"Only that there isn't a moment to waste," she said finally, and hurried out of the kitchen.

Melinda Carr lived with her husband in a tastefully restored hundred-year-old house along the south fork of the St. Lucie River. The place was very charming in that sort of grandma-ish, doilies-and-lace way that many historic homes and B&Bs are famous for. As for Melinda herself, she was as stiff and humorless as the house's creaky floors. I guessed she was in her fifties, a tall, thin brunette with the best posture—and vocabulary—I'd ever seen. When she opened the door to let me in, shoulders back, head erect, she spotted the gardening tools her husband had forgotten to remove from the front steps, frowned, and said apologetically, "He was endeavoring to effectuate all of his chores before shaking off the yoke of domestication and escaping to the golf course. Pardon the detritus."

"No problem," I said, thinking Melinda was probably a killer at Scrabble.

We sat next to each other on the white wicker loveseat in her sunroom, sipped tea, and got down to the business of the job at the Historical Society.

"Your mother indicated that you're contemplating a move to the Stuart area," said Melinda, "and that you'll be looking for work, if you do move here. Are you familiar with the House of Refuge?"

"Oh, yes," I said. "My father used to take me there to see the turtles they had in the aquarium back then. Afterwards, we'd go swimming at Bathtub Reef Beach, so I could check out the surfers."

"How nice," said Melinda with a note of condescension. Perhaps surfers were detritus, in her opinion. Or was it the turtles? "Actually, I was inquiring whether you were familiar with the building's historical significance, its raison d'être, if you will."

"Well, I know that it's the oldest standing structure in Martin County," I ventured, "and that it was built as a place where shipwrecked sailors could come out of bad weather."

"Yes. After each storm, its keeper would walk the beach to search for survivors."

"Is that what you'd want me to do as a keeper? Search for survivors after storms?" Maybe I wasn't qualified for the job after all. I'd failed Junior Lifesaving in summer camp.

"No," said Melinda. "When we use the term *keeper* now, we mean a site manager or caretaker. Jody Callahan operates the museum, Betty Newcombe recruits and trains our volunteers, Linda Rubin runs the gift shop, and Doreen Keefer approaches the people in Tallahassee about grant money. What we would need you to do is live in the cottage adjacent to the House of Refuge, to keep an eye on things and to contact the county building maintenance department when there are problems. It's a restful, undemanding job. *If* you're the type of person who doesn't mind being alone a good deal of the time."

"I don't mind being alone," I said, having just told my mother the same thing.

"Do I assume correctly that you're unattached?"

"Yes."

"No beau in the picture?"

"No beau."

"No disgruntled ex-husband who might come to town and provoke an unfortunate situation?"

I laughed. "No. Why would you ask that?"

"Because the Historical Society has an impeccable reputation in the community. If the keeper of the House of Refuge were to bring unwanted publicity to the building or to our organization, it would be unpleasant for everyone."

"Not to worry," I said. "I lead a very quiet life."

"Excellent. According to your mother, you've been a scrivener up in New York."

"A what?"

"An inditer."

"I don't—"

"A *writer*."

"Oh. Yes. I've been a writer for *From This Day Forward*. It's a daytime drama. A soap opera."

Melinda's jaw dropped.

Well, there goes the job, I thought, figuring Melinda had pegged me for the kind of person who would bring ignominy and disgrace upon the Historical Society, because of all the sordid storylines I'd dreamed up for some low-brow television program. I was tempted to inform little Miss Priss that *From This Day Forward* had won numerous Emmys and that some of our most avid fans were members of the clergy. But before I could get a word out, she said, "Your mother didn't mention that you write for that particular program. You see, I've been watching it since I was twenty and videotape every single episode."

I heaved a sigh of relief. "It's nice to meet a loyal viewer."

She nodded, then pumped me for information about the actors on the show. When she got to Philip, I cut her off. "About the keeper's job. I'm definitely interested. The problem is, I don't know when I'm going to make the move to Florida. I may get cold feet once I'm back in New York. Do you have a deadline for filling the position?"

"The current keeper is leaving at the end of this week, and we'd like to have the new keeper settled in by the beginning of March, although we'd be willing to wait for the right candidate." She paused. "Let me be direct, Deborah. You're exactly the sort of mature, dependable person we're looking for. The House of Refuge would be in responsible hands if you were caring for it, I'm certain. We wouldn't have to worry about any bacchanalia with you installed on the property."

"No, Melinda. I wouldn't be having any wild parties," I reassured her. "In any case, I'll keep in touch with you over the next few weeks and let you know whether I'm really heading South. How's that?"

"Perfect."

We got up from the loveseat and walked to the door.

"Thanks for seeing me on such short notice," I said as we shook hands.

"Thank you for coming—and for the soap opera gossip. I must admit that the other applicants I've interviewed for the position haven't provided nearly the divertimento that you have."

"Divertimento?"

"Yes. You know. *Divertissement.*"

"You're saying you had fun, is that it?"

"Irrefragably."

I navigated my mother's Delta 88 into her driveway and found her out in front of the house, weeding. She was wearing sunglasses, a wide-brimmed hat, and loose-fitting clothes to protect her from the midday sun, but her face was flushed and damp with perspiration and she seemed a little out of breath.

"Tell me what happened with Melinda," she urged, wiping her brow. "I want to hear every detail."

"I'll give you a blow-by-blow account over lunch and a swim," I suggested. "I'll make us some sandwiches, and we can load the cooler, beach chairs, and umbrella into the car and drive over to Bathtub Beach. And while we're in the vicinity, I'd like to pass by the House of Refuge, so I can get a look at the keeper's cottage. What do you say?"

"Oh, Deborah." She beamed. "Does that mean Melinda offered you the job?"

"Irrefragably," I told her.

The keeper's cottage, I observed as I peeked out the car window, was a little white dollhouse, perched smack atop a craggy stretch of land overlooking the Atlantic. It had seen better days and it wasn't the first place you'd choose if you wanted to be out of harm's way during a hurricane, but it was everybody's idea of a romantic retreat—a picturesque, loaded-with-charm beach bungalow that screamed peace and quiet and solitude, literally a "house of refuge" for a stressed-out city girl.

"If you decide to take up painting again, dear, I can't imagine a more scenic spot," said my mother.

"Neither can I," I agreed, recalling from my college years how beautiful the beach looked at night, when the sightseers were gone and the place was deserted. Even on a stormy night, *especially* on a stormy night, the sea was magical.

"But it might be lonely living all the way out here," said my mother.

"Lonely? Nah. I'll be a happy hermit, just like Glenn Ford in the movie *A Stolen Life*. He played a lighthouse keeper, remember?"

"I don't think I saw that movie."

"Sure you did, Mom. Bette Davis played identical twins, one nice, one bitchy."

"Deborah. This isn't leading up to another discussion of your relationship with Sharon, is it?"

"No," I laughed. "It really was a movie. Both sisters were in love with Glenn Ford."

"I see. A love triangle. Did he have to choose between them in the end?"

I shook my head. "Things got extremely complicated in that movie. There was a shocking death that spun the story in a whole different direction."

She chuckled. "Real life isn't nearly as eventful as a Bette Davis movie, is it?"

"Not usually," I said, clueless that mine was about to be.

After a relaxing afternoon at the beach, we returned to my mother's house so I could pack. At four o'clock, I came downstairs with my suitcase and suggested to her that I should take a taxi to the airport, instead of letting her chauffeur me as she usually did. I was surprised when she didn't object.

"Our excursion must have tired me out more than I realized," she said. "Ordinarily, I'd love to have the extra hour with my little girl before she flies away again."

I felt a lump in my throat suddenly. There was something in her tone that sounded so poignant, so wistful. "I'll be back," I assured her. "You know that, Mom."

When the taxi arrived, we said a tearful goodbye. I promised to call as soon as my plane touched down at LaGuardia, to let her know I had made the trip safely—a ritual in our family. Then off I went, home to the land of Monday meetings.

Chapter Five

While Woody had held his Monday meetings in his apartment, the "Gruesome Threesome," as Helen had dubbed our new head writers, conducted theirs in a suite at the fabulously expensive Four Seasons Hotel on East 57th Street. So much for the budget cuts they kept shoving down our throats.

The day of this particular Monday meeting also happened to be "Take Your Daughter to Work" day, where career mommies give their nannies a few hours off and actually bring their little girls to the workplace in order to boost their self-esteem.

Please.

None of us breakdown writers brought our children to the meeting, either because, like me, we had no children, or because, like most sensible adults, we understood that when children are present, no work gets done.

The Gruesome Threesome, on the other hand, did bring their daughters to the meeting, some of whom were terrible twos. They wheeled these little cherubs into the hotel suite in their strollers, unfastened them, and turned them loose—for the next eight hours. Trust me, it was a nightmare.

"I wonder how Philip puts up with that one," said Helen, nodding at the child who belonged to the former Harlequin editor, the single mother he was dating. The kid was crayoning on the walls—in red.

"You know Philip," I said with a shrug. "Anything for his career, including little miss Picasso."

It wasn't just the children that got on my nerves that day, or even Helen's relentless gossiping. It was the distance I felt from my job, the utter detachment. I really was out of the loop now, disenfranchised. The network had hired the Gruesome Threesome because they wanted us to abandon the audience we'd spent years cultivating for younger, hipper viewers. But it was I who was made to feel unyoung and unhip. I mean, had I ever heard of Daft Punk? Well, my bosses had. "They're our favorite rock group," one of them explained, while her daughter was severing the head of her Barbie. "But we like Rusted Root and Nine Inch Nails too."

Daft Punk. Rusted Root. Nine Inch Nails. I ask you: How was I supposed to contribute to *that* conversation? By holding fast to my affection for James Taylor? I could no more relate to my bosses than I could to the teenagers we were trying to lure to the show.

Move to Florida, I told myself as the three women chatted about an alternative band called the Foo Fighters. You'll feel young there, surrounded by all those seniors. When they rave about Julio Iglesias, at least you'll know who they're talking about.

I hadn't gotten around to replacing the computer that had been ripped off from my apartment, so I spent the week commuting to and from the production office, where I wrote my breakdown on the machine there. When Saturday rolled around and I finally had a minute to breathe, I intended to go out and shop for a new computer, a TV, a VCR, and the other gadgets that had been stolen, but something stopped me. And it wasn't the words of the cop who had warned me that as soon as I replaced all this stuff, they'd be back to clean me out again. No, it was the sense that I wouldn't be in town much longer, so why bother? It was the notion that I was definitely getting out, moving on, packing up. I had made a decision, I realized that Saturday: I was heading South. My lease on the apartment was about to expire. My contract with the show was up for renewal. I had nothing and nobody tying me to New York. I was free. The time was right. It was only the circumstances that were wrong, as it turned out.

I was fast asleep on Saturday night, absolutely conked out, when the phone rang. It took me a couple of seconds to come to, and after I did, I turned on the light and checked the clock on the night table: 3:00 A.M.

I wondered who in the world would have the nerve to call me at such an ungodly hour.

"It's Sharon," said my sister.

I bolted up in bed. "What's wrong?" Something had to be for her to pick up the phone and dial my number.

"Mom's had a heart attack," she said.

"She *what?*" My own heart stopped.

"She had a heart attack, but she's stable," said Sharon, who blew her nose, then took a few seconds to collect herself. "I just talked to the cardiologist. We had her moved to the intensive care unit about a half hour ago."

"You're at the hospital now?"

"Mom had them call me right after she got to the emergency room. I jumped into the car and drove like a madwoman."

I nodded silently as I sat there in my dimly lit bedroom, stunned, numb, barely able to process what Sharon was telling me. My father had always been my hero, but my mother had always been my rock. For the first time in my life, I was forced to confront her mortality.

Sharon went on to explain that my mother had been having chest pains for months but didn't tell anybody; that she'd been watching TV in bed that night when she began to feel *really* awful; and that when she didn't feel better after twenty minutes, she called 911.

"Once she got to Martin Memorial, they paged the cardiologist on call," said Sharon, "a doctor named Jeffrey Hirshon. He has a practice in Stuart and lives in Sewall's Point, around the corner from Mom."

"Is he supposed to be any good?" I asked, my eyes flooding with tears.

"Good? He's terrific. He saved Mom's life," Sharon replied. "He took one look at her cardiogram, started her on tPA, this drug that dissolves blood clots, and an hour later she was asking when she could go home. Of course, she's not out of the woods yet. Dr. Hirshon said she has to be watched carefully. He's keeping her in the hospital for at least four or five days."

I started to cry in earnest and blotted my eyes with the sleeve of my nightgown.

"A heart attack." I sobbed. "I can't believe it. She seemed fine when I saw her last weekend."

"Well, you know Mom," said Sharon. "She's not a kvetch."

"Still, she should have—"

"Look, Deborah," Sharon cut me off. "I've got to run back to the ICU to check on things. Why don't you roll over and try to get some sleep. It's not as if there's anything you can do from up there."

I bristled at her remark but willed myself to remain civil to her. "Is Dr. Hirshon with Mom now?"

"Yes, and he'll be monitoring her throughout the night. I'm staying too, naturally."

"Naturally, but you must be exhausted after all the worrying and waiting around."

"I am exhausted, but *someone* from the family has to be here for Mom. Her other daughter is too busy in New York to—"

"Stuff it up your ass!" I exploded. So much for civility. "Just tell

Mom that I love her, that I'm catching a flight out tomorrow, and that I'm taking the job with the Historical Society."

"Job? What job?"

"None of your business. Give Mom my message, can you manage that, Sharon? *Can you?*"

She sighed. "I'm the one who manages everything, Deborah. What else is new?"

On Sunday morning I telephoned one of my three bosses (not the one who was seeing Philip; God forbid *he* should answer the phone) and informed her that I wouldn't be renewing my contract with the show because I was moving to Florida. Then I called the Salvation Army and arranged for them to haul away my beat-up furniture and everything else in my apartment that wouldn't fit into the two suitcases and carry-on bag I was taking with me. I also buzzed the super in the building and asked him to forward my mail to my mother's house until I had a more permanent address.

"You were real pesty, calling me all the time to fix things, but I'll miss you," he said.

"You were real surly, complaining all the time about having to fix things, but I'll miss you too," I told him.

I secured the last seat on an afternoon flight out of LaGuardia and I was outtathere.

Upon my arrival at Palm Beach International Airport at three-thirty, I collected my suitcases, hopped into a taxi, and gave the driver my mother's address. I still had the extra key to the house she'd made for me the previous week (did she have a premonition that I'd need it?), so when I got to the house, I let myself in, ran upstairs to the guestroom, and shed the heavy clothes I'd worn on the plane, depositing them on the floor along with my luggage. As I was tearing back downstairs, I noticed that the other guestroom was also occupied. Neatly. Three Louis Vuitton bags were stacked in perfect alignment in the corner of the room; a comb, hairbrush, and makeup case were laid out on top of the dresser; and a pale pink nightgown and matching peignoir were draped across the foot of the bed, a pair of gold satin slippers resting on the floor below.

Great. Sharon and I will be roomies, I thought, picturing the two of us cooking breakfast together. I'd compliment her on her fluffy poached eggs and she'd say my sausage patties looked like roadkill.

I quickly reminded myself that my sister was not my immediate concern and headed straight for the garage, to the Delta 88, the keys to which my mother always left in the ignition. I started up the old boat and chugged out of Sewall's Point. As I crossed the bridge onto East Ocean Boulevard, I realized with a shudder that the ambulance transporting my mother had followed the same route only hours before.

Please let her be all right, I prayed. Please let this Dr. Hirshon be everything Sharon says he is.

Martin Memorial Medical Center, the second-largest employer in Martin County, is a community-owned, not-for-profit hospital with a professional, albeit "just-us-folks," atmosphere. Like most small-town facilities, its staff and patients tend to know each other, live near each other, play golf or go fishing with each other. Unlike most small-town hospitals, it sits along the St. Lucie River, affording many of its patients a sensational water view.

Of course, my mother, a patient in what they call the Medical Intensive Care Unit (MICU), wasn't one of them; the window in her little cubicle on the first floor overlooked the roof. Still, she was lucky to even get a bed. February is high season in Florida, not just for hotels and restaurants but for hospitals too.

One of the MICU nurses—her name was Vicky—escorted me down the corridor, where we passed a half dozen "rooms" that were open to the nurses' station yet separated from each other by a curtain. I had expected there to be a sort of hush over the place, given the seriousness of the patients' illnesses, but between the televisions blaring, the electronic monitoring devises beeping, and the visitors visiting, there was more of a nonspecific hum than a hush.

"Here's our Mrs. Peltz." Vicky smiled, stopping when we arrived at the room at the end of the hall.

My mother didn't hear us at first; she appeared to be napping. Sharon was sitting in a chair to the right of the bed, flipping through an issue of *Modern Bride*. She looked up at me and faked a smile, one of those square, clenched-teeth jobs that are meant to make the other person feel like, well, detritus. I ignored her and focused on my mother, her body hooked up to a half dozen contraptions, her complexion frighteningly pale.

I had prepared myself for this moment. During the entire two-and-a-half-hour flight to Florida, I had coached myself. *Don't fall apart when you see her. Don't say anything to upset her. Be cheerful.* But when I actually came face to face with my poor little mommy in that big hospital bed, I totally lost it.

"Mom!" I blubbered, rushing to her side, arms flailing in the air, tears pouring down my cheeks. "Oh, Mom!"

I woke her up, obviously, but she didn't seem to mind.

"Deborah," she said, patting my head as I bent down to kiss her. "You didn't have to come, dear. It must have been a lot of trouble for you."

"I wouldn't be anywhere else, Mom," I said. "How are you feeling? Any more chest pains?"

"No," she said tentatively, as if not to trust her luck. "Dr. Hirshon is taking good care of me. He has a very good reputation, I hear."

"Sharon told me," I said. "I'm looking forward to meeting him."

"He's stopping by tonight," said Sharon, perking up considerably. "Within the hour, I think."

"I'll be here," I said, eager to shake the hand of the man who had saved my mother's life.

I sat in the visitor's chair on the other side of the bed and asked my mother about her condition—what medications she was taking, what dietary restrictions she'd been given, what sort of tests she would have to undergo over the next few days, whether she was scared.

"A little scared," she admitted. "Even if I survive this heart attack, there's always a chance I'll have another. Uncle Bernie had a triple bypass, remember, dear? There's a history of heart problems in our family. I feel as if I'm doomed."

"You're going to be just fine," I insisted, startled by my mother's pessimism. Lenore Peltz had never been one to complain or give up or lose hope, never one to let life's vicissitudes get her down, not even after my father died. But now she sounded down, sounded as if the heart attack had knocked the fight out of her. "The only thing is, I wish you'd told me about the chest pains when we were together last weekend. Maybe I could have done something."

"Like what?" Sharon challenged.

"Like taken Mom to the doctor," I said. "Like *helped* her."

"Helped her?" she scoffed. "The way you helped her by charging into her hospital room and *boo-hoo*-ing?"

"I wasn't *boo-hoo*-ing. I was showing my emotions," I said defensively.

"You were hysterical," said Sharon.

"I was *human,*" I said. "Do you know what it means to be human? To have feelings?"

"Oh, I have plenty of feelings. You just don't want to hear what they are."

"You can say that again. The last thing I—"

"Shut up already! Both of you!"

Sharon and I froze.

"I've had enough of your nonsense! Ee-nuff!"

We turned to look at our mother, to calm her down, make sure she was all right, apologize, but before we knew it, Vicky, the nurse, had bounded into the room.

"Out! Out! Out!" she said, shooing us into the corridor. "You're upsetting my patient and I won't have it. Go cool off in the visitors' lounge and I'll come and get you when your mother's feeling better."

Reluctantly, we left Mom in Vicky's hands and walked wordlessly across the hall, to the extremely crowded visitors' lounge. As we stood in the doorway, we saw that there were two empty chairs but that they were not together.

"Here. Take mine," said a man seated next to one of the unoccupied chairs.

Thinking he was doing us a favor, he started to get up, so Sharon and I could sit side by side in our time of need.

"No! Don't!" we responded simultaneously, wanting to be as far away from each other as the size of the room would permit.

The man shrugged and sat back down. Sharon took the seat next to him. I sat on the other side of the room, next to a woman whose husband had been stabbed in the stomach during an argument with his mistress.

"You must love him very much to stand by him like this," I told her. "Some women aren't so forgiving."

"What's to forgive?" she said. "It's not as if he slept with my sister or anything. I don't even know the girl."

I nodded, wondering if we had reached a new low in the tolerance department in our country. According to this woman, it was fine for a married man to have a mistress as long as the mistress wasn't his sister-in-law. I mean, really.

I laughed to myself. And then I tried to imagine how I would feel if I had a husband and he slept with *his* sister-in-law, who, of course, would be Sharon. I stopped laughing.

About fifteen minutes after Vicky had thrown us out of intensive care, she stuck her head in the lounge and motioned for us to come back.

"Your mother's blood pressure went sky-high," she scolded us. "She's all right now, but she won't be if you keep this up. Your bickering is very disturbing to her."

"But she's never spoken to us about it before," said Sharon.

"She's always pretended we're the Bobbsey Twins," I explained.

"Your mother has had a life-threatening event," said Vicky. "That can change a person profoundly. She may not be concerned about pleasing everybody the way she used to be. She may be focusing more on herself, on her own welfare. I'd be prepared for some straight talk from her if I were you two."

Sharon and I thanked Vicky for being so candid with us, and, chastened, hurried back into our mother's room.

We took our seats on either side of her bed.

"We were horribly insensitive, Mom," said Sharon.

"We're sorry for arguing in front of you like that," I agreed.

"Good," said my mother. "Then you can just sit there, keep your traps shut, and listen for a change."

Yikes. The New Lenore Peltz wasn't especially subtle.

"I want my girls to patch things up," she announced. "Once and for all. If you don't, I'll have another heart attack and die, and my last memory will be of you two insulting each other. Is *that* what you want for me? Is it?"

"Of course it isn't," Sharon and I said in unison.

"Fine," said my mother. "Then put aside your differences and behave like sisters. For my sake. For my *health*."

For her health. Well. There was only one thing to do then.

I got up from my chair, walked around to the other side of the bed, where Sharon was sitting, and extended my hand to her. "Truce?"

She rose from her chair but merely stared at my hand for several seconds. It was beginning to cramp from all the tension when she finally reached out and grasped it. "Truce," she said, a tad begrudgingly.

"Give me a break," my mother snapped. "I'm talking about a real kiss-and-make-up, not a business handshake. Do you girls want me to live or don't you?"

This time, Sharon and I did the deed. There were quick pecks on the cheek, followed by an honest-to-goodness hug, followed by several pats on each other's back. My mother kvelled. It was a Kodak moment.

And then, as if on cue, someone applauded.

All three of us turned toward the nurses' station, in the direction of the applause. Leaning against the desk, clapping his hands together and smiling broadly, was a tall, dark, bearded man in a white lab coat—a man whose kindly expression reminded me of my father.

"Dr. Hirshon!" Sharon exclaimed, quickly disentangling herself from me so that she could have both hands free to fluff her hair.

Dr. Hirshon, I mused, finding my mother's cardiologist unexpectedly appealing at first glance and, therefore, giving my own hair a fluff or two.

Chapter Six

Jeffrey Hirshon wasn't conventionally handsome, certainly not in the way Philip was. He was over six feet tall, like Philip, and had a similarly perfect, Chiclets smile, but his features were slightly out of proportion with his face—his nose too big, his lips too thin, his eyes a little droopy. Still, this doctor, whom I figured to be in his mid-fifties, was exceedingly attractive to me, perhaps because of his dark curly beard with its patches of gray, his broad shoulders and chest, his hearty, ho-ho-ho laugh—all of which lent him a jolly, avuncular air, as if he were someone I'd known for years, as if he were a person I could lean on, a person I could trust. Of course, the fact that he didn't have a *tan* contributed to this perception. I'd assumed that the cardiologists in Florida spent more time hitting golf balls than they did diagnosing myocardial infarctions.

"Isn't this nice," he said as he made his entrance, stethoscope around his neck, shirt and tie underneath his lab coat. "A hospital room where everybody's smiling."

"It's all because my two girls are by my side, helping me get well," my mother said proudly.

"That's what I like to hear," said Dr. Hirshon, "family members coming together to promote the patient's recovery. Very important, in my opinion. Doctors can dispense drug after drug, perform surgical procedure after surgical procedure, but it's the healing power a patient derives from his or her loved ones that truly makes the difference between sickness and health."

Ah, so he's one of those touchy-feely holistic types, I mused, impressed that a small town like Stuart had such a forward-thinking doctor, a man of science who was also spiritual, soulful, sensitive.

"Speaking of loved ones, you've already met my older daughter, Sharon," said my mother, nodding at my sister.

"*Older?*" Sharon chuckled but looked mortified. "You make me sound positively ancient, Mom."

My mother went right on. "And this is my younger daughter, Deborah."

"It's a pleasure," said Dr. Hirshon as we shook hands. He had a warm yet firm handshake, I noticed, and the droopy, puppy-dog eyes were a rather captivating velvety shade of brown.

"Same here," I said. "From what I've heard, you were a hero last night. Obviously, I'm very grateful."

"*I* had to tell Deborah the whole story over the phone, long-distance," Sharon explained to the doctor, insinuating herself into our conversation. I expected her to finish the sentence with "Because she lives in New York where she writes for a *soap opera.*" But after glancing at my mother's heart monitor, she said instead, "We're very close, my sister and I. We tell each other everything."

"That's as it should be," said Dr. Hirshon. "I see so many siblings who allow petty misunderstandings to come between them. They hang on to these grievances and hang on and hang on, and before they know it they've stopped speaking to each other. It's hard to imagine that kind of shortsightedness, isn't it?"

Sharon and I agreed that yes, indeedie, it was very hard to imagine it.

Dr. Hirshon smiled and moved closer to the bed. "Now, how are you feeling this evening, Mrs. Peltz? Any pain? Shortness of breath? Tightness in the chest?"

"No, nothing like last night," she answered. "I think I'm just nervous, you know, about having another heart attack. I feel very fragile all of a sudden."

"That's perfectly normal," said Dr. Hirshon, who patted my mother's arm and then spoke of the psychological aftershocks she would likely experience, of the support groups available to her, of the fact that he would be available to her. Eventually, he asked Sharon and me to step out of the room while he examined her.

"Dr. Hirshon seems like a caring person," I commented as my sister and I sat together in the visitors' lounge.

"Very caring," said Sharon. "You should have seen how he watched over Mom during the night. He was so competent, yet so gentle. He was clearly in charge of the situation, but he didn't club anybody over the head with that God-almighty-authority-figure bullshit. He reminds me of Daddy in that way."

"I had the same impression the minute I saw him," I admitted. "Daddy with a beard."

Sharon was pensive. "I didn't see a wedding ring, did you?"

I shook my head in amazement. "You're incorrigible, Sharon. Mom is lying in a hospital bed and all you think about is marriage. Checking men for wedding rings is probably a reflex action for you at this point."

"Oh, spare me the marriage lecture for once. I'm as worried about Mom as you are—I'm the one who spent the entire night at this place, remember?—but I'm not comatose. When an attractive man— and a Jewish doctor to boot—walks into my life, I pay attention. Tell me you didn't look to see if he was wearing a ring, Deborah."

"I didn't."

"Sure."

"I didn't. Honest."

"But you think he's attractive too. You blushed when he came into Mom's room. And you turned even redder when he shook hands with you."

"Did I?"

"Beet."

Beet? Well, I did feel a quickening of my pulse when I was intro-duced to Jeffrey Hirshon, but I figured that I was just overwhelmed by what had happened to my mother, that my emotions were out of control, that I was so relieved that she was alive that I was ready to deify the man who had saved her.

"Let's change the subject," I said quickly. "We promised Mom we wouldn't argue."

"You're right," she agreed. "Let's talk about something else."

Something else. There was an awkward silence. We'd spent so many years feuding that we were at a loss how to talk to each other *without* feuding.

Finally, I asked Sharon how her wedding-planning business was doing. She said, "Great. We're scheduled through the summer." I asked her if she still liked living in Boca. She said, "Of course. It's home." I asked her if she had read any good books lately. She said, "No. Who has time?" She wasn't exactly effusive in her answers, but at least she wasn't cursing me out. It wasn't until I asked her how Norman was handling military school that she managed to string several sentences together.

I should have remembered that he was the key to her heart, the secret to getting her to loosen up. For all her neurotic nonsense—her martyr complex, her perfectionism, her impulsive, self-destructive behavior when it came to men—she was a surprisingly good mother, a devoted single parent who showed her son the affection she had such difficulty showing me. Whenever she opened up about Norman, her face softened, lost its pinched, burdened quality.

And so it was on this occasion. Her usual tightness melted as she told me laughingly how freshmen at the Citadel are called knobs; how their dreadful haircuts are called knobcuts; how she missed Nor-man terribly now that he was out of the house, shaved head or no shaved head; how having a son like him more than made up for the hell she went through with his polygamist father.

She was a different Sharon when she spoke of her child, a sharing Sharon, a woman I could relate to. For a few moments in that hospital visitors' lounge, I forgot that for most of our lives we were at war. For a few moments there, I actually liked my sister.

Eventually, though, she brought up Dr. Hirshon again.

"You know," she said, "even if he is single and available, I won't act on my attraction to him. Not if you want him."

"Sharon," I said, forcing my tone to sound benign, unprovocative. "It's really premature to—"

"Face it, Deborah. The issue is going to come up sooner or later. As you pointed out before, we promised Mom that we wouldn't fight with each other over anything or anyone, so I'm simply saying that if it ends up that Dr. Hirshon isn't married or gay or otherwise spoken for and that he's as interested in us as we are in him, I'll bow out and let you have him. To keep the peace."

"You'll *let* me have him?" I laughed.

"Yes. I'm your older sister. It should be my decision whether or not to step aside and let you have him."

I shook my head again. "That's very generous of you, Sharon, but since you're the one who seems obsessed with him, I think you should take him."

"Obsessed? You're the one who practically swooned when he walked into Mom's room. No, Deborah. *You* take him."

Jesus. Now we were bickering over how to avoid bickering.

"Why don't we just relax and let the situation play itself out," I suggested. "I'm sure we'll be seeing a lot of Dr. Hirshon over the next few weeks, what with having to drive Mom to his office for her followup tests once she leaves the hospital and consulting with him if she runs into problems. Maybe, as we get to know him, we'll both decide he's not what we want."

"What do you mean, we'll be seeing a lot of him over the next few weeks?" asked Sharon. "I'm the one who'll be seeing a lot of him. You're going back to New York as soon as Mom is feeling better, to that soap opera you write for."

"Wrong. I'm staying in Florida. I've quit the show and I'm taking a job in Stuart, with the Historical Society. I'm the one who'll be seeing a lot of Dr. Hirshon, Sharon. He's going to be my neighbor."

When he was finished examining my mother, Dr. Hirshon stopped by the visitors' lounge, to fill us in on her condition.

"Your mother's doing reasonably well, considering what she's been through," he began, stroking his beard. "The tPA appears to have dissolved the clot that caused the heart attack. Tomorrow morning, we'll send her down the hall for an angiogram, so we can find out which of the coronary arteries is clogged or narrowed. If all goes well, she'll spend another night or two in intensive care, then we'll move her to telemetry."

"What's that?" I asked.

"Telemetry? It's on the fifth floor," he said. "There's a little room there—we call it 'Heart Beat Central'—where technicians sit in front of computers that monitor the heartbeats of every single patient on the floor, whether they're taking a walk, being transported down to X-ray, or sitting in the lounge. Think of it as air traffic controllers monitoring incoming and outgoing planes." He *ho-ho-ho*-ed. "Your mother can be completely ambulatory, yet the technicians will be able to pick up the signals from the electrodes she's hooked up to, wherever she is in the hospital."

"How long does she have to stay there?" asked Sharon.

"Two or three days," he replied. "We'll start her on a cardiac rehab program—exercise, diet, new medications. On the fifth day, we'll put her on a treadmill for a stress test. If there's no pain or shortness of breath, we'll send her home."

"Just like that," I said, marveling at how quickly a life-threatening illness can be treated.

"Over the short term, it *is* pretty routine," he agreed. "The artery is like a pipe, and removing what's clogging the pipe is like putting Drano in your sink. The problem is, people who have clogged arteries are subject to recurrences. I've explained that to your mother."

"How did she react?" I asked. "She's not used to being incapacitated. She's always been very independent."

"And she will be again," said Dr. Hirshon. "But she's bound to experience some depression at first. She'll have to face her own mortality. She'll probably be angry—the 'Why me?' syndrome. She'll wonder why she was cursed with a bad family history. She might even blame herself for holding in her emotions for so many years. And, of course, she'll have to learn to live freely without a cloud hanging over her head. But I'll be there for her. All *three* of us will be there for her, won't we?"

Dr. Hirshon reached out and placed his left hand on my shoulder and his right hand on Sharon's, a coach huddling with his star players, urging them on.

"We will," Sharon and I told the doctor, who then continued his touching and talking and coaching, reminding us that we were a team and that, together, we would restore Lenore Peltz to good health.

Boy, this guy's not like any doctor *I've* ever been to, I thought. No abrupt bedside manner. No playing the Lord of the Manor. No running off to escape the patient's family. He's everything you could want in a physician, maybe even everything you could want in a man.

Stop that! I scolded myself. You're not going to do anything to blow the truce you've made with Sharon, no matter how delicious Jeffrey Hirshon's hand feels on your shoulder.

"So, you two can go back in and see your mother now," he advised us. "I'm going home, but I'll look in on her in the morning."

"What if she feels worse during the night?" I asked.

"Not to worry. The hospital will call me," he said.

"Or you could give us your home number and we could contact you directly," Sharon said brazenly. "Although we wouldn't dream of disturbing your wife and children."

Dr. Hirshon smiled as he shook his head. "No wife. No children. Just a big house in Sewall's Point that I got to keep in the divorce. My wife got the place in Aspen."

I refused to make eye contact with Sharon.

"Still," he went on, "it's best if the hospital calls me. What's more, I don't expect your mother to have any major problems during the night. And as for you two"—he nodded at Sharon and me—"I'm prescribing a good night's sleep. You've both had a lot to deal with over the last twenty-four hours. The saving grace here is that you've got each other."

"You betcha," I said, giving old Sis a pat on the back.

"Without a doubt," she echoed, elbowing me in the ribs.

"Your mother's a lucky woman to have such loving daughters," he said, appraising us. "Loving—and lovely-looking, I might add."

Chapter Seven

Sharon and I spent another hour with Mom. At some point, Vicky, the nurse who had thrown us out of the room for our bad behavior, came in to inform us that her shift was over, that she was going off duty, and that the night nurse would be taking over. We thanked her profusely for attending to our mother and said we'd see her bright and early on Monday morning.

Not long after that, we decided it was time to let Mom get some rest. We kissed her goodnight and left the hospital. We were both exhausted, drained, starving, and so before heading home, we stopped for dinner at the Prawnbroker, a popular Sewall's Point eatery.

The restaurant was packed—typical for Florida in February—but we were seated within twenty minutes and served our meals within another twenty. Too pooped to talk, we ate in virtual silence, except for the flurry of conversation regarding my move to Stuart. I told Sharon about the job Melinda Carr had offered me. She was shocked that I was abandoning a career in television to babysit "some broken-down building on the beach," as she referred to the House of Refuge. I explained that I needed a change of scenery, that the keeper job had fallen into my lap, and that I was glad to be settling in Stuart because I'd be closer to Mom in case she got sick again. Well! The part about being closer to Mom provoked a mini hissy-fit. Sharon said that she was the one who'd always looked after Mom while I was the one who'd always looked after myself and what did I know about looking after anybody, anyway? What she'd meant, of course, was that I was a threat, barging into town and usurping her long-standing role as the Good Daughter.

The woman is terrified, I realized, as I listened to her do her martyr number. You'd think she would have welcomed the chance to share the burden of caring for our mother, but she was scared to death that after years of having Mom practically to herself, *I* would be horning in.

God, I thought. It's the competition for Daddy all over again.

It was close to nine o'clock by the time we paid the check and got up from the table. We were walking toward the exit, past the restaurant's handsomely appointed bar, when Sharon nudged me.

"What?" I said.

"Over there," she said, pointing at the two people sitting at the end of the bar, a man and a woman who appeared to be having a heated argument of their own. The man was gesturing wildly and the woman was dabbing at her eyes with a cocktail napkin and neither of them was drinking the champagne in front of them.

I squinted. "I can't see—"

"It's Dr. Hirshon," she said, nudging me again.

Sure enough, there was our mother's cardiologist, minus the lab coat. There, too, was Vicky, our mother's nurse, wearing a rather fetching red dress.

"And he told us he was going home," said Sharon as we stood together by the door, observing.

"Looks like he and Florence Nightingale are seeing each other," I said.

Sharon peered at the couple. "Not for much longer. I'm no lip-reader, but I could swear he's breaking up with her."

"Vicky does seem pretty distraught," I acknowledged. Vicky had just thrown her soggy cocktail napkin at Dr. Hirshon's face, where it attached itself to his beard, then dropped to the floor. "Come on, let's give them some privacy, Sharon. Ending a relationship is hard enough without people staring at you."

I turned to go, but she wouldn't budge.

"You don't think we should walk over and say hello?" she asked. "It might give Dr. Hirshon moral support to know that we're hot for him. I mean, *here* for him."

"We can be here for him tomorrow, at the hospital," I offered.

"I suppose." She cast a final stare at the bar before permitting me to drag her out the door.

W hen we saw Dr. Hirshon the next morning, he looked as chipper as he had the day before.

Vicky, on the other hand, looked dreadful.

As for my mother, she was much improved, physically, according to her array of monitoring devises; emotionally, however, she was a wreck, convinced that every muscle spasm, every gas pain, every twinge and twitch signaled another heart attack.

Dr. Hirshon was extremely understanding. He sat beside her on the bed, stroked her hand, told her in a soft, reassuring tone that she was right to ring for the nurse if she felt discomfort—any discomfort. He was kind and gentle with her, which touched me immensely and led me to believe that he was not a heartless cad for breaking up with Vicky at the Prawnbroker, but was a gentleman for bringing to a merciful end a relationship that was not to be.

Wow, now he really is free, I thought as I watched him try to jolly my mother out of her anxiety. Now, he'll be in the market for a *new* lady friend.

As if reading my mind, Dr. Hirshon winked at me.

———

My mother's angiogram showed that she had suffered only minor damage from the heart attack and that no further procedures were necessary. On Tuesday afternoon, she was moved to the telemetry unit of the hospital, where she spent three days in a private room overlooking the St. Lucie River and ate baked scrod until it was coming out of her ears. Dr. Hirshon checked on her each day, once in the morning and again at night. Not coincidentally, my sister and I were always present on those occasions.

On Thursday evening, after examining Mom, he said he was taking a break from his rounds and stopping in the hospital coffee shop for a quick bite. He asked Sharon and me if we wanted to join him. Surprise, surprise; we said yes. Over tunafish sandwiches and iced tea, he recounted the rather mawkish story of how he came to be a cardiologist. At the conclusion of the story, he suggested that we call him Jeffrey.

On Friday morning, he pronounced my mother well enough to leave the hospital. While she was putting on her clothes, he wrote prescriptions for her—for tenormin, Lipitor, and nitroglycerin—and instructed us that she should also take one baby aspirin per day, plus a vitamin E capsule.

"You can buy the aspirin over the counter, of course, but you can only buy the vitamins from my office," he said. "They're specially formulated for me under the brand name Heartily Hirshon."

"Heartily Hirshon?" I repeated.

"The name's corny, I know." He chuckled. "But the vitamins themselves are the real deal—my foray into the world of the doctor-as-entrepreneur. I set up a little company with a partner, after my patients kept telling me how overwhelmed they were by all the different types of vitamins in the health food stores. I wanted to offer them pure, unadulterated vitamin E—no synthetic substances, no preservatives, no baloney."

"That's very industrious of you, *Jeffrey*," Sharon said admiringly. "But why vitamin E and not one of the others?"

"Vitamin E is an active antioxidant, which means it prevents and dissolves blood clots, lowers blood pressure, and promotes general cardiovascular health. It also keeps people looking younger, by the way, not that either of you ladies needs to worry about that."

He scribbled something else down on the prescription pad. "Which reminds me: I think it's time you both had my home phone number. Feel free to call if something comes up."

"But you said you prefer it when your service contacts you at home," I reminded him.

He smiled. "I changed my mind."

He held out the piece of paper. Sharon and I practically dove for it, but she got there first, folded it into tiny squares, and slipped it into her purse.

Having Mom home brought new challenges. Sharon and I had assumed that she'd bounce back once she returned to familiar surroundings, that after resting up for a day or two, she'd be her old independent, don't-fuss-over-me self, even return to her job as a mediator. But while she took her medicine without objection and put up with the low-fat, low-cholesterol, low-sodium diet Dr. Hirshon had prescribed and walked obediently on the treadmill we'd bought her, she wasn't her old self; she had metamorphosed into a frightened child, a seventy-five-year-old who acted as if she'd been given a death sentence instead of a clean bill of health.

"Maybe we should call Dr. Hirshon," Sharon suggested that first weekend after my mother complained of chest pains.

So we did. Or, should I say, Sharon did. She dialed his home number, and when he answered she described the situation to him. He told her it was probably nothing to worry about but that she should bring Mom to the emergency room and he would meet them there. I would have gone along, but I had made plans to meet with Melinda about moving into the keeper's cottage. Besides, Sharon and I had agreed that we would take turns accompanying Mom to the doctor, the hospital, the grocery store; that once Sharon had resumed her life in Boca she would drive up to Stuart twice during the week (she was busy with her weddings on weekends) and that I would help out whenever she wasn't around. It was such a mature arrangement for us, I thought, this sharing of responsibility for our mother's care. Or was it something else we were sharing? *Someone* else?

The excursion to the emergency room that Sunday was uneventful, thank God, at least in terms of my mother's heart. As for my sister's heart, well, that was another matter.

"He asked me out!" she said while my mother was napping.

"Who?" I asked, as if I didn't have a clue.

"Jeffrey, of course. I was sitting in the waiting room at the hospital and he came and sat down next to me, to explain that Mom is going through a stage, psychologically. He looked divine, by the way. No lab coat, just khakis and a forest green polo shirt. Sort of a casual Sunday outfit, you know?"

I nodded, experiencing a peculiar feeling in the pit of my stomach.

"Anyhow," she chirped, "he mentioned that he had two tickets for some opera at the Lyric Theatre in downtown Stuart and wanted to know if I'd go with him."

"What did you tell him?" I managed, trying my best to look curious as opposed to covetous.

"I told him I couldn't go," Sharon replied with a sigh of regret. "For one thing, the concert is next Saturday night and I've got a wedding down in Delray Beach that starts at seven-thirty. For another, I'm stepping aside and letting you have Jeffrey, remember?"

"Sharon," I said, "it sounds like it's you he's pursuing. I don't want to stand in the way of—"

"I'm doing this for Mom," she cut me off, "so we won't upset her. If there's no man to come between her 'girls,' that's one less thing for us to fight about, right?"

I regarded my sister. She really was taking the high road this time. I wondered if I would have been so magnanimous if *I* had been the lucky recipient of Jeffrey Hirshon's invitation.

On Monday afternoon, a couple of hours after Sharon had packed up her Louis Vuitton bags and headed back to Boca, my mother was convinced yet again that she was having a second heart attack. I was torn. I didn't want to pester the doctor, given that he had examined

Mom only the day before, but I also didn't want to do anything to jeopardize her health. So I telephoned his office. The receptionist put me on hold for what seemed like an eternity. Finally, a woman introducing herself as Dr. Hirshon's nurse came on the line, asked me what the problem was, and told me to bring Mom into the office. My mother and I piled into the Delta 88 and off we went. I knew she wasn't her old self because she let me drive.

Dr. Hirshon's office was on Osceola Street, a quaint, charming, tree-lined street in downtown Stuart, near the hospital. Unfortunately, the office itself was neither quaint nor charming. It was a huge, impersonal building, because Dr. Hirshon, like many physicians trying to eke out a living in the age of managed care, did not have a solo practice; he was in a sixty-doctor group of multispecialists—urologists, dermatologists, gastroenterologists, you name it. When we walked in the door, I felt as if I'd stepped inside a Home Depot for hypochondriacs.

While Dr. Hirshon examined my mother, I chatted outside his office with his nurse, the one I'd spoken to on the phone. Her name was Joan, she was in her fifties, and she had mousy, light brown hair worn off her face, in a rather severe bun. She had, she confided to me, worked with the doctor for ten uninterrupted years.

"So you knew his wife," I ventured at some point in our conversation, seeing as Joan had initiated the girl talk. "His ex-wife, I should say."

"Francine?" She rolled her eyes. "I knew her all right. Poor thing. She's an addict."

"Oh. I'm sorry. What is she addicted to?"

"Shoes."

"Excuse me?"

"She buys shoes, expensive shoes. Can't help herself. She has a problem with handbags too. I guess you could say she's addicted to accessories. Nearly bankrupted the doctor."

"That *is* sad," I said.

"What's sad is the way she keeps harrassing him for money, even though he gave her everything—except, of course, the Porsche, the Hatteras, and the house here in town."

A sportscar, a boat, and a million-dollar house on the river. Clearly, Dr. Hirshon wasn't suffering.

"Well," said Joan. "I'd better get back to work or the doctor will have my head. He's got some temper."

"You've stayed with him for ten years. How bad a temper could it be?"

"Bad," she said. "But this job has other compensations."

I was about to ask "Like what?" when the doctor himself emerged. Joan scurried back to her desk.

"Our patient will be out in a minute," he informed me. "She's dressing."

"I appreciate your seeing her this afternoon," I said, feeling my cheeks flush, just as they had when I'd first met him. Perhaps it was his resemblance to my father that overwhelmed me. Perhaps it was that we were all placing my mother's life in his hands that made him appear Godlike to me. Perhaps it was even that Sharon had found him attractive initially and, as a result, out of habit, I viewed him as a trophy. Or perhaps it was that I hadn't had a boyfriend since Philip, who didn't really count; that I was hungry for male companionship, for someone to love.

Whatever the reason for my hot, red face, I couldn't deny that I felt alive when I was in Jeffrey Hirshon's company.

And so I listened attentively to his diagnosis of my mother's condition. "As I suspected, it's not a physical problem; it's the mortality issue," he said. And then I asked if there was anything I could do to distract her from her morbid thoughts. "It would be wonderful if you could stay in town for a while, Deborah," he said. "I know Sharon lives in Boca, but I really think your mother could use someone close-by. Someone to talk to, do things with." I smiled and told him I would be in Stuart for the foreseeable future; that within a week or two I was moving into the keeper's cottage at the House of Refuge. "That's fantastic," he said with enthusiasm. "I'm so pleased." He paused as if an idea had just come to him. "Deborah," he said, "I've got two tickets to a local opera company that's performing at the Lyric on Saturday night. How about being my date? If you're not busy."

Busy. As if.

I wanted to go out with Jeffrey in the worst way. It didn't matter that he had asked Sharon first. It didn't matter that he neglected to mention that he had asked Sharon first. It didn't even matter that I hated opera. But, of course, I declined his invitation. If my sister could resist him for my mother's sake, so, goddamn it, could I.

Chapter Eight

On Monday night, I called Sharon to report the emergency trip to Dr. Hirshon's office (I left out the bit about him asking me out). I told her I was concerned about our mother's mental state and that I thought we needed a more structured plan for taking care of her—just until she got her sea legs back. Sharon agreed. So we convinced Rose, who cleaned for Mom on Tuesdays, to come in on Fridays too. Sharon said she would drive up and spend Wednesdays and Thursdays at the house. And I would be on duty Saturdays through Mondays.

The plan worked. By the end of the week, my mother felt less anxious because she had people around her on a regular basis. She started eating and sleeping better, visited with her friends, even tended to her garden again. Rose was happy that she was earning an additional day's pay. And Sharon was relieved that she could go back to work without having to worry about Mom. The only problem was me. I missed New York. I missed the show. I was desperately lonely.

I was so lonely that I called Woody. His "manservant" said he had rented a villa in Tuscany and wouldn't be back in Manhattan for a month.

I was so lonely that I called Helen. She said that Philip had moved in with the ex-Harlequin editor and that they were talking about adopting a baby from Romania. "But I've only been gone a couple of weeks," I said. "How could all that have happened so fast?" "Philip's a fast worker, remember?" she clucked and then dished more dirt that I didn't particularly want to hear.

I was so lonely that I even called the super at my apartment building, to see if he was forwarding my mail the way he'd promised, since I hadn't received any. "Always so pesty," he snarled, surly as ever. "Maybe nobody's writing to you. Ever think of *that?*"

I was so lonely that on the following Monday night, after my mother mentioned that she had strained her arm weeding, I called Dr. Hirshon. At home. To make sure that she wasn't having another heart attack. "I remembered that the pain can radiate down the left arm," I said, shoveling the you-know-what. "I didn't want to take any chances." He said that, seeing as we were neighbors, he'd be right over.

I felt like the scheming heroine of an old movie—the type of pathetic woman who fakes the vapors to get the guy to pay attention to her, only in this case it was my *mother's* vapors I was faking. Still, I had accomplished my mission: Jeffrey Hirshon was on his way over to my mother's house, and Sharon was an hour-and-a-half away in Boca.

While I waited for him to show up, I wondered what he would think of the house, my father's Shangri-la. It was pretty rustic compared to his place, which I had walked by a few times, hoping he'd be out there mowing the lawn or something. He lived in the Highpoint section of Sewall's Point, at the southernmost tip of the peninsula, in a two-story, peach-colored, metal-roofed house that had wraparound verandahs and porches, window boxes overflowing with impatiens, and, from what I could see by peeking through the trees, a swimming pool, outdoor Jacuzzi, and boat dock. Not bad for a man whose ex-wife had nearly "bankrupted" him, according to his nurse.

"Great place," he said when I opened the door for him. "Sort of your own private Shangri-la."

I stared at him.

"Something wrong?" he asked.

"Not at all." This man and I are meant to be, I thought. The hell with Sharon.

I led him upstairs, to my mother's bedroom. He talked to her more than he actually examined her, asking her where it hurt, asking her if she was short of breath, asking her if she was taking the medications he had prescribed. After a few minutes, he determined that the pain in her arm was due to muscle strain, not cardiac arrest, but he said he was glad we had gotten in touch with him, as a precaution.

When he and I were alone, he praised me for being so solicitous of my mother, so caring. "You're a terrific woman, Deborah," he said. "Sharon is too, as I've discovered from the long phone conversations she and I have had over the past week." Long phone conversations? Funny, she never uttered a word about them. "I know patients are supposed to develop crushes on their doctors, but I think I've got it backwards; *I've* developed a crush on my patient's *daughters.*"

Jeez. He's coming on to both of us, I thought, feeling slightly creeped out.

"It's still early," he said, checking his watch and then his beeper. "Want to go to a movie? Or have dinner? I'm a fan of the food at the Flagler Grill. I could see if they've got a table. Or maybe you'd like to come back to my place." He grinned. "We could sit and relax, have a drink, discuss this silly crush of mine." He was standing next to me now, standing over me, really. The tip of his beard was tickling the top of my head.

Oh, go out with him, I thought. When are you ever gonna get an opportunity like this? A nice man. A nice-looking man. A doctor who saved your mother's life. A doctor who called your father's Shangri-la a Shangri-la.

No! I chided myself. A deal's a deal. You and Sharon agreed not to go out with Jeffrey Hirshon. You must be strong. You must not succumb to his compliments. You must not jeopardize your mother's health by fighting with your sister.

"I'd love to, Jeffrey, but I've got to be up early in the morning," I said. "I'm moving to Hutchinson island to start the job I told you about."

"Right. With the Historical Society," he said. "Sounds romantic, living in that beach cottage. Let me know when you're ready for company."

I'm ready now! I wanted to scream. *Take me!* Instead, I thanked him for coming over and watched him drive off in his Porsche.

On Tuesday morning, just after Rose arrived, I loaded my bags into the '82 Pontiac I'd bought off a used-car lot on Federal Highway. The thing had over a hundred thousand miles on it and wasn't exactly in showroom shape, but it had been cheap—amazingly cheap—and I figured it would be fine for tooling around Stuart.

I kissed my mother goodbye, reminding her that I'd be just over the bridge if she needed me, and took off. As much as I loved her, I couldn't wait to be on my own again.

The Pontiac and I chugged across the causeway to Hutchinson Island. It was a glorious day—bright blue sky, moderate breezes, temperature in the eighties—and as I turned right at the Indian River Plantation, the area's only major hotel-and-golf resort, and drove down MacArthur Boulevard, toward the House of Refuge, I felt like a kid again—a college kid on spring break, heading for the beach in my broken-down jalopy, radio blaring, wind in my hair, the whole bit. All that was missing was a surfboard.

Melinda Carr was waiting for me at the gate to let me in, since it was still early and neither the House of Refuge nor the adjacent gift shop were open for business yet.

"I'm thrilled you've accepted the position," she said, after inquiring how my mother was. "Absolutely exhultant."

"I'm pretty exhultant myself," I said as we trotted toward the little white cottage that was to be my new home. As we walked, I glanced out over the beach and felt a smile spread across my face. The sand was a soft, creamy beige, the natural promontory a craggy maze of cavelike rocks, the ocean a deep, almost navy blue. And then, of course, there was that fabulous smell—the briny, salty sea smell that clears the mind as well as the sinuses. I can't believe that the Historical Society is actually paying me to wake up to *this* every morning, I thought, not missing New York in the slightest, suddenly.

When we got to the cottage, Melinda paused before unlocking the door.

"Now I've warned you, Deborah. This isn't Mar-a-Lago," she said, referring to Donald Trump's enormous mansion-cum-private club in Palm Beach. "What's more, the previous keeper didn't take very good care of the furniture. It's a tad shabby, I'm afraid."

"That's okay," I told Melinda, feeling like a bride impatient to be carried over the threshold. "Let's see it already."

Melinda finally opened the door.

We entered through the cottage's kitchen, which was about the size of my galley kitchen in New York with similarly miniature appliances, and proceeded into the living room, where there was a rather beat-up sleep-sofa, a coffee table made out of driftwood, and a couple of futons—all resting on badly stained wall-to-wall carpeting that was a shade I'll call Gulden's mustard. Above the sofa were three large windows overlooking the ocean, the room's main attraction. The bedroom was small but faced west, in the direction of the Intracoastal Waterway, and I anticipated that the sunsets on that side of the cottage would be as spectacular as the living room's sunrises. In addition to a bathroom and an office/storage area, there was a porch that spanned the front and back of the cottage and provided a truly spectacular view of the sea, the beach, and the Intracoastal; I knew instantly that I would spend much of my time there, reading, contemplating my future, fantasizing about my mother's cardiologist.

"As we've discussed," said Melinda after the tour, "you'll be our caretaker here, our *castellan,* so to speak. If there are problems with any of the buildings on the property, you're to call Ray Scalley, the supervisor at the Martin County Building Maintenance Department, and have him send me the invoices for whatever work is done." She handed me his business card. "If there are problems with intruders, you'll call nine-one-one, of course."

"Intruders?"

"Yes. Malfeasants."

"I knew what the word meant, Melinda. I was just surprised that anybody would break into this place. As you pointed out, it's not exactly Mar-a-Lago." I looked down at the stained carpet.

"Oh, I wasn't talking about your little cottage. I was referring to the other buildings. Many people have keys to the gate—the maintenance staff, the volunteers, et cetera—and every once in awhile, they decide to use them in the middle of the night, for goodness sake. For a lark, I suppose. And then you'll get the occasional drunk who decides to climb over the gate and peek inside the buildings. Or the hormonal teenagers who are bound and determined to have sexual intercourse up in the observation tower. It's nothing to be frightened about, believe me."

I believed Melinda, but I had just fled New York after my apartment had been broken into and trashed. I thought I had traded murder and mayhem for peace and quiet.

"Now, unless you have any questions, I'll leave and let you get settled," said Melinda, handing me the keys to the gate and the buildings and then moving toward the door of the cottage. "The volunteer staff will be arriving shortly. I'm sure you'll find them very helpful, very pleasant."

We shook hands. "I'm lucky that this job came along," I told her. "The timing was perfect."

"For me too," she said. "As I indicated at our initial meeting, the Historical Society was searching for someone like you, someone who knows how to conduct herself in a mature, responsible way."

"I'll do my best to live up to the organization's high standards," I said, feeling as if I'd just enlisted in the marines.

After I unpacked my things, I inspected the cottage more closely. It needed a thorough cleaning and some paint touchups, but my mother had loaded me up with paper towels, Fantastik, and other essentials, and I was prepared to do battle. The important thing was, I loved my little place by the sea, felt at home the minute I walked in the door.

Now, I thought, if I can just get the gas stove to light, the toilet to flush properly, and the window in the bedroom to open, I'll be a happy gal.

I picked up the business card Melinda had given me and dialed the number of Ray Scalley, the county building and maintenance supervisor who was supposed to fix things. I hoped he'd be less surly than my super in New York.

I got a recorded message.

"Hello," I said. "My name is Deborah Peltz and I'm the new keeper at the House of Refuge, having recently moved to Stuart from Manhattan. Melinda Carr from the Historical Society suggested that I call Mr. Scalley if there are problems with any of the buildings here. Please call me back." I left my number. I repeated it twice, in fact.

While I waited for the call-back, I scrubbed the kitchen, dusted the furniture, vacuumed the carpet, made the bed, ate the lunch my mother had packed for me, and sat on the porch gazing at the ocean. In other words, Ray Scalley did not return my call with great urgency. Actually, he did not return the call at all; he showed up.

"Ray Scalley. Howareya," he said, stepping past me, into the cottage. "I was down the street at the Elliott Museum when I checked in at the office for messages. They gave me yours. What's the trouble?"

"It's nice to meet you too," I said dryly. Well, he wasn't quite as surly as my old super, but he wasn't Mr. Charm either. "I'm Deborah Peltz."

"Right. From New York. That's what you said in your message."

His accent was southern as opposed to the super's, which was Serbian. Also, he was younger than "Ivan the Terrible," as I used to refer to the super, in his late thirties or early forties, I guessed. He had reddish-brown hair, about the same color as my mine, and it hung straight, down around the collar of his light blue button-down shirt, which was tucked inside a pair of well-worn blue jeans. He was of medium height and medium build and was great-looking, if your idea of great-looking is the Marlboro Man. No, he wasn't wearing a cowboy hat, but he had the swagger of a cowboy, of a loner, a rugged outdoorsy type, complete with a scar on his chin an inch or two below his lower lip.

"I'd offer you something cold to drink, but I only moved in a few hours ago and I haven't gone grocery shopping yet."

"Tap water's fine," he said. "We're not afraid to drink ours here."

Oh, I get it, I thought. He hates New Yorkers. He's probably a hick who's never been out of Martin County.

I got him a glass of water. He thanked me.

"Now, maybe you'll tell me what needs fixing," he said. "Diane."

"Deborah," I corrected him. "The problems are here in the cottage. First, there's the stove. When you turn on the gas, nothing happens. Also, the toilet only stops flushing if you jiggle the handle. And then there's the window in the bedroom that won't open. It's stuck or something."

Ray Scalley stared at me as if I had two heads. "You called me over here for this, Diane?"

"It's *Deborah*," I said, becoming annoyed. "You must be bad with names."

"No. I'm pretty good with names," he said. "I'm just bad with yours."

"I'm flattered. About the toilet—"

"Get a plumber."

"And the stove?"

"Call the gas company."

"What about the window? Or shouldn't I ask?" This guy was making my old super seem positively charismatic.

"Look, Deborah—"

"There. That wasn't so hard, was it?"

He actually managed a smile. I wanted to break open a bottle of champagne. Over his head.

"Deborah," he repeated. "It's your first day on the job, so you don't have the lay of the land, as they say. I supervise all the county-owned buildings, including the House of Refuge, which is over a century old and needs major renovations from time to time. When Melinda Carr gave you my number, she didn't mean for you to call me about the toilet in your cottage. She meant for you to call me if there's a leak in the roof of the museum or rotting in one of the columns or damage to the siding following a storm. I'm not some redneck handyman who chews tobacco and high-cracks his customers. I not only eat with a knife and fork, I take a shower every now and then. What's more, I have a degree in building construction from the University of Florida with specialties in historic preservation, quantity surveying, site development, and business law. In other words, I'd be privileged to take a look at your stove, your toilet, and your window while I'm here, but next time, reach out and touch somebody from the Yellow Pages, huh?"

Sheesh! Was this person full of himself or what? Touchy, too.

I replayed his rant, to try to figure out what I had done to set him off, and then I started to laugh. When he asked me what was so funny, I said, "I used to write for a TV soap opera. That little lecture you just gave me reminded me of a scene I wrote a couple of years ago where the female character asks the male character if he'd mind changing her flat tire. He responds by telling her to change the damn tire herself. He says, 'What do I look like? A car mechanic?' You see any similarity here?"

"Vaguely. What happened in your next scene? Did the guy change the lady's tire and end up in bed with her? That's how it usually works on those shows, doesn't it?"

"Yeah, but not this time. The guy changed her tire and then he shot and killed her."

"Why on earth did he do that?"

"The actress's contract wasn't being renewed. We had to write her out of the show."

He laughed. "Sounds like some job you had up there in New York. What made you chuck it all to be a caretaker in little ol' Stuart?"

"My mother lives here," I said. "She had a heart attack and is recuperating. I wanted to be close-by." I didn't mention that another reason I had abandoned my life in New York was my raging midlife crisis.

"Sorry about your mother. Sorry about the lecture, too. I had no right to hammer away at you. How were you supposed to know who does what around here?"

"Or who has a chip on his shoulder?"

He laughed again. "You're a pretty straight shooter, aren't you?"

"I try to be."

"I admire that." He shook my hand. "Ray Scalley. Nice to meet you, Deborah. We might as well start over, right?"

"Right." Maybe he doesn't have an attitude, I thought. Maybe he's just shy.

"You say your mother's doing better?" he asked.

"Much better, thanks."

"Who's her doctor over at Martin Memorial?"

"Jeffrey Hirshon." I tried not to blush.

"I was afraid of that. But then Hirshon does a booming business in town."

"Do you know Jeffrey?" I asked tentatively, thinking it unlikely that the two men traveled in the same circles.

"Oh, I know him," Ray replied. "Too well." He looked distressed suddenly, as if the mere mention of Jeffrey's name had touched a nerve. "I realize I could be sticking my nose where it doesn't belong, but my advice to you is to keep your mother away from the bastard."

"Bastard?" I said, stunned by his reaction. "That's a little harsh, isn't it? I have no idea why you feel the way you do, but Dr. Hirshon saved my mother's life. He's a good doctor. A good friend, too."

Ray nodded. "Forget I said anything." He set the glass of water I'd given him down on the kitchen counter. "Now, how about showing me the things that need fixing?"

"Oh, that's not necessary, Ray. I'll call the appropriate people."

"I'm happy to help," he said. "And then I'll be on my way."

I showed him the things that needed fixing and he fixed them. And then he was on his way.

Chapter Nine

Later that afternoon, I drove to Stuart Fine Foods and bought groceries. I loaded them into the trunk of the Pontiac, got into the car, and put the key in the ignition. Unfortunately, the engine refused to turn over, even after several attempts. I realized that the battery must be dead. Swell. I sat there like a doofus, trying to decide what to do, until I caught Jeffrey Hirshon's Porsche zipping into the lot. My heart thumped in my chest as I hopped out of the car and waved him down.

"Deborah. Is something wrong?" he asked, leaning out of the Porsche. He was still wearing his lab coat. Perhaps he was taking a break between patients.

"Nothing serious," I said. "Just car trouble. Do you think you could give me a jump start?"

"My pleasure," he replied with his nice-guy smile.

"Thanks. You're becoming a regular knight in shining armor. First, you rescue my mother. Now, you rescue my car, although I'm not sure the car is worth rescuing. I've only had it a week and it's been in the shop three times."

"Sounds like you've got a lemon."

"Or else I've got a new strain of that psychological disorder."

"Which disorder is that?"

"The one where a woman makes her child sick on purpose so she has to keep taking it to the hospital."

"You mean, Münchausen by Proxy."

"Right. I think I've got Münchausen by Pontiac."

He laughed. "Let's get this Pontiac humming."

While we waited for my battery to charge, Jeffrey asked me how Mom was doing, how I liked my new digs on Hutchinson Island, and whether I was free for dinner that night.

"I'll be seeing patients at the hospital until about eight-thirty," he said, "but after that I'm all yours."

All mine, I thought greedily—and then I remembered the Promise.

"I can't go out," I said reluctantly. "It's my first day on the job. I should probably hang around the cottage."

He shook his head. "I'm not reading you, Deborah. I get the distinct impression that you like me, and yet every time I ask you out you turn me down."

"I do like you, Jeffrey. Very much. It's just that—" I stopped. How could I explain about my pact with Sharon, about our fragile truce after years of intense sibling rivalry, about how antsy she was to snag another husband? How could I make him understand that going out with him even once could set off another estrangement from her and upset my mother terribly? How could I tell him that I was weak and vulnerable and lonely and was exercising every ounce of restraint I had by saying no to him? How?

"Ah, the picture's coming in clearer now," he said, studying me. "This has to do with your sister, doesn't it? You're leery about going out with me because I've shown an interest in her, too. You're afraid I'm playing games with the two of you."

"As a matter of fact, you did say you had crushes on both of us, and you did ask Sharon to the opera before you asked me, so I—"

"Let me stop you," he said, placing his forefinger across my lips. "I want to state, right here right now, that I like Sharon very much but she isn't you, Deborah. *You're* the one I want to spend time with. *You're* the one I want to get to know better. I made that flip remark about the crushes because I thought you both needed cheering up, given the situation with your mother. As for the opera, I invited Sharon first because she seemed more—" He paused, as if searching for the precise word.

"More what?"

"Eager. Or should I say: *willing.*" He winked. "You, on the other hand, have been sending me mixed signals."

So he likes me better than Sharon, I mused. A Pyrrhic victory.

"I'm not trying to confuse you, Jeffrey. But, for reasons I can't go in to, I have to pass on the dinner date tonight," I said evasively.

"Then how about tomorrow night? The weather's supposed to be a carbon copy of today, and I'll be home earlier, around seven. We could take the boat out, go for a moonlight cruise. What do you say?"

God, this was hard. "I'm sorry," I answered. "I can't tomorrow night either."

He shrugged. "I don't get it, but if you change your mind, I'll be home. Just come on over."

I thanked him again and ducked into the Pontiac.

When I got back to the cottage, the volunteers were closing up the House of Refuge and gift shop. One of them, an elderly man named Fred Zimsky, offered to carry my groceries into the kitchen for me. At first, I resisted his help—he was stooped over and quite frail-looking and I was afraid that heavy lifting might do him in—but he was full of pep and personality and insisted that he was up to the task.

He deposited the bags in the kitchen and proceeded to tell me the story of how he came to be a volunteer at the museum.

"My beloved wife, Ellie, had Alzheimer's and I had to put her in a nursing home," he said. "I was lost without her. A mess. My neighbors at the condominium thought I needed a distraction, because I was sitting, day after day, in that nursing home with a wife who didn't recognize me anymore. One of them made a few calls and found out they needed volunteers here. Well, I had always loved history—nautical history, especially—and what's bad about working so close to the ocean, right? So I started volunteering, three hours every afternoon, and the next thing I knew I was feeling great. My Ellie passed away last year and I miss her, naturally, but this place brought me back to life, what with giving tours, telling the tourists about the shipwrecked sailors, and all that. Talking to them gives me a big kick, reminds me how important it is to connect with people. Now I work out at a gym twice a week. I catch the latest movies. I belong to a reading group at the library. Eighty-four years old and I'm a kid again."

"No doubt about that," I said, energized from listening to him. "I only hope the House of Refuge proves to be a tonic for me, too."

"It will if you let it." He turned to go.

"Fred?"

"Yes?"

"Are you seeing anyone? A woman, I mean?"

He laughed. "You're not coming on to me, are you, Debbie?"

"No. But I've got a mother with the most extraordinary blue eyes. Want to meet her?"

"Sure. Give me her number," said Fred. "I'm between girlfriends."

After Fred left, I called my mother to make sure she was okay about sleeping alone for the first time since getting out of the hospital. She said she was fine. I told her she might be hearing from a a man named Fred Zimsky. "What about?" she asked.

"A blind date," I said. "I thought it would be nice if *one* of us had a social life."

———

As for my first night in the cottage, it was magical. No drunks. No hormonal teenagers. No midnight trespassers. Just waves lapping against the rocks, the occasional splish-splash of fish jumping in and out of the water, and the vast, cloudless sky, dotted with stars. The scene outside the cottage was so beautiful and the night air so mild that I pulled the down comforter off the bed, dragged it out to the chaise longue on the porch, wrapped myself in it, and slept there.

On Wednesday, Sharon arrived in Stuart for her two-day stint. Around 2:30, she stopped by the cottage, to see "what you've gotten yourself into," she said. After giving the place the once-over, she conceded that the view was divine but added that if the cottage had been in Boca, it would have been bulldozed years ago. "Yeah, to make way for more McMansions," I said under my breath.

"I saw Jeffrey this morning," she informed me as we were sitting on the porch. "I swung by his office to drop off a thank-you note. I wanted to show my appreciation for everything he's done for Mom."

"A thank-you note," I said dryly. "How Emily Post."

"Actually, it was a thank-you poem. A thank-you *limerick*. 'There once was a doctor named Jeff—"

"I'm sure it was very clever," I cut her off.

"Jeffrey thought so. He said that no one had ever written him a limerick before. Can you imagine?"

"Vividly."

"Anyhow, we ended up talking and talking and talking. I hate to say this, knowing how you feel about him, but I think *I'm* the one he's interested in, Deborah."

I didn't respond. How could I, after what Jeffrey had told me just the day before?

"For example," Sharon went on, "I mentioned that I had a son and he insisted on hearing all about Norman, as busy as he was with patients. I said to myself, Would this man make a fabulous father for my child or what? I have to admit, Deborah, it's getting more and more difficult to stick to our little bargain and keep myself from marching right over to his house and letting nature take its course."

Tell me about it.

My mother called and asked me if I would join her and Sharon for dinner that night, but I begged off, saying I was still settling in at the cottage, still had a lot of unpacking ahead of me. The truth was, there was a sensational sunset building across the Intracoastal—the sky was an exquisite canvas of yellow and gold and pink—and all I wanted to do was sit on my porch, have a glass of wine, and stare at it. Besides, the thought of having to put up with Sharon for an entire evening, of having to pretend we were bosom buddies for my mother's sake, was more than I could bear. I knew the subject of Jeffrey would come up—*she* was sure to bring it up—and I would be forced to act as if I didn't care about him, as if he hadn't told me flat out that he cared about me, as if I didn't feel like I'd been strait-jacketed by my peace pact with my sister.

And so I sat with my wine on the porch. And when I drained the glass, I poured myself another. And another. I sat there drinking and looking out over the water; sat there watching the sun go down and the moon come up; sat there thinking about Jeffrey and his boat, about the cruise he'd offered to take me on.

Suddenly, I remembered what Aunt Harriet had said at my mother's birthday party: how I'd been hiding my light under a bushel, so I wouldn't outshine Sharon; how I'd been afraid to go after my Mr. Right for fear of offending my Dreaded Sibling.

And then I snapped.

Not that I'm blaming Aunt Harriet for what happened that night, any more than I'm blaming the wine I consumed. All I know is that one minute I was sitting there on the porch, in that intensely ro-mantic setting, musing that Jeffrey was only a bridge ride away, and seconds later I was rushing into my bedroom, changing my clothes, and applying makeup, perfume, and a squirt of breath freshener. And then I was out the door.

A girl's got to do what a girl's got to do, I thought as I bounded into the Pontiac and prayed that it would start. Why should I deny myself a little pleasure, a little solace during this turbulent time in my life? How will it hurt? Who will it hurt? Sharon won't find out, which means my mother won't find out. *Nobody* will find out, because it's only going to be one night, one intimate night between two mature, consenting adults. One night. What's the harm?

My hands were trembling as I drove down MacArthur Boulevard to the bridge linking Hutchinson Island to Sewall's Point. At the traffic light, I made a left turn onto South Sewall's Point Road and stayed on that street instead of crossing over to South River Road, where my mother lived. (God forbid, she or Sharon should look out the window and spot my car.)

I continued on until I approached Jeffrey's house, and then I slowed down, my palms so clammy they were practically sliding off the steering wheel. It had suddenly occurred to me that, after I'd declined Jeffrey's invitation, he might have asked someone else to join him; it was entirely possible he was not alone.

I stopped in front of his house, poked my head out the Pontiac's window, and peered at the place. It was dark on the street, in spite of the moon, but I could tell there wasn't another car parked in the driveway. I figured the coast was clear and pulled in.

Jeffrey's outside lights weren't illuminated, I noticed with relief, so I assumed he wasn't expecting company. But the darkness made it difficult to see up his front walk, and I hoped I'd make it to the door without slamming into a palm tree.

Maybe he's not even home, I thought, as I drew closer to the house, my entire body tingling with excitement—and guilt. Yes, I was feeling guilty now, tremendously guilty that *I* was the one who wasn't living up to my agreement with Sharon.

You should be ashamed of yourself, I said to myself. Bad girl.

And then I heard something near the front door. A rustling in the trees.

I jumped, still spooked by the memory of the crooks who'd cleaned out my apartment. After a few seconds I realized it was probably just a raccoon, a possum, or one of the other nocturnal creatures that bedevil the residents of Sewall's Point by digging up their landscaping and defecating in their swimming pools.

I stepped closer to the door, my hand poised to lift the brass knocker, when the rustling grew louder.

I gasped in earnest this time, particularly when I saw that the creature in the trees wasn't a raccoon—it was Sharon.

"What the hell are *you* doing here?" she hissed as she emerged from the thicket, picking off the dead palm fronds that were clinging to her extremely clinging sweater. Judging by all the cleavage, she was not dressed for tree trimming.

"What the hell am *I* doing here?" I said, trying—and failing—to keep my voice down. *"You're* the one who's been skulking around in the bushes like some thief in the night."

"I wasn't skulking. I was walking," she said defensively. "Yes, that's it. I was taking an after-dinner stroll in the neighborhood and happened by Jeffrey's. When I heard someone drive up, I thought he might have company. So I, uh, got out of the way."

"You *hid,*" I said accusingly. "When you saw it was me, you hid. Because you knew you were breaking our agreement."

"I was breaking our agreement?" She glowered. "What about you? You told Mom you couldn't come over for dinner tonight because you had *sooo* much unpacking to do. Unpacking, my ass. You've been drinking. You smell like the inside of a wine bottle."

So much for the breath freshener. "Look, Sharon, you may as well know the truth. I came here because Jeffrey *asked* me to. He invited me on his boat. For a moonlight cruise. I hate to break this to you, but I'm the one he's interested in."

She laughed. *Cackled* was more like it. "I hate to break this to *you,* Sis, but Jeffrey told me just this afternoon that *I'm* the one he wants. He said he was only being nice to you because of Mom. And because you seemed so—"

"What?"

"Eager. No. *Willing* was the word I think he used."

I staggered back. It couldn't be true. What Sharon was saying simply could not be true. Jeffrey would never hand us the same line of bullshit. Or would he?

"You've resented me for years," I said, as we stood nose to nose at the front door. "You'd do anything, say anything to hurt me."

"What about your resentment of me?" she said. "You're the only one in the family who didn't go to Norman's graduation, let's not forget."

"I had the flu that day," I shouted. We were both shouting now. "I had a one-hundred-two-degree fever."

"Oh, really?" She smirked. "The last time you brought up your famous 'fever,' you claimed it was one-hundred-three."

"Whatever. The point is, you're always criticizing me, always on my back. I can't do a fucking thing without taking a load of crap from you about it. If it isn't Norman's graduation, it's my lifestyle or my job or your demented notion that you're a better daughter than I am."

"Now I'm demented. Isn't that rich," she said. "Obviously, *you're* the one who constantly attacks *me*. Have you ever heard yourself on the subject of my ex-husbands? So I've had a couple of bad marriages. So what?"

"Not a couple. Three."

"Whatever. You're the one who's always on my back about that. And now you're on my back about Jeffrey. Dear, sweet Jeffrey. You're wondering if I'll marry him too, aren't you?"

"No, Sharon. I'm wondering if you're still stuck in a competition for Daddy."

"Daddy? What's he got to do with this?"

"You once told me that he died for you the day I was born. Do you remember saying that, Sharon?"

"No."

"Well, you did. You said that the minute I came into the world, he stopped paying attention to you. And you've held it against me ever since. Now, first of all, it's not my fault that I was born. Second of all, it's not my fault that Daddy noticed. Third of all, the older I got, the less he was home, and after a while, he didn't pay attention to me either."

She was quiet for a minute. Then she shook her head. "What *I* remember is the cheerleading."

"Cheerleading? How did we get from Daddy to cheerleading?"

"I remember that I tried out in high school and didn't make the team. I also remember that you tried out and did make the team. And if *that* wasn't enough of a slap in my face, you went around the house practicing back flips and cartwheels and splits, not to mention those dumb cheers. *Rah rah rah! Sis boom bah!* God, it made me sick."

"And *you've* held that against *me* ever since?"

"I don't know! I don't know! I'm too cold for a psychodrama." She wrapped her arms around herself and shivered.

"Of course you're cold," I said. "That skimpy sweater you're wearing doesn't cover much."

"Jeffrey won't mind." She batted her eyelashes.

"Sharon, Jeffrey really did invite *me* over here tonight. He said he wanted to get to know me better."

"He told *me* the same thing," she maintained. "I wouldn't be here otherwise."

"Then he's been dishonest with both of us," I said, realizing we'd been had. And Jeffrey had seemed so nice, so different from the others.

"Dishonest? Jeffrey?"

"I think we were wrong about him, Sharon. I think we should go inside and confront him."

"You mean, ask him point-blank if he's been toying with our emotions?"

"Yes. Or are you afraid of the truth?"

Her nostrils flared. "I'm ready if you are," she said, and reached for the brass knocker.

She knocked on the door. We waited. No answer.

"Let *me* try it," I said, giving her a little shove out of the way before banging the knocker against the door. Again, we waited. Again, no answer.

"You didn't bang it hard enough," Sharon said, pushing me aside and pounding the knocker three times.

As the knocker struck the door the third time, the weight of the blow—and our leaning on it—caused the door to open, and before we could stop ourselves, we were tumbling inside the house.

"He must have gone out and forgotten to lock up," I said as we peered into the foyer, which was not as grand as Sharon's but was pretty grand nevertheless.

"No. He told me he would be home tonight," she insisted.

"Maybe he's watching TV or listening to music, and can't hear us." She called out to him. *"Jeffrey? Hello! It's Sharon Peltz!"*

"And Deborah Peltz!" I added, in case I really was the one he wanted.

There was silence, except for a series of very faint beeps.

"It could be his answering machine," I said. "Maybe he's got messages."

Assuming Jeffrey had, indeed, gone out, we flipped on some lights and followed the beeping sound through the first floor of the house, through the living room, past the dining room, into the family room. We were on the threshold of what appeared to be a den or office, the room from which the beeping was emanating, when I spotted something.

"Sharon," I said, nudging her. "What's that on the floor? Next to the desk?"

She switched on a light—and then she screamed.

I would have screamed too, but nothing came out.

"Deborah! He's been shot!" cried Sharon, motioning at the body splayed on the sisal carpet—the body of Jeffrey Hirshon, M.D.

He was lying in a pool of blood, face up, a bullet hole through his chest, through his *heart,* ironically, but there was no gun around, at least not that we could see. What we did observe was that he was ghostly pale—even his beard looked wilted—and he was utterly still.

Shaking off our shock and fear and nausea, Sharon and I rushed to his side and knelt on the floor next to him. Neither of us was proficient in CPR, so we improvised, Sharon breathing into his mouth, I pushing down on his chest. I had written many such scenes for *From This Day Forward,* yet never imagined I'd be starring in one.

When our efforts to revive Jeffrey failed, I picked up the phone in the office. I was poised to dial 911, but there was no need, it turned out. Miraculously, the police had already arrived.

"Oh, thank God. I was just about to call you," I said with relief, as one of Sewall's Point's Finest stormed into the den.

"Freeze!" he yelled, pointing a gun at Sharon and me. "Drop that phone! Hands in the air! Nobody move!"

I stuck my hands in the air and looked obedient. Sharon put hers on her hips and pouted.

"What are you shouting at *us* for?" she scolded the officer. "We were trying to help the poor man."

"I said 'Freeze!'" he barked.

"I *am*," she muttered through chattering teeth. "Somebody should turn down the air conditioning in this place."

The barking cop was not amused. He kept his gun on us, even as another officer came thundering into the den with his gun drawn. I felt like some hardened criminal—until I reminded myself that the only crime I'd committed was falling for a man who had, apparently, thought nothing of two-timing me with my own sister.

"Check him for a pulse," the first cop said to the second cop, referring, of course, to Jeffrey.

The second cop returned his gun to his holster and knelt beside the body. "Forget EMS," he said when he found no pulse. "This guy's ready for the body bag."

From there, the situation really began to deteriorate. The first cop radioed for still more cops—a cast of thousands, it seemed to me. Before I knew it, there were deputies from the Martin County Sheriff's Office, a couple of detectives, the chief of the Sewall's Point Police, the county medical examiner, and a vanload of evidence collectors. Also swarming the scene were members of the local media, who'd picked up the action on their police scanners, plus neighbors, lots of neighbors, several of them in their pajamas.

At some point during this nightmare, one of the cops was instructed to take Sharon and me outside, into a patrol car. When Sharon resisted, complaining that she had a terrible headache and wanted to go back to my mother's, his superior said, "'Cuff her."

Sharon didn't care for that idea either. "Handcuffs!" she balked. "Are you aware that this diamond tennis bracelet I'm wearing could get scratched?" She held up her right wrist.

The cop clamped the handcuffs on her. On me, too.

"Look. You don't think *we* shot Dr. Hirshon," I protested.

"If you didn't shoot him then what are you doing here, covered in blood, raising a ruckus?" asked the handcuffer.

"Raising a ruckus?" I said.

"Yeah," he said. "A neighbor reported a disturbance—two women arguing outside the doctor's house. The officers over there came to see what the trouble was. When they saw that the front door was open, they figured they were dealing with a burglary, not a homicide."

A homicide, I thought, as it was all beginning to sink in. A *murder*. Jeffrey Hirshon had been offed. Jeffrey, the cardiologist. Jeffrey, the charmer. Jeffrey, the lying, cheating son-of-a-bitch.

Yes, I was hurt and angry that he had turned out to be a rat, but I didn't want him dead! And I certainly didn't want to be caught standing over his dead body!

My, won't Melinda Carr be thrilled to hear about this, I mused, remembering her little speech about the Historical Society and the impeccable reputation it demanded of its employees.

Of course, it was my mother, not my job, I was most worried about. I hoped she wouldn't hear what had happened—at least not until Sharon and I had a chance to talk to her first.

"Get 'em outside already, so we can secure the crime scene," the cop who seemed to be in charge ordered the cop who was herding us out the front door. "Let 'em cool their heels before we drive 'em down to the station for questioning."

For questioning. In the murder of Jeffrey Hirshon.

Sharon and I looked at each other, first helplessly, then cautiously.

As we were being stuffed into the backseat of a patrol car, it suddenly occurred to us that, no matter how dysfunctional our relationship had been, no matter what had happened between us in the past, we could no longer afford to be each other's enemy; we were now each other's alibi.

Part
Two

Chapter Ten

While Sharon and I sat in the backseat of the patrol car for what seemed like a lifetime, our friendly cop stood guard outside the car, watching our every move—and, unbenownst to us, taping our every word.

"I can't believe this," I said to my sister. "It's a disaster."

She nodded dully. "Now we'll never know which of us Jeffrey wanted."

I stared at her in amazement. Clearly, she was still in shock. I would have grabbed her by the shoulders and shaken her, but the handcuffs made that a bit cumbersome. "He didn't want *either* of us," I reminded her. "The guy was a liar, Sharon. He didn't mean any of the things he said to us."

"Yes, a liar," she repeated. "I forgot. It's this damn headache. A premenstrual headache. They're the worst, don't you think? Especially in combination with the bloating?"

Jesus. "Listen, Sharon. I feel funny asking you this, but how long were you in the bushes before you saw me walking up to Jeffrey's house?"

She shrugged. "A minute or two. Who remembers?"

"Did you see anybody else coming or going from the house?"

"No."

"Hear anything?"

"No."

"Did you go inside the house at any point before I got there?"

"No."

"So you had no idea that Jeffrey was—"

"*No!*"

"Okay. Okay. I'm just asking."

"You're doing more than that. You're insinuating that *I* killed Jeffrey before you showed up. Admit it."

"Sharon, I'm trying to piece things together. That's all."

"Well, piece *this* together. I had dinner with Mom at seven-thirty. She went to the bedroom to watch television at eight-thirty. I changed my clothes and walked over here about nine. The rest you know. I didn't kill Jeffrey. What's more, I can't believe my own sister suspects me of killing him."

"Keep your voice down," I shushed her, nodding at the cop keeping vigil outside the car. "I don't suspect you of killing Jeffrey. Honest."

"Thank you." She eyed me. "Now, why don't you tell me *your* story?"

"My story?"

"Yes. It was about nine-fifteen when you pulled into Jeffrey's driveway, wasn't it?"

"I guess so."

"Was that your first trip over here tonight?"

"What are you implying?"

"Well, maybe you came over earlier. To confront Jeffrey about his feelings for you. Maybe he gave you the brush-off and you got mad and shot him. You ran out of the house and then remembered that you left the gun next to the body. So you drove back to get it. Which is when you saw me. Maybe *you're* the one who killed him, Deborah. How do you feel about *that?*"

I shook my head. Things were worse than I thought. "Do I look like the sort of person who goes around shooting people? I don't own a gun. I don't even know how to work a gun."

She thought for a minute. "I believe you," she said finally. "People who shoot people probably don't say '*work* a gun.' It sounds amateurish."

"I appreciate that. Look, Sharon. We've had our problems, but let's at least agree that neither of us murdered Jeffrey."

"Agreed."

I sighed with relief. "Let's also agree that the best way to handle this pickle we're in is to tell the truth."

"No. The best way to handle it is to get a lawyer. Mom works for the court system. She must know some lawyers."

"The lawyers she knows are small-claims lawyers, Sharon. Their clients are dry cleaners accused of ruining people's favorite garments. They don't defend murder suspects."

"Then we'll find a lawyer who does. There may not be any in this one-horse town, but I bet there are plenty in Boca."

Before I could respond, the cop opened the door of the driver's side of the car, got in, and announced that he was taking us down to the Martin County Sheriff's Office, where we would be interviewed about the murder.

"But it's late, and I'm not feeling well," Sharon whined. "Couldn't we do this tomorrow?"

He snickered and drove off.

There had never been a homicide in Sewall's Point. The "crimes" in my mother's exclusive little hamlet, aside from the occasional robbery, involved driving over the thirty-five mph speed limit, walking a dog without a leash, and mowing the lawn before 8:00 A.M. As a result, there was some confusion as to which branch of local law enforcement would handle the investigation. Technically, Sewall's Point's chief of police was overseeing the matter, but it was the Martin County Sheriff's Office that had experience in dealing with murderers and, therefore, was taking charge of the case. So across the bridge to Stuart we went, to the sheriff's office on Monterey Road, where a detective was waiting to question us.

"Let the games begin," I said to Sharon, after she had asked that our handcuffs be removed so she could massage her aching temples. (They were removed.)

While one cop in the office was fingerprinting us, another was running background checks on us, to find out if we had any "priors."

"Why would they care about my ex-husbands?" Sharon whispered.

"That's not what they mean by priors," I said tolerantly.

We were also given something called a GSR test, to determine if there was any gunshot residue on our hands.

And then we were read those notorious Miranda Rights, which sent Sharon into a tizzy.

"I'm not talking without my lawyer present," she insisted.

"So call your lawyer," said the detective, whose name was Frank Gillby, a short, stocky man with a full head of carrot-red hair.

"I don't have one," she said. "Yet."

"Sharon," I said. "We're innocent. We have nothing to hide. We should cooperate with the police as best we can so that whoever killed Jeffrey will be caught. The last thing we want is some psycho running around loose in Sewall's Point, right? Not with Mom living here all by herself."

"Fine," she said. "I'll talk. And then I'll hire a lawyer. If that's *okay* with everybody."

"It's great," said Detective Gillby. "Now. Which of you wants to go first?"

"I will," I said, eager to get the whole business over with.

I was led into an interrogation room and told to sit down opposite the detective. Sewall's Point's head honcho, Chief Avery Armstrong, was there too, since the homicide occurred in his jurisdiction. But it was Gillby who asked the questions, which ran the gamut from, "How long have you known Jeffrey Hirshon?" and "Were you having an affair with him?" to "What were you and your sister fighting about outside his front door?"

Answering the last question was complicated, obviously. How could I make the detective understand about Norman's graduation? About Daddy? About cheerleading?

I couldn't, but I tried. And in my effort to be totally forthcoming about my relationship with Sharon, I must have bored the poor detective to death, because he actually nodded out. So did Chief Armstrong.

"Hey, guys," I prodded them, after having just completed the story of the high fever that had kept me from attending my nephew's special day. "Are you going to arrest me and my sister or not?"

Detective Gillby opened his eyes. "Say it again?"

I repeated the question.

"I don't know yet," he replied. "Have a seat outside, while I bring your sister in. I've gotta hear what she has to say about all this."

So it was Sharon's turn in the interrogation room, and she was in there much longer than I was. I assumed it was because she had a better memory than I did when it came to dredging up past slights.

Eventually, we were reunited and told that we were not going to be arrested—for the moment.

"I'm gonna let you ladies go for now," said Detective Gillby. "It'll take a couple of days before we get the results of the GSR test, which will tell us if either of you pulled the trigger and shot the doctor. In the meantime, you haven't got any outstanding warrants or priors. And you don't strike me as a threat to the community—except maybe to each other." He elbowed Chief Armstrong. "The problem is, there's still a lot of stuff we don't know. Like approximately when Dr. Hirshon died and where you two were at that particular time. Like why there was no sign of forced entry into the house. Like how you really felt when you figured out he was coming on to both of you. Like whether you got mad enough to hire someone to kill the doctor."

"Hire someone?" Sharon said, taking umbrage at the very notion.

"Come on, Detective. We hardly knew Jeffrey Hirshon," I said.

"Then why did your sister admit, on the record, that she hoped to marry him?" he challenged.

"Because there isn't a man my sister *doesn't* hope to marry," I said, utterly exhausted.

Sharon must have been exhausted too, because her only response was to glare at me.

Detective Gillby arranged for us to be driven home—Sharon, to my mother's; me, to the cottage. He promised he would have the Pontiac dropped off too, as soon as the forensics people tested it for blood, hair fibers, and other goodies.

"Maybe they can change the battery while they're at it." I sighed. And then I remembered that Jeffrey had jump-started the battery. The last time I saw him. The last time I saw him *alive*.

We decided that the cop should drive us both to my mother's house, so we could break the news of Jeffrey's death—and our involvement—together.

When we walked in, we braced ourselves, expecting her to be frantic, since Sharon had been gone for so long. But she had fallen asleep in her bedroom with the TV on and didn't even know my sister had left the house.

We woke her.

"Oh. It's my two girls," she said, rubbing her eyes, still a little groggy. "What are you both doing here? And Sharon, that sweater you've got on is a little skimpy, dear. Stained, too."

"Mom, there's something we have to tell you," I began, helping her to sit up in bed.

"Yes. It's about Dr. Hirshon," said Sharon. "He's—" She stopped and looked at me. I looked right back at her. Hey, she was the oldest. Let *her* drop the bomb. "He's dead," she said finally.

My mother gasped. "Dead? But how? Was he in some sort of an accident?"

I reached for her hand and held it tightly, wondering where the nitroglycerin was in case she went into cardiac arrest.

"He was murdered, Mom," said Sharon. "In his house."

"No! Not in Sewalls Point! No one gets murdered here."

"It's true," Sharon said. "They found him in his den. Well, to be totally accurate, *we* found him in his den."

"Who's 'we'?"

"Deborah and I found him, Mom. He'd been shot." Sharon paused and then laid out the entire story, leaving nothing out, not even the part about the cheerleading.

My mother gasped again. Louder this time. I asked her if she wanted some water, her pills, anything. She shook me off.

"I'm sure there are other cardiologists in town," I said reassuringly. "We could ask around at Martin Memorial. Or maybe one of the internists in Jeffrey's practice could recommend someone. We'll find you another doctor, Mom. Don't worry."

"For goodness sake, Deborah. I'm not worried about me," she said. "I'm worried about my girls."

"You mean, because we're murder suspects?" asked Sharon.

"No, because you're mental cases!" she said irritably. "Why you two can't behave yourselves is beyond me."

Sharon and I stared at the floor. We were still trying to get used to our mother's new practice of speaking her mind.

"Did the police say what their next move is?" she asked.

"Sharon and I are supposed to go back to the sheriff's office tomorrow, for more questioning," I said.

"Which is a complete waste of time," said Sharon. "They should be out combing the streets, searching for the real killer. Besides, I have to go back to Boca tomorrow afternoon. I have a business to run."

"I hope you still *have* a business," said my mother. "Sewall's Point's first murder is going to make headlines in every paper in south Florida. The publicity might scare your brides and grooms away."

"Not a chance. The minute I get home, I'm finding a criminal defense lawyer," said Sharon. "Someone to advise me and protect me and clear my name."

"What about you, Deborah?" asked my mother.

"I'm not a fan of lawyers," I said.

"All right, but what about *your* job? Do you think Melinda will let you stay on at the cottage? The Historical Society isn't an especially broad-minded organization."

"I know, but I'm planning to make Melinda an offer she can't refuse," I said, an idea dawning on me. "And then I'm going to find out who killed Dr. Hirshon."

"You?" Sharon scoffed.

"That's right," I said. "I didn't spend the last ten years in the soap opera business for nothing. I just might be able to spin out a few scenarios that wouldn't occur to the police."

Chapter Eleven

Thursday's editions of the *Stuart News* and the *Palm Beach Post,* both of which serve the residents of the Stuart area, featured a front-page story on Jeffrey's murder, complete with a photograph of the doc in his lab coat and stethoscope. Part crime report, part obituary, each article gave the bare essentials of the case—that Jeffrey had been found dead in his Sewall's Point home, the apparent victim of a gunshot wound; that the results of an autopsy and other tests were pending; that the police discovered the body after receiving a distur-bance call from a neighbor; and that the two women found at the scene were Deborah Peltz of Hutchinson Island and Sharon Peltz of

Boca Raton, the only daughters of Lenore Peltz and the late Dr. Henry Peltz of Sewall's Point.

Nice of them to include my parents, I thought, wondering why they didn't drag Aunt Harriet, Cousin Jill, and the other branches of the family tree into the story.

Both articles also provided retrospectives on Jeffrey's life and career, as he was a local big-shot and his death was said to be a terrible loss to the community. They reported where and when he was born and raised, where and when he attended college and medical school, where and when he moved to Florida and opened his practice, and where and when he married and divorced his wife, the former Francine Fink, who currently resided in Aspen, Colorado. (They did not mention Francine's addiction to shoes and handbags.)

There were references to Jeffrey's philanthropy, his years of service to the people of Martin County, his love of boating and fishing, and his air of accessibility and kindly manner.

"Dr. Hirshon's death is a tragic loss," the CEO of the hospital was quoted as saying. "He was a skilled physician, a sensitive, caring human being, and a dear friend. He will be missed."

Not by me, I mused, as I sat in the sheriff's office at eleven-thirty that morning, reading and rereading the articles while I waited my turn to be interrogated. Since I was car-less, Sharon had picked me up and driven us over for what was to be our second and, I fervently hoped, final session with Detective Gillby and company.

This time, the media was camped outside the office, and we were forced to barrel through everybody, heads down, muttering "No comment." A small-town version of a tabloid nightmare.

The other difference between this interrogation session and the one that had taken place the night before was that Sharon had arranged for her lawyer to be present.

"I've engaged an attorney," she'd informed me on our way to the sheriff's office.

"How did you manage that so quickly?"

"It's fantastic, isn't it? The truth is, I didn't even have to engage him. *He* engaged *me*."

"What are you talking about, Sharon?"

"He tracked me down at Mom's early this morning and offered

his services. He's a criminal defense attorney from Boca, and read about the case in today's *Post*."

"You mean he just picked up the phone and called you? Like some ambulance chaser? How can you trust this guy? You're a perfect stranger to him."

"No, I'm not. That's the best part," she enthused. "He's the brother of a woman who hired me to coordinate her daughter's wedding a few years ago. He was at the wedding. I remember meeting him. He's gorgeous, by the way. And *single*."

I didn't even start. Who had the energy?

"Does this person have a name?" I asked.

"Barry Shiller. He's been divorced twice, according to his sister, but only because he's so driven, so in to his work. Some women don't know how to deal with a man like that, you know?"

Barry Shiller appeared at the sheriff's office at ten o'clock, just in time to escort Sharon into the interrogation room. He was a slick piece of work—Armani suit, deep tan, lots of mousse on the shoe-polish brown hair, lots of rings on the manicured fingers—and he was wearing enough cologne to marinate a leg of lamb. Sharon's idea of "gorgeous," maybe, but not mine, thank God. The last thing we needed was another man to fight over.

When he and Sharon emerged from the interrogation room, he asked me if I wanted him to represent me too, now that he was "up to speed" on the specifics of the case. I told him I appreciated the offer but that I was fine on my own.

"Your call," he said with a smarmy smile. "I'll be hanging around in case you change your mind." He turned to Sharon. "While they interview your sister, why don't you and I have lunch? They must have at least a couple of decent restaurants in Stuart, huh?" He laughed, because he was from Boca and people from Boca think people from Stuart are hayseeds who wouldn't know a decent restaurant from a pig's trough.

"Take him downtown to the Jolly Sailor," I suggested to Sharon. "They're open for lunch, and they have indoor plumbing in case he has to drain the lizard."

She scowled at me. "Want us to bring you back anything, Deborah? You know how cranky you get when you're hungry."

Cranky. My sister invented the word. "No, thanks. You two have a nice lunch."

And off they went.

My interrogation by Detective Gillby was basically a rehash of what we'd already discussed. No, I wasn't having an affair with Jeffrey Hirshon. No, I didn't have a grudge against him. No, I didn't kill him. Blah blah blah.

Afterwards, I was given a sort of lie detector test, only this one was called a CVSA, which stands for computer voice stress analyzer. Basically, they ask you questions and test the stress level in your responses. I tried to stay calm throughout the procedure, but it was like trying not to blink; the more you think about it, the harder it gets.

Eventually, I was told I could go home.

"You know very well that my sister and I didn't kill Dr. Hirshon," I said to Detective Gillby, while we waited for Sharon and her new lawyer to return from lunch.

"Maybe you did. Maybe you didn't," he said. "What's not debatable is that *somebody* did—with a twenty-two caliber bullet."

"Jeffrey was killed by a single bullet?"

"Looks like. Why?"

"Then whoever did it must be a pretty good shot, which rules Sharon and me out. Neither of us even owns a gun."

"So you've claimed. But we'll be searching your place, your sister's place, and your mother's place."

"My mother's place?"

"Sure. You could have stashed the gun there. We'll be talking to your sister's kid too."

"Norman?"

"Right. She said he goes to military school. He must know something about guns."

"Yes, but the school is in South Carolina. He was nowhere near Stuart when Jeffrey was murdered."

"Then he's got nothing to worry about. It's all part of our investigation, Ms. Peltz. We've questioned you and your sister, and now we're going to interview your mother, your nephew, Dr. Hirshon's neighbors, his business associates, his friends, everybody."

"I'd be happy to lend a hand," I said earnestly. "With Jeffrey's neighbors, business associates, and friends, I mean. I don't have a very demanding job. I could snoop around."

He laughed, as if I were nutty. A nutty killer. "Tell you what: you think of anything that could shed some light on the case, you call me," he said. And then he laughed again.

Sharon picked me up at the sheriff's office after what she termed a very "successful" lunch with Barry Shiller.

"He really knows the justice system," she said as she drove me back to the cottage. "I'm so grateful that he agreed to take my case."

"You didn't exactly have to beg him, Sharon. He contacted you. Don't you find that a little strange, a little sleazy?"

"No. I find it reassuring. Now I have someone to lean on for a change. Did you hear that the police intend to question my Norman? The boy was in school last night, for God's sake. He doesn't come home for vacation—or do they call it a *furlough?*—for several weeks."

"I'm sure it's just a formality," I said. "You don't need Barry Shiller to defend Norman. He can take care of himself."

"Even so, I'm glad Barry's on our side. Did I tell you that he lives in the Sanctuary, one of Boca's ultra high-end communities, and that we're having dinner tomorrow night?"

"When's the wedding?" I said sarcastically.

"For your information, I'm interested in Barry for his legal expertise. Of course, he *is* quite a catch. A woman could do worse."

I wasn't so sure, but I kept my mouth shut.

The minute I got back to the cottage, I called Melinda. Not surprisingly, she was extremely troubled by the publicity surrounding my involvement in the murder of one of Stuart's most prominent citizens. "Nettled" was the word she used.

"I'm fond of you, Deborah," she said. "I'm fond of your mother too. But, under the circumstances, I don't see how I can keep you on the Historical Society's payroll."

"Whatever happened to 'innocent until proven guilty'?" I asked. "I had nothing to do with Jeffrey Hirshon's death. Neither did my sister."

"Still, the sordidness of it all. The unseemliness. The indecorousness."

"How about the tawdriness?" I added.

"Yes, yes. You understand my predicament then."

"I do, but here's the deal, Melinda. I just moved into the cottage. I like it here. I'm staying."

"Not if I instruct you to vacate the premises."

"You won't."

"Oh? And why is that, pray tell?"

"Remember when we met that first time? When you interviewed me for the job?"

"Of course."

"Remember when I told you I wrote for *From This Day Forward* and you gushed that you've been watching the show since you were twenty and never miss a single episode?"

"Gushed? I'm not certain that I—all right. Yes. I remember."

"Well, if you let me keep my job at the House of Refuge, I'll arrange for you to spend a day on the set, be right there while the show is taped, meet the cast members."

Melinda was silent, but her breathing was labored. "I feel as though I'm being blackmailed," she said finally.

"Nonetheless, I could make one phone call and get you behind the scenes of your favorite soap opera."

"You're saying that I would be mingling with Holden Halsey, for instance? Or, rather, that British actor who plays Holden Halsey?"

"That's what I'm saying."

She sighed. "What if it's the board members of the Historical Society who balk at keeping you on?"

"You're the boss, Melinda. I have faith in your powers of persuasion."

My next order of business was to call my mother, to see how she was handling the fact that her name had been sullied in the press.

"Are your neighbors picketing outside your house?" I asked, half-jokingly.

"No, dear. My friends have been very supportive."

"That's a relief. Are you feeling okay? Any chest pains?"

"None. To tell you the truth, this whole situation has perked me up. I'm upset about what happened to Dr. Hirshon, obviously, and I'm furious that the police are accusing my girls of a crime. But in a strange way, the murder has forced me to forget about my own problems, to stop dwelling on every little ache and pain."

"That's great, Mom. Maybe you'll be able to go back to work as a mediator soon."

"I won't have time," said my mother.

"Why not?" I asked.

"Because I'll be helping you help the police solve the murder," she said matter-of-factly. "I've lived in this town a long time, and I know plenty of people with loose lips. In the past, I never paid much attention to all their gossiping, but maybe it's time I started."

Loose lips. Gossiping. I thought of Helen, suddenly. Where was she when I needed a *real* busybody?

"I want to protect you, Mom. I think you should stay out of this mess."

"You're not hearing me, Deborah," she said. "This 'mess' has taken my mind off the heart attack. I don't feel like a cardiac cripple anymore."

After I hung up with my mother, I sat down and made my list of possible suspects in Jeffrey's murder.

First, there was Vicky, the ICU nurse, who had argued with Jeffrey at the bar at the Prawnbroker. She had taken excellent care of my mother and had seemed like such a decent, reasonable person during the two days I'd observed her at the hospital that I hated to even imagine that she might be capable of murder. But she *had* thrown her cocktail napkin at Jeffrey, which indicated a certain lack of control, in my opinion. So I scribbled down her name, vowing to learn more about her relationship with the deceased.

Then, there was Joan, the nurse in Jeffrey's office, the one who said that she'd worked for him for ten straight years, the one who claimed that he had an explosive temper. I had found the latter piece of information difficult to believe at the time, given how kind and gentle Jeffrey had always appeared. But what I had found even more puzzling was Joan's response when I'd questioned her about it. His temper was bad "but this job has other compensations," she'd said. Like what? I wondered now. Money? Was Jeffrey paying Joan more than the going rate for nurses in doctors' offices? Was he paying her so much that she was willing to put up with his frequent and possibly violent fits of pique? Or had she been referring to another type of compensation? Compensation of a romantic or sexual nature? She wasn't particularly attractive and hardly looked the part of the femme fatale, with her unstylish bun, matronly figure, and matching set of jowls. But who was I to say what turned men on? Maybe she and Jeffrey *were* lovers, either before, during, or after his marriage.

Speaking of marriage, I quickly added Francine Fink Hirshon to my list. According to Joan, Jeffrey's ex-wife, the shoe-and-handbag addict, had supposedly "bankrupted" him with her free-spending ways and yet she continued to harrass him for money. Did it gall Francine that Jeffrey was living the good life in Sewall's Point while she was "roughing it" in some condo in Aspen, poor thing? Was she angry at him for refusing to fork over more dough? Was she angry enough to hop on a flight to Florida and shoot him? It was entirely possible that she had kept a key to the house, which would account for the lack of forced entry. But if she killed him, she'd never be able to wheedle money out of him. Unless, of course, she discovered that he had forgotten to change his will and that she was still his sole beneficiary.

I put my pen down for a moment and tried to come up with other suspects, encouraging myself to think creatively the way I used to when I'd sit at my computer, cranking out my weekly breakdowns. "What if they did this?" I'd ask myself of the characters on the show. "Or this? Or this?"

Think, Deborah, I pushed myself as I flashed back to the scene in Jeffrey's den, to the sight of his leaky, lifeless body. Piece together who could have done this. Who?

Maybe it's one of the other doctors in Jeffrey's sixty-man practice, I mused, writing the notion down on my notepad. Maybe one of them had an ax to grind against him—a professional rivalry of some sort.

Or maybe the killer is a disgruntled patient, I thought. Someone whose acid reflux Jeffrey had misdiagnosed as severe angina.

No. If nothing else, Jeffrey was an excellent doctor. My mother was proof of that.

I pondered the matter further, trying to remember if I'd met anyone in town who was not a member of Jeffrey's fan club, anyone who'd spoken negatively about him, even in passing.

And then it came to me: Ray Scalley, the head of the county building maintenance department, Mr. I'm-Not-a-Handyman.

Ray and I had been standing in the kitchen, talking about my mother's heart attack, when he'd asked me who her doctor was. I'd told him she was being treated by Jeffrey Hirshon and he'd called Jeffrey a bastard, warned me to keep my mother away from him but never explained why.

Was Ray Scalley the murderer? I wondered. Did he despise Jeffrey enough to kill him? Did he show up at Jeffrey's house on Wednesday night minutes before Sharon and I did, jimmy the front door open with one of his handyman tools, and fire a single bullet into the heart doctor's heart?

Could be, I decided, as I added Ray's name to my list of suspects—placed his name at the *top* of my list, actually. I was putting the finishing touches on the "y" in "Scalley" and wishing I could see Ray again, to feel him out about his relationship with Jeffrey, when I heard footsteps outside the cottage. I froze momentarily, afraid that my visitor was either a reporter sniffing out a story or a cop brandishing a search warrant. And then came a knock.

"Hey, Deborah. You in there?" a man called out.

"Who is it?" I yelled, not recognizing the voice.

"Ray Scalley. Stuart's answer to Bob Vila."

Be careful what you wish for, I thought, grabbing my notepad and sticking it in a kitchen drawer.

"Coming," I said, and hurried to the door to let him in.

Chapter Twelve

R ay. What a pleasant surprise," I said, trying to sound casual. "I was just thinking about you."

"Why? Is your toilet on the fritz again?" he said, stepping past me and escorting himself into the kitchen.

"No. My toilet's fine," I said. "I was thinking about you in an entirely different context."

He looked perplexed. "What context was that?"

"Oh, just something to do with the House of Refuge," I lied. "Why don't you tell me why you're here?"

"Fair enough, since I barged in without calling first. I came for two reasons, as a matter of fact. One: I heard about Hirshon's death and remembered your saying you were a friend of his. I wanted to offer my condolences."

"Your condolences," I said skeptically.

"That's right."

"You met me once, Ray, and the encounter didn't last more than twenty minutes. What's more, you warned me to keep my mother away from Jeffrey, even called him a bastard. So let's try your second reason, okay?"

He smiled. "Reason number two: the article in today's paper said you and your sister were at Hirshon's house when the cops found the body. They must have grilled you pretty hard down at the sheriff's office last night. I thought I'd stop by to see how you were holding up."

Now I was confused. Either Ray Scalley was a nice man who was genuinely attempting to be my friend, or he killed Jeffrey and came over to pump me for information about the case.

The only way to find out is to pump *him* for information, I decided.

"Why don't we sit out on the porch and chat," I said, "if you're not too busy rescuing the county's buildings from dry rot, that is." There was a tacky but large lamp on the porch. I figured that if Ray was a murderer and suddenly became violent, I could hit him over the head with it.

"I'm not too busy," he said. "It's five-thirty. I'm through for the day."

Great, I thought. Plenty of time to squeeze a confession out of him. Who needed that sleazy Barry Shiller when *I* was about to get Sharon and me off the hook?

"Do you feel like talking about what happened at Hirshon's house?" Ray asked once we were seated on the porch. "I realize it's a touchy subject and we hardly know each other, but you're new in town and I'm a good listener so you're free to use me as a sounding board if you want to."

"That's very clever—I mean, *kind*—of you, Ray," I said, thinking the sounding board bit was probably a ploy, to get me to fill him in on the status of the police investigation. "But to be honest, I'd rather talk about you. It would be a welcome distraction after the trauma I've suffered." I placed the back of my hand on my forehead. For dramatic effect.

"Oh, hey. I can understand that. What would you like to know about this here country boy?"

"How about a little bio? The Cliff Notes version of the Ray Scalley Story."

"Well, I live downtown, on Seminole Street, in a house that was built in 1925 and renovated top to bottom by yours truly."

"I'm impressed. Were you born and raised in the area?"

"Yup. I'm a genuine local. There are a bunch of us still around, believe it or not. We're mixed in with all the snowbirds now, but you can pick us out if you look closely enough."

"Were your parents born here too?"

"In Florida, but not in Stuart. They came to town after they were married, when my father opened his first store just north of here in Port St. Lucie."

"*First* store?"

"Yeah. He owned a chain of hardware stores in south Florida. Made a lot of money too. Fortunately, he was a smart investor and held on to the money, even after a national building and home supply retailer—you know the one—came in and put him and most of the other Mom-and-Pop stores out of business."

"So he's retired?"

"No, he's dead. Both my parents are."

"I'm sorry."

"Thanks. I'm not alone in the world though. I've got an older brother in Palm Beach Gardens, in BallenIsles, golf community to the stars. His name's Doug. Or, as he prefers to be called, *Douglas*."

I smiled, catching the tone in his voice. I knew sibling rivalry when I heard it. "And what does Doug do?"

"He's the 'Douglas' in Douglas's Menswear. He's got six shops, from Miami up to Jupiter."

"Sounds like he takes after your father, the big businessman. How did you come to be an expert in historic buildings?"

"How did I come to be the black sheep in the family, you mean?"

"Is that how you see yourself?"

"Only in the sense that, unlike my brother, I work for the county, I don't make a lot of money, and I don't play golf."

"No golf?" I pretended to look horrified.

"No. I'm a Gators freak."

"Excuse me?"

"The Gators. The football team of my alma mater, the University of Florida."

"Oh, right. You mentioned that you went to school there."

"And I've rooted for the Gators ever since. College football sort of stays in your blood, or, at least, that's how it's been for me."

I nodded, underwhelmed by this news. While Ray's background was all very interesting, I needed to fast-forward to the present, to the reason he hated Jeffrey, to where he was on the night of the murder. The question was: How to segue? "You know, Ray, I think Jeffrey Hirshon was a Gators fan too," I said, winging it. "Is that how you two met? By sitting next to each other at some local sports bar one night and yelling: 'Go, Gators!'?"

Ray's expression grew serious. "I met Jeffrey Hirshon in the emergency room at Martin Memorial."

"Really? Did you have a heart problem?"

"No. My wife did."

His wife. So there was a *Mrs.* Scalley. If Sharon had been doing the questioning, she would have unearthed that detail first.

"Look," Ray said, "the guy helped your mother, and you and your sister were friendly with him, so you don't want to hear why I—"

"Yes," I interrupted. "Yes, I do."

"You sure?"

"Positive."

He cleared his throat. "My wife and I had been trying to have children since we first got married," he said, speaking more slowly than before. "Six years ago, she finally got pregnant." He stopped abruptly.

"What's the matter?"

He got up from his chair. "This is silly, Deborah. I shouldn't be dumping this on you. You've got your own problems. Not only that, we don't really know each other, like I said."

"Yes, but we've got to start someplace, don't we? I'm the keeper at the House of Refuge. You're in charge of the buildings here. We'll be working together on a regular basis. Why not share a few confidences?"

"I don't hear *you* sharing any."

"That's because we're concentrating on you this time around. My turn will come. Now. Go on with your story. Your wife got pregnant. What happened next?"

Ray sat back down. "The pregnancy was uneventful. We were preparing for our new life with our baby. She went into labor. I took her to Martin Memorial, as planned. The obstetrician showed up. Everything was fine, completely normal. Then, out of the blue, she had a heart attack. Boom. A healthy—or so we thought—thirty-six-year-old woman. The cardiologist on call that night was your pal Hirshon, which is how I met him and why I despised him. The long and short of it, see, is that he couldn't save my wife, which complicated the delivery of the baby, which resulted in the death of both my wife *and* my baby. All in all, not a happy ending."

I was speechless momentarily. The man sitting opposite me had lost his wife and child at the same time. He must have been devastated. Anyone would have been. But were the deaths of his loved ones Jeffrey's fault? Did he kill Jeffrey to exact revenge? And if so, why did he wait six years to do the deed?

"The hospital conducted a thorough investigation," he went on. "They're a class outfit, Martin Memorial. No coverups. No doubletalk. It turned out that Beth—that was my wife's name—had a congenital heart defect that had gone undiagnosed for years. The stress of the labor was the straw that broke her, literally. What I'm saying is that Hirshon was cleared of any negligence."

"Then why the anger and resentment toward him?" I asked. "When his name came up the other day, you—"

"Wouldn't *you* be angry and resentful toward him?" he cut me off. "I'm not a fool. I understand—intellectually, anyway—that there was probably nothing Hirshon could have done to save my wife and child. But he was on the scene. He was the one who said the words 'Your wife didn't make it.' He was the one who was *there.* How do I know that another cardiologist wouldn't have found a way to prevent the situation? How do I know that if, by some twist of fate, Hirshon *hadn't* been on call that night, things wouldn't have turned out differently?"

"You don't know," I said softly, looking out over the Intracoastal Waterway, the sun beginning its descent into the water. "How could you know?"

And how in the world am I supposed to proceed with my little inquisition after *that* tragic tale? I wondered, thinking it would be cruel to question Ray about an alibi, under the circumstances.

Still, I wasn't about to go to prison for a crime I didn't commit.

I was on the verge of asking Ray about the night of the murder when he volunteered a juicy tidbit.

"You'll probably find this hard to believe after the story I've just laid on you," he said, "but when that cop walked into the Black Marlin last night and told everybody at the bar that Hirshon had been murdered, I was actually sorry. Sorry! It was like, with him gone there'll be nobody for me to blame anymore, no way to hold on to the past. I felt sort of empty, as if the air went out of me. Maybe that's why I'm here, Deborah. I had to talk to somebody who knew the guy."

"Yes. Of course you did," I said in a soothing tone. "And I'm glad you chose me to confide in. But do you mind if I back up a second? The Black Marlin is that restaurant in downtown Stuart, right?"

"Yeah. Next door to the Ashley, on Osceola Street."

"And you say you were there last night?"

"Is there some reason why I shouldn't have been? I had a date. I thought I'd take her there, if that's okay with you."

So he was dating again. And why not, after six years? "I was just curious," I said. "I've never been to the Black Marlin. You and your date had dinner there?"

"Yeah. Grilled snapper. Roasted potatoes. Some kind of squash thing I wasn't crazy about. Now, why don't you tell me why you're asking me about my dinner at the Black Marlin when I just got through spilling my guts about my wife and kid?"

He was pissed off at me. I glanced over at the big tacky lamp. In case.

"Forgive me," I said. "I was totally insensitive. Chalk it up to my lack of sleep."

I must not have sounded very convincing, because Ray glowered at me, his mouth in a tight line. And then he said, "I think I get it now."

"Get what?"

"Get why you're so interested in me and my dinner. You're wondering if I killed Hirshon, because of the way I talked about him the other day. You want to know if I have an alibi."

I shrugged, caught. "So the thought crossed my mind. So shoot me." I bit my lip, wishing I could take back that last one.

"Fine. For your information, I *have* an alibi," he said hotly. "From seven to about eleven-thirty, I was in the company of Willow Janson."

"You're actually dating a woman named Willow?" I asked.

"She said it's a childhood nickname. Because she's always been thin and *willowy.*"

How nice for her, I mused, sucking in my stomach. "Listen, Ray. The police think I'm involved in Jeffrey's murder. I have a vested interest in finding the real killer, so you'll have to excuse me if I'm suspicious of everyone around here. Particularly someone who expressed negative feelings toward Jeffrey. I apologize. Really."

His scowl receded gradually. "Apology accepted."

"Thank you," I said, mentally crossing Ray Scalley's name off my list of suspects—for the time being. I mean, he could have killed Jeffrey *before* he and Willow went out for dinner. "How about this great weather we've been having?"

He smiled. "The weather's swell. Now, I think I'm entitled to ask *you* a couple of questions. What *were* you and your sister doing at Hirshon's house last night?"

I sighed and told Ray what had happened.

"I wasn't in love with him by any means," I said as a footnote. "I guess I was drawn to him because I was scared I was going to lose my mother and he was so reassuring about her prognosis and in some ways he reminded me of my father, who was also a doctor, and my sister liked him too, which played into our rivalry. Plus, I was lonely."

"I don't doubt it. It's tough to move to a new town. This part of the world must seem like another planet compared to New Yawk."

I laughed at his southerner's attempt at a New York accent.

"It *is* different here, but I was ready for a change," I said. "What I wasn't ready for was a murder. The thing that gets me is that my sister and I probably missed the killer by an hour or two—at the most."

"What makes you say that?"

"I'm no forensics specialist, but when I worked for *From This Day Forward*, I wrote enough scenes with dead bodies in them to learn about lividity and rigor and stuff like that. Last night, I was kneeling right next to Jeffrey's body, and I promise you there was plenty of blood but hardly any lividity or rigor. He was dead all right, but he hadn't been dead for long. Someone shot him and left the house, and then Sharon and I stumbled onto the scene, too busy bickering outside his front door to notice anything."

"You mentioned a rivalry. You and your sister don't get along?"

"That's an understatement. And now this shifty lawyer has glommed onto her. God knows what advice he's been giving her."

"You haven't hired a lawyer?"

I shook my head. "I'm not guilty. I don't need one. Besides, I'm going to nail the killer myself."

I expected Ray to tell me I was out of my element, but he didn't. "Shouldn't be too hard to do," he said. "Sewall's Point's like Peyton Place. Everybody's into everybody else's business and nobody's shy about sharing what they know. Even the people who don't live in Sewall's Point gossip about what goes on there. So you might very well 'nail the killer' yourself."

"Thanks for the vote of confidence."

"Welcome. Hungry?"

"What?"

"Are you hungry? It's practically dinnertime."

"Oh. Yes, come to think of it."

He nodded. "We'll go to the Black Marlin. Since you're so *curious* about the place."

I smiled. "I'm sorry about all that," I said, wanting to stay on his good side. "I'm especially sorry about your wife and baby, Ray. I hope you believe me."

He nodded. "Let's get fed," he said, pulling me up from my chair.

"No date with Willow tonight?" I asked.

"Nope," he said, and left it at that.

Chapter Thirteen

I was a little apprehensive about going out for dinner, about going out in *public,* for that matter. No, the newspapers hadn't run a photo of either Sharon or me in their articles about Jeffrey, but they might as well have, as far as I was concerned. Just having my name printed in connection with the murder of an upstanding doctor in the community made me feel exposed, vulnerable, as if everybody would be staring at me, pointing at me, thinking she's the one! She killed him! Let's lynch her!

And so, before entering the Black Marlin, I quickly combed my hair forward until it literally covered most of my face.

"What in the world are you doing?" Ray asked as we stood on the street.

"Nothing," I said.

"You're trying to hide behind your hair," he persisted. "Either that, or the Bride of Frankenstein Look is big in New Yawk."

"Okay. I *was* trying to hide," I admitted. "I started having a panic attack at the thought of people in the restaurant whispering about me."

"If you don't fix your hair, they *will* whisper about you. The important thing is that you're innocent, Deborah. What do you care what a bunch of strangers say about you?"

I fixed my hair, grateful for Ray's pep talk. "Actually, it's you they'll probably whisper about. Two nights at the Black Marlin with two different women. Imagine."

"Oh, yeah. That's me. The big stud," he said, his tone self-deprecating.

"Did you enjoy your date with Willow last night?" I asked.

"Not especially. A buddy of mine at work fixed it up. He tries that a lot, usually with better results."

"So you date pretty often. I sort of assumed it would be hard to have a social life down here, since most people are either married or my mother's age."

"It *is* hard, but I'm a guy. We're a hot commodity. Especially if we wear tight jeans and a carpenter's tool belt."

"Is that right?" I said wryly.

"Sure. I think it has something to do with the hammer and tape measure and nail pouches we carry around. Very *manly*."

I laughed, fully aware that he was pulling my leg. "Well, I'll be living vicariously through you then. I don't see myself back on the dating scene any time soon, not with Jeffrey's murder hanging over my head."

"I wouldn't be so sure. Maybe my buddy at work will fix *you* up too."

"Yeah, and maybe we could double date." I smiled, thinking that Ray was a good sport for dragging me out to dinner, for being a pal to someone he barely knew—provided his motives were pure.

———

The Black Marlin is a dark, cozy place with a nautical theme, a busy bar, and better-than-average pub food. To my enormous relief, nobody stared or pointed or fired accusations at me as we were seated at a booth. Ray, on the other hand, was recognized by several people, including our waitress, Kimmy, who kissed him on the cheek and then handed us our menus.

"Looks like you're a regular," I commented.

"I come over after work now and then," he said. "They've got TVs at the bar, as you can see, so if there's a sports show on and they're covering the Gators—"

"You're here," I said.

"You bet," he said.

We ordered drinks and dinner and talked; Ray asked me about my work in television; I asked him about his work for the county. We also touched on his relationship with his father and brother and mine with my mother and sister. It was sort of a novelty for me, I realized, to sit and trade stories with a man I wasn't dating, a man who didn't make me feel as if I had to be "on," a man with whom I would not be having sex. An added bonus was that Ray wasn't recoiling in horror because I had spent the previous evening in the company of the police.

Not that there weren't constant reminders of the murder throughout the meal. As I've said, there had never been a homicide in Sewalls Point, and Jeffrey's was the talk of the town. The people sitting in the booth directly behind me, for example, spoke of nothing else. *Maybe it was a drug hit. Maybe it was a woman scorned. Maybe this. Maybe that.*

"I think I need to go home," I said, after Ray had suggested that we order another cup of coffee. "I haven't had any sleep and I'm dying to crawl into bed and let the sound of the ocean lull me into dreamland."

"Not a bad plan," he said, signaling to Kimmy for the check, which she brought right away and placed in front of him. He tallied it up, passed it over to me, and said, "I figured we'd split it. Your half comes to twenty-fifty."

"Oh, sure," I said, reaching for my wallet, relieved that Ray didn't appear to consider our evening a date any more than I did.

He drove me back to the cottage. We stood outside the door for a few minutes, talking and admiring the view. "What's your next move?" he asked at one point, referring to my own little murder investigation.

"I'm going to have a chat with a nurse at the hospital," I said.

"Which one? Maybe I know her."

"Her name's Vicky, and she works in the Intensive Care Unit."

"Nope. Sorry."

"Well, Jeffrey knew her. He had an argument with her recently, and now he's dead."

"Have you told the police this?"

"I tried, but Detective Gillby doesn't seem all that interested in my theories about the case. I'm not giving up on him though. He told me I could pass along whatever I learned, and I intend to."

"Atta girl." Ray patted my shoulder.

"Well, you probably have to be up early tomorrow," I said, suddenly uncomfortable when I realized that I didn't know how I wanted to say goodnight to him, to a man who was neither a date nor a business colleague, to a man who was being very nice to me but, for all I knew, could have killed Jeffrey.

"You're the one who needs sleep," he said. "I should let you get some."

"Yes, I do. Need sleep, I mean."

"Okay. I'll say goodnight then."

"Goodnight, Ray. I really enjoyed dinner."

"Me too. We'll have to do it again. Just give me a holler."

"I will."

"Look forward to it."

God, you have to picture this. As if our back-and-forth wasn't banal enough, we were standing at the door to the cottage, inches apart, hands at our sides, like a couple of uptight imbeciles.

Why is this so awkward? I asked myself. After spending an evening with my friend Helen, we'd always kiss each other on the cheek and that was that. Now, there I was with Ray, and I was practically paralyzed.

He's no different than Helen, I decided finally. I leaned over and kissed him on the cheek, then went inside the cottage.

The next morning, just after I had completed my walk through the House of Refuge and gift shop to make sure the buildings were intact (a twice-daily routine that was part of my job as keeper), Detective Gillby and friends showed up with a search warrant. They rummaged through my belongings, hunting for the murder weapon, but all they found was a can of mace. "What are you doing with *this?*" Gillby asked suspiciously. I reminded him that I had just moved to town from New York City, where I used to jog occasionally in Central Park. I explained that if you jog in Central Park you equip yourself with either a can of mace or a pit bull and that I had opted for the mace.

When the cops didn't find the gun they were looking for, they moved on to my mother's house. I was worried that the stress of their visit might give her chest pains, that she would clutch her heart and fall to the ground and it would be my fault, mine and Sharon's, but she was quite cheerful as she reported the incident to me. "I told the officers they had no business accusing my girls of any wrongdoing," she said. "And then I offered them coffee and cholesterol-free bagels."

Sharon was less than thrilled when her McMansion in Boca was searched. She called Barry Shiller in a snit the minute the cops darkened her door, and without hesitation he left his office and rushed right over to supervise the police's activities. "He's utterly committed to my defense," she said. "He has made himself available to me day or night." Unable to resist, I asked her if she had made herself available to him day or night. She hung up on me.

Melinda phoned soon after the cops left the cottage.

"Has the Historical Society made a decision?" I asked.

"Yes. You may stay on as keeper," she said. "After a rather fractious meeting, the board members conceded that one is innocent until proven guilty."

"Good for them," I said. "Now, when would you like to fly up to New York for the taping of the show?"

"As soon as possible!" she said, her previous crispness morphing into giddy enthusiasm.

"I'll call my friend Helen to arrange it," I promised.

I showered, dressed, and, since the police had impounded my Pontiac, called a taxi. As I was leaving the cottage, I ran into Fred Zimsky, the octogenarian volunteer. I expected him to shun me, given the situation, but he shuffled over and hugged me.

"If someone as sweet as you killed that doctor, Debbie, he must have had it coming," he said, patting me.

"Thanks, Fred, but I didn't kill anyone," I said, sensing that he meant well. "Dr. Hirshon was already dead when my sister and I got to his house."

"I still say he must have had it coming," Fred repeated.

"Why?"

"People talk. I've heard whispers."

The taxi had arrived. I was in a hurry now. "Do you know something about Dr. Hirshon, Fred?" I asked. "Something that's germane to the case?"

He nodded.

"Are you going to tell me?" I said, eager to move the conversation along.

"All right," he replied. "But it's a terrible thing. The worst thing you could say about a man, maybe."

"Yes?"

He leaned closer to me. "The doctor hardly ever visited his mother."

"That *is* terrible," I agreed. Although not the kind of "terrible" I was hoping for. "Actually, I didn't know Dr. Hirshon had a mother in town."

"Minnie Hirshon was his mother," said Fred. "Before she passed away, she lived at the same nursing home as my wife."

"So you met Dr. Hirshon there? At the nursing home?"

"No. That's the point. I never saw him at the nursing home, because he hardly ever came. If you ask me, a son who doesn't visit his poor, sick mother isn't worth a damn."

What's more, the image of Jeffrey as an uncaring, neglectful son doesn't jibe with the image most people seem to have of him, I thought—the image of the sensitive healer, the generous philanthropist, the all-around good guy.

Of course, *I* knew, from his treatment of Sharon and me, that Jeffrey Hirshon wasn't so sensitive; that, judging by the way he had pitted us against each other, he was careless with people's feelings. The question was: *how* careless and with *whose* feelings?

I had not called ahead to the hospital to determine if Vicky was on duty. I was afraid of scaring her off, afraid that she'd refuse to talk to me. So I took my chances, had the taxi drop me off at Martin Memorial, and found my way to the MICU/CC unit on the hospital's first floor.

"Yes? May I help you?" asked the head nurse when she spotted me.

"Hi. I was wondering if Vicky is here this afternoon," I said, wishing I could remember Vicky's last name, in case there were two Vickys working the unit. "She took care of my mother recently and I wanted to say a quick hello and thank her."

Fortunately, the head nurse was so busy that she not only didn't recognize me, she didn't grill me about who my mother was, how she was feeling, and why my sister and I were at Dr. Hirshon's house the night he bought the farm. She simply said, "Vicky's over there," and pointed to one of the rooms. "She's with a patient who's just been cathed."

"Great. I'll wait outside the room," I said, tiptoeing down the corridor.

Before long, Vicky emerged, her eyes widening at the sight of me.

As she started to back away, I whispered, "Wait. Please. I didn't kill Jeffrey. Honest."

"What are you *doing* here?" she asked, apparently unconvinced by my declaration of innocence.

"I was wondering if you had a couple of minutes to talk," I said. "I know you knew Jeffrey and—"

"Of course I knew Dr. Hirshon!" she said defensively. "We were colleagues."

"You *knew* Jeffrey," I said, making my meaning clearer. "My sister and I saw you two at the Prawnbroker one night, having quite an argument. Since I have more than a passing interest in the events leading up to his death, I'd like to ask you about your relationship. Or would you prefer that someone from the sheriff's office asked you?"

Vicky grew pale. She was a reasonably attractive woman, I noticed on closer inspection. Thirties, strawberry blond hair, green eyes, a little on the chubby side but nevertheless well proportioned. It wasn't a stretch to imagine her the object of Jeffrey's—or any other man's— libido.

"Look. I'm about due for my break," she said finally. "I'll meet you in the visitors' lounge in five minutes."

"I was hoping you'd see things my way," I said, sounding like the sort of tough-as-nails gun moll I was going around town trying to prove I wasn't.

According to Vicky, whose last name turned out to be Walters, she and Jeffrey had what she described as a brief affair.

"How brief?" I asked.

"Three months," she said.

"Did people at the hospital know?"

"Probably, in spite of our efforts to keep it to ourselves."

"Why keep it to yourselves?"

She shrugged. "The secrecy was Jeffrey's idea. I tried to persuade him that we were both adults, both single; that there was nothing improper about our relationship. But he felt that it wouldn't be right for us to be seen together in public, because we both worked at the hospital. He said, 'Let's give ourselves time to find out if this thing is serious. If it is, then we'll shout it from the rooftops.' "

"Speaking of shouting, if Jeffrey was so intent on keeping the relationship a secret, what were you two doing at the Prawnbroker, shouting at each other in full view of practically everyone in town?"

Vicky's eyes pricked with tears. "It was my birthday. I asked Jeffrey if we could go out for dinner—just that once. I was tired of sneaking around the way we always did. You can understand that, can't you?"

"Sure."

"So he said okay, he'd take me somewhere, but he wasn't happy about it. We ended up at the Prawnbroker, since it was near his house. During dinner, he barely spoke to me. When I suggested we have an after-dinner glass of champagne at the bar, he agreed, but he wasn't happy about that either. He made a nasty remark and then I made one back, and before I could stop myself, I was yelling at him. I said, 'Here it is my birthday and you act like I'm invisible.' I asked him if he was ashamed to be seen with me, after the society women he was used to dating."

"Society women?"

"Well, Stuart's version of society women. He dated a lot of them once he was divorced."

I made a mental note: investigate Jeffrey and society women.

"You're a registered nurse, Vicky," I said. "You work at a very reputable hospital. You're a lovely, intelligent woman. Why would anyone be ashamed to be seen with you?"

"I don't know, but that's the way Jeffrey *made* me feel. All he wanted to do was screw. You'd think I was his whore, when what I dreamed of being was his wife."

"You wanted to be his wife?" I said, wondering if Vicky, like Sharon, was delusional when it came to collecting husbands—yet another serial marrier.

"I did want to," she said sheepishly. "I was a fool. Jeffrey didn't care about me. He was using me. For his own sexual gratification. He told me as much that night at the Prawnbroker. I was pretty upset about it, as you saw."

"Nobody likes to get dumped," I said, trying to display real empathy. "But Vicky, how upset were you? I mean, well, I might as well come right out and ask this: Did Jeffrey ever give you a key to his house?"

"Yes, but what does that have to—"

"Then I have to ask you another question," I cut her off, my excitement building. "Where were you the night Jeffrey was murdered?"

She lowered her eyes.

"Vicky? Tell me."

"I can't."

"Oh, Vicky. Yes, you can."

She shook her head.

"You can do it, Vicky," I said, urging her on. "Embrace your fears. You go, girlfriend." I know. I was a little heavy on the Oprah. "If you confess, the police will take it easier on you. In fact, I bet they won't even ask for the death penalty in the case."

"The death penalty? What are you talking about?"

"I'm talking about the fact that you don't have an alibi for the night Jeffrey was killed."

"But I do," she maintained.

"Fine. What is it?"

She inhaled deeply. "I was with Peter Elkin."

"Who?"

"Dr. Elkin, one of the internists in Jeffrey's practice. He and I were together all night, at his place. He and his wife split up recently."

I nodded. So Vicky got around. "Why didn't you just tell me this the first time I asked?"

"Because people still have this ridiculous, insulting notion that nurses are promiscuous," said Vicky. "The last thing I want to do is play into that stereotype."

Chapter Fourteen

As soon as the cab dropped me off at the cottage, I called Detective Gillby.

"I've got a lead for you in the Jeffrey Hirshon case," I said.

"You mean, you're gonna confess?" he said dryly.

"Of course not."

"How about your sister?"

"Detective, you told me I could call you if I learned something. Do you want to hear it or not?"

"I'm all ears."

"There's a nurse named Vicky Walters, who works in the Intensive

Care Unit at Martin Memorial," I began. "She was having an affair with Dr. Hirshon during the three months prior to his death—a secret affair, I might add." I passed along Vicky's explanation of why they hadn't gone public with their relationship; then I reported the argument at the Prawnbroker, my conversation with Vicky earlier in the day, the fact that she admitted having a key to Jeffrey's house, and her supposed alibi. "She was dumped by the doctor. She was angry at him. She could be the killer."

"You just said she was with another guy the night of the murder," said Gillby. "A Dr. Peter Elkin."

"Yes, that's what she *said*, but how do I know if she was telling the truth? If I were you, I'd check it out, Detective. Give her one of your Voice Stress Analyzer tests. Talk to this Dr. Elkin to see if he corroborates her story. Maybe you'll find out that he's the one who committed the murder, with Vicky's help. Maybe he and Hirshon had a professional and/or personal rivalry. Maybe he wanted his associate out of the way, permanently."

"You have a vivid imagination, Ms. Peltz."

"If I'm imagining this then why are you taking notes, Detective? You *are* jotting everything down, aren't you?"

He mumbled that he was.

"Oh, I almost forgot. There's another alibi you might want to confirm, although this one seems pretty ironclad to me."

"From your vast experience, you mean."

I ignored the sarcasm. "A man named Ray Scalley—he's the head of the county building maintenance department here in town—had sort of a grudge against Dr. Hirshon. But he's a nice guy, not a killer type. And he says he was with a woman named Willow Janson the night of the murder. Normally, I wouldn't even mention the two of them to you, but just to dot the *i*'s and cross the *t*'s . . ."

"Ray Scalley isn't a suspect."

"I don't think he is either, but how do you—"

"Because Willow Janson is my niece."

"Your niece?"

"My sister's daughter. Now, if you're finished, Ms. Peltz, *I* have an announcement to make."

"Please."

"The results of the GSR tests you and your sister took came back an hour ago. They were negative."

"See? I told you we were innocent."

"Could be. But another possibility is that you washed your hands before we administered the tests. You can get rid of gun residue with soap and water."

"Come on, Detective. You don't really think one of us shot Dr. Hirshon and then wandered around the house looking for the powder room."

"Okay. You might have been wearing gloves when you fired the gun."

"Did you find any gloves with gun residue on them when you searched our houses? Did you find any gloves, period? I, for one, left mine back in New York."

"Yeah, yeah, yeah."

"Now, I have an important question for *you*, Detective. When can I have my old Pontiac back? The taxis around here charge a fortune."

"Monday, probably."

"So I have to go the whole weekend without a car?"

"You'll survive. Pretend you're a teenager and you have to borrow your mother's car."

"That's not a bad thought," I said, figuring I could always press the Delta 88 into service.

My mother was so excited about lending me her car, especially when I told her that I needed it to do a little sleuthing, that she insisted on driving me wherever I wanted to go.

"Wow, Mom. You must be feeling as good as new," I said, remembering how she loved to be behind the wheel, perched atop that telephone book.

"Not quite, but I'm getting there." She smiled.

On the way over to Jeffrey's office, to see Joan, his nurse, I explained to my mother the purpose of the visit—to worm out of Joan what she had meant when she'd said that her job had "other compensations."

"I think that woman's hiding something," I said.

"Like what, dear?"

"I don't know. With any luck, we'll find out."

As expected, Joan was not thrilled by my appearance at the office. Neither were the cops who were busily searching Jeffrey's files, interviewing his co-workers, proceeding with their investigation.

"You must be crazy, showing up here at a time like this," Joan hissed as my mother and I accosted her at her desk. "The place is swarming with policemen."

"I didn't kill the doctor, Joan," I said. "I'm perfectly free to roam the streets of Stuart."

"Then roam another street," she snapped.

"Please don't speak to my daughter in that tone of voice," my mother piped up. "Deborah only came to this office because I asked her to. I'm out of the vitamins that Dr. Hirshon prescribed for me and Deborah graciously consented to drive me here so I could buy some more."

I looked at my mother with shimmering respect. She was a natural at this make-it-up-as-you-go-along stuff.

"Very well," said Joan. She went to a nearby closet, fetched a bottle of Heartily Hirshon Vitamin E capsules, and handed it to my mother. "We take checks or cash for the vitamins. Which will it be, Mrs. Peltz?"

"I'll write a check," said my mother.

While they were transacting their business, I tossed around various scripts in my mind, all designed to regain Joan's trust. Eventually, I decided to go the condolence route.

"I want to express how terribly sorry I am about the doctor," I said. "How sorry both my mother and I are. We can only guess at your grief, since you worked for him for ten years."

Joan's lower lip quivered. "I wasn't planning to come into the office," she said. "But there's so much paperwork. Dr. Hirshon had such a thriving practice."

"And why not," I said. "My mother's living proof of what a skilled doctor he was."

Joan regarded my mother and nodded. She was thawing slightly.

"You must have gone into shock when you heard he'd been murdered," I said.

" 'Shock' doesn't begin to describe it," said Joan. "When you've worked for someone day after day, year after year, and then—poof!—they're gone, it's like the rug has been pulled out from under you. I still can't believe he's dead."

I patted her hand. "Just out of curiosity, did Dr. Hirshon have any enemies that you know of? Any disgruntled patients? Any overly aggressive medical malpractice lawyers?"

"No," she said defensively. "Not Dr. Hirshon."

"Even though he had a bad temper?" I said, reminding her of the comment she'd made.

"He had many more positive qualities than negative," she said. "Not the least of which was the gentlemanly manner in which he handled the constant badgering he took from his ex-wife."

"Francine?"

"Yes. No matter who much money he gave her, it was never enough."

"Not for all those shoes and handbags, huh?"

"She's a leech, that woman. The doctor couldn't get rid of her."

Maybe, but did *she* get rid of *him?* I wondered. "By any chance, do you know if Francine has a key to the doctor's house?" I asked.

"I assume she does, because he never bothered to change the locks after she moved out. Doctors are notoriously disorganized when it comes to their personal lives."

I nodded, pondering whether he never bothered to change his will, either. Mostly what I pondered, though, was why Joan had brought Francine up both times I'd talked to her, had bad-mouthed Jeffrey's ex to a complete stranger. Was she threatened by Francine? Did she view the former Mrs. Hirshon as competition, either for her boss's money or his love?

"Well, we've taken up enough of your time, Joan," I said, linking my arm through my mother's. "Although there is something else that's been nagging at me."

"And that is?"

"The last time I was here, I asked you why you had stayed with the doctor for ten years and you said it was because the job had 'other compensations.' What did you mean?"

She gathered herself up. "Not that it's any of your business, but I was extremely well paid, as far as office nurses go. I was also given more responsibility than most office nurses. The doctor trusted me without reservation, allowed me to manage personal matters for him as well as assist him in his practice, treated me like family. We had what can only be characterized as—"

"Yes?"

"—a special partnership."

I nodded, intrigued by her choice of words. Intrigued enough to try to get in one more question. "You really do have our sympathies, Joan. For someone as close to the doctor as you were, hearing that he was murdered must have been like hearing that Kennedy was assassinated—you know, one of those major events where you remember exactly where you were and what you were doing when you found out."

"It *was* like that," she acknowledged.

"Where were you when you heard, by the way?"

"About Kennedy or Dr. Hirshon?"

"Dr. Hirshon."

"I was at home."

"Alone?"

"No. With my precious little Sheldon."

"Your child?"

"My cat."

"Oh. How did you hear about the murder?"

"On the *Eleven O'clock News*. I almost fainted when they put that unflattering photograph of the doctor on the screen. I have so many wonderful pictures of him at home and they had to use that one."

God, this Joan was more than devoted to her boss. She obviously worshiped the man. But was it Jeffrey's charisma that bound her to him for a decade or the tidy sum of money he kept paying her?

As my mother and I left the office, I felt just as suspicious of Joan as I had before the visit. Maybe more so.

——————

I called Detective Gillby from my mother's house.

"I've got another lead for you," I told him. "Two leads."

"We're on top of the case, Ms. Peltz," he said.

"Undoubtedly, but I spoke with Dr. Hirshon's long-time nurse today, Joan . . . Joan . . . I didn't catch her last name."

"It's Sheldon."

"No, that's the name of her cat."

"It's also the name of her late husband."

"His name was Sheldon Sheldon?"

"No," Gillby said impatiently. "His name was Samuel Sheldon. And Joan's name is Joan Sheldon. As you can see, we've already talked to the lady."

"Of course you have. I mean no disrespect, Detective, but did you know that she has no alibi for the night Dr. Hirshon was killed? She was home alone, with Sheldon."

"We didn't ask her what she was doing the night of the murder because she's not a suspect, Ms. Peltz. She had no motive. She was extremely loyal to the doctor. She worked for him for ten years."

"Yes, but when you interviewed her, did she reveal that he paid her very handsomely, more than the typical salary for an office nurse?"

"No. Actually, she didn't."

"Well, she wasn't shy about telling me. She referred to their relationship as a 'special partnership.' I'm going out on a limb here, Detective, but I think the two of them were having sex."

He laughed. "Ms. Peltz, the only people who have sex are the characters on that soap opera you used to write for. Nobody has it in real life."

"You must be married," I said.

"Correct," he said.

"Let's say they *were* having sex, just for the heck of it. Maybe Joan got wind of Dr. Hirshon's fling with Vicky and killed him in a jealous rage. Or, there's another possibility—that all the money he was paying her was hush money. Maybe she was his accomplice in some shady activity. Have you considered that they might have been engaging in Medicare fraud, Detective?"

"It wasn't the first thing that came to mind, no. But this office is very thorough, Ms. Peltz. If there was fraud, we'll uncover it. In time. These things take *time.*"

"I understand."

"I appreciate that. Now, you said you had two leads. Let's have the other one."

"Well, according to Joan, Dr. Hirshon's ex-wife, Francine, was always nagging him about money."

"What are ex-wives for?"

"I'm serious, Detective. She harrassed him about money. No matter how much he gave her, it was never enough. What do you think of *that?*"

"We've already spoken to the doctor's ex-wife, Ms. Peltz. We're aware that she had disagreements with him."

"Okay, but did you ask her if she still has a key to her ex-husband's house? Because—now this is only a theory—she could have been so upset with him that she let herself into the house and shot him."

"She was in Aspen the night of the murder, Ms. Peltz. We ruled her out."

"She could have given the key to a hit man. Did you rule that out?"

There was no response.

"Oh, and I was wondering," I pressed on. "Have you interviewed Dr. Hirshon's attorney?"

"His attorney?"

"Yes. Whoever did his estate planning. You might want to ask him or her if Dr. Hirshon forgot to change his will after the divorce, the same way he forgot to change his locks. If it turns out that Francine's still the sole beneficiary, it certainly would shed new light on the case."

"Ms. Peltz. Do you mind if I ask *you* something?"

"No."

"Why are you involving yourself in this investigation?"

"*You* involved me, Detective Gillby, the minute you read me my Miranda Rights."

"But most murder suspects go out of their way to avoid talking to the police. You, on the other hand, seem to have my phone number on speed dial."

"Are you saying that none of my information is useful to you? Not the fact that Vicky Walters was having a secret affair with the doctor or that Joan Sheldon was involved in a 'special relationship' with him or that Francine Hirshon was desperate for money and might stand to inherit a bundle from his will? Do you really want me to buzz off?"

Silence.

"Detective?"

"You call whenever you've got something, Ms. Peltz."

I smiled and bid him a pleasant evening.

Chapter Fifteen

My mother insisted I stay for dinner Friday night. We feasted on boneless, skinless chicken breasts, baked potatoes topped with salt-free, cholesterol-free, fat-free cheese product, and salad with ranch dressing that was made with yogurt, not sour cream. By the end of the meal, I had an insatiable craving for an egg yolk.

During dinner, we traded theories about who killed you-know-who.

"Vicky told me that Jeffrey dated a lot of 'society women' after his divorce," I said at one point. "What sort of society women does Stuart have?"

"They're not the dowager-types they have in Palm Beach," my

mother explained. "For the most part, they're pretty, young girls from Stuart's old, moneyed families. They play golf or tennis, serve on planning committees for charity balls, and ride around in expensive convertibles. And some of them look like they're straight out of a Talbot's catalog."

"I get the picture," I said. "I wonder if one of them could have murdered Jeffrey. As a retaliation of some sort."

"Given the way he treated my daughters, I think he probably provoked angry feelings in a lot of women."

"Definitely, but the question is, which of these women did he provoke angry feelings in and how do I find them?"

My mother chuckled. "That's an easy one, dear. I'll give Celeste Tolliver a call. She's the society editor at the *Stuart News*. She's been covering the scene for years, knows who goes where and with whom. If Dr. Hirshon was the philanthropist people say he was, he attended the big fund-raising events in town—and brought a lady friend to each function, undoubtedly. I'll bet Celeste will not only give us the names of the women; she'll show us the photographs she took of them."

I smiled, enjoying this new side of my mother. She'd always had a knack for solving problems, but solving *crimes* was something else again. "How do *you* know Celeste, Mom? I don't remember you attending many charity galas."

"This is a small town, Deborah. You live here long enough, your path crosses with just about everybody."

We agreed that my mother would try to reach Celeste Tolliver on Monday morning at the newspaper. I was about to say goodnight and head back to the cottage when the phone rang.

"I'll get it," I said, eager to spare her from either an intrusive media person or an intrusive salesperson. "Hello?"

"Oh. It's you, Deborah," said Sharon, sounding disappointed when she heard my voice. "Aren't you supposed to be on Hutchinson Island, watching over those derelict buildings?"

"I'm a caretaker, not a security guard, Sharon. I'm allowed to leave the premises."

"Whatever. How's Mom?"

"She seems fine. We've just been sitting here plotting our next move in the investigation. This afternoon she drove me over to Jeffrey's office, so I could question his nurse. Now she's setting up an interview for us with a woman who works at the *Stuart News*."

"I cannot believe—can*not* believe—that you're dragging our mother into this lunacy of yours, Deborah. Have you completely forgotten that she's been seriously ill?"

"Of course not. She *asked* me to involve her. She said helping me takes her mind off her health, makes her feel useful."

"Well, I'm against her traipsing around like some amateur private eye. I'm concerned that the stress could bring on another heart attack."

"No, Sharon. You're concerned that you're not up here running the show, the way you've always been."

"That's a lie."

"No, it isn't."

"Yes, it is. Besides, this 'investigation' you've undertaken is a fool's errand, according to Barry. He's been advising me that the best strategy for us to take right now is to *stop* talking to people about the case. He says we should let the dust settle, let the smoke clear, let nature take its course."

"Does he charge you by the hour or by the cliché?"

"Very amusing. The point he was making is that we should keep a low profile. As for what he charges me, we haven't discussed his fee. He told me when he called me that first time that he simply wanted to be there for me, to steer me through the tangled web of the justice system."

I tried not to gag. "Where is Barry tonight? I thought you two were having dinner."

"We are. I'm at a pay phone at La Vieille Maison. We're between courses." I practically drooled when I pictured all that cream sauce. "He's been telling me fascinating stories about his background. For example, he's from New Jersey, originally, but he got his B.A. at the University of Miami—class of sixty-three—and liked it so much that he went to law school there too. And he's been living in south Florida ever since."

"Boy. What an adventurer. I can see why you were riveted."

"What is it with you, Deborah? You've done nothing but make snippy remarks about Barry from the minute you met him."

"You're right. I'm sorry," I said, remembering that it was my snippy remark about Lester, Sharon's most recent ex-husband, that set off our two-year estrangement. Still, there was something about Barry Shiller that caused me to want to take a shower.

"Look, is Mom there?" Sharon said. "I called to tell her that the police have talked to Norman and confirmed that he was at school the night of the murder. I'm relieved that they don't suspect him of anything, but I hate that they bothered him with this nonsense."

"I don't blame you. Give him my love when you speak to him, would you?"

"I'll try, but it may come out sounding forced."

I bit my tongue. "I'll get Mom." I put down the phone and told my mother it was her other daughter, Miss Congeniality, on the line. And then I kissed her goodnight and went home.

Saturday was a gray day at the beach, the sky ominous with rain clouds, but that didn't keep dozens of tourists from stopping by the House of Refuge and having a look around.

I saw Fred Zimsky as he was coming on duty, and he introduced me to a couple of the other volunteers, both of whom said they had read about me in the newspaper and wasn't it an awful thing that such a nice doctor was murdered in his own house.

"He wasn't a nice doctor," Fred told them. "He hardly ever visited his mother in the nursing home."

Not in the mood to listen to them debate the issue, I escaped inside the cottage, where I read, watched a little TV, and pondered my future—my professional future, mostly. I knew, deep down, that Gillby would let Sharon and me off the hook eventually and that he would nail the real killer in time. And so I tried to project what I would do with myself after the murder was solved. Since I had written for a living once, I considered writing for a living now: a novel; a column for one of the local newspapers; advertising copy for golf communities. When none of those options appealed to me, I went out on the porch and stared at the ocean, which was as unproductive as it was enjoyable.

The sea was churning and white-capped by late afternoon, and a gusty, southeasterly wind had developed. I didn't have to be a meterologist to figure out that we were in for a storm, possibly a nasty one, and that it would be my first since I'd moved in to the cottage. I was grateful that my job description didn't include rescuing shipwrecked sailors after all.

I went into the kitchen and took an inventory of my rations, should the electricity go out. I had bread and tunafish and salad fixings, and two bottles of Chianti. An embarrassment of riches.

At about seven o'clock, just after the rain started coming down in sheets, along with a few rumbles of thunder, I heard a knock at the door. Slightly paranoid since the murder, I considered not answering it. But then I recognized Ray Scalley's voice.

"Hey, Deborah!" he yelled. "I see the lights on. I know you're in there."

I opened the door.

"What are you doing out in this rain? You're soaking wet," I said, pulling him inside.

He shook the water off of him, like a dog after a bath. "I was driving back from Jensen Beach and thought I'd stop in, check out how you're doing," he said. "I know it's Saturday night, but since you told me you're not interested in dating, I figured it was a safe bet you'd be here all by your lonesome."

"That's very sweet of you, Ray. I'm happy to have the company, although you seem to have an aversion to using the telephone."

"I do tend to show up without calling first, don't I?" He laughed. "Sorry about that. It must be a childhood thing. When I was growing up, my brother was always hogging the phone. I probably decided somewhere along the line that I could survive without ever using one."

"Siblings are such fun," I said. "Now, how about something to drink? The choices are Chianti and water."

"Normally I'm a beer guy, but I'll suffer with the Chianti."

I poured us each a glass and we took our wine into the living room.

"You've got the floodlights on out there, which makes this sofa a great spot for storm watching," said Ray. "Have a seat." He patted the cushion next to him.

I sat. We drank the wine and talked. I filled him in on my Jeffrey-related encounters, and, as a finale, performed what I thought were brilliant imitations of Detective Gillby, Vicky Walters, Joan Sheldon, Barry Shiller, and my sister. Ray laughed, which made me laugh, and after we'd gotten All Things Jeffrey out of our system, we pledged not to mention him or the investigation for the rest of the evening. (I also made a silent vow to stop waiting for him to suddenly reveal himself as the murderer and just be grateful for his company.)

We gazed out the windows at the rain and sea and swaying palm trees, just kicked back and let nature's pyrotechnics entertain us. I had forgotten that thunderstorms at the beach, particularly thunderstorms at night, are so dramatic, and I felt lucky both to have a front-row seat and to be snug and warm and dry at the same time.

It wasn't a hardship having someone to share the experience with, either. I had been so accustomed to experiencing everything alone, was so used to being by myself, that having Ray there, listening to the low timbre of his voice as he commented on the storm, on how the weather in Florida has become more unpredictable over the last few years, on how the water and salt and wind take their toll on wood-frame buildings like the House of Refuge, was soothing.

Not that I mean to make Ray sound like a glass of warm milk, because he certainly wasn't soothing as in *boring*. He kidded me and I kidded him back, and there were moments when we sparred like a couple of prizefighters. But there was something so easy, so natural about the way our conversation moved, the way it meandered. This was a different sort of intimacy, I realized, this having a person to watch rain storms with, this having a person who drops over to your house, unannounced, simply because he feels like it.

"Ray. We haven't had dinner," I pointed out when it was eight o'clock.

"What're you offering?" he asked.

"Tuna on whole wheat with lettuce, tomato, and mayo."

"Sold, minus the lettuce and tomato."

"You don't eat vegetables?" I said, remembering how he'd wrinkled his nose at the zucchini he'd been served at the Black Marlin.

"No," he said. "Unless you count ketchup as a vegetable. I eat that."

We gobbled up the sandwiches and sipped more Chianti while we waited for the rain to stop.

"Tell me about your wife," I said when he had finished a story about his family. "If the memory isn't too painful."

"The memory of Beth's *death* is painful. The memory of her life is one of my real pleasures."

I nodded. "Did she work?"

"She was a high school English teacher. She loved kids and loved books, so she and the job were a perfect fit."

"How did you two meet?"

He smiled. "Through my brother, indirectly. I was trying on a pair of pants at Doug's Palm Beach Gardens store and Beth was there, buying a tie for her father. I thought she was great-looking and wanted to strike up a conversation with her, but you know me. I'm not the smoothest guy on the planet when I first meet someone."

I laughed, recalling *our* first meeting. "You're what they call an acquired taste," I said dryly. "Did you give Beth the kind of lecture you gave me?"

"Not exactly. The lecture I gave her had to do with ties—basically, how men hate wearing them and why she shouldn't buy one for her father. She asked me what, in my opinion, she *should* buy for her father, and I said, 'Tell me about your father.' And she told me. Over dinner at Captain Charlie's Reef Grill in Juno Beach. We were married six months later."

"How romantic."

"It was romantic. And it stayed romantic. I'm not saying we didn't have our rocky periods, but they never lasted. We had too much fun with each other. We didn't want to waste our energy fighting, almost as if we had a hunch that our time together was going to be short."

"I'm so sorry, Ray. I can't even imagine what it must be like to have the kind of relationship you and Beth had and then lose it. But you've survived, which goes to show how resilient people are."

"I don't know how resilient I am. I just get on with it. What's the alternative?"

Ray stayed until about ten-thirty, when the rain finally let up. I was walking him out to his car when we heard voices coming from the observation tower between the House of Refuge and the gift shop.

"I think you've got trespassers," said Ray.

"Melinda Carr warned me about them," I said. "She also indicated that it was part of my job to get them off the property."

"Then away we go."

We headed toward the tower.

"Hey, you!" Ray shouted. "Come down off there or we're calling the police."

"Don't have an aneurysm, Pop," a young male voice shouted back. "We're done."

Within a few minutes, two teenagers, a boy and a girl, scampered down the steps of the tower, flung themselves over the gate, and fled into a car.

"I think I'd better have a look, to make sure they didn't do any damage," said Ray, who went to his own car, fetched a flashlight, and mounted the tower. When he came back down, he was carrying something. "She forgot her panties," he said, dumping them in the trash bin in the parking lot. "Ah, to be young again."

I laughed. "Goodnight, you old geezer. Thanks for stopping by." I kissed him on the cheek—without agonizing over it this time.

"See ya," he said. "Stay out of trouble, huh?"

I said I'd try.

Chapter Sixteen

At two-thirty on Monday afternoon, my mother picked me up in the Delta 88 and drove us to the *Stuart News*.

"We have an appointment with Celeste Tolliver," she told the receptionist who sat behind a desk in the lobby of the snazzy white office building.

"May I have both your names, please?" asked the receptionist.

"Mrs. Lenore Peltz and her daughter Deborah."

We were instructed to take a seat until "Miss Tolliver" came for us, which she did after a ten-minute wait.

"Lenore," said the society editor after descending a staircase and making her way over to us. "It's been too long."

As she and my mother air-kissed each other, my initial impression of the sixtyish Celeste Tolliver was that she was the pinkest person I'd ever seen—pink dress, pink cheeks, pink lipstick, even a pink tint to her tightly curled gray hair. My second impression of her was that, despite all the pink and the candy-sweet innocence the color suggested, she was in no way candy-sweet or innocent. After my mother introduced us, Celeste, who was heavily perfumed, looked me over as if I were crawling with lice, and said, "I understand that *you're* the one who found the body. You and your sister, the wedding planner from Boca."

"Yes, Miss Tolliver," I acknowledged. That was the third thing about her—she was definitely a *Miss Tolliver*. "But there's a lot more to the story, and my mother suggested that, because of your position in the community and your familiarity with its most socially prominent residents, you might be able to help us fill in the blanks."

"Indeed," she said, her eyebrows arching. I sensed that she was flattered by the importance we were bestowing upon her. She was someone people sucked up to on a regular basis, and she obviously relished the part. "You realize, of course, that I'm not a crime reporter for this newspaper."

"No, but by letting us ask you a few questions, you could have a hand in bringing a killer to justice," I said. "That would boost your readership, wouldn't it?"

"If you weren't new to Stuart, Deborah, you would know that my readership is rather devoted as it is," she said. "However, I must admit that in all the years I've been covering the social scene in Martin County, no one has ever thought to plumb the depths of *my* experience in order to solve a murder. I'm quite taken with the idea, to be perfectly frank."

I winked at my mother as Celeste turned and led us up the staircase, to a conference room on the second floor, her perfume trailing behind her.

When we were all seated, I explained why we—and not the police—were poking around in Jeffrey's personal life and assured her more than once that Sharon and I had nothing to do with his murder. "What we'd like you to tell us," I said, "is which social functions Dr.

Hirshon attended within the past year and which ladies he escorted to each of them."

"Which ladies." Celeste rolled her eyes. "There were so many. Jeffrey Hirshon played the field, as they say."

"Yes, but can you possibly give us the names of these women?" I asked.

"I suppose so, but not off the top of my head," said Celeste. "I would have to search through my files to be absolutely accurate, but if you wait here, I'll bring the ones that may be pertinent."

She was gone for twenty minutes. I wished I had brought along a deck of cards or, at the very least, a magazine.

"Now then," she said, returning with several boxes, as well as folders, in her arms and setting them down on the table. "Our social season gets underway in October with Junkanoo."

"Jew Canoe?" I said, wondering if this was a soirée sponsored by the local Cadillac dealership.

Celeste practically passed out at my ignorance. "*Junkanoo*—the word means 'Bahamian Festival'—raises money for Hibiscus."

"The Hibiscus Center is a shelter for abused children, dear," my mother said, tipping me off before I committed another, even more embarrassing social gaffe.

"A very worthy cause, obviously," said Celeste. "The party itself is held at Mariner Sands Country Club every year, has a lively tropical theme, and is widely supported within the community. My guess is that Jeffrey Hirshon was in attendance."

She flipped through a folder, rereading the newspaper column she'd written about the party. "Yes, here's his name," she said excitedly. "Now, let's see if I've got a photograph of him. He may not have made it into the column, but I keep all the photos I take, even the rejects." She rummaged through one of the boxes. "Ah. I thought so." She pulled out a snapshot and displayed it proudly.

"That's Jeffrey," I said, peering at the photo. He was dressed in a festive Hawaiian shirt, as opposed to a white lab coat, but he was wearing that same warm, open smile that had reeled Sharon and me in. And there was a good reason he was smiling—two good reasons, actually. In one hand, he was holding a tall, umbrella-ed cocktail. In the other, he was holding a tall, curvaceous blonde. "Who's the babe?"

"Why that's Didi Hornsby," Celeste remarked, tapping her finger on the table. "I had forgotten that she dated the doctor."

"Is she Ted and Audra Hornsby's daughter?" my mother asked, referring, I guessed, to the babe's parents.

"She's their eldest," said Celeste. "Divorced. Two children. Lives in Snug Harbor."

"And she dated Jeffrey for a while?" I confirmed.

"Yes, it's coming back to me now," said Celeste, "although there was talk that it was just a summer fling."

"A summer fling that carried over into the fall, apparently," I mused. "It didn't, by any chance, carry over into the winter too, did it? Right up until the murder?"

Celeste shook her head. "I doubt it. They weren't together at the Chrysanthemum Ball in early November. That I do remember."

My mother leaned over to interpret. "The Chrysanthemum Ball is a black-tie party to benefit the hospital, dear. It's held at a private home each year."

"Indeed. Last year it was held at Jeffrey Hirshon's Sewall's Point home, as a matter of fact," said Celeste. "If I'm not mistaken, his date that evening was Suzie Kendall." She fished into another folder. "Yes. Here they are. An attractive couple, don't you agree?"

She placed the newspaper column on the table for our viewing. Sure enough, there was a photo of Jeffrey in a tuxedo, his arm wrapped around the waist of a woman wearing a sequined blue dress, serious eyeshadow, and big black hair piled on top of her head, Ivana style. "What's the story with Suzie Kendall?" I asked. "Other than her desperate need for a fashion makeover."

"Old family. Lots of quiet money. *Railroad* money," Celeste confided.

"Divorced?" I said.

"Twice," said Celeste. "She and the doctor were awfully chummy at the party, but, if memory serves, the romance fizzled even more quickly than the liaison with Didi."

"Do you have any idea why?" I said.

"No. Perhaps the answer is in another of my folders," she said. I could tell she was beginning to enjoy this little game. "Yes, here's Jeffrey Hirshon's name, linked with Lucinda Orwell, in my column on the River Dayz Festival."

"We're trying to save the St. Lucie River from pollution," my mother translated yet again. "There's an annual street fair in downtown Stuart in late November to build awareness of the problem."

"That's very noble, Mom," I said. "But what gets me is how Jeffrey pops up everywhere, like Forrest Gump. You start to wonder when he had time to practice medicine."

"Look!" Celeste interrupted. "I've got a nice photograph of the doctor at River Dayz. He's standing next to Lucinda, who, as you can see, is one of Stuart's fairest flowers."

I stifled a laugh and zeroed in on the picture. Lucinda Orwell was a knockout, I had to admit. Long blond hair, green eyes, gigantic tits.

"I suppose *she's* why the romance with Suzie Kendall broke up," said Celeste slyly. "Although what these women saw in Jeffrey Hirshon, I cannot fathom. He seemed so *new* money."

"As opposed to quiet money, you mean," I said.

"That's it exactly," said Celeste, nodding.

"What *I* can't fathom is how many young, single women there are around here," I said. "And I thought it was competitive in New York."

Celeste didn't respond. Her head was back in her folders. "What about this!" she said triumphantly, pulling out two newspaper clippings. "Dr. Hirshon took Lucinda to the Red Cross Ball at Willoughby in December, but he brought Roberta Ross to the Heart Ball at Sailfish just the other week."

"Just the other week?" I said, astounded. At the same time he was shtupping Vicky *and* coming on to Sharon and me?

"Yes, indeed. I have the evidence." She shoved both columns at me. "And to think that the ink was barely dry on Roberta's divorce papers."

Didi. Suzie. Lucinda. Roberta. I was dizzy with Jeffrey's women, couldn't figure out how he juggled them all in such a small town, couldn't imagine how a cardiologist, a man people trusted with their lives, could afford to have the reputation of a lothario.

"It's rather ironic that the doctor's final event was the Heart Ball," said Celeste. "Given his profession."

"It is," I said. "But getting back to Roberta, you mentioned that she'd just been divorced when she went to the party with Jeffrey. Who was she divorced from? Someone with new money? Quiet money? Any money?"

"How interesting that you should ask," said Celeste. "Roberta's ex-husband was in the same medical practice as Dr. Hirshon. He's an internist named Peter Elkin. You must know him, Lenore. He lives in Sewall's Point, too."

That little tidbit stopped me cold. Dr. Elkin was the man Nurse Vicky claimed to have been with the night of the murder.

"Oh. You're wondering about Roberta's last name," said Celeste, mistaking the reason for my stunned expression. "She's a successful real estate agent in town. She's always used her maiden name, Ross, even during her marriage to Dr. Elkin."

God, Ray was right, I thought. Sewall's Point *is* a Peyton Place. Talk about six degrees of separation.

"Well, Miss Tolliver, you've given us more than enough to chew on," I said. "I assume the four women you mentioned are in the phone book, in case I want to ask them a few questions?" Roberta Ross, in particular.

"I'll give you their numbers," she said, "but I'll deny that you got them from me if I'm ever asked."

"Understood," I said.

"I doubt they'll speak to you though," she added. "You *are* a suspect in the murder of a man they cared about."

"If they truly cared about Jeffrey, they'll want to see his killer caught," I said. "I have a feeling that they'll squeeze me in between charity balls."

My mother and I thanked Celeste for her help and left the building.

An hour after I was back at the cottage, I received a call from Detective Gillby.

"We're ready to return your car," he said. "It's clean."

"Oh, that's very thoughtful, Detective, but you didn't have to wash it for me."

"No, it's *clean,* as in *evidence-free.* No blood, no gun, no nothing. Although we did find a couple of hairs that match the hair of the deceased—his beard hair. They were down on the floor, under the steering wheel. Do you have any idea how they landed there, Ms. Peltz?"

"Sure. The day before he was killed, Dr. Hirshon helped me jump-start the Pontiac in the parking lot of Stuart Fine Foods. After he opened the hood and hooked me up to his jumper cables, he got into the car on the driver's side and started her up. I guess he shed a few beards hairs while he was at it."

"That was the one and only time he was in your car?"

"He owned a Porsche, Detective. Under other circumstances, he wouldn't have been caught dead in my Pontiac." I regretted the *dead* naturally, but it was too late to take it back. "How about the other lab results?" I asked. "Do we know any more about the crime scene?"

Gillby laughed. "Even if we did, *we* wouldn't share it."

"Why not? *I* share all my information with *you.*"

"So you do." I sensed that, while Detective Gillby was very professional and, therefore, couldn't rule me out altogether as a suspect, he was developing a tolerance, if not an actual fondness, for me. "All right. Here's a nugget for you, since you're so interested," he said begrudgingly. "The autopsy report came back with no evidence of drugs or alcohol in the doctor's bloodstream. And the analysis of his stomach contents—and his kitchen—showed that he had eaten dinner at home shortly before he was killed: pasta in some kind of tomato sauce, plus a green salad and—"

"You can skip that part," I said, my own stomach turning over. "How about the skin under his fingernails? Don't you guys usually check for that? To determine if there was a struggle?"

"We didn't find any," said Gillby. "But then we've pretty well determined that there wasn't a struggle. For one thing, the crime scene suggests that the killer is someone Hirshon knew, because his front door was open when you and your sister found the body."

"Then you think the killer did have a key to the house."

"Either that, or the doctor invited him in. Also, our photos of the scene tell us that nothing in the house was disturbed or out of place, not even in the den where the doctor was shot. Whoever pulled the trigger was probably sitting in that room, having a nice little chat with Hirshon, when he surprised him with the gun, fired off a twenty-two-caliber bullet, and then left the house the same way he entered—out the front door."

"What about fingerprints, Detective? Did you find some?"

"Yeah. Yours and your sister's."

"Swell. Anybody else's?"

"Look, you and I both know I shouldn't be discussing the specifics of the case with you, Ms. Peltz. Let's just say that we're moving ahead with the investigation and that you and your sister are not our primary focus at the moment."

"I'm relieved to hear that. I've got another question though. Do you think it's important that Jeffrey was shot in his den?"

"Run that by me again?"

"Do you think it's some sort of clue that he was killed in his den, as opposed to, say, his bedroom or bathroom or boat? From the brief look I got at the room, it seemed as if it doubled as his home office. It just occurred to me that if the murder were a crime of passion, an office would be an odd backdrop for it."

"*Backdrop.*" Gillby chuckled. "I realize that you're coming to us straight from the glamorous world of show business, Ms. Peltz, but we're not dealing with a stage set here. We're dealing with a real-life homicide."

"I'll remember that," I said, trying to sound chastened. "I'll speak to you soon."

"I have no doubt of it."

Chapter Seventeen

On Monday night, I placed calls to Didi Hornsby, Suzie Kendall, Lucinda Orwell, and Roberta Ross. I did not pretend to be a market researcher, nor did I say I was with AT&T or MCI. I told them exactly who I was and why I wanted to talk to them, and used the fact that my mother was a long-time resident of Sewall's Point (as well as a contributor to the charitable organizations in which they were involved) to prove I wasn't some social gate crasher.

To my surprise, all of them—even Roberta, the real estate agent and former Mrs. Elkin—said they'd make time for me. I was beginning to realize that people around town had few inhibitions when it came to sharing intimate details of their lives, even with a total stranger. I assumed this was either because of the glut of confessional talk shows on television today or because of the friendly, open manner that small towns foster. Of course, it could also have been because everyone likes to offer his or her two cents' worth about a murder.

The next morning, my mother drove me to the sheriff's office so I could reclaim the Pontiac. The car looked just as sorry as ever and smelled worse, thanks to whatever chemicals the cops sprayed it with in order to ferret out beard hairs and other traces of Jeffrey.

"You sure you don't want me to go with you, dear?" my mother asked as I set off for my appointments with the "Sirens of Stuart," as I came to call them.

"Positive," I said. "I'm saving you for another mission, Mom."

"Oh?" Her blue eyes twinkled.

"Now that Jeffrey's gone, you're going to need a new doctor," I said. "Somebody like Peter Elkin, for instance."

"I get it." She smiled. "You want me to have a checkup."

"Right. And while you're there, you'll slip in a few questions, which I'll write down for you in advance."

"That's very clever, Deborah, but Dr. Elkin's an internist, not a cardiologist. He takes care of people with all sorts of medical problems."

"Well? Didn't you say your stomach was acting up? Or was it your arthritis?"

She laughed. "Tell me the symptoms I'm supposed to have and I'll have them, dear."

My first stop at ten o'clock was Didi Hornsby, who lived in a scenic section of Stuart known as Snug Harbor. Set along the St. Lucie River, across the bridge from Sewall's Point, Snug Harbor boasted lovely homes, plus a marina and tennis court for members of its neighborhood association. Didi's house, a brick residence of a style more typically found up north, screamed *kids*. There were beach balls and frisbees and bicycles in the driveway and toys of various colors and shapes scattered about the front lawn. I stepped gingerly out of my car, so as not to slip and impale myself on a Mighty Morphin Power Ranger.

When I rang the doorbell, I was greeted by the sound of many large barking dogs. I considered getting back in the car.

"Deborah?" said a blond woman after opening the door a crack.

"Didi?"

"That's me. Come on in," she said, at which point four Great Danes the size of horses attempted to trample me. "Inga! Pipi! Sonja! Eva! Down!"

It took several of Didi's *down!*s, but eventually the dogs left me alone.

"They get, like, creeped out by new people," Didi said apologetically, her accent a mixture of southern belle and valley girl. "Let's go and sit in the family room."

As I followed Didi into the room, I studied her from behind. She was wearing a purple-and-black tank top and matching spandex shorts, the sort of costume you see at gyms and health clubs. (She explained that she'd just returned from hers.) She was in fabulous shape, there was no question about that. With her blond hair, lightly tanned complexion, and glistening muscles, she looked very much the outdoorsy type—sort of like Meryl Streep in that movie where she white-water rafted for two straight hours. Yes, Didi Hornsby was a woman who would have enjoyed working out with Jeffrey, I surmised, and vice versa.

"Evian?" she offered me, stopping at the wet bar.

"No, thanks."

She poured herself a glass, dipped her fingertips into it, and spritzed her face with the water.

"It's important to keep the skin moist," she said, as she continued to flick droplets of water on herself. "People forget to, because Florida is so, like, humid."

She peered at the skin on my face, then flicked Evian on *me.*

"There," she said. "How does that feel?"

"Wet," I said, blinking the water out of my eyes.

We sat on her sofa after she cleared away some of her childrens' toys.

"I appreciate your making time for me this morning," I began.

"That's okay. The kids are with the au pair. I have a lunch date at twelve-thirty, but the rest of the morning is, like, totally free. Oh, except for my massage at eleven."

"Great. As I said on the phone, I want to talk to you about Jeffrey Hirshon. My sister and I met him when our mother had a heart attack, and, in the course of her hospitalization and follow-up treatment, we struck up a friendship with him. Shortly after that, he was murdered and we were the ones who found his body, which was an incredibly traumatic experience, as you can imagine. Ever since then, I've become obsessed with learning more about him, about who could have hated him enough to kill him. I mean, the man saved my beloved mother's life! The least I can do is try to find out who took *his!*" I should add that I performed this speech while clutching my hands to my bosom, and, I'm afraid, I pretended to cry.

Didi seemed concerned. "Can I get you some herbal tea, Deborah?"

I shook my head, fearing she might spritz my face with the hot liquid. "I'll be all right if you'll tell me about Jeffrey, how you felt about him, whether you were aware of anyone who was angry at him."

"Who could be angry at Jeffrey? He was a super guy, a real sweetheart. That's the crazy part of this," she said. "We dated for six months and it was a blast."

"If it was such a blast, why did you two break up?"

"Because it stopped being a blast."

"Yes, but *why*, Didi?" I asked, realizing she wasn't particularly introspective.

She shrugged. "It just did. We had fun and then we didn't. So we moved on to other people."

"You're saying that the spark died, is that it?"

"Yeah, kind of. You know how you go through periods where you, like, can't eat too many softshell crabs? And then the season's over and you think, I'll never eat one of those critters again? That's what happened between Jeffrey and me. We ODed on each other or something."

"So it was a mutual decision to end the relationship."

"Totally. We stayed friendly after we broke up. I was the one who suggested he take Suzie Kendall to the Chrysanthemum Ball last year."

"Really. Who did you go with?"

"Suzie's ex-husband Chip."

I sighed, trying to conceive of this sort of overlap going on in New York. "Wasn't that a little awkward for everybody?" I asked.

"Not at all," said Didi. "Chip was Suzie's first ex-husband. Now, if I'd shown up at the party with Hartley, her second ex-husband, it would have been a different story. She's still hurting from *that* breakup."

I tried to keep my eyes from crossing. "So you remained on good terms with Jeffrey after you stopped seeing each other."

"Oh, yeah. I told you, he was a super guy."

"But staying with him would have been like eating too many softshell crabs."

"Exactly."

I asked a few more questions, but it was a waste of time. Didi Hornsby didn't know anything—and I do mean *anything*. Besides, her house smelled of Great Danes, and I needed some fresh air. I thanked her for talking to me and left.

Next, it was back to Sewall's Point for a visit with Suzie Kendall, who lived in an enormous, gated, pistachio-colored house in a relatively new subdivision aptly named Castle Hill. So much for Suzie's "quiet" railroad money.

Before being admitted inside the house, I had to press the intercom outside the gate.

"Yes?" came a female voice.

"It's Deborah Peltz."

The gate swung open and the Pontiac and I were in.

Waiting for me at the front door was Suzie herself, a vision in a lime-green sundress. She wasn't as bouncy as Didi, nor was she a cover girl for a fitness magazine, but she was pretty (or would have been without all the eyeshadow) and the pouffy black hair from the Chrysanthemum Ball photo had given way to a more casual (and flattering) ponytail.

We shook hands and she invited me inside the house. We sat in her living room, which had been decorated in an African safari motif, complete with dead animals peering at us from over the fireplace. I wondered immediately if Suzie was a hunter and owned a gun. So I asked. She said that it was her ex-husband (Hartley, not Chip) who hunted and that she, on the other hand, was frightened of guns.

The subject of guns and the shooting of living things led us straight into a discussion of Jeffrey. I gave her the same sob story I'd thrown at Didi, but Suzie wasn't nearly as cavalier about the way her romance with him had ended.

"He didn't even have the courtesy to tell me he was seeing another woman," she said bitterly. "He just stopped calling. I felt so abandoned, which is how I felt after Hartley left me. I'm at the stage now where I have no self-esteem whatsoever." I tried to squeeze in a question, but she kept going. "I know I shouldn't look to men for validation, for my identity; that I should love myself and nurture myself and figure out what *I* want in life and then pursue it. The question is: What *does* Suzie Kendall want out of life? Who *is* Suzie Kendall?" Before I could ask why she was speaking of herself in the third person, she was at it again. "Suzie Kendall doesn't have a career. Suzie Kendall doesn't have children. All Suzie Kendall has is a very large trust fund."

Let me whip out the Stradivarius, I thought, as she whined about the gobs of money she'd been saddled with by her forebears.

At some point, there was a break in the action and I said, "Getting back to Jeffrey Hirshon, how long did you two go out?"

"Three months," she said. "Three months of kissy-kissy and then nothing, as if I didn't exist. I'd call his house and his answering machine would pick up. I'd call his office and that witch of a nurse—"

"Joan."

"—Joan would tell me he was with patients. I couldn't reach him. He froze me out, and I had no idea why. And then one Sunday I opened the *Stuart News* to Celeste Tolliver's column and who did I see but Jeffrey, arm in arm with Lucinda Orwell, at the River Dayz Festival."

"You must have been hopping mad," I said, wondering whether I had ever used that expression before and, if not, why I had used it then.

"I was hurt and humiliated and didn't go out of the house for two weeks."

"Two weeks? Boy, you either have a lot of fruit trees on your property or you had a lot of pizzas delivered."

"I have a wonderful cook. She shops too."

"That *is* fortunate. Did you ever see Jeffrey again or talk to him about what happened between you?"

"I saw him at the Heart Ball recently, but I didn't confront him," said Suzie. "He was much too *busy*."

"With Roberta Ross, you mean."

"Yes." Suzie looked at me. "You know, for a newcomer in town you're very up-to-date on the social scene, Deborah."

"My mother clips all of Celeste Tolliver's columns," I explained. "Sort of the way other people clip coupons. I read them the other day. In one sitting."

"Because you were so fond of Jeffrey."

"Yes, and because my mother doesn't subscribe to *People*."

"Well, I may have had my ups and downs with him, but I was devastated when I heard he'd been murdered."

"Can you think of anyone who was upset with him? Beside you, that is."

"You're asking if I can think of anyone who might have killed him."

"Yes."

"What about Lucinda Orwell?" said Suzie. "Jeffrey dumped her for Roberta. Maybe she didn't take it as well as I did."

"Do you know Lucinda, Suzie? I mean, are you two social acquaintances?"

"Of course I know her," said Suzie. "She's my first husband's second ex-wife."

I felt lightheaded after my chat with Suzie, so between appointments I bought a sandwich and a Diet Coke at the Harbour Bay Gourmet and wolfed them both down in my car.

Fortified, I proceeded down South Sewall's Point Road to another exclusive subdivision, this one called the Archipelago. Developed more than twenty years ago to resemble a chain of islands in the South Pacific, it consists of three narrow streets, its houses fronting either the wide Intracoastal Waterway or a picturesque lagoon. Separated from the rest of Sewall's Point by two little bridges, the Archipelago has a mystique to it, and its residents, some of whom are a bit eccentric or like to think they are, contribute to that mystique.

Lucinda Orwell's house was on Simara Street. Modest, certainly by Boca standards, it was reminiscent of the Polynesian, thatched-roof huts found in Tahiti, Bora Bora, or, at the very least, that old TV series *Adventures in Paradise.*

There were steppingstones leading up to the house and a cowbell hanging from a rope instead of a doorbell. I yanked it.

Lucinda answered. She was an exquisite creature, I noticed right away, with shoulder-length flaxen hair, emerald green eyes, and a tall, shapely figure. She was casually dressed in bare feet, cut-off blue jeans, and a white T-shirt (no bra), and she wore no makeup, not even lip gloss.

"Welcome," she said as she let me inside. "I'd shake hands but mine are wet." She displayed her palms, which were dotted with several shades of oil paint.

"Are you an artist?" I asked as she dashed into a mud room so she could wash her hands

"Yes," she called out. "I'll show you, if you like."

She took me upstairs to her studio, a large sky-lit loft area that made up the entire second floor of the house. "A lot of my stuff is at the Profile Gallery in Habour Bay Plaza, but there are a few pieces here. Bahamian scenes, mostly."

I was no art critic, but Lucinda's work was beautiful—colorful and atmospheric.

"I take it you go to the Bahamas frequently," I said. "For inspiration."

She nodded. "Jeffrey and I went together a few times. You did come here to ask me about him, didn't you?"

"Yes," I said, and gave her the same spiel I'd given the others.

"We saw each other for three or four months, I don't remember exactly," she said. "He liked going to the Bahamas on his boat on long weekends, if he wasn't on call, and I was happy to hitch a ride."

"Why'd you break up?" I asked. "Suzie Kendall suggested that Roberta Ross might have been the reason."

Lucinda laughed. "Suzie Kendall is about as out of touch as it gets. Jeffrey and I broke up because of Gwen Ladd."

"Who?" Celeste never mentioned anyone by *that* name, I thought. She gave me and my mother the distinct impression that Jeffrey had transferred his affection directly from Lucinda to Roberta.

"You don't know Gwen?" said Lucinda, seeming surprised.

"No. Should I?" I said.

"Yes, if you have any interest in the art scene here. She's got a show going on at the Norton in Palm Beach. She does glass sculptures." Lucinda walked over to a table and carefully held up a large piece of brown-tinted glass. It seemed to me to be in the shape of a portobello mushroom.

"That's one of Gwen Ladd's?" I asked.

Lucinda nodded. "She's amazing, isn't she?"

"I'll never look at a mushroom the same way again," I agreed. "But I must say, Lucinda. You're an incredibly good sport. Never mind that you own one of your rival's pieces; you place it right where you can see it day after day."

"Gwen and I aren't rivals. She does her art. I do mine."

"No. I meant, your rival for Jeffrey. You told me that you and he broke up because he left you for Gwen."

Lucinda laughed again. "Jeffrey and I broke up because *I* left *him* for Gwen."

"I'm sorry?"

"Gwen and I are a *couple*."

"Oh." I took a second to regroup. "Was Jeffrey muffed—sorry— miffed that you dumped him for another woman?"

"Not that I could tell. He started dating Roberta Ross about a week after Gwen and I moved in together. I ran into them at a reception at the Cultural Courthouse one night, and they seemed very compatible."

Interesting, I mused. Celeste Tolliver prided herself on knowing who went out with whom, but maybe her reach only extended to heterosexual twosomes.

"Well," I said. "I'll ask my last question and let you get back to work, Lucinda. Can you think of anyone who might have wanted to kill Jeffrey?"

She shrugged. "Anyone. Everyone. He wasn't a particularly nice guy."

"Then why on earth did you go out with him?"

"Hey. Haven't *you* ever misjudged a man?"

I sighed. "Lucinda, honey, I wouldn't be here if I hadn't."

Roberta Ross lived in a four-bedroom townhouse in Sailfish Point, a gated, guarded, notoriously expensive country club community on the southernmost tip of Hutchinson island. A sprawling maze of condos, townhouses, and truly immense homes, as well as a beachside clubhouse and restaurant, tennis courts, a marina, and a fabled golf course, "Sailfish" boasts CEOs, Wall Streeters, and other newly minted folks, many of whom fly back and forth to their primary residences in their very own little Gulfstreams.

Roberta's townhouse, a Mediterranean-style building with brick courtyard, plunge pool, and fireplace, was her temporary home, she explained as she led me inside.

"I'm renting until I find something I want to buy," said Roberta, a stunning brunette dressed in a career-woman, canary-yellow suit. "The real estate market's been so hot that we don't have a lot of inventory right now. Speaking of which, I'm showing a house across town in a half hour. Will this take long?"

"No. I'll get right to the point," I said. "As I told you on the phone, I want to talk to you about Jeffrey Hirshon." I did my song-

and-dance. "Since you and he were dating shortly before he was murdered, I figured you might have some thoughts about who could have killed him."

"Truthfully, I didn't know Jeffrey all that well. Wait—let me amend that. I knew him casually for years, because he and my ex-husband were in the same medical group. But it wasn't until Peter and I split up that my relationship with Jeffrey took a romantic turn. The minute he heard I'd left Peter, he started calling me."

"That doesn't show much sensitivity on Jeffrey's part. Toward your ex-husband, I mean. They *were* colleagues."

"Yes, but they never got along. For one thing, Peter was envious of Jeffrey's success. Whatever Jeffrey had, Peter wanted. The money, the car, the boat, the women. Peter is incredibly immature that way."

"Is that why you left him? Because of his immaturity?"

"I left him because I found him in bed with a nurse. From the Intensive Care Unit at the hospital, would you believe. I walked into our bedroom and there she was, caring for him intensely."

Vicky Walters, I realized. Whatever Jeffrey had, Peter wanted—and got, apparently.

"That must have been quite a shock," I said. "Every woman's nightmare."

"It wasn't great," she admitted. "I guess that's why I went out with Jeffrey, as a payback. I knew it would drive Peter crazy. Of course, the reason Jeffrey asked me out in the first place was to tweak Peter."

"So you only dated Jeffrey briefly?"

"Yes. We went to the Heart Ball together. He took me to dinner a couple of times. We did an overnight on his boat. That was about it. We were hardly the love match of the century. In fact, I don't know why Peter was so envious of him. There wasn't a lot to the man, in my opinion. Not when you got up close."

"Roberta," I said. "This is a touchy question, but I'm going to fire away, okay?"

"Go ahead."

"Given the animosity between the two men, do you think there's any chance that Peter killed Jeffrey?" Yes, I know. Peter was with

Vicky the night of the murder, according to Vicky. But she was a dedicated nurse by day and an insecure slut by night, and I wasn't sure if I trusted her.

"I doubt it," said Roberta. "Peter's not the violent type at all. In the eleven years we were married, I couldn't get him to kill a single palmetto bug."

"Any other ideas as to who could have done it?"

She shook her head. "I hate to run, but I've really got to show that house now."

"I understand."

"Although there is something I'd like to ask you, Deborah."

"Please."

"You said on the phone that your mother lives on South River Road in Sewall's Point. It's that two-story, blue-gray one on the water, isn't it?"

"Yes."

"Is she interested in selling?"

"Selling? Absolutely not. She adores the house."

Roberta handed me her business card. "If she changes her mind, see if she'll call me, would you?"

"You want to buy the house?"

"No, I want to list it. I told you: we don't have a lot of inventory, especially when it comes to waterfront properties in Sewall's Point."

"Well, my mother's house is not for sale," I said. "But there is another house in the neighborhood that I'd go after if I were you."

"Really? Whose?"

"Jeffrey's. You and he may not have been the love match of the century, Roberta, but you were his last girlfriend, as far as we know. If any realtor in town should get the listing, it's you."

Chapter Eighteen

When I got back to the cottage on Tuesday afternoon, there were two messages on my answering machine. One was from my mother, saying that she had wangled an appointment with Peter Elkin for the very next day.

"I made it sound like an emergency." She giggled in her message. "But what got me in, I think, was that I was a patient of Dr. Hirshon's, so the office already had my file. The nurse said she'd ask Dr. Elkin if he'd take me right away, and fifteen minutes later she called to say he'd squeeze me in at two-thirty. Mission accomplished, dear!"

What Jeffrey had, Peter wanted, I thought, remembering Roberta's assessment of her ex-husband and wondering if the rivalry extended to their patients.

The second message was from Ray, which surprised me, given his antipathy toward the telephone.

"How about dinner tonight? My place," said the message. "You made the tuna sandwiches last time. I'll make 'em this time. The address is Thirty-nine Seminole Street. Seven o'clock. Let me know." He left his home phone number.

I smiled as I rewound the tape. Ray Scalley was definitely growing on me.

His house was a two-story, white-shingled bungalow that he had lovingly and painstakingly renovated in his spare time. He had bought it two years after Beth died, thinking he needed a change of scenery as well as a project that would take his mind off his loss.

On a narrow, palm tree-lined street in downtown Stuart, behind and between the city's commercial buildings, the house was an old Florida jewel set along one hundred feet of the St. Lucie River, complete with yellow pine floors, tongue-and-groove ceilings with exposed beams, handsome moldings, and a fireplace made of original coquina. Also on the property were a small outbuilding, which Ray used as a workshop, and a detached garage.

"This house is terrific," I said after he had given me the tour. We were standing in his kitchen, which wasn't a lot bigger than the one at the cottage but boasted gleaming new appliances and custom-built cherry-wood cabinets. In fact, the entire place was gleaming and polished and showed off Ray's splendid woodworking skills—skills so splendid I suspected that he had run out of areas to renovate, out of ways to fill his lonely hours.

"Thanks. I'm pretty happy with the way it turned out," he said, handing me a glass of white wine and then reaching into the refrigerator for a Heineken for himself. "And I like living downtown. It's not like New Yawk, but there's always something going on, always a little hustle-bustle, whether it's a train coming through or a concert at the Lyric or just the restaurant traffic. Down here, you never feel like you're alone."

"As opposed to my little cottage in the middle of nowhere, you mean."

"Hey, don't get me wrong. I love it out at the beach. But there are times in your life when it's good to be smack in the heart of civilization. That's what my well-meaning friends tell me, anyway."

Ray was smiling, but his grief over the death of his wife and child was still palpable, even after six years.

"Tell me about these tunafish sandwiches you're making," I said, trying to lighten the mood. "Are you a Bumble Bee man or will it be Starkist tonight?"

"Oh. Jeez. I forgot to start the fire." He hurried out of the kitchen and returned several minutes later with charcoal all over his hands. "If you hadn't reminded me, we would have starved to death."

"Are you grilling something on the barbecue?"

"Yeah. Fresh tuna. I bought it this morning, hoping you'd be able to come over. We're having it with pasta, garlic bread, and some broccoli for you, since you're the vegetable fan. Sound okay?"

I wagged a finger at him. "You said we were having tuna *sandwiches* and now I find out you're going to a lot of trouble."

"What trouble? You're my new buddy. I'm making dinner for you. Sit back and count your lucky stars."

I laughed and took my wine into the living room, a lovely spot with wall-to-wall windows overlooking the river. Ray had furnished it with white slip-covered chairs, lamps that had been converted from kerosene lanterns, and a rectangular, richly varnished teak coffee table that, I assumed, he had designed and built himself. I wondered if the pieces had moved with him from the house he and Beth had shared. There were no framed photographs of her in the room, I noticed. No wedding pictures. No shots of the two of them frolicking in the sun and surf. No evidence that she had existed, as far as I could tell; only photos of Ray's parents and brother, judging by the strong family resemblance, and souvenirs from Gators games, along with a stack of periodicals called *Gator Bait*. Nothing whatsoever that said "Beth." But then I had no idea whether the floral needlepoint pillow resting on one of the chairs held special memories of her, or whether the art books displayed on the coffee table had been meaningful in some way to their relationship. Perhaps Ray derived a measure of comfort in keeping his reminders of his wife to himself. I had never suffered the kind of tragedy he had; I couldn't imagine how he managed to mourn *and* cope at the same time.

After a few minutes, he joined me in the living room, parking himself on the arm of my chair. He asked me what was new with the investigation. I told him about my visits with the Sirens of Stuart.

"I ran into Frank Gillby this morning," he said when I'd finished chronicling my adventures. "He can't figure out what to make of you."

"As long as he doesn't send me off to jail, I don't care what he makes of me."

"He's a good man, Deborah. So's Avery Armstrong, Sewall's Point's chief cop. They've got a tightrope to walk with this case. Everybody in Sewall's Point is screaming for an arrest—they're worried their property values will go down from all the publicity, I guess. But Frank and Avery want to take their time, to make sure there are no mistakes, no rushes to judgment. I wouldn't want to be in their shoes, believe me."

"Did Detective Gillby say whether he was following up on any of the information I gave him?"

Ray smiled. "He said he thought your information was *interesting*."

"Oh. In other words, I should muzzle myself."

"No. In other words, he's glad to have your input."

"Really?"

"That's what he told me."

I felt better knowing that my shlepping to people's houses so I could ask them impertinent questions wasn't for nothing.

At eight o'clock, Ray announced that dinner was served and motioned for me to follow him into the small but cozy dining room. He served the tuna steaks hot off the grill while I dished out the pasta and garlic bread and helped myself to the broccoli.

"You're not a bad cook," I remarked after taking a bite of the fish.

"Self-taught. Beth used to do the cooking when we were married. After she died, I decided it was time I became a big boy and learned how to fend for myself."

"Well, I'm impressed. Everything's delicious."

"Even the broccoli?" He made a face.

"Especially the broccoli," I said, flattered that he had prepared something he didn't like just to please me.

We ate and talked, not about Jeffrey or the police, but about Ray's job and some of the people he worked with, about the Historical Society and the politics that went on there, about the debate raging in Stuart between those who welcomed development and those who sought to stem the tide of "progress."

After we cleared the table and did the dishes, Ray asked me if I was up for a little excitement.

"That depends," I said. "Can you be more specific?"

"No problem." He grabbed my hand and led me outside to the detached garage, an old building that he had also renovated.

He opened the doors and grinned. "She's pretty sweet, huh?"

I followed his adoring gaze to the right bay of the garage, where a motorcycle was parked.

"Well, what do you know?" I said. "Ray Scalley's a biker."

"No, Ray Scalley's a collector," he corrected me. "Come see."

He waved me over to the object of his obvious affection.

"It's a 1948 Indian," he said proudly. "A 'Chief,' their top-of-the-line model."

"What? Not a Harley?" I teased.

"Nah. Every yuppie and his brother's got a Harley now," he said. "Indians are classics, very hard to get your hands on. The company started making them in the twenties and stopped production in the fifties. I've been working on this baby for a long, long time, especially the engine, which is seventy-four cubic inches and took me forever to rebuild. Naturally, it's much more reliable than a Harley."

"Naturally," I said, getting caught up in Ray's enthusiasm.

"The Indian itself weighs about four hundred fifty pounds, which means it's really powerful but relatively light for such a big bike. With all due modesty, I think it's the finest-looking machine on the road."

"It's shiny, I'll grant you that. I've never seen so much chrome. And those fenders." I whistled.

"They're called skirted fenders, and they're the Indian's distinguishing feature, the way the metal continues down the sides of each wheel."

"Spiffy."

"Yup. And what about the leather? Feel it."

I reached out and stroked the motorcycle's black leather seat. It was as soft and smooth as velvet. "Feels comfortable," I conceded.

"Good. Then we'll go for a spin."

I gulped as Ray reached for a couple of helmets. I had always viewed motorcycles with a mixture of Wow-They're-Cool and Yikes-They're-Dangerous. I had never ridden one, figuring I was too bourgeois, leaving it to bad-ass chicks with tattoos and nose-rings to ride them for me.

"You look terrified." Ray laughed.

"You noticed."

"It'll be okay, I promise." He handed me one of the helmets and helped me strap it in place before slipping on his own. And then he stradled the seat of the Indian and rolled the bike out of the garage.

"Your turn." He patted the seat behind him and told me to sit. I sat—hesitantly, to say the least. "Come on, Deborah. I won't bite." He pulled me closer. "Just hang onto me and away we'll go."

I followed his instructions, wrapping my arms around his waist, pressing my legs against the back of his, noticing how hard and warm his body felt and trying not to be distracted by my own yearning to be held.

Ray kick-started the motorcycle, at which point the seat vibrated so forcefully I thought I'd lose my teeth. "Hang on," he said again, his voice rising with the giddiness of a kid playing with his favorite toy.

He steered us out of the driveway and off we went, down Seminole Street, onto Osceola, and, eventually, over to Riverside Drive and its lushly landscaped homes along the St. Lucie. At first, I clung to Ray so tightly that he complained that my fingernails were digging holes in his sides. "If you ease up a little, you might actually enjoy yourself," he called out. "It's not like I'm taking you on I-95. I'm just doing the quiet streets. Slowly. So you'll get your feet wet."

"I appreciate that," I shouted in response and relaxed my grip a tiny bit.

It was a balmy, starry evening, with only an occasional light breeze—a perfect night to be out zipping around the neighborhood—and as I became more comfortable with the fact that I was perched atop the seat of a motorcycle, as opposed to, say, a garden-variety bicycle, I did begin to enjoy myself. It really was liberating to be zooming along, the sweet, soft air in my face, my body formfitting Ray's. That was the part I liked best, I must admit—the physical contact, the sense of literally hugging Ray without having to feel awkward about it.

"Yee-hah!" he cried out as we left a Jaguar in the dust at a traffic light, the luxury car no match for the Indian.

"You're a juvenile delinquent," I kidded him.

"What?" he yelled.

"Never mind." I laughed.

Ray's sheer joy, his unadulterated pleasure at being able to cruise around in the classic cycle he had resurrected and labored over and tinkered with, was contagious. I caught the fever, the fun, the sense of freedom he was experiencing. I was having such a good time that I almost forgot there was a killer on the loose—right there in river city.

About ten o'clock, Ray brought us back to his house.

"Well?" he said as he helped me off the motorcycle. "Liked it? Didn't like it? None of the above?"

"Liked it," I said, "although I think it'll take a while for my heart rate to return to normal."

Remembering that Ray had to be on the job early each morning, I told him I thought I should get going.

"That was a great evening," I said as he walked me to my car. "Thanks for inviting me over, Ray."

"It's a standing invitation," he said, leaning over to kiss *me* on the cheek this time. "See you later in the week?"

"Sure."

As I was driving home, I realized that Ray and I were settling into a routine of sorts. We were forging a friendship that appeared, at face value, to be based on the simple fact that we liked each other. We didn't have a lot in common in terms of our backgrounds, nor were our personalities especially similar. But he was pulling me closer, I could feel it. And I wasn't resisting, I could feel that too.

My nice, mellow mood darkened the minute I opened the gate and let myself in. There were at least a dozen empty beer bottles strewn across the path leading to the House of Refuge, some of them smashed and in pieces, and shaving cream had been sprayed across the building's windows. The museum itself hadn't been broken into, thank God, nor had any damage been done to the gift shop or to my cottage, but a bunch of drunken, mischievous kids had apparently thought nothing of hopping over a locked gate and defacing public property.

Melinda had prepared me for the pranksters and trespassers and hormonal teenagers who would likely cause trouble now and then, just as they had a few nights before, up on the observation tower, so I was merely annoyed by this particular group's disorderliness more than I was rattled by it. Still, it was my job to report any acts of vandalism. I called 911 and waited for the police to show up.

Since Hutchinson Island is beyond Stuart's city limits, it was two of my friends from the Martin County Sheriff's Office who responded. They arrived within five minutes, saw that it was the infamous Deborah Peltz who had summoned them, and made a couple of "Oh-you-again"-type cracks, as if I spent my every waking moment placing calls to the police. But their visit was mercifully brief. They checked "the premises," asked me a few questions, and wrote up a report. And then they moved to go.

"Wait," I said. "What about the beer bottles and the shaving cream? Somebody has to clean this mess up."

"You're the caretaker here, right?" said one of the officers.

"Right," I replied.

"Then *take care* of it." He smirked.

And off they went.

I was perfectly capable of picking up the beer bottles and tossing them in the trash, as well as wiping the shaving cream off the windows, but it was late and I was tired and all I wanted to do was go to bed. But the cop had a point: I *was* the keeper there and seeing as Melinda had allowed me to stay on, the least I could do was do my job.

I could have left everything until morning, but, afraid I'd oversleep and the volunteers (or worse, Melinda!) would come upon the scene first, I got to work. After retrieving the powerful flashlight that Ray had insisted on lending me, plus a large plastic garbage bag, a roll of paper towels, and a bucket of water, I trudged back outside and began the cleanup. I started at the north end of the building and worked my way south. I was just about to rinse off the last window, the one closest to the cottage, when I noticed that the shaving-cream graffiti artist hadn't sprayed the stuff haphazardly. He had actually written something with the foamy lather. Something in a broad, loopy script. Something that, on closer inspection, was clearly intended to intimidate me:

Hey, Soap Queen! Mind Your Own Business or
This Won't Be Your Last Close Shave!

I gasped as I stood back from the message, my heart hammering in my chest. Obviously, whoever wrote it knew I'd worked for a soap opera. Just as obviously, whoever wrote it knew I'd been scooting around town, asking a lot of questions about Jeffrey. And most obviously, whoever wrote it knew I lived at the cottage, probably even knew I lived there alone.

I considered going back inside and calling 911 again.

But what if a member of the police force is behind the threat? I reminded myself? A cop who's familiar with Jeffrey's case and my background and the fact that I've been talking to people and passing information along to Detective Gillby? What if it's someone who sees me as competition, someone who wants to be a hero and solve the murder by himself?

I grabbed the bucket of water and splashed the shaving cream off the window. When it didn't all come off the first time, I removed the rest with the paper towels.

And then I did go inside and make a phone call—to Ray.

" 'Lo?" he said, sounding as if I'd woken him up.

I apologized and told him what had happened.

"Nope. I don't see a cop doing something like that," he said after asking me if I was okay. "It was probably a pack of kids out for a good time."

"A pack of kids with knowledge of my employment history?" I challenged. "And what was that bit about minding my own business?"

"Maybe they read about your TV career in the article that ran in the paper," Ray theorized. "Maybe their parents talked about you over dinner. Or maybe they heard about you from one of those women you went to see today. Anything's possible. This is a—"

"—small town. I know," I interrupted, thinking it was getting smaller and smaller by the minute. "It could have been a prank, I guess, but I have a feeling it was a genuine warning, Ray. I wonder if my interest in the case is making Jeffrey's killer nervous."

"Jesus, Deborah. I'm more comfortable with the idea of the kids on a prank. What are you going to do now?"

"The same things I've been doing. I'm going to ask questions, look for leads, and give them to Gillby. The sooner the murderer is caught, the sooner I can get on with my life."

"In other words, you're ignoring the warning, if that's what it was."

"I'm not ignoring it, exactly. I'm just not letting it freak me out. Much."

He laughed. "Do you want me to drive over there? Sleep on your couch? Sing you a lullaby?"

"That's sweet. No, I'll be fine. I just had to tell someone about this. Not my mother, because I didn't want to upset her. And not my sister, because I didn't want her to upset me. That left you, Ray. Sorry."

"Why sorry? I'm glad you called. That's what friends are for."

Chapter Nineteen

The next morning, I made up a list of questions for my mother to ask Peter Elkin during her checkup. They ran the gamut from the innocuous ("It's such a shame about Dr. Hirshon, isn't it?") to the gently probing ("Were you two close personal friends as well as colleagues?") to the downright nosy ("Where were you the night of the murder?").

I knew my mother would balk at the last one, so I put an asterisk next to the question with a note below, advising: Ask this in an offhand, nonthreatening manner after telling him where *you* were the night of the murder; the idea is to seem as if you want to trade stories about Jeffrey—i.e., if you share *your* memories of him, maybe Elkin will share *his.*

In addition, I included a few queries about Elkin's love life, as in "Both my daughters are single, are you?" And "Oh, you're divorced? Well, if you're not going out with anybody, I'd be happy to introduce you to my girls." The point of all that was to get Elkin either to admit that he was seeing Vicky or to pretend that he wasn't.

Of course, I warned my mother that the internist might be wary of telling her anything other than her temperature and blood pressure, given the fact that her "girls" were suspects in Jeffrey's murder. But it was also possible, I reasoned, that our notoriety in connection with the case could work in our favor; that if Elkin believed that the police were pinning the murder on Sharon and me, he might be inclined to let his guard down.

"I'll do my best," my mother pledged as I drove her to the appointment. "I've come up with loads of aches and pains, so I should be in the examining room with him for a good half hour."

While she was indeed being examined by Dr. Elkin and after one of the nurses in the bustling Grand Central Station-of-a-medical-practice mistakenly left open the door between the patients' waiting room and the doctors' offices, I slipped past everybody and tiptoed down the corridor to Jeffrey's office. Once inside, I locked myself in and prayed that no one would come looking for me. (I hadn't planned this part of the caper, but when I saw opportunity knocking, I couldn't just sit there in that waiting room and thumb through a six-month-old issue of *Redbook,* could I?)

As luck would have it, no one did come looking for me, not even Joan Sheldon, Jeffrey's long-time gate keeper, who, I later learned, had taken the day off. And so I inhaled deeply and began searching the office for anything that might be *important.*

The room's decor was pretty basic—a big leather-top desk with matching (and swiveling) leather chair, two upholstered visitor's chairs, a pair of filing cabinets, and a credenza on which Jeffrey had displayed photos of himself—on his boat, in his Porsche, in his lab coat and latex gloves.

Taped to the wall of the room was standard cardiologist propaganda: a large diagram of the heart and its coronary arteries and a full-color "Healthy Heart Diet" poster that attempted to make vegetables, fruits, and legumes look as appetizing as steak, cheese, and white chocolate mousse. There was also a map—or, perhaps, it was a boater's navigational chart—of the islands of the Bahamas, Jeffrey's favorite getaway spot, apparently.

And then there were the requisite diplomas on the wall. The college diploma. The diploma from medical school. The diploma indicating the hard-earned specialty. You know the ones. I studied all of Jeffrey's offical-looking documents, picturing him as a young man, imagining the twists and turns his life could have taken for him to end up the way he did.

I was focusing on his undergraduate diploma from the University of Miami, class of sixty-three, when I suddenly heard someone fiddling with the door, jiggling the handle, trying to get in.

I stayed absolutely still.

"I think it's locked," said a woman's voice. "Joan of Arc must have locked it."

"What an incredible bitch," said a second woman. "The good news is, now that Hirshon's gone, maybe she'll work someplace else."

"Don't I wish."

"What should we do in the meantime though? The files we need are in there."

"She'll be back tomorrow. We can get them then."

The two women—nurses, presumably—gave up on the door and went away.

Boy, that was close, I thought. Too close. Maybe this wasn't such a swell idea after all, particularly if somebody finds me in here and calls the police.

I pressed my ear to the door to make sure the two nurses—or anyone else, for that matter—weren't standing nearby. When I determined that the coast was clear, I quickly unlocked the door, scampered down the hall, and, as nonchalantly as I knew how, reentered the waiting room, as if I had merely gotten up to use the facilities.

Damn, I cursed silently, grabbing the dreaded dog-eared copy of *Redbook* off the magazine rack. I was actually alone in Jeffrey's office and didn't find a thing. Of course, if I'd had time to poke around in his files . . .

Well, there was no use blaming myself about that, I decided. So I read the *Redbook*, a *McCall's*, and a *Ladies' Home Journal*, and was studying a recipe for meat loaf in *Better Homes and Gardens* when my mother emerged.

"All set," she winked, waving a wad of prescriptions at me. "Let's beat it, dear."

Peter Elkin was very thorough, according to my mother. He listened to her heart, palpated her abdomen, rapped her kneecaps with that stupid little hammer, you name it. And during the examination, she quizzed him, moving down the list of questions I'd given her with the skill of a professional investigator.

"What did he say when you asked him where he was the night of the murder?" I pumped her.

"He didn't answer that one at first," she replied. "I had to use my feminine wiles."

"What do you mean?"

"*My womanly charms,*" she explained. "I may be seventy-five, but I still have them, Deborah."

I smiled. "Sure, you do, Mom. I was only wondering how you used them. To make Elkin talk."

"Oh. Well, I told him that he was much too young and handsome to tie himself down so soon after his divorce."

"Wait a second. You're saying you got him to talk about his divorce?"

"Yes, while he was checking my lymph nodes."

"And you got him to admit he was seeing Vicky?"

"In so many words."

"How many words, Mom? This could be crucial."

"He said he was seeing a nurse from the hospital. Exclusively. I assumed he was referring to Vicky."

"A reasonable assumption. Okay, then what?"

"This is where the feminine wiles come in."

"I'm ready."

"I tugged on his stethoscope and said, rather coquettishly, 'Why you're much too young and handsome to tie yourself down so soon after your divorce, Dr. Elkin.' 'You think so?' he said. 'Absolutely,' I said. 'You're one of Stuart's most eligible bachelors now, and instead of going out and painting the town the night poor Dr. Hirshon died, I bet you were stuck at home with this nurse of yours.' I tsked-tsked, to register my disapproval."

"What did he say to that?"

"He said I was right—he *was* home with her the night Dr. Hirshon was murdered. That's what you wanted to know, wasn't it, dear? Whether or not he would confirm Vicky's alibi?"

I nodded. Apparently, my mother, the mediator, was just as capable of being my mother, the Mata Hari.

Later that day, Sharon blew into town for her midweek visit, but she wasn't alone. She brought Barry Shiller along. Or, more accurately, *he* brought *her* along—in his gold Corniche. It seemed that Barry had a client in Vero Beach, an hour north of Stuart. The plan was for him to have dinner with my mother, Sharon, and me (his treat), drive to Vero after dinner, meet with his client on Thursday, and then buzz by Stuart on his way back to Boca so he could take my sister home. What a guy.

"I'm busy tonight," I told my mother when she reported this.

"Deborah."

"I am. I'll be sitting in my living room, staring out at the beach and counting grains of sand."

"Nonsense. You're trying to avoid Sharon. And after you promised me you two would get along."

"No comment."

"I'd like to point out that tonight will be my first evening at a restaurant since the heart attack. That's a special enough occasion for you to un-busy yourself, isn't it, dear?"

I sighed. "Where's the Barrister of Boca taking us?"

"I suggested Guytano's, that nice, casual place next to Stuart Fine

Foods. You can either meet us at the house and we can drive over together, or you can go straight to the restaurant and we'll see you there."

"I'll go straight to the restaurant, thanks. When is this party?"

"The reservation is for seven-thirty. Under the name Shiller."

"I suppose he'll be dispensing all sorts of legal advice while we're eating, so he can pay the check and then bill Sharon for his time."

"Let's give him the benefit of the doubt, Deborah. Your sister says he's been extremely attentive to her."

"For three hundred dollars an hour, even *I'd* be attentive to her."

"Deborah."

"See you soon."

The three of them were seated at the table when I arrived at the restaurant. Barry rose from his chair to greet me, impossibly over-dressed in yet another Armani suit, his brown hair soggy with the latest "styling product," his skin bronzed and burnished and scented with a fragrance that was heavy on the musk. Sharon looked "done," as always, but on this particular evening, she also looked radiant, like a new bride. Of course, *I* would have looked radiant too, if I had spent the day in a beauty salon, having a facial, a manicure and pedicure, and a touch-up to the old roots. But, since I had not, I looked my usual, thrown-together self. As for my mother, she looked ecstatic just to be alive. This was her first night out, as she had reminded me, and she was enjoying the attention being paid to her. Friends she hadn't seen in a while stopped by our table, to inquire about her health (and to sneak a peek at the daughters who were at Jeffrey's house the night he was murdered, I suspected). She was having such a good time that she didn't seem to mind that Barry kept excusing himself, so he could go outside and smoke his big fat cigar, or that Sharon and I almost came to blows over the difference between tortellini and tagliatore.

Mostly, our conversations involved Barry's exploits on the golf course, Barry's frustration at not being able to find a car mechanic who truly understood Rolls-Royces, Barry's decision to sell his house in the Hamptons after many "unbelievably great" summers there, and Barry's friendships with nationally known lawyers of the type who appear regularly on *Geraldo*.

Not that Sharon and I didn't get in a word or two.

"I'm doing the Traubman wedding the weekend after next," she announced with some fanfare.

"Who are the Traubmans'?" I asked.

She stared at me, as if I were a moron. "They own half of Boca," she said.

"Really? Who owns the other half?" I said.

She turned to Barry. "You see what I have to put up with?"

He patted her arm, his diamond-and-sapphire pinky ring a sight to behold.

Sharon went on and on about the food she had ordered for the Traubman wedding, the flowers, the music, the "intangibles." (These included seating the mother of the bride at the other end of the dais from the mother of the groom, as they had each insisted on wearing Vera Wang.)

She was waxing poetic about the poem she had written for the bride and groom to recite to each other, as part of their vows, when I excused myself.

"I'm going to powder my nose," I said.

"Come to think of it, mine needs powdering too," Sharon said purposefully, eyeing me with bad intent.

We got up and went to the ladies' room. I braced myself.

"You're being disrespectful to Barry," she blasted me as we stood outside the restroom door. "I've watched the way you ignore him, and I won't have it. He's very special to me, Deborah."

"Oh, please," I said. "You just met him."

"So? We've become extremely close in a short time. It's kismet."

"No, it's bullshit. You don't know him. You don't know anything about him."

"That's not true."

"Right. You know where he grew up and where he went to school, but what do you know about *him*? About his *character*? Why rush into another mess, Sharon?"

"I'm falling in love with him, that's why," she said defiantly. "If our relationship continues to develop as quickly as it has, I just might marry him."

"Marry him? Sharon, he's a snake. What's the matter with you? I realize that you're still hurt by what you perceive to be Daddy's neglect of you and that your knee-jerk response has always been to marry the first man who *doesn't* neglect you. But Barry Shiller? Even *you* can do better."

"There you go. Criticizing me *and* my choices in men. As if you should talk."

"I admit I've made mistakes when it comes to my own relationships, but I'm trying to change, Sharon. The disaster with Jeffrey was a wake-up call in a way. I see how important it is to take my time, to make sure the guy is right for me, to make sure the guy has scruples, for God's sake."

"Well, while *you're* doing all that waiting, *I'll* be enjoying myself. With Barry."

She did an about-face and stormed into the ladies' room. I decided I could live without powdering my nose. I was heading back to the table when Barry slithered toward me, having just returned from another smoke.

"Deborah," he said. "Got a minute?"

"I guess so. What's up?"

He coughed, spraying me with his stogie breath. "I'd like to offer you some free legal advice."

"Free legal advice? Now there's an oxymoron."

"That's very funny. I'll have to remember it."

"Be my guest. Look, you're Sharon's lawyer, Barry. I don't need any legal advice, free or otherwise. I'm kind of going it alone."

"A bad move."

"Is that why you took me aside? To convince me to hire you if the police arrest me?"

"No. I took you aside because I think you should stop talking to people about the case."

I regarded him as he fingered one of his massive gold cufflinks. "Stop talking to people? What people?"

"People in Stuart. Sharon tells me you've been asking a lot of questions around town. That could come back and bite you, Deborah. I've seen it happen. I'd keep my mouth shut if I were you. Let the police do their job."

"*That's* your free legal advice?"

"Yeah. And you ought to take it."

I smiled. He was such a thug. "I appreciate your interest," I said noncommitally. "So. How about dessert?"

He shrugged, as if he thought I were a fool not to listen to him. "After you," he said, bowing unctuously.

He followed me back to our table. It wasn't until he was helping me into my chair that I suddenly recalled something Sharon had told me—that Barry had gotten his B.A. at the University of Miami, class of '63, the same year that Jeffrey had gotten *his* undergraduate degree from the school.

I faced Barry as he sat down next to me. "Did you know Jeffrey Hirshon?" I asked.

"Know him? What do you mean?"

"It's a simple question, Barry. Did you *know* Jeffrey? Were you friends? Fraternity brothers? Acquaintances?"

"What are you nuts? If I knew the guy, I would have told your sister before I took her on as a client."

"But you and Jeffrey *were* in the same class in college. Class of 1963."

"Were we? Miami's a big school. Hirshon could have gone there, but if he did, it's news to me."

"Still, if you both did go there, it would be quite a coincidence, wouldn't it, Barry?"

He was about to respond—or, at least, I think he was—when Sharon returned to the table, having applied fresh lipstick and run a comb through her shimmering golden hair.

"What did I miss?" she said, gazing into his eyes.

"Your sister's interested in dessert," he said.

"My sister's always interested in dessert." She smiled. "Judging by her waistline."

Chapter Twenty

On Thursday morning, I had a phone call from Detective Gillby.
"I'm still innocent," I said.

"That's not why I'm calling," he said. "I'm following up on the vandalism you reported on Tuesday night. I understand there wasn't any major property damage to the House of Refuge, just a mess to clean up. Is that right?"

I debated whether to tell Gillby about the shaving cream note. Barry Shiller had advised me not to talk to anyone about anything, but was I going to listen to that sleaze?

"Actually, something else happened that I didn't tell the officers about," I said. "The person who was responsible for the shaving cream and the beer bottles left a threatening message on one of the windows." I gave him a full account. "It could have been a kid, having a grand old time with me. Or it could have been the killer, trying to scare me."

"Why would the killer want to scare you, Ms. Peltz?"

"I don't know. I *have* been poking around, as you're well aware. Which reminds me, I'm pretty sure I can confirm for you that Peter Elkin, the internist in Dr. Hirshon's medical group, really was with Vicky Walters, Dr. Hirshon's former girlfriend, on the night of the murder. Talk about sloppy seconds."

"You asked Dr. Elkin about this?"

"No. My mother asked him. I hope nobody sprays shaving cream on *her* windows now."

"I hope not. Is there anything else you want to tell me, Ms. Peltz? I have a hunch you're not finished here."

I smiled as I remembered what Ray had told me—that Frank Gillby welcomed my input and that I shouldn't be put off by his brusque manner. "Well, let's see. Yes, I spoke to some of the other women Dr. Hirshon was going out with before he died. One of them, Suzie Kendall, is still upset about the way he dumped her. She was so upset when she found out he was dating someone else that she didn't come out of her house for two whole weeks. I'd call that kind of behavior a little extreme, wouldn't you, Detective?"

"What did you say her name was?"

"Suzie Kendall. Of the *railroad* Kendalls. She lives in Sewall's Point, in Castle Hill. I asked her about her breakup with Dr. Hirshon, but I never got around to asking her if she had an alibi for the big night. Sorry."

"What? Can this be true? You forgot to ask her if she had an alibi?" he said sarcastically. "Luckily, the sheriff's office can handle that part of it."

"Luckily. Oh. Suzie *did* tell me she was afraid of guns, which would make it unlikely that she shot Dr. Hirshon. On the other hand, maybe she wasn't afraid of guns until she pulled the trigger on the murder weapon and realized how much trouble she was in. What's your opinion?"

"Who has time for an opinion?" he said. "I'm too busy listening to yours to have any of my own, Ms. Peltz."

"Ms. Peltz. Ms. Peltz. Don't you think it's time you called me Deborah?"

Silence.

"Detective?"

"I'm sticking to Ms. Peltz, Ms. Peltz."

"Up to you. Would you rather I didn't call you Frank then?"

"You can call me whatever you want. You will anyway."

"Thanks. Have a terrific day, Frank."

"You too, Ms. Peltz."

The rest of the day was uneventful, other than a brief spat I had with Sharon when I'd called her at my mother's before she went back to Boca. I had urged her yet again not to throw herself into a romance with Barry, and she had told me yet again that I was a jealous, spiteful spinster.

Later that afternoon, I wandered into the museum, where Fred Zimsky was winding up his shift and preparing to go home. After we chatted about this and that, I asked him if he had any children and whether they got along.

"I have four daughters," he said. "Beautiful girls, every one of them."

"Yes, but do they get along?" I repeated, eager to know if Sharon and I were freaks of nature or if it was common for sisters to carry on the way we did.

"They get along great," he replied. "Just not with each other."

"So they fight a lot?"

"I don't know how to describe what they do. They're on the phone to each other and they're over at each other's houses and they watch out for each other's kids—they're joined at the hip. And then bam! Out of nowhere, one of them gets crazy about something another one did, and it's World War Three. Two of them stop speaking to the other two or three of them gang up on the one; it varies. Then, all of a sudden, the war's over and everybody's at everybody's houses again. Who can figure what goes on between sisters?"

"You know what I think?" I said. "I think having a sister means always having to say you're sorry."

Fred hugged me. "You're a sweet girl, Debbie. I'm going to ask your mother for a date."

I nodded with approval, even as it occurred to me that if Fred and my mother met and fell in love and got married, I'd have five sisters instead of one—a truly terrifying thought.

On Friday, Ray stopped by, but I must have been at my mother's house when he came. He slipped a note under my door asking if I wanted to go dancing at Conchy Joe's on Saturday night. "They've got good reggae, good grouper, and good atmosphere, and I could meet you there at seven-thirty. You in?" read the handwritten invitation. I left a message on his answering machine, saying I was in.

Conchy Joe's is one of those big, raucous, honky-tonk places on the water for which southern coastal towns are famous—part Tiki bar, part restaurant, part "scene," the Florida equivalent of a New England lobster pound. Housed in an unprepossessing building between a couple of bait-and-tackle shops along Indian River Drive in Jensen Beach, the next town north of Stuart, Conchy Joe's is the kind of joint where you take your out-of-town guests to show them the "real Florida." In other words, if you go inside and survey the customers, you'll probably find more tourists than locals. As an example, in all the years I'd been coming to Stuart, I'd never eaten there.

Ray was waiting for me by the door when I arrived.

"God, it's packed," I said, having circled the parking lot three times before finding a spot.

"It's Saturday night, in season," he reminded me, raising his voice in order to be heard over the din. "They told me it'll be a thirty-to-forty-minute wait. We can have a drink at the bar and they'll call us when the table's ready. Is that okay?"

"Sure." He looked cute, I thought. Sexy. He had nicked the side of his neck, shaving, and, as ghoulish as this must sound, the tiny cut on his otherwise smooth, lightly tanned skin was a turn-on—a hint of the teenager inside the macho man.

I followed him past the hostess's station, past the shelves filled with Conchy Joe's T-shirts and Conchy Joe's sweatshirts and Conchy Joe's fishing hats, into a dark, noisy bar room, complete with big-screen TVs, hanging buoys, and giant marlin mounted on the wall.

"What'll y'all have?" asked a waitress as she wiped down the small round table Ray had commandeered, the only one that was unoccupied.

"I'll have a nice, cool margarita," he told her. "Cuervo Gold, lots of lime juice, salt on the rim."

I smiled. "I thought you said you were a beer man."

"Yeah, but when in Rome. This place cries out for something a little more Jimmy Buffet than a plain old beer."

"You're absolutely right." I studied the specialty drinks menu. Listed were alcoholic concoctions with names like Guana Grabber, Goombay Smash, Latitude Adjustment, and Hemingway Daiquiri (this one was described as "Papa's recipe as served in the Floridita Bar in Havana").

"Have you decided?" the waitress demanded in a tone that suggested I was taking sixty years instead of sixty seconds to make up my mind.

"I'll have a margarita," I said.

"Atta girl," said Ray. "It'll put hair on your chest."

"Just what I've always wanted," I said.

"How about an appetizer while we wait?" said Ray as he perused the Bar Menu. "They've got conch fritters, buffalo shrimp, alligator tidbits . . ."

"Alligator tidbits?"

"Don't tell me you've never had alligator, Deborah. With all those swanky restaurants in New Yawk?"

"The 'swanky restaurants in New Yawk' are into elk and venison and wild boar, not alligator. In New York, people have alligator shoes and handbags and belts, not tidbits."

"Their loss. Alligator's good eating."

"Please. Now you're going to tell me it tastes like chicken."

He laughed. "The truth is, I've never had it. I was planning on ordering a shrimp cocktail."

"Make it two," I said.

The margarita gave me an extremely pleasant buzz, which, in turn, made the shrimp taste extremely fresh and the cocktail sauce extremely tangy. It also enabled me to ignore the cigarette smoke that was coming at me from the next table and the fact that the waitress bumped the back of my chair every single time she passed.

"So here we are on a Saturday night," I said. "A couple of dateless wonders."

"*I* could have had a date tonight," said Ray. "My friend at work wanted to set me up with someone named Laurel."

" 'Laurel' is certainly a step-up from 'Willow,' as far as names go," I said. "But what is it with your friend? Are all the women he fixes you up with named after trees? The next thing I know you'll be going out with someone named 'Elm.' "

"I already have. It was short for 'Elmira.' "

"You're joking."

"I'm joking."

I reached across the table and tossled his thick, auburn hair. "So why didn't you go out with this Laurel tonight?"

"I thought it would be more fun hanging out with you: No pressure. None of that Does-she-like-me? stuff."

"In other words, you don't wonder if *I* like you?"

"Nope. If you didn't like me, you wouldn't keep going places with me."

"Unless I was desperate for company."

"If you were desperate for company, you wouldn't live way out there on the beach by yourself, without another house in sight."

"Point taken. I feel the same way about being out with you tonight, by the way. None of that Does-he-like-me? stuff. It's obvious that you're *mad* about me."

He laughed. "You must have been great at that soap opera writing. You can make almost anything sound dramatic."

"It's in the blood, I guess. I've only been away from the show a few weeks and I miss it already. Not the behind-the-scenes politics and not the people who are running the show now. I miss Woody

Davenport, the former head writer, and Helen Mincer, one of the other writers, and, mostly, I miss the work itself. It feels weird not to be grinding out an episode per week."

"Uh-oh. I hear a little homesickness in that speech. But I'm warning you: You can't move back up there. Not after I've invested all kinds of time and money in you."

"What money?" I said. "We split the check the one and only night we went out for dinner."

"Yeah, but I'm thinking ahead to tonight's tab. I'm treating, or didn't I mention that in my note?"

"You didn't mention it, but it doesn't matter, Ray. I'm perfectly glad to pay for myself."

He shook his head. "It's my birthday and I'll pay if I want to." He sang the line, taking off on the old Leslie Gore song.

"Your birthday?" I said, surprised. "Today?"

He nodded. "My forty-fifth. A biggie."

"And you wanted to spend it with *me?*" Ray had lived most of his life in Stuart. He had to have zillions of friends in the area, zillions of pals to celebrate with. So what am I doing here? I wondered.

Not for the first time, I was wary of his interest in me, suspicious of it. But then I reminded myself that his old friends knew him when he was married to Beth, knew him *with* Beth, as half of a couple. Maybe he felt comfortable being with me precisely because I was new in town; because I hadn't lived his history; because he sensed that when I looked at him, the first thing I saw *wasn't* a man in pain.

"Your table is ready, Mr. Scalley," said the waitress, handing him the check for our drinks and appetizers.

"To be continued." He winked at me, then paid the bill.

We were seated at a table in the "band room"—i.e., the room in which the establishment's long-time house band, a Jamaican group called Rainfall, entertained the customers.

Soon after we sat down, Ray pointed out that our table was wobbly.

"Oh, good," I said, relieved. "I thought it was the margarita."

"No, it's the table or the floor or both. When you go to Conchy Joe's, you take it for granted that you'll have to bring a matchbook with you."

He pulled a matchbook out of his pants pocket, bent down and wedged it under one of the table's legs, and then rocked the table to see if he had solved the problem. He had.

"Done," he said, sitting back in his chair. "In the carpentry trade, the matchbook would be known as a shim."

"A shim," I repeated. "I'll make sure I've got one with me the next time I come here."

We ordered grouper sandwiches, as well as beer for Ray, white wine for me. While we were waiting to be served, the band started up with a Bob Marley tune.

"How about it?" he asked, motioning toward the small dance floor.

"It's your birthday," I said. "You want to dance? We dance."

Ray led me onto the floor, where we were quickly joined by a half dozen other couples, most of them my mother's age. Reggae music can be danced to any number of ways, most of them not involving touching one's partner, but Ray had other ideas. He took me in his arms and steered me side to side, back and forth, as if we were doing a combination waltz-tango-fox trot. I didn't have a clue what he was doing or how to follow him, but I did my best, managing not to step on his toes fewer than three or four times.

As he held me, I remembered the feeling I'd had on his motorcycle, when our bodies had conjoined atop the bike's leather seat. This was even nicer, this sensation of being enveloped by him, of being wrapped inside his grasp, of timing our footwork to the pulsating, base-driven rhythm of the music.

There was a moment while we were dancing when Ray drew his face very close to mine. My heart started to pound as I thought he might actually lean over and kiss me, kiss my lips.

Wait! I wanted to yell out. *We're just friends! Don't ruin this!*

But I didn't have to. Ray did lean over but only so he could shout something in my ear. The music was so loud I wouldn't have heard him otherwise.

"How do our dreadlocked friends stack up against the bands at your New Yawk clubs?" he asked with a sardonic smile.

"I didn't go to a lot of clubs when I lived in New York," I said. "I spent a lot of time in front of the television set, working."

He nodded and wheeled me around the floor, around and around and around. I felt lightheaded, giddy, happy. A dancing fool.

"There's something I've been meaning to ask you," I said as we danced. "How did you get that scar?" Letting go of his hand, I took my index finger and traced the scar, which was about an inch in length, just under his lower lip.

"I had it tattooed on," he teased. "I figured if it worked for Harrison Ford when it came to getting girls, it could work for me."

"Ha ha. Now, how did you really get it?"

"I knocked myself in the chin with a two-by-four."

"On purpose?"

"No, silly. It was an accident. It happened while I was renovating the house. But it could just as easily have happened on a job. Occupational hazard."

"Well, I think it gives you character."

"You do, huh?"

"Yes. Character and a sort of rugged, lived-in quality."

Ray seemed flattered by my remark. He tightened his grip around my waist and rubbed the small of my back. I realized that I was still stroking his face, still tracing the scar with the tip of my finger. Embarrassed that I had initiated such intimate contact, I quickly pulled my hand away.

"So," I said, hoping he didn't pick up on my discomfort. "How about dessert?"

And then I laughed to myself, recalling that I'd made the same request to Barry Shiller a few nights before. *My sister's always interested in dessert,* Sharon had sniped. *Judging by her waistline.*

"Maybe you want some birthday cake?" I said. To hell with my waistline. "We could tell them to put candles in it and get the band to play 'Happy Birthday,' Reggae-style."

"Thanks, but I've never been a fan of sitting there like a stooge while a bunch of strangers sing 'Happy Birthday' to you. I'd rather keep dancing."

And so we did.

It was 11:30 by the time we left the restaurant.

"Do you want me to follow you home, in case the beer-swilling, shaving-cream vandals have put in another appearance?" Ray asked as we stood in the parking lot, the lights from across the bridge, from the high-rises on Hutchinson Island, twinkling at us.

"No. I'll be fine," I assured him.

"But you'll call me if there's any problem at the cottage, right?"

I smiled. "By 'problem,' you don't, by any chance, mean a problem with my toilet or my air conditioner or something of that nature?"

"I guess I'll never live that day down, will I?"

"Nope."

"So, I repeat, you *will* call me if you need me? We've established that?"

"I'll call you, I'll call you." I laughed.

"Good. Thanks for being with me on my birthday," he said. "It's not everyone who's willing to watch you take that next step toward geezerhood."

"Thanks for asking me to," I said.

Ray reached for me then, encircling me in a bear hug. We held each other for several seconds, swaying to the music as the band played its final number.

Chapter Twenty-one

I awoke to a fabulously sunny Sunday morning, the sunrise over the ocean a spectacular canvas of red and yellow and pink. I ate breakfast out on the porch and spent a lazy few hours sipping coffee, reading, watching the seagulls. At eleven o'clock, the phone rang. I contemplated not answering it, such was my vegetative state, but I thought better of it, given my mother's heart attack.

"Hey, Reggae lady," said Ray.

"Hey, yourself," I said, delighted to hear from him so soon.

"I'm having dinner with my brother down at Jetty's in Jupiter tonight, but I was thinking about going to the beach this afternoon."

"It is a perfect beach day," I agreed.

"And, since you've got a beach right in your own backyard, I was hoping I could invite myself over and we could do the beach together."

"A great idea. What time do you want to 'do the beach'?"

"One. One-thirty. Something like that. I'll bring us a couple of sandwiches from the Pantry over by the Indian River Plantation. Turkey okay?"

"Sure, but I could make us lunch, Ray."

"Nope. You contribute the beach. I contribute the lunch. See ya."

After he hung up, I hurriedly straightened up the cottage, jumped in the shower, and rummaged through my dresser drawer in search of a bathing suit that wouldn't make me look like a beached whale. Actually, I had lost a few pounds since leaving New York, and my figure reflected that. I wasn't exactly a waif, but I wasn't a whale either.

With an hour to go before Ray arrived, I remembered that it had been his birthday the day before. Deciding I wanted to buy him a present, I hopped into the Pontiac and drove over to The Gate, a shop in Sewall's Point that sells unusually appealing home accessories and gifts—virtually something for everybody.

Relieved to find the store open on a Sunday, I went inside and browsed, trying to come up with just the right gift for Ray. We hadn't known each other that long, so I didn't want to spend an extravagant amount of money. And we were friends, not lovers, so I didn't want to buy anything ultra-romantic. I was in the market for a gift that would be utilitarian yet whimsical, good-looking yet not too froufrou, stylish yet classic—like Ray's motorcycle, like Ray's house, like Ray himself.

I knew the minute I spotted the small brass weather vane that I had lit on the perfect present. It was an old piece, or so it appeared, the brass a deep, rich antique color as opposed to a shiny gold, the rods pointing north, south, east, and west each a little distressed, a little dinged, the wind arrow fashioned in the shape of a tiny sailboat. It was a stunning item that anyone would be proud to display. I could easily picture Ray placing it in his living room, on one of his handsome built-in bookcases.

Yes, he'll love this, I thought as I paid the saleswoman. She wrapped it, I scribbled "Happy 45th Birthday" on a gift card, and when the transaction was complete, I rushed back to the cottage.

Ray arrived at one-thirty, bearing gifts of his own: turkey sandwiches, a couple of bags of chips, a six-pack of Pepsi, and two large beach towels.

"Hubba hubba," he said when he walked in the door and saw me in my bathing suit—a black one-piece number that really did hide a multitude of sins.

"You don't look so bad yourself," I said. He was wearing light blue swimming trunks, flip-flops, and no shirt. I'll be honest here: I've never been big on men with hairy chests, but Ray's was definitely not a liability. Yes, his body hair was so thick it was more like fur, but with his broad shoulders, flat stomach, and muscular arms, the total package was extremely attractive, and my overriding feeling when I took him in was, this guy is adorable. And so I blurted out the question that had been on my mind ever since he'd told me about Beth. "Why haven't you remarried, Ray?"

He was clearly taken aback. "Where'd that come from?"

"I don't know. I was wondering, I guess. It's been six years since Beth died. That's a long time to go it alone."

"Look who's talking," he said. "You've never been married, not even once."

"You sound like my sister."

"I didn't mean it as a criticism."

"It sounded like one. No, I haven't been married, but I was thinking about *you,* about the fact that you had a successful marriage but not a remarriage. I read somewhere that men who are happily married tend to remarry fairly quickly after their spouse dies. And yet you've stayed single. You don't even date, except when your friend at work fixes you up. Why is that, Ray? Are you afraid of getting involved again? Afraid that if you let yourself love another woman you'll lose her too?"

Ray scratched his head. "I could have sworn I came over here to go to the beach, not to be psychoanalyzed. If it's okay with you, I'd like to get out there before it starts raining."

"It's not going to rain, Ray. This is the sunniest day we've had since I moved here."

"Great. Let's enjoy it instead of standing here picking apart my love life."

"You're annoyed."

"Sort of."

"Then this is our first fight."

"I don't want to fight with you, Deborah. You're my friend."

"Am I?" It seemed odd that he could be so buddy-buddy with me one minute and so hands-off the next. Was he just protective of his emotions or did he have something to hide?

"You know you are," he said. "Sorry I barked at you."

"You'll be even sorrier when you open this." I handed him the gift-wrapped box.

"Hey. What is it?" He held it next to his ear and shook it.

"Only one way to find out."

He read the card, then tore off the wrapping paper and opened the box. His eyes widened as he lifted the weather vane out and brought it up to the light. "It's beautiful—really sharp-looking, Deborah. But you didn't have to buy me a birthday present."

"I *wanted* to. Is that all right or do you get as weird when people buy you birthday presents as you do when they ask you to reveal your innermost feelings?"

He didn't answer.

"Ray?" I pressed him.

"I really do love the weather vane," he said. "There. I've just revealed an innermost feeling."

I sighed. "Is this a man thing—to shut people out?"

"I don't know. Is it a woman thing—to nag?"

"Why don't we go to the beach."

"An excellent idea."

I made sure to keep the conversation light for the rest of the afternoon. Not that we talked all that much. We ate lunch and soaked up the sun and watched the other beachgoers, and I went combing the sand for shells while Ray went swimming in the ocean. At four o'clock he collected his towels and his weather vane and said he was going home to shower and change for dinner with his brother.

"I'm crazy about my present," he told me as he was getting into his car.

"Where are you going to put it?" I asked.

"I was thinking about the living room, on the bookcase."

"I pictured it there too."

"Thanks again." He gave me a quick hug and was off. I sensed that what had happened between us earlier was still upsetting him. I hoped not. I didn't want anything—particularly anything *I* did or said—to drive a wedge between us.

After he left, I cleaned myself up and was about to head over to my mother's for the evening when Helen called.

"How's the weather in New York?" I needled her, having read that Manhattan had been blanketed by its third big snowstorm of the winter.

"Rotten," said Helen. "I suppose it's gorgeous there."

"You don't want to know."

"Well, I'm calling to tell you I've made contact with that nut-job boss of yours from the Hysterical Society, Melinda Carr."

"I really appreciate it, Helen. When's she flying up for the taping?"

"In a couple of weeks. By the way, does she always talk like she just stepped out of a dictionary?"

"I'm afraid so. She's a little stiff, but you'll take good care of her, won't you, Helen?"

"Sure."

I asked her how the show was going and she was full of gossip as usual. The only interesting tidbit, as far as I was concerned, was that Philip and the ex-Harlequin editor had broken up, that the breakup had been ugly, and that Philip—through his agent—was rumored to be making overtures to *Days of Our Lives*.

"Listen, Helen. Before I let you run off, I want to talk to you about the murder down here, the one I told you about."

"Oh, right. Are the police still harrassing you?"

"No, it's not that. I just wish I could figure out who did kill Jeffrey. Solving this thing has become an obsession with me. Which is where *you* come in."

"Me? How?"

"You've been writing for the soaps a long time. Longer than I did."

"Too long."

"And in all those years, you've written hundreds of storylines revolving around a murder, the murder of a man, specifically."

"So?"

"So which character generally has the motive for his murder? In other words, who turns out to be his killer most often?"

"I don't know about 'most often,' because I've never sat down and actually done a study. There've been way too many murders for that."

"Okay. Then, off the top of your head, give me some examples of characters who've ended up being the guy's murderer."

"Well, there's the wronged woman."

"Swell. Jeffrey wronged practically every woman in town."

"There's the wronged son or daughter."

"Nope. Jeffrey didn't have any children."

"There's the wronged space alien."

"Helen."

"Don't tell me you forgot *that* storyline, Deborah. Our ratings went through the roof."

"I'm serious about this. I want realistic scenarios."

She thought for a minute. "There's the wronged business associate."

"The wronged business associate," I mused.

"Yeah, you remember. We had that storyline two or three years ago where George Latham, Mr. Social Register, was secretly dealing in something illegal—dope, prostitution, whatever. He was about to double-cross Billy Olson, the punk he was in the illegal business with, but Billy bumped him off and went into hiding and wasn't caught until Sweeps Week. Of course, even though George was dead, technically, we brought his character back a month later—as a ghost—so he could haunt Billy in prison and seduce Billy's wife."

"It's coming back to me now."

"Do you think it could help you with your murder?"

"Who knows? I haven't really delved into the business aspect of

Jeffrey's life, other than to question the nurse who ran his office and one of the doctors who worked in his practice."

"Maybe you *should* delve into it," she urged.

"The wronged business associate, huh?"

"The wronged business associate," she confirmed.

"I can't see it somehow. Not in this case."

"Why? You said your guy was a womanizer."

"Yes, but he had a squeaky clean reputation, professionally."

"Deborah, when you first told me about this doctor, you said he was two-timing you with your sister. If he was a double-crosser in his personal life, he could have been a double-crosser in his professional life. True?"

"True. It's just that Stuart is such a small town. If Jeffrey was involved in some sort of illegal business dealing *and* he was double-crossing his partner in crime, everybody around here would have heard about it. Even *I* would have heard about it."

"Maybe you did hear about it but you weren't paying attention."

"Helen. I may be a little dense sometimes, but I'm not stupid."

"Who said you were? Look, you wear glasses, right?"

"Yes. For reading. But what does that have to—"

"Haven't you ever driven yourself crazy looking for your glasses? You're positive that you've lost them, so you go through every drawer, every handbag, every pocket, and you still can't find them, right? And then, what do you know: they're on your face, exactly where they're supposed to be. Do you get what I'm saying, Deborah?"

"You're saying that the key to solving the murder is in front of my face."

"It's a possibility."

My mother and I went out for dinner, to the Flagler Grill in downtown Stuart—the same restaurant Jeffrey had mentioned the very first time he'd asked me out. The Flagler is one of the town's most popular eateries and boasts terrific food in a relaxed yet sophisticated setting. I was delighted that my mother had suggested it.

"You're really back to your old self," I commented after we were seated. She looked lovely in a blue silk blouse that matched her eyes.

"I'm better than my old self," she said. "I told Rose she doesn't have to come twice a week anymore, and I told Sharon she doesn't have to drive up every Wednesday, and now I'm telling you not to feel you have to babysit me on weekends, dear. I'm over the hump."

"Maybe I like being with you on weekends, Mom."

"Yes, but I'm sure you'd rather be with that young man you went out with last night, the one who works for the county."

"Ray and I are just friends. We're not dating."

"Oh. Well, apropos of dating, the gentleman who volunteers at the House of Refuge called me this morning."

"Fred?"

She nodded shyly. "He said you were a sweet girl and sweet girls usually have sweet mothers. He invited me to go to the movies next week."

"Mom! That's great!"

She shrugged. "We'll see. In all these years, I've never bothered with other men; I loved your father and that was that. But you can do one of two things after you've had a heart attack. You can either crawl in a hole and wait to die, or you can decide you're going to live the rest of your life to the fullest. So I told this Fred I'd have a date with him. At my age, can you imagine?"

"What have you got to lose?" I said, thinking *I* was the one who would lose if they hit it off, my visions of Fred's four daughters threatening to spoil my appetite.

My mother ate grilled salmon (sauce on the side), while I threw caution to the wind and went for the lamb shanks. We were midway into the meal when she said she had forgotten to take her medications.

She reached into her purse for her pills and retrieved her baby aspirin, her beta blocker, her cholesterol-lowering drug, and her Heartily Hirshon Vitamin E capsule.

"There," she said after swallowing them down with some water. "Now I can get back to this delicious salmon. How is your lamb, dear?"

I didn't answer.

"I asked you about the lamb, Deborah," she repeated. "Is it tender?"

Again, I didn't respond. I couldn't. I was too preoccupied, too busy replaying my conversation with Helen, too caught up in the notion that Jeffrey's murder might have something to do with his lucrative sideline, his auxiliary income, his *vitamin business.*

For God's sake, I scolded myself, as I tried to make sense of my thoughts. How could I have been so single-minded in my efforts to flush out the murderer? How could I have allowed myself to be diverted by Jeffrey's peccadilloes with women? How could I have completely overlooked another aspect of his life—the company he'd formed to produce and sell his "specially formulated" vitamins? How could I have forgotten that he had told Sharon and me that the pills were his foray into the world of the doctor-as-entrepreneur, and—here's the part that made me feel really dim—that he had a *partner* in the venture? Wasn't it more than possible that Jeffrey and this partner had a falling out—over the business, over the product, over money—and that it was the partner (or, as Helen had put it, "the wronged business associate") who had wiped Jeffrey out?

"Deborah," my mother was saying. "What is it dear? Are you all right?"

"I'm fine, Mom," I assured her. "I thought I'd lost my glasses, but it turns out they're sitting smack on my face."

She looked at me. "You're not wearing glasses, dear."

"I guess I'd better explain," I said, and served up my latest theory.

Chapter Twenty-two

I spent the next week stewing over my suspicion that Jeffrey's vitamin business was somehow central to his murder, the expression "follow the money" playing over and over in my head. But I was frustrated in my attempts to actually go out and *do* anything about my hunch for a number of reasons. First, the Pontiac was out of commission yet again, this time for a busted water pump, which meant that I didn't have my own wheels. Second, my mother and the Delta 88 went down to Boca to stay with Sharon for a couple of days, which meant that I didn't have *her* wheels either. Third, several sections of wood decking behind the House of Refuge were rotted and needed to be replaced, and Melinda insisted that I be present while the work was done.

Of course, the person overseeing the work was Ray, so I didn't really mind being grounded. We ate lunch together at the cottage each of the three days he and his crew were on the property, and chatted about a wide range of subjects. Ray was good company as always, but there was no mistaking the distance between us, the distance *he* seemed to be placing between us.

Was he still annoyed with me because I'd asked him why he hadn't remarried? I wondered. If so, what was the big deal? It was true that he and I had known each other for barely a month, but I felt closer to him than I did to any of the men I'd left back in New York. He was my first friend in Stuart at a time when I desperately needed one. I'd shared aspects of my life with him that I hadn't shared with anyone, including my tormented relationship with Sharon. So wasn't I permitted one measley question about *his* life?

No, this little chill between us will melt, I decided. Ray's just preoccupied with his job.

Well, his *job* appeared to be the last thing on his mind on Wednesday night, the night my mother returned from Boca and the two of us went to dinner at the Black Marlin. We were in the middle of our meal when Ray walked in with an attractive—and very youthful-looking—woman. After they waited at the bar for ten minutes or so, the hostess seated them in the booth directly opposite ours. Naturally.

He didn't see us at first, but when he did, he jumped up and made his way over to our table. Wearing blue jeans and a tan denim shirt, he looked scrubbed and shaven, his often unruly hair neatly combed. A combination cowboy/altar boy. "It's a pleasure to meet you, Mrs. Peltz," he said after I introduced him to my mother.

"It's lovely to meet you too, dear," she said, shaking hands with him. "I understand you've been very kind to Deborah."

"Kind? He's been a saint," I said. "A *boy scout.*" There was a definite edge to my voice; for some reason, I was doing an excellent imitation of my sister. "So, who's the lucky lady tonight, Ray?" I nodded at his companion.

"That's Holly," he said, waving at her. She waved back. She had small hands, I noticed. A child's hands.

"Holly," I mused. "You're dating another tree."

He laughed. "I guess I am, now that you mention it. You doing okay, Deborah?" He touched my arm.

"I'm great. My mother's great. We're both great. But don't let us keep you," I said, shooing him away. "We wouldn't want Holly to get restless. You know kids and their short attention spans."

My mother shot me a disapproving glance.

Ray, on the other hand, seemed amused. "Actually, I came pre-pared—I brought crayons and a coloring book, in case little Holly gets antsy. Enjoy the rest of your evening, Mrs. Peltz. You too, Deb-orah."

When he was out of earshot, my mother leaned across the table and asked me why I had been so rude to someone who had been so nice to me.

"I'm a bad person," I said, hanging my head in self-loathing.

"You're no such thing," she said.

"Okay. Then *you* explain it."

She smiled. "It's possible that you're angry at Ray for going out with another woman tonight. In other words, you're jealous."

"No, you don't understand, Mom. Ray and I are just—"

"—friends. You told me."

"That's right." I paused. "However, I admit that I won't be shat-tered if it turns out that he and Holly decide not to see each other again."

"That remark doesn't strike me as something one would say about a friend, Deborah. Friends want each other to be happy."

"True, but friends also want what's best for each other. I don't happen to think Holly is what's best for Ray."

"You're an authority on Holly?"

"No."

"Then what makes you think she's not an appropriate match for Ray?"

I shrugged. "Women's intuition. And the fact that she doesn't look old enough to drive a car in most states."

My mother shook her head. "As I said before, you're jealous, dear. Either get over it or do something about it."

Do something about it. As if Ray had any interest whatsoever in being more than pals with me. As if *I* didn't have other, much more pressing matters with which to concern myself.

On Thursday morning, after picking up the Pontiac and learning that the car's radiator hose, fan belt, and wheel bearings were, in the mechanic's professional opinion, "about to go," I sat down and plotted my next move in my investigation into Jeffrey's murder—my not-so-magnificent obsession, as I had come to regard it.

Following up on Helen's Wronged Business Associate theory, I reviewed my conversations with Joan Sheldon, recalling that *she* was the one who handled the sales and fulfilled the orders of Jeffrey's vitamins; that *she* was the one who collected the cash and checks from customers and, presumably, deposited the money in the bank; that she was the one who described her relationship with the doctor as a "special partnership." But was she the actual *partner* Jeffrey had referred to when he'd told Sharon and me about his vitamin business? Was it *her* share of the profits from the company that represented her "other compensations?" Was *she* the wronged business associate who shot and killed Jeffrey Hirshon?

If you don't ask, you don't get, I thought, reaching for the phone.

I called Joan at the office, assuming she was still holding down the fort there.

"I wonder if you would meet me after work tonight," I said, getting right to the point. "Someplace quiet, where we wouldn't be disturbed."

"Why in the world would I do that?" she said rather belligerently. "You and your sister are implicated in Dr. Hirshon's murder. You don't really expect me to be alone with you and put *myself* in jeopardy."

"Oh. Then you haven't heard. The police have completely ruled us out as suspects." Well, it *felt* true.

"No, I didn't hear that. Have they figured out who did kill the doctor?"

"Not yet, and that's one of the reasons I'd like to sit down with you, Joan. I was hoping that you and I could knock around a few ideas, since the police don't seem to have any."

"Nope. I'm not saying anything to anybody. Not about Dr. Hirshon."

"You used to talk about him," I pointed out, citing several of the gossipy tidbits she had shared when I'd stopped by the office.

"Well, I'm not talking about him now," she said firmly.

"Why? Has someone told you not to discuss his case?" I asked, thinking of the shaving-cream warning I'd received.

"I said I'm not talking and I meant it."

Clearly, a different tack was in order. If I couldn't get through to Joan's passion for justice, I would appeal to her passion for financial security. "Listen, Joan. What I really want to talk to you about is Heartily Hirshon."

Silence.

"Are you there?"

"Yes."

"I said I want to talk to you about the vitamin company."

"What about it?"

"How it got started, whether it's been a successful business, that kind of thing. Ever since I left my job in New York, I've been trying to decide what to do with myself here in Stuart, career-wise. It occurred to me that I could start my own vitamin company, with one of the doctors in town, and that we could hire you as a consultant, to get the project up and running. Would you be interested in making some extra money? Now that poor Dr. Hirshon's gone?"

Another silence.

"Joan?"

"I'm still not talking."

She hung up.

Spoiled sport, I thought, as I leafed through the phone book, hoping her home number and address were listed.

Ah, yes, here we go, I smiled when I came upon the information. *J. Sheldon.* The only J. Sheldon in the book.

I scribbled down the address. Coincidentally, Joan owned a home not far from where Ray lived—on Valor Point, a cul-de-sac off Riverside Drive near the hospital, one of the streets down which he and I had ridden on his motorcycle.

I decided I would pay Nurse Sheldon a visit later in the day—and that, to ensure that *I* wouldn't be alone with a killer, I would ask Ray to accompany me.

I thought you were mad at me," he said after I'd contacted him at work and requested his presence at seven o'clock that evening.

"I thought *you* were mad at *me*." I said. "Ever since we went to the beach last Sunday."

"If I was, I'm over it," he said. "Now, about showing up unannounced at Hirshon's nurse's house. Have you considered that this ambush of yours might piss her off—enough for her to call the cops?"

"If she's Jeffrey's killer, she won't call the cops."

"If she's his killer, she might kill *us*."

"That's why I'm inviting you along on this outing," I said. "There's safety in numbers, right?"

"Not always."

"Look, you're supposed to be my friend. Are you coming or not?"

"It depends."

"On what?"

"On whether you're gonna apologize for that crack you made about Holly."

"Holly. You mean the child you were out with last night?"

"She's thirty-nine, Deborah. That's not exactly jailbait. She takes care of herself, that's all."

"Really? Does she bathe in formaldehyde or something?"

"Your fangs are showing."

"Sorry. I'll behave."

"You will if you want me to go to the nurse's house with you tonight."

"Okay. Just one last question, because my curiosity is getting the best of me. Are you going to see Holly again?"

"I haven't decided."

"I think you *should* see her again. I want you to find someone,

Ray. I want you to fall in love and be happy." I wished my mother could have heard that little speech. She would have been proud of me.

"Holly will be relieved to know she has your blessing," he said wryly. "Can I go back to work now?"

Joan's house was vintage '70s ranch and, therefore, undistinguished, architecturally. But it was on the water; it was sprawling, as if it had been added on to in recent years; and it was expensively landscaped. I had hoped to surprise Joan so that when Ray and I rang her doorbell, she wouldn't have time to peek out the window and pretend she wasn't home. But thanks to the Pontiac's muffler, which the mechanic hadn't even bothered to mention because it so obviously needed to be replaced, we pulled into Joan's driveway with the subtlety of a garbage truck.

Still, we tiptoed up her front steps. I rang the bell.

We waited for several seconds before we heard Joan padding through the house.

"Who is it?" she called out.

Ray and I kept silent.

"Anybody there?"

Just as I'd hoped, she couldn't resist opening the door and sticking her head out, at which point Ray forced the door open farther, allowing us to slip inside the house.

She scowled at me as we all stood in her foyer. "I said I wasn't talking." It was only seven-fifteen, but she was already in her nightgown, and her hair was hanging loosely around her shoulders instead of in its usual tight bun. And then there were her slippers—the huge, fluffy kind that resemble Plush toys; hers were in the shape of cats, not unlike her real-life cat, Sheldon, a cute little tabby that was gray with black stripes.

"Won't you give us a few minutes?" I pleaded. "I really am considering starting up a private-label vitamin business and I'd be extremely grateful for your input."

"Then what's *he* doing here?" she said, nodding at Ray. Did she know him? I wondered. Did she recognize him as the husband of Jeffrey's former patient, the woman who'd gone into cardiac arrest during the birth of her child? There was only one way to find out.

"He's my accountant," I said with a straight face.

Ray picked up the thread beautifully. "Bob Kleinfeld," he said, pumping Joan's hand. "I'm a CPA down in West Palm Beach. Deborah asked me to advise her about the tax ramifications of launching her own venture."

Joan sighed. "I'm not up on tax ramifications, but I'll give you five minutes. That's it."

"We appreciate it," I said.

She flipped on a few lights and led us into her den, a room filled with clutter, not to mention cat litter. The stench was so bad I attempted to talk and hold my breath at the same time, which is instinctive under such circumstances but ultimately impossible.

"What do you want to know about the vitamins?" Joan asked after the three of us were seated. "As I told you, I had nothing to do with the ins and outs of the company; I just sold the pills to the patients who wanted to buy them."

"Yes, but you are a registered nurse, aren't you?" I said.

"I am," she confirmed.

"Then you could tell us about the medicinal benefits of the vitamins, why the doctor prescribed them so enthusiastically," I suggested, realizing we had to start somewhere.

"Well, the most significant feature of Heartily Hirshon vitamins is that they're water dispersible, *dry* capsules, as opposed to the oil-based softgels more commonly distributed," Joan explained.

"Why the dry capsules?" Ray asked.

"Because Dr. Hirshon wanted the best for his patients," she declared, "many of whom are elderly and cannot tolerate oil."

"Is that why his vitamins are so much more expensive than the ones sold in drugstores?" said Ray. "Because they're the dry kind?" He wasn't guessing about the cost of the pills. I had prepped him. Very well, apparently.

"Yes, although a lot of drugstores don't even stock powder-based vitamin E," Joan said. "It's usually the health food stores that carry the product."

Ray quizzed Joan on the actual ingredients in Heartily Hirshon Vitamin E capsules. She spoke of tocopherols and IUs and D-Alpha, and expounded on the reason people should take the vitamins religiously, each and every day. (The short answer: because the actual vitamin content remains in the body for only a brief period before it's excreted. Fascinating stuff.)

My eyes glazed over as Ray continued to elicit this sort of quasi-technical information out of Joan, so I took the opportunity to look around the room, hoping against all hope that I'd find something to link her to Jeffrey's murder.

Aside from the aforementioned cat debris, the place was crammed with knick-knacks, I observed, as well as photographs in cheap plastic frames. I stole a furtive glance at the snapshots displayed on top of the round, skirted table next to me.

There were photos of a man I assumed was Samuel, Joan's dearly departed husband, as well as photos of their two children—another assumption, based on their similar facial features.

There were photos of Sheldon, the beloved cat, curled up in Joan's lap, curled up on her bed, curled up in one of her Plush cat slippers.

There were photos of Jeffrey throughout the ten-year period that Joan had worked as his nurse; he was pictured with and without his beard.

And, tucked way in the back, behind all the others, there was a single photo—a slightly out-of-focus shot—of Joan, Jeffrey, and a man I couldn't identify, though there *was* something oddly familiar about him.

I was dying to reach out and yank the picture off the table so I could study it, study the man. Instead, I squinted at it in an effort to sharpen my vision.

What I *could* see was that it was a relatively dated photo, taken a few years ago when Joan was younger and thinner and Jeffrey was not only beardless but minus any glints of gray at his temples. I could also see that the man was older than his cohorts; he had a full head of silvery hair, heavy bags under his eyes, and leathery, wrinkled skin. And, finally, I could make out that three of them—Joan and Jeffrey and the man—were standing together, arm in arm, Joan in the middle, on a white sandy beach, palm trees in the background, crystal-clear turquoise water beyond.

Where were they when the picture was shot? I wondered, having never known Florida's waters to be such an intense blue-green or its beaches to consist of such snowy, powdery grain. And who was the man? Was he one of the other doctors in Jeffrey's medical group? Had I run into him at the office on Osceola Street? In the photo, he seemed awfully chummy with Jeffrey and Joan. Was it possible that *he* was the silent partner in Heartily Hirshon?

No, I decided. A doctor would never be a partner in a business that promoted another doctor, would he? With those big egos doctors have?

If only I could divert Joan's attention away from me, I thought, away from where I'm sitting, I could grab the damn picture off the table and get a good look at the guy.

Suddenly, I felt something rubbing up against my legs.

I was startled until I realized it was only Sheldon, the cat. I leaned down and petted him, and as I did an idea came to me.

"Sheldon. You're such a sweetie pie," I cooed. I was hardly a cat person; cats made my eyes itch. Nevertheless, I continued to stroke the animal and murmur loving words to him, even as I kicked Ray, to signal him to keep Joan talking about the vitamins. "Come here, you darling kitty. Come to Deborah, Sheldon." I picked up the cat, gave him a few kisses and hugs and purring opportunities, and then, when Joan wasn't watching, set him down on top of the skirted table, where he proceeded to knock over all the photos.

"Oh, my! I'm sorry! He's so frisky he just jumped out of my arms," I said apologetically as Joan sprang to her feet to gather up the cat and prevent further destruction. "Let me put everything back," I offered. "You help too, Ray. I mean, *Bob*."

"No. I'll take care of it," Joan insisted.

"But it was my fault," I protested, while Ray and I scrambled to set the plastic frames in order.

Naturally, I tried to take my time with the photo of Joan, Jeffrey, and the mystery man before placing it right-side up on the table. Who *is* this person? I said silently, racking my brain for an answer. I *know* I know him.

Before I could figure out *how* I knew him, Joan snatched the photo out of my hand and flung it onto her chair.

"I've told you about the vitamins," she said testily. "I have nothing to add. Please leave."

"We will, Joan," I promised, "but I wonder if I could ask you who—"

"Out," she barked. "Now."

She marched herself and Sheldon out of the room, which was our cue to follow her. When we got to the door, I decided to go for broke.

"Just tell me this," I said. "Were *you* Jeffrey's partner in Heartily Hirshon?"

"Don't talk nonsense," she snapped. "I was Dr. Hirshon's nurse."

"What about the man in the photo?" I said. "Was *he* the other half of Heartily Hirshon?"

Joan pretended not to understand which masterpiece in her "gallery of photos" I was referring to.

"You and Dr. Hirshon were with this man on a beach," I persisted. "It was just the three of you. In the Caribbean, maybe. Since you all seemed like friends, I thought the man might be—"

"That's enough," said Joan, who proceeded to throw me out of her house. Ray-Bob too.

Chapter Twenty-three

After getting booted out of Joan's house, Ray and I grabbed a pizza at Luna's, an Italian place next door to the Flagler Grill. He said he was heading north for the weekend on his motorcycle—to Daytona Beach for the last few days of the annual March ritual known as "Bike Week." I told him I'd miss him. He told me not to meddle in Joan's or anyone else's affairs until he got back and could pose as my accountant again.

On Friday, my mother asked me to go with her to the Treasure Coast Mall so she could buy a new outfit for her date with Fred.

"He's taking me to a movie and dinner tonight," she said. "He must be very sophisticated."

"Fred? He's sweet, but I don't know about sophisticated."

"When a man his age says he's taking you to a movie and dinner— not dinner and a movie—that's sophisticated. It means he doesn't care if he misses the early bird special."

After plowing through the racks of the other women's clothing stores in the mall, we ended up at Dillard's, where my mother spotted dozens of outfits she wanted to try on. Leaving her in the hands of a perky young saleswoman, I dashed over to the shoe department, hoping to find a pair of sandals. I was perusing the "sale" table when I literally bumped into another woman.

"Are you hurt, Mrs. Hirshon?" asked the salesman who'd been trailing after her and the shopping bags she was toting.

Mrs. Hirshon? My head shot up when I caught the name, obviously.

"I'm fine," she told him in a rather tough, no-nonsense manner, then glared at me.

"Please forgive me," I apologized to her, as I tried to remain calm. "I must not have been watching where I was going."

"Okay, okay. Don't worry about it." She turned to the salesman and dangled a beige Bruno Magli pump from her index finger. "Do you have this in a six double-A?"

"I'll check, Mrs. Hirshon," he replied. "Is there anything I can help *you* with, ma'am?" he asked me.

"Yes. I'll have what she's having," I said quickly. I hadn't worn a size 6 shoe since I *was* 6.

He gave me a funny look and disappeared into the back room.

"It's a beautiful pump," I commented, following her as she made her way around the table.

"They're all beautiful." She sighed wistfully, then took a seat. I took the seat next to her.

She was a petite little thing, about Sharon's height and weight, with one of those extremely short unisex haircuts women are wearing now. Her hair was dark and so were her eyes—big, brown eyes that had a sad, haunted quality. An addict's eyes.

"I hope you don't mind my asking," I said, "but are you by any chance Francine Fink Hirshon, the late Dr. Jeffrey Hirshon's former wife?"

"What of it?" she said, her tone nonchalant but her expression surprised, as if she didn't expect to be recognized, having moved away from Stuart years before. "Do we know each other?"

"Yes," I lied. "I'm Cathy Mayer. I lived down the street from you in Sewall's Point. We used to go shopping together when you were still married to the doctor. My condolences, by the way."

She stared at me. "I don't remember you."

"Oh, that's okay." I shrugged. "I probably wouldn't remember me, either. I've changed a lot since you left town. Time hasn't been so kind to me. I've had my own marital troubles, if you know what I mean."

"Let me guess. Your husband left you."

"For a twenty-year-old."

"God. I hope you nailed him for every dime he was worth."

"Is that what you did, Francine? Nail your ex-husband?"

She smiled. "Let's just say he's no longer cheating me out of what belongs to me."

"Is that so?" Maybe it was Francine who was Jeffrey's partner in Heartily Hirshon, I thought, wondering how I could have forgotten about her. Maybe she got sick and tired of begging him for her cut of the profits. Maybe she really did hire a hit man to kill him while she kept a low profile in Aspen. Maybe she came back to Stuart to collect—and while she was here she popped into Dillard's for a few pairs of shoes. "How did you manage to turn your financial picture around, Francine? I wouldn't mind a few pointers."

She stared at me again. "I still don't remember you, Carol."

"Cathy."

"You were a neighbor?"

"Yes. My children loved coming over to your house, especially at Halloween. They said you gave out the best candy."

"Your children are deranged. Jeffrey and I always spent Halloween in the Bahamas. On our boat. Make that, *my* boat. Make that, *my* house. Make that, *my* everything in Jeffrey's estate."

My jaw dropped. "He left you all his assets in his will? Even though you're divorced?"

She leaned closer. "Listen, toots. Do yourself a favor. Get cozy with your ex's lawyer. Sleep with him if you have to. Just make sure he doesn't change a word of hubby's will, no matter what hubby wants. The truth is, men don't really care about the will, unless they plan to remarry. They're too busy fucking. So they forget all about the piece of paper. Then they die—and you're rich. Of course, I got lucky. I didn't have to wait it out. Mine died sooner rather than later."

"That *was* lucky," I said, amazed at Francine's heartlessness. I couldn't wait to tell Detective Gillby.

"Here we are, ladies," said the shoe salesman, scurrying toward us carrying two boxes.

"You have the six double-A?" said Francine excitedly.

"I have *both* the six double-A's," he said, beaming.

Francine grabbed her pair and tried them on. "Oooh," she moaned with pleasure. "They fit like they were made for me. I'll take them."

"Tell you what," I said. "You can have mine too."

And then I scrammed.

Before meeting my mother back in women's dresses, I found a pay phone and dialed Gillby's number. He wasn't in his office, so I left a message.

Later that night, while my mother was out on the town with Fred, I was alone at the cottage, trying and failing to place the man in Joan's photograph. Even if Francine did inherit Jeffrey's estate, even if she did hire a hit man to speed up the probate process, there was still the matter of Jeffrey's secret business partner, and I couldn't shake the feeling that Joan's beach pal was the guy. There had to be something fishy about him or she wouldn't have reacted the way she did, snatching the photo away from me, pretending not to know what I was talking about when I asked who the man was, ordering Ray and me to leave so abruptly. But what was the real story? *I* certainly couldn't make sense of it.

On Saturday morning, my mother called to tell me about her date.

"It was very pleasant," she said.

"Pleasant? That's it?"

"Well, it was more than pleasant, but I don't want to jinx it by rhapsodizing about it."

"Ah, so you liked Fred, and he liked you."

She sighed. "He told me I had eyes the color of the Florida Marlins' uniforms."

"That's very romantic, but the Marlins' uniforms are teal," I pointed out.

"Deborah. He meant blue and you know it."

"Of course he did. I'm glad the date went well, Mom. When do you think you and Fred will see each other again?"

She lowered her voice to a whisper. "I'm seeing him right now, dear. He's out on the porch, reading the paper and drinking his orange juice and Metamucil. He stayed over last night."

"Mom!" I was shocked.

"I can guess what you're thinking," she said unashamedly. "That I'm behaving like Sharon, jumping into a relationship with a man I just met. But your sister has a history of being pathologically impulsive when it comes to men; I've lived alone, always denying my need for companionship. There's a big difference."

"Yes, there is," I conceded, still taken aback by my mother's new candor and straightforwardness.

"Heart attacks really do change you," she went on. "They force you to realize that you'd better seize the day or it might seize you."

"I can appreciate that, Mom, but—God, I don't know how to ask this of my own mother."

"Go ahead and ask, dear."

"Well, I'd heard that it's not uncommon for people who've had a heart attack to be afraid of having sex, afraid it might bring on another attack."

"Yes, but who said anything about my having sex? I simply said that Fred stayed over last night."

"Oh. I misunderstood." Boy, was I was relieved. Nothing against Fred, but it's creepy to imagine your parent having sex. I don't care how grown-up you are.

"Now, for the second reason I called. Fred has requested that you have dinner with us tonight, dear. He wants us all to go to 11 Maple Street. I *told* you he was sophisticated."

"You may be right." The food at 11 Maple Street is considered on a par with the best restaurants in south Florida, its setting a charming historic house in Jensen Beach. I had eaten there on special occasions over the years and was ecstatic to be invited back. "I doubt we'll get in though. It's Saturday night, in season. They're usually booked a week in advance."

"Fred says we won't have any trouble reserving a table, dear. One of his grandsons is a waiter at 11 Maple Street—his oldest daughter's boy."

More small-town overlap.

When I returned home from the restaurant on Saturday night, having gorged myself on three rich, worth-every-calorie courses, I was met by Detective Gillby. He was standing at the entrance to the property, along with several other officers, all of them looking extremely grim.

"I take it you're not here to apologize," I said, opening the gate. "You never did return my phone call from yesterday."

"Let's go inside," said Gillby. It was a directive, not a suggestion, and he was not in a joking mood.

He followed me into the cottage; the others remained outside. I asked him if he wanted something to drink while I downed an Alka Seltzer. He declined. We went into the living room.

"Where've you been this evening, Ms. Peltz?" he said finally.

"Why?" I said.

"Please answer the question." He was speaking in his monotone *Dragnet* voice—the voice he'd used to interrogate me the night Jeffrey was murdered. Not a good omen.

"I was with my mother and Fred Zimsky, a volunteer here at the House of Refuge. We were having dinner at 11 Maple Street."

He nodded, writing in his little notebook. "And your sister? What was she doing tonight?"

"I don't keep tabs on her as a rule, but I happen to know that she was coordinating a wedding for the Traubman family."

"Who?"

"The Traubman's. They own half of Boca," I said, parroting Sharon.

Gillby wrote in his notebook again.

"This feels like a formal interview," I commented. "As if we're right back where we started, Frank. Maybe you could explain why that is, explain why my sister and I would need an alibi for this particular night, since Jeffrey Hirshon was killed over two weeks ago."

"He may have been killed over two weeks ago, but his nurse was killed less than two hours ago."

"What?"

"You heard me."

"You're saying that Joan was—?"

"Correct."

I felt my mouth go dry and my stomach churn. I sank into one of the futons. "How?" I managed, still trying to process this stunning development. "What happened?"

"It'll take a day or so for the autopsy results, but if I had to guess, I'd say Ms. Sheldon was shot with a single twenty-two calliber bullet."

"Where?"

"In the chest."

"No. Where was she when she was shot?"

"In the den of her house on Valor Point," said Gillby. "A neighbor reported hearing a gun go off. When we got there, we found no sign of forced entry and no sign of a struggle. Same scenario as the other homicide, basically."

I held my head in my hands and wondered how on earth I had stepped into such a soap opera. Ha ha. "Any idea who did it? Now that you've crossed *my sister and me* off the list?"

"Sorry about that, but I had to ask. Because of the Hirshon case."

"I understand. Why don't you sit down, Frank. You look exhausted."

He sat on the futon next to mine and cracked his knuckles. "No, I don't have any idea who did it. What I have are a lot of dead ends."

I nodded, imagining how frustrated he must be.

"Do *you* have any idea who did it, Ms. Peltz? You're usually full of ideas."

"Actually, I do have something to confess," I said sheepishly.

"So confess."

"I *was* in Joan Sheldon's house—in her den, as a matter of fact. But it was Thursday night, not tonight, and Ray Scalley was with me."

Gillby stared at me, shaking his head. "What the hell were you two doing at her house?"

I explained my theory—Helen Mincer's theory—about the wronged business associate; how Jeffrey's vitamin company may have figured in his murder and how Ray and I had gone to Joan's house hoping to get her to open up about the business.

"She didn't want to talk about Heartily Hirshon, per se, just the health benefits of the vitamins," I said. "She denied being Jeffrey's partner in the company, but I got the feeling she knew everything there was to know about it—including who the real partner is."

I went on to describe the photograph of the man who had looked vaguely familiar to me.

"Where was this photo?" asked Gillby.

"On the skirted table in Joan's den, toward the back, mixed in with the others."

He scratched his head. "Funny. There weren't any photos in the room when we arrived at the crime scene. Not one."

"No photos? The woman had a million of them."

"Not when we got there."

"Then that *proves* the man standing with her and Dr. Hirshon in the picture was someone I wasn't supposed to see! Joan probably hid his photo and the rest of them the minute Ray and I left the house."

"Or maybe the killer took them, so he wouldn't be linked with Ms. Sheldon and Dr. Hirshon."

"Why would he take all of them?"

"He was probably in a hurry, Ms. Peltz. Why pick through dozens of pictures when you can pile the whole bunch into a bag and beat it?"

"True."

"Chances are, if the killer and the man in the picture are the same person, he panicked that Ms. Sheldon might give him up."

"You mean, he killed her because she knew too much."

"And because she talked too much. You did say she was a talker."

"Yes, but who isn't in this town? I've never met so many people who are willing to spill their guts."

"Well, Ms. Sheldon won't be doing any more spilling."

"Poor woman. She wasn't a barrel of laughs but she didn't deserve to die. Have her children been told? I think she had a few."

"Two. We notified them about an hour ago. They were pretty shaken up."

"I'm sure they were. Her cat must have been freaked out too. She was very attached to him."

"He was freaked out all right. Wouldn't let any of us near him. It took three of our guys to grab him and bring him in."

"Bring Sheldon in? Why would you do that?"

"Evidence. The kitty was up to his little paws in blood. Most of it's got to be the deceased's, but some of it could be the killer's."

"If the cat scratched or bit him?"

"Right. Even the most cuddly animal can get spooked by the sound of a gun going off, not to mention the sight of his owner lying on the floor, unconscious. If the cat tangled with the guy, there should be traces of the killer's blood and/or skin under his claws, which would be a nice break for us."

"Let's hope."

"Getting back to the man in the photograph. If he's the partner in the doctor's vitamin company, he shouldn't be that tough to track down. The business has to have an address, a warehouse, and a bank account, and there should be financial records, tax returns, the works." He got up from the futon, looking more upbeat than he had earlier. "We'll find the guy, Ms. Peltz," he said.

"I know you will, Frank," I said.

"We've got to," he added as he moved toward the door. "Or I'll be out of a job."

"Before you go," I said, "there's something else."

He rolled his eyes. "What?"

"Francine, Jeffrey's ex-wife. She's back in town. She was buying shoes at Dillard's yesterday. That's why I called you."

"I'm a busy man, Ms. Peltz. You don't have to inform me of everybody's shopping habits."

"She told me she inherited Jeffrey's money, Frank. Apparently, he really did forget to change his will after the divorce, exactly the way I hypothesized a couple of weeks ago. Remember?"

He nodded, cracking his knuckles again.

"It might be prudent to interview her a second time," I suggested. "Just to be thorough. Where there's money, there's motive, right, Frank?"

When Ray returned from his motorcycle odyssey and called to check in, I told him about Joan. He was as shocked as I had been—or so he seemed. A little later in the conversation, when I asked him about his trip, he was vague about it, wouldn't say anything specific about it, leaving me to wonder: did he actually *go* to Daytona?

Of course he went, I laughed at myself, laughed at the sad fact that I had become suspicious of everybody. Ray was honest and decent, for God's sake. Ray was always there for me. Ray was my friend.

Still, it was interesting that he was out of town the weekend Joan was murdered. Interesting that he had been inside her house only two nights before she was killed. Interesting that he hated Jeffrey and, perhaps, by extension, he hated Jeffrey's nurse too.

Talk about hate. I despised myself for even considering the possibility that Ray could harm anyone. But, given the mayhem swirling around me, I wasn't taking any chances. I decided to stay away from him for a while. Just until the picture got clearer.

Chapter Twenty-four

It was several days before I spoke to Detective Gillby again. I understood how much pressure he was under, plus I remembered that it took awhile for forensic test results to come back, so I didn't bug him for bulletins. But when I couldn't stand the suspense any longer, I called his office.

"Any news?" I asked.

"Yeah, but it isn't good," he said. "First off, we can't locate Francine Hirshon."

"Damn. She probably grabbed her inheritance and beat it for Beverly Hills." I pictured her cruising the leather-goods shops on Rodeo Drive.

"Could be. Problem number two: Heartily Hirshon doesn't exist."

"What do you mean? Of course, it exists."

"Well, according to the label on the vitamin bottles, the product was produced less than an hour from here, in Riviera Beach. We went down to the address and, lo and behold, it wasn't a pharmaceutical operation; it was a Laundromat."

"You're kidding."

"I wish I were. Not only that, we searched Dr. Hirshon's office, his home office, and Joan Sheldon's home and office, and we couldn't find a single scrap of paper having to do with the vitamin company—no bookkeeping records, no deposit slips, nothing."

"I can't believe this."

"Believe it. There's more. We got hold of Hirshon's tax returns and guess what: no profits from a company called Heartily Hirshon. Not even a hint that there's ever *been* a Heartily Hirshon."

"So he was cheating the government," I said, astonished. "Every penny he was making from those pills was going straight into his pocket."

"It looks like."

"And Joan was in on it."

"Most likely."

"Which brings me to the partner. Any updates there?"

"Nope. At the moment, we're trying to get the real story on where the vitamins were manufactured and where the cash and checks from the business were deposited. My guess is, we're talking about money coming and going from an offshore bank account, say, in the Caymans or the Bahamas."

"The Bahamas," I said excitedly. "Jeffrey took his boat there on long weekends. There's even a navigational chart of the islands hanging on the wall of his office. Plus, Francine told me that the two of them used to go there together, in happier times."

"Could be a lead. I'll keep in touch, Ms. Peltz."

"Good luck, Frank. I'm rooting for you."

The following week, Norman, my nephew, came home for his spring break. Our little family was a-twitter with his arrival, since we hadn't seen him since Christmas. On a Wednesday afternoon, Sharon drove him up to Stuart so he could spend a couple of days with his grandma. They arrived in Barry Shiller's Rolls-Royce—chauffeur driven, according to my mother, who explained that Barry himself had wanted to make the trip but was very busy with a case and, therefore, insisted on offering his car and driver to Sharon and her son. Yech.

The first night of Norman's stay, I was permitted to join everybody for dinner at my mother's.

"Norman," I said, hugging him. "You look great."

"Great" may have been overstating it a bit, but he did look better than he had at Christmas. Always on the short, scrawny side like his mother (one of the reasons, I suspected, that he had chosen to attend military school—so he could prove he was a manly man despite his slight build), he had seemed even skinnier in December. But now he had filled out somewhat and walked with a more confident stride. Even his haircut—his "knobcut"—wasn't as pitiful anymore. "How're you doing, Smoothie?" I joked as I ran my fingers over the shaved portions of his head.

"I'm doing fine, Aunt Deborah," he said. "I can't believe you're living down here in a cottage on the beach. That's too cool."

"For someone *your* age, Norman, it's cool," said Sharon. "For someone your *aunt's* age, it's peculiar."

"If you've got time tomorrow, maybe you'll borrow your grandmother's car and drive over," I said, ignoring my sister. "We could take a walk on the beach, catch up."

"Sounds like a plan," he said, high-fiving me.

During dinner, Norman told us stories about life at the Citadel. I asked him if the male cadets were as abusive to the female cadets as the media led us to believe. "Not any more abusive than the male cadets are to each other," he replied, proudly lifting his shirt to show me his battle scars.

After the meal, he went into the den to watch an old John Wayne movie; my mother went into the kitchen to do the dishes. When they were both gone, Sharon and I found ourselves alone with each other—always a tricky business.

"You must be happy to have Norman home," I said.

"Ecstatic," she said. "I'm especially pleased how quickly he's bonded with Barry."

"Do you really think that's wise?" I asked. "Norman has seen so many of your men come and go."

Sharon stiffened. "I'm not a hooker, Deborah. 'My men,' as you put it, weren't customers. They were husbands."

"Exactly. The last thing Norman needs is to form another emotional attachment to a man who ends up leaving."

"Leaving? What makes you think Barry's leaving? He and I are growing closer by the day. Look at how he sent us up here, with his car and driver. Even when he's meeting with clients, he makes sure I'm taken care of."

"Who *are* his clients?" I asked. "Other than you, of course."

"He's not at liberty to discuss them with me," she said. "Attorney-client privilege."

"So you don't know anyone else he represents?"

"No. But I know that he must be extremely competent because he lives like a king—and treats me like a queen, by the way. Can you say the same thing about this carpenter you've been seeing?"

"He's not a carpenter," I said, wishing my mother hadn't told Sharon about Ray. "And I'm not seeing him. We're friends."

"Whatever. My point is that Barry is a wealthy man, but he's also a generous man. I really believe he could be The One."

"The Fourth, you mean."

"That's hilarious, Deborah."

"Sharon." I sighed. "Snap out of it. Barry's a sleaze."

"*You* should have such a sleaze in your life."

"I'm doing fine, thanks."

"With the carpenter. What do you two do for entertainment? Watch *This Old House?*"

Just then, my mother came into the room, eyeing us. "I could have sworn I heard you two bickering," she said. "But since you promised there wouldn't be any more bickering—out of love for me and concern for my *health*—I must have been mistaken. Isn't that right, girls?"

Sharon and I smiled and said, "Yes, Mother."

On Thursday afternoon, Norman drove the Delta 88 over to the cottage for a visit. I made him lunch, showed him around the House of Refuge, bought him a House of Refuge T-shirt, and introduced him to Fred Zimsky, who clutched Norman to him and said, "Your grandmother is some kind of woman, kid."

Later, Norman and I were taking a walk on the beach, trolling for shells, when he asked if I would do him a favor.

"Sure. Name it," I said.

"Watch out for my mom," he said.

"Why? Is she about to swoop down from the sky on her broomstick?" I said, pretending to duck.

"No, I didn't mean it that way. I meant, take care of her for me. Look, I know you and she haven't always gotten along, Aunt Deborah, and she can be a pain in the butt, no doubt about it, but she's my mom and I love her, and since I'm going back to school tomorrow, I won't be able to—"

"Norman," I cut him off, realizing he was serious. "Slow down. Tell me what's worrying you about your mother."

He shrugged.

"Norman?"

"Okay. It's the guy she's going out with."

"Barry Shiller?"

He nodded. "My father was a crook, and I've had to live with that my whole life. The last thing I expected is to come home and find this new crook hanging around."

"What makes you think Barry is a crook?"

He shrugged again. "I just don't trust him."

"There must be some reason, Norman. Be specific."

He thought for a minute. "He's always on the phone, whispering about stuff. And when he does pay attention to my mother, he only wants to hear about the murder you and she got mixed up in—if she remembers anything about the night the doctor got shot, in case he has to defend her or something. He's, like, so *into* being a lawyer."

"Your mother did say that he was very driven, very focused on his law practice, and that his marriages broke up as a result. That makes him self-absorbed and one-dimensional, but it doesn't make him a crook."

"Okay. How about this? He had plastic surgery."

I laughed. "Plastic surgery isn't a crime, Norman. You'll understand that better when you're my age."

"Maybe, but none of the guys at the Citadel would ever have it."

"No, I don't suppose they would."

"Well, this clown had the fat sucked out of his face *and* he had— wait, what do you call it?—a chemical pull."

"A chemical *peel*."

"Right. Oh, yeah, and he dyes his hair. Talk about a girlie man."

"His hair is sort of a muddy brown. What color did it used to be?"

"Gray. Like Grandma's."

"How do you know all this, Norman? People aren't usually so forthcoming about their nips and tucks and tints."

"From my mom. When she met Barry a few years ago at some wedding, she thought he was much older. She must have mentioned that to him because he gave her the name of his surgeon. He does his hair himself, he told her. Grecian Formula."

"I guess appearance is important in his line of work."

"Then he's gonna have to skip work for a while. His face is a mess."

"Why? Did he have another chemical peel?"

"No, he had a wrestling match in his garden with a bougainvillea. That's what he *said*, anyway. If you ask me, Aunt Deborah, he was on the wrong end of a woman's fingernails." Norman shook his head. "The guy's got a lot of balls, acting so interested in my mom and then looking like he's been in a goddamn cat fight."

"A cat fight."

"Yeah."

"Because Barry's face is full of scratches?"

"Yeah."

"He claims he got them from bougainvillea thorns?"

"Yeah. Fat chance, right?"

"Fat chance."

My heart was racing so fast at this point that I thought I might actually pass out. But I didn't pass out. I held on. I had to. I didn't want to scare my poor, sweet nephew. He'd had enough to deal with in his young life. And now there was about to be more for him to handle. A lot more. Because it finally dawned on me that his mother hadn't merely latched on to yet another loser in Barry Shiller; this time, she'd landed a cold-blooded killer.

"Aunt Deborah? You okay?"

No! I wanted to scream. *No!*

If only I'd put things together sooner, I berated myself, my mind reeling, my breathing coming in fast, uneven gasps.

If only I'd followed my instincts, remembering that even after I'd learned that Barry had gone to the same college as Jeffrey, even after I'd *confronted* Barry about it, I still didn't take the link between the two men seriously, still didn't consider the possibility that Barry had only insinuated himself into Sharon's life in order to stay one step ahead of the police investigation. But, of course, now it all seemed so obvious, so clear, the way it always does once the missing pieces of a puzzle reveal themselves. *Barry* was the partner in Heartily Hirshon. *Barry* was the gray-haired beachgoer in the photograph in Joan's house. *Barry* was the person who had wrestled, not with a bougainvillea or with a woman, but with Joan's cat. *Barry* was the one whose blood and skin Frank Gillby would find under Sheldon's claws. *Barry* was the man who had shot both Joan and Jeffrey in their own homes. I knew these things as surely as I knew my own name. What I didn't know was, why?

"Aunt Deborah?"

"I'm fine, Norman," I managed. "Just a little dizzy from being out in the hot sun."

He took my arm in a gentle yet commanding way. "Here. Lean on me," he insisted, so mature, so take-charge. As we walked together across the sand, toward the cottage, I gazed at him with love and pride, and I thought, He sure isn't "little Norman" anymore.

"I wanted to be at your graduation," I said wistfully as we strolled along. "I hope you believe that."

"I do. You had a fever that day," he replied, still guiding me by the arm. "You were too sick to be there."

"Your mother's never forgiven me for not coming. But then she's never forgiven me for so many things."

"She just needs to bust your chops every once in awhile. That's the way she is. Who knows why."

"It doesn't matter why," I said. "Not anymore."

When we got to the cottage, Norman glanced at his watch and said he'd better go.

"You won't forget what we talked about, right?" he asked. "You'll watch out for Mom while I'm away at school?"

I pulled Norman to me and hugged him tightly. "I love your mother," I said with conviction. "And I'll watch out for her. You have my word."

But she's not going to make it easy for me, I thought as I released him. Not our Sharon.

Chapter Twenty-five

The minute Norman left, I called Detective Gillby, praying he would be in his office this time. He was. As calmly as I could under the circumstances, I blurted out everything I had on Barry. Gillby was skeptical, at best.

"You think he was the guy you saw in Ms. Sheldon's photo," he said. "Before his makeover."

"I don't think. I know."

"Yeah, well we never found this photo, so we can't prove he's the same guy."

"What about the scratches on his face? Can't you do tests on the cat?"

"I don't have any samples from Mr. Shiller. I can't confirm the presence of his blood or skin under the cat's claws if I don't have any of *his* blood or skin to match 'em up with."

"How about fingerprints at both crime scenes?"

"If Mr. Shiller has no priors, I won't have a match there either."

"You're saying the fact that Barry and Jeffrey went to college together and then Jeffrey gets murdered and then, miraculously, Barry turns up as my sister's lawyer and then Joan gets murdered in exactly the same way as Jeffrey did doesn't raise any red flags here?"

"Nothing I can haul him in for, Ms. Peltz. Where's the motive, for instance? Even if he did have a connection to both Dr. Hirshon and Ms. Sheldon, why kill them?"

"Over the vitamin business," I offered. "I'm positive that Barry and Jeffrey were partners in the company, a company we've already established looks pretty questionable. So—you want motive? Maybe Jeffrey was cheating Barry out of his share of the profits, and Joan took Jeffrey's side. Maybe Jeffrey got scared that the IRS would catch onto their scheme and wanted out, and Barry said, no way. Maybe Jeffrey and Joan had something on Barry and were threatening to blackmail the guy. I can come up with a thousand maybes."

"I can't arrest people on maybes."

"Really? You were going to arrest my sister and me on a lot less."

"But I *didn't* arrest your sister or you, Ms. Peltz. I'd keep that in mind."

I sighed. "You're right, Frank. I'm sorry. I'm just—"

"—worried about your sister."

"Yes. Does that seem odd to you, since you have it on record that we fight like a couple of lunatics?"

"My wife has a sister, Ms. Peltz, and the two of *them* fight like a couple of lunatics. But if I make one comment, one innocent little remark about my sister-in-law, my wife gives me the silent treatment."

"Then you understand about sisters."

"I understand. Look, what I'm gonna do is get somebody to dig into Mr. Shiller's background, pay him a visit, see what he knows. Maybe we'll get lucky and stumble on a bona fide link between him and Dr. Hirshon and Ms. Sheldon."

"That would be great. Then we could go after Barry and rule out the other suspects."

"Other suspects?"

"Yes. Francine Hirshon."

"Right, but you said suspects, plural. Who else did you mean, Ms. Peltz? My department has already ruled out Ms. Walters, Dr. Elkin, Ms. Hornsby, Ms. Kendall, Ms. Orwell, and Ms. Ross."

"I meant—" No, I wouldn't mention Ray's name. There was no reason to. *Barry* killed Jeffrey and Joan, I was sure, and Gillby would find a way to prove it soon enough.

"Were you about to say something, Ms. Peltz?"

"No, Frank. I was just thinking, it would really move things along if we could get more information on Heartily Hirshon. All we have now are the stupid vitamins."

"Well, wait a minute. Dr. Hirshon must have sold your mother the pills, since she was his patient."

"He did."

"Then depending on how she paid for them, she may have a cancelled check—with the name of the bank where the money was deposited. That would give us a lead."

I brightened. "I'll get back to you, Frank."

I called my mother. There was no answer. I drove over to her house. There was no one home. Sharon's car was gone, so I assumed she and Norman had already headed down to Boca. I panicked as I imagined her spending the night with Barry only hours after Norman boarded the plane for South Carolina the next afternoon. If I wasn't able to convince her not to, my pain-in-the-ass sister would be rushing into the arms of a murderer, completely clueless, utterly helpless, with no one but me to rescue her. Talk about a twisted turn of events.

"Where in the world is my mother?" I muttered to myself as I paced back and forth outside her front door, my nerves fraying.

Probably with Fred, I decided, thinking it was a helluva time for her to get a life after seventy-five years.

I was about to give up and go home when she pulled in the driveway. When she emerged from the car, I saw that she was wearing sneakers, a pink leotard, and matching leggings.

"Mom! Where have you been?" I said as I followed her inside.

"At the Y," she said. "Working out. It wouldn't do *you* any harm to spend a little time there, dear. You're looking stressed out. You might consider doing some yoga."

"I might," I said. "But first, I want to talk to you about Heartily Hirshon Vitamins."

I explained what Gillby had learned about the company, and asked her to track down her cancelled check for the pills she'd bought (I omitted any reference to Barry). Within ten minutes, she found it.

I thanked her and high-tailed it to the sheriff's office. I presented the check to Gillby, who smiled after examining it.

"What?" I asked. "Tell me."

"Have a seat, Ms. Peltz."

And then he vanished down the hall. I waited anxiously. Waited. Waited. When Gillby returned, he was still smiling.

"Okay. What?" I said.

He told me that my mother's check had been deposited in a Bahamian bank in Nassau and paid to the account of the Blue Waters Corporation . . . the same corporation that owned the Laundromat in Riviera Beach, where Jeffrey's vitamin E pills were supposedly manufactured . . . the same corporation that owned the title on Barry's house in Boca.

"*Yesss!*" I said, jumping up from my seat. "There's the link! He did it, Frank! Barry Shiller really is the murderer! You can go and arrest him now, right?"

"I can't arrest him just yet, but I've sure got plenty to question him about."

"Good. When are you going to question him?"

"As soon as you stop questioning *me*, Ms. Peltz."

I hopped into the Pontiac and sped over to Ray's house, my mind a jumble of emotions. I was terrified that Sharon had involved herself with a killer, but I was also extremely relieved that *I* had not; that Ray was innocent; that I had been wrong to suspect him of anything.

When I stopped the car in front of his house, he was standing at his mailbox, leafing through the latest issue of *Gator Bait.*

"Hey," he said, his eyes lighting up when he saw me. "Where've you been keeping yourself? I dropped by the cottage a couple of times but missed you, I guess. Have you been avoiding me?"

In response, I practically flew out of the Pontiac, throwing my arms around him, knocking the newspaper out of his hands. "Please say you're not busy." I had no intention of admitting that I *had* been avoiding him or why. I was too ashamed.

He laughed, seeming perplexed and pleased by my display of affection. "I'm not busy."

"You're not about to go for a ride on your motorcycle?"

"Nope."

"Or pick up a date?"

"No date tonight."

"Good. I'd like to talk to you, to my best friend."

He took my hand and led me inside the house.

We were two steps into his foyer when I began to weep on his shoulder, my chest heaving with deep, wet sobs. I felt lost suddenly, out of control, my adventures of the past few months finally getting to me. It was as if my problems at *From This Day Forward,* the break-in at my apartment, my mother's heart attack, my move to Florida, my squabbles with Sharon, my entanglement in a murder investigation, my doubts about Ray, and my discoveries about Barry had congealed into one giant load that was too heavy, too burdensome, for me to carry. "Oh, Ray," I said, realizing I was staining his nice blue-and-white striped shirt with my big sloppy tears. "You don't need this."

"How do you know what I need?" he said softly, stroking my hair. "Why don't we sit down and you can fill me in?"

I nodded, and moved myself and my tears into the living room.

"I don't want my mother to find out yet," I said after reporting the Barry story, winding up with Gillby's reluctance to arrest him until the evidence was more conclusive. "The same goes for Norman. My mother will worry herself sick, and Norman will feel torn because he has to get back to school. Besides, it's Sharon who has to be told; Sharon I've got to warn. Unfortunately, by warning her I'll be setting off another war between us."

"Why a war?" said Ray. "All you have to do is wait until Norman leaves tomorrow and then call her and tell her to stay away from the guy."

"She'll never buy it. She'll accuse me of belittling her choice in a man, the same way she always does. She'll turn whatever I say into a thing, a conspiracy, a putdown of *her*. She'll insist that I'm trying to smear Barry not because he deserves smearing but because I'm jealous. God, I can write the script."

"I remember now. You two have been this route before."

"This exact route. The last time we really got into it, we didn't speak for two years."

"Still, you've got to call her."

I nodded. "Tomorrow afternoon. After Norman's gone."

"Would it help if I sat there next to you when you made the call? For a little moral support?"

"I'd love it if you were there, Ray. Whether it'll help or not remains to be seen."

At five-thirty the next day, Ray and I plunked ourselves down on the futons in my living room, poised and ready for the call.

"Break a leg," he said as I dialed Sharon's number, the phone in my lap.

I mouthed the word "Thanks" and waited while there was one ring, then two. On the third, Sharon's assistant, the Roaring '20s flapper from my mother's birthday party, answered.

"Weddings by Sharon Peltz," she said breezily.

"Hi, Paula. This is Sharon's sister, Deborah. Is she there?"

"Oh. Deborah. Let me check."

I turned to Ray. "I'm on hold. The assistant is asking Sharon if she wants to take the call. Sharon will make gagging noises and say she'd rather eat stale wedding cake than talk to me, but she'll pick up the phone, because I could be calling about my mother's health."

"You know her pretty well," he remarked.

"Yes, I'm afraid I do."

"Sharon will be with you in a moment," said Paula, coming back on the line.

I thanked her and gave Ray the thumbs-up sign.

And then I waited forever while dear Sharon decided to make her baby sister twist in the wind.

At last, she greeted me with, "What is it, Deborah? I'm swamped. I'm doing the Glasserstein wedding *and* the rehearsal dinner in two weeks."

I did not ask who the Glassersteins were. "There's something very serious I have to discuss with you, Sharon."

"This isn't about Mom, is it?"

"No. It's about Barry Shiller."

She snorted. "You've figured out what a fabulous catch he is and you're dying to know if he has a brother for you, is that it?"

"Not exactly. Sharon, this will come as a terrible shock to you, but I have reason to believe that Barry may have killed Jeffrey, as well as Jeffrey's nurse, Joan Sheldon."

"Excuse me?"

"You heard me. I'm so sorry to be the one to—"

"Wait. Just wait. Have you completely lost your mind, Deborah? I mean, you did move to Florida to have a nervous breakdown, according to Mom, but surely you're being treated with medication now. Prozac? Zoloft? St. John's Wort?"

I pressed on. "Barry was Jeffrey's partner in the vitamin company. He never told you that, did he?"

"Of course not. Because it isn't true."

"It *is* true."

"Prove it."

"I can't."

"There. You see?"

"I can't, because he and Jeffrey hid their profits from Heartily

Hirshon in a bank account in the Bahamas. The government can't touch the money. He never told you about that either, I assume."

Sharon sighed, in an attempt to sound bored. "I do hate to ruin your little game of cops and robbers, Deborah, but if Barry has a bank account in the Bahamas, it's probably because he has a house in Nassau. In Lyford Cay."

"In what key?"

"Lyford. It's a private club. Extremely exclusive. Sean Connery has a place there."

"I'm impressed beyond words."

"You should be. Lyford is home to movie stars, captains of industry, members of various royal families—a Who's Who of the rich and powerful. Barry has owned there since the seventies."

"So he's been burying his money in the Bahamas for over twenty years," I mused, "and then laundering it through Laundromats, vitamin businesses, and God knows what else. He was the one who probably put up the money for Heartily Hirshon and came up with the plan to hide the company's assets. Why else would Jeffrey have needed a partner? He was the doctor. He could have sold vitamins to his patients on his own. But he had to have a backer, someone who knew the ins and outs of offshore banking."

"What in the world are you rambling about now?" said Sharon.

"They must have stayed in touch after college," I went on. "Or they ran into each other a few years ago, during one of Jeffrey's boat trips to the Bahamas, and hatched the vitamin scheme over a few Goombay Smashes."

"That's enough. I'm not listening to any more of this ridiculousness," said Sharon. "I will not have you insulting Barry or insinuating that he's done anything wrong or trying to come between me and marital bliss."

"Marital bliss? Sharon, you can't marry Barry. He's a murderer, not to mention a tax cheat. He's going to prison for a long time. It would be nice if he didn't kill you first."

She actually laughed. "He's a wealthy attorney, he's single, and he's in love with me. You can't stand that, can you, Deborah?"

"Sharon. Pay attention. This is not about Daddy. This is not about cheerleading. This is not about sibling rivalry. *Do you understand?*"

"What I understand is that you are intent on undermining my happiness."

"No, I'm intent on saving your life. Norman's father was a criminal. Barry Shiller is a criminal. There's a pattern here. You're a smart woman who makes foolish choices."

"And you're a woman who dresses badly, weighs too much, and can't get a man."

"I am not."

"Are too."

"Am not."

"Are too."

Click.

I looked helplessly at Ray. "She hung up on me."

He nodded. "I had a feeling the conversation was heading in that direction."

"I let her get to me, Ray. I promised myself I wouldn't do that."

"What was said was said. Now you'll have to dust yourself off and try again. I think we should give Sharon the rest of today to calm down and then we should drive to Boca tomorrow and talk to her in person."

"We?"

"Yeah. I don't work on Saturdays."

"I know, but are you sure you—"

"Positive."

I thanked him. And then, suddenly overcome by a sense of dread, I asked, "What if Barry hurts her, Ray? What if he goes berserk when he realizes that the police are investigating him, and he blames my sister for tipping them off? What if he's as crazy as he is cunning?"

"We can't make her stay away from him."

"We can't?"

"Well, not unless we kidnap her."

I smiled, relieved. "Then that's what we'll do."

Part Three

Chapter Twenty-six

We had planned to be in Boca by noon, at the latest, but the gods were definitely not with us on Saturday morning.

First, my Pontiac wouldn't start. I called Ray, who drove over in his Honda, took a peek under the Pontiac's hood, and found that the alternator was shot.

"Can't you fix it?" I asked.

"No, you need a real mechanic," he said.

"I *have* a real mechanic," I said. "What I need is a real *car*."

We decided to take Ray's Honda, only to have it not start.

"I never have trouble with this car," he muttered, after not being able to diagnose what was wrong.

"Well, you have trouble with it now," I said, growing more and more agitated.

Ray suggested we call my mother and see if we could borrow the Delta 88. I nixed that idea. "I don't want her to know anything about this," I said. "If fighting with my sister is bad for her heart, imagine what *kidnapping* Sharon will do to it."

"There is another option," said Ray. "We could take the Indian."

"Your motorcycle?"

"It's transportation, Deborah. It made it up to Daytona Beach last weekend. I'm willing to bet it can make it down to Boca today."

"Yes, but can I?" I said. "I'm not sure I'm ready for an hour-and-a-half ride on it, beautiful as it is. Tooling around locally is one thing; speeding along I-95, dodging tractor-trailers, is another."

"You'll be fine," Ray assured me. "Perfectly safe."

"Okay then, what about Sharon? Where on earth would we put her after we kidnap her? On the handlebars?"

"No problem. I've got a sidecar that attaches to the bike. We could strap her in there. She'll be nice and snug."

"Nope. I don't see it. If there's one thing Sharon isn't, it's a biker chick. She wouldn't be caught dead in one of those helmets, for example; it would flatten her hair."

Ray took hold of my shoulders. "I hate to bring this up, but if we don't hurry and get to Boca, Sharon could be dead, period."

He had a point.

We left both our faithless vehicles at my house, called a taxi, and zipped over to Ray's house to pick up the Indian. As I donned the helmet and the black leather jacket he lent me, I forced myself not to wail or whine or wimp out. I was on a mission to rescue my sister, and if I had to risk my life on the back of a motorcycle to do it, then that's what I would do.

By the time we arrived at the entrance to Sharon's ritzy country club community, it was nearly three o'clock. I must say, we caused quite a stir as we vibrated up Broken Sound's long, palm tree-lined driveway, Mr. and Mrs. Easy Rider.

The minute he saw us, the tall, uniformed, armed guard stepped out of the gate house (which was only slightly smaller than *my* house) and asked if we were lost.

"No," I shouted so as to be heard above the idling motorcycle. "We're here for Sharon Peltz."

"Is Ms. Peltz expecting you?" he said, eyeing us suspiciously.

"No, but I'm her sister," I explained. "My name's Deborah Peltz." I reached into the back pocket of my jeans, pulled my driver's license out of my wallet, and passed it to him. For I.D.

He studied it, then handed it back to me. "I'll give her a call, but I think I saw her go out about three hours ago."

"Oh, no," I said, clutching Ray's hand in dismay, hoping the guard had mistaken Sharon for one of the other bottle blonds in the community, hoping she was still home, out of harm's way, out of *Barry's* way.

Ray and I waited while the guard went back inside the gate house and dialed Sharon's number. A few seconds later, he emerged, shaking his head. "Nobody's there," he said. "She went out, like I told you."

"And you think she left about three hours ago?" I said.

"Yeah. Maybe four," said the guard.

"Was she alone?" asked Ray.

"Alone with a driver," said the guard. "They were in a black Lincoln Town Car. One of those airport limos, it looked like."

"Airport limos?" Ray and I said simultaneously.

By this point, a short line of cars had formed behind us.

"I've gotta move things along," said the guard. "You can try again later, but now I've gotta have you leave."

"What should we do?" I asked Ray.

"Just what the man said," he replied. "Try again later."

We drove around Boca, stopped for some iced tea, and dialed Sharon's number from a pay phone, to make sure she wasn't there after all. Unfortunately, the guard was right: she wasn't home.

At five-thirty, we went back to the gate house. The guard swore he hadn't seen Sharon come in but humored us by calling her again. Still no answer.

"She could be at Barry's," I said to Ray.

"Then why the airport limo?" he said.

"Okay, then maybe she took a business trip," I theorized. "Maybe someone wants her to coordinate a wedding out of the state, and she's scouting locations."

"Would she tell your mother if she was going away for an extended period of time?" asked Ray.

"Probably."

"Then call your mother."

We drove to another pay phone.

"Mom," I said when she answered. "Just curious: did Sharon go out of town by any chance?"

She giggled. "Yes, but she swore me to secrecy."

"Why?"

"My lips are sealed."

"Well, unseal them, Mom," I said. "I really have to get in touch with her as soon as possible."

"Deborah, dear. I'm so happy that you feel close to your sister at long last. You know how much I've wanted that. If you need to speak to Sharon, I'm sure she'd want me to tell you where she can be reached."

"I do need to speak to her," I said emphatically.

"Well, then." My mother giggled again. "She's flown off to Nassau with that nice Barry Shiller."

I grabbed Ray's arm, feeling faint. "She didn't."

"Oh, yes she did, dear. Apparently, he has a lovely house in Lyford Cay and insisted she come and spend a few days."

"But she's doing some big shot's wedding in a couple of weeks," I recalled. "Isn't this trip awfully sudden?"

"Yes, and that's the best part. Sharon suspects that Barry is whisking her off to the islands because he intends to propose."

"Propose."

"Marriage, dear. Oh, I can guess what you're thinking—that Sharon's deluding herself again. But this time, the man she's set her sights on seems to have set his sights on her too. A whirlwind courtship if ever there was one. Imagine our Sharon finding a mate as impulsive as she is."

"I'm imagining." What I imagined, of course, was that Barry was whisking my sister off to his romantic Bahamian retreat, not because he was madly in love with her and wanted to propose marriage to her, but because he was feeling squeezed by the cops and wanted to flee the country—go on the lam, in police parlance—and take Sharon along as insurance . . . as a hostage.

"I do hope her little vacation goes smoothly for her," said my mother.

"Listen, Mom. You don't happen to have Barry's phone number at Lyford Cay, do you?"

"No. Sharon didn't give it to me. Do you need to speak to her that urgently?"

"That urgently."

"Perhaps if you call his law office, his secretary could—"

"On second thought, I shouldn't bother the lovebirds," I interrupted, not wanting to tip Barry off that I was on to him.

"That's very considerate of you, dear. As I said, I'm delighted about the way you and your sister have worked things out between you. I'm very proud of my girls."

I told her we were proud of her too and hung up. I turned to Ray. "Is there any way you could take a day or two off from work?"

"Because?"

"Because I'm inviting you to fly over to Nassau with me."

"Why? So we can storm Barry's house and rescue Sharon? You told me Lyford Cay is a private club. They'll never let us get within a mile of the place."

"Then we won't storm his house and rescue Sharon. We'll *sneak* into his house and rescue her. We'll figure out how once we get there."

He shook his head. "Barging into the nurse's house here in Stuart was one thing. Flying all the way to Nassau to be shut out of some private club is another."

"All the way to Nassau? From what I've seen, people in south Florida commute to the Bahamas like people from New York commute to the Hamptons. It's no big deal. Jeffrey used to go there on his boat, for long weekends."

Ray wasn't committing.

"Come on," I coaxed. "I bet Nassau's beautiful this time of year. You could use a change of scenery, couldn't you?"

"Sure, but why not let Gillby fly down and arrest Shiller? Then after he's got him in custody, we'll go and bring Sharon home."

"Gillby isn't ready to arrest Barry. He's still gathering evidence against him. That's the problem."

I was frustrated now. Either Ray was in or out.

"If you don't want to go, then tell me," I said.

In response, he reached out and stroked my cheek with the back of his hand. "I don't want you to go, don't you get it?"

"Not exactly."

"You're so into the drama of this, as if it's just another episode on your soap opera, that you don't see the danger. Barry Shiller's a bad guy, Deborah. A rich and powerful bad guy. If you mess with him, you could be the next person to catch a bullet in the chest. I'm not real keen on letting that happen."

I smiled, enjoying the feel of his fingers against my skin, enjoying his concern for my welfare, for me. "Then come with me," I urged. "Nothing will happen if you're by my side. You're my friend, my buddy, my pal."

"I'm more than that and you know it."

"Do I?"

"If you don't, maybe this will convince you."

He leaned forward and kissed me on the mouth—a kiss that was sudden and lasted only a moment but definitely put a new spin on the nature of our relationship.

At first, I was too startled by the kiss to register anything but bemusement. "That felt weird, like kissing my brother," I said, running my fingertips along my lips, as if to confirm that the kiss had actually occurred.

"You don't have a brother," said Ray. "Maybe I'd better try it again."

He kissed me a second time, longer, more passionately, pulling me closer and encircling me in his arms. It was that second kiss that did it; when it was over, I hardly viewed Ray as a brother. I was so hot for him, so electrified by the sensations his kisses had unleashed, that I thought my insides would melt.

"How about now? Still feel weird?" he asked, his voice low, husky.

"No. Not weird at all."

I became the aggressor then, taking his face in my hands, folding my mouth into his, folding my body into his, as if I couldn't get enough of him once I'd had my first taste.

"I don't want anything to happen to you," he reiterated as we continued to paw each other in broad daylight, oblivious to the traffic along Yamato Road, one of Boca's main thoroughfares.

"You won't lose me, Ray," I said breathlessly between nibbles on his lips. "You won't."

He protested, murmuring something about Beth, but I silenced him with another kiss. Ignited or liberated or a combination of both, he began to move his hands along the front of my body, down, down, down, touching, rubbing, massaging my breasts, my abdomen, my—

"Ray," I said, forcing myself to break away, just as his palms had made contact with my pelvic bone. "We're worse than those horny teenagers up in the observation tower. Let's at least do this in the car."

"We don't have a car," he moaned, nodding at the Indian.

I laughed, picturing us trying to keep our orgy going on the seat of the motorcycle.

"If there isn't a lot of traffic, I can get us back to Stuart in just over an hour," he said, practically panting as he returned his hands to my body, as if there were a powerful magnetic field between us and he couldn't help himself.

"And then what?" I said through half-closed eyes, finding it almost impossible to concentrate on anything but the feel of him.

"We'll do more of *this*." He kissed me again—this kiss, like the others, bearing the unmistakable mark of a man in lust.

"What about Sharon and Barry and Nassau?" I asked, pulling away from him. "I'm serious about flying over there, Ray. I'm afraid for my sister, afraid she doesn't have a clue what she's walked into this time, and I can't sit by and do nothing. Once and for all, I've got to prove to her that I care about her, that I've always cared about her, that I'm not out to take anything away from her. She and I will never be able to co-exist peacefully unless I make some sort of grand gesture."

Ray nodded. "Infiltrating Lyford Cay and dragging her out of there would qualify as a grand gesture, no doubt about it."

"Then you'll go with me?"

"Tell you what," he said, taking my hand and leading me over to the motorcycle. "When we get back to Stuart, we'll talk about Nassau, come up with a game plan."

I threw my arms around him. "Oh, thanks, Ray. You won't be sorry. I swear it."

"But the first thing we're gonna do when we get home is finish this other business we've started. Do we have a deal?" He pressed himself against me. He was, as they say, aroused.

I smiled. "You drive a hard bargain, baby."

Chapter Twenty-seven

We made it back to Stuart in record time, propelled, in part, by the kind of euphoria only a new romance can inspire. We pulled into Ray's driveway, all worked up about hopping off the bike, tearing off our clothes, and engaging in lewd and lascivious behavior. There was a slight problem, however.

"Holly!" said Ray, when he spotted her sitting cross-legged on his front steps. She looked even younger—and thinner—than she had the night I'd seen her with him at the Black Marlin, and she was dressed entirely in white. A vestal virgin. "What are you doing here?"

"Waiting for you," she said, glancing at her watch. "It's eight o'clock. You invited me for seven-thirty."

Ray looked stricken. "Jeez, Holly. I was going to make you dinner, wasn't I?"

"Grilled tuna, you said," she reminded him. "With pasta and garlic bread."

The same menu he cooked up for me, I thought, minus the broccoli. What a coincidence.

Coincidence, my ass. I was incensed by this turn of events. Instantly furious. Smoke-coming-out-of-my-ears pissed off. My anger zooming from zero to ten in a matter of nanoseconds. I mean, there I was, totally turbo-charged, sexually speaking, anticipating my first intimate evening with a man I genuinely cared for, my first intimate evening with a man in ages, as a matter of fact. And what do you know? Ray already had plans for the evening—dinner at his place with one of his goddamn tree-women.

Never mind that I had encouraged him to see Holly again, encouraged him to fall in love and be happy. That was *then*—before I realized that the woman I was encouraging him to fall in love and be happy with was me.

"I'm really sorry," he told Holly. "Something came up and I completely forgot about our date."

"Some*thing?*" I said, glaring at him. "My, that's flattering." I strode over to Holly and pumped her hand, not wanting to be rude. This mess wasn't her fault. It was Ray who'd led me to believe he wasn't dying to go out with her again; Ray who'd given me the impression that he didn't especially enjoy dating; Ray who'd morphed into another Jeffrey Hirshon before my very eyes. "I'm Deborah Peltz," I said to Holly. "We met at the Black Marlin. How are you?"

"Hungry," she said. "My stomach's growling. I skipped lunch today." Holly may have had a pleasingly youthful appearance, but she had the voice from hell, it turned out. A sort of Fran Drescher honk.

"Did you hear that? She's hungry, Ray," I said. "Better get right into the kitchen and feed her."

"But I—we—she—" he stammered.

"Well, you've certainly got your pronouns down," I said as I started back up the driveway, in the direction of the street. I figured I'd walk the couple of blocks into town and call myself a cab.

"Wait! Where are you going, Deborah?" said Ray, rushing toward me, his expression full of what-should-I-do? As if I was supposed to bail him out.

"I'm going home," I replied as I kept walking. To take a cold shower.

"Won't you at least stay until I straighten this out?" he pleaded.

"What's to straighten out?" I said. "Three's a crowd."

Ray was about to respond when Holly called out to me. "Nice meeting you, Deb! Have a beautiful evening!"

"You too, Hol!" I said. "Don't do anything I wouldn't do!"

"We've got to talk about Nassau," said Ray, as he followed me onto Seminole Street. "I'm flying over there with you, remember."

"Just grill your tuna," I said. "I'm flying over there by myself."

By the time I got to the cottage, I was so jazzed up I didn't know what to do first—eat dinner? Call the airlines? Reserve a hotel room? Punch a hole in the wall? Besides which, I didn't have a clue about Nassau, had never been to the Bahamas, and I wasn't in the mood to run out to the nearest bookstore and buy a Fodor's guide.

And then there was another wrinkle: my job. The Historical Society was paying me to caretake the House of Refuge, not to go gallavanting on some island. I would have to tell Melinda I was leaving town on a family emergency. But if I did that, she would run to my mother to find out *what* family emergency, and I'd be stuck having to fess up to Mom about Barry, which I was not about to do.

Of course, Frank Gillby wouldn't be too crazy about my rushing off to Barry's Bahamian palace and taking the law into my own hands. But there are times when you can't please everybody. (There are also times when you can't please anybody, which was about to be the case here.)

Ultimately, I decided to confide in Fred Zimsky. He would not only cover for me at the House of Refuge, I hoped; he would keep my scheme a secret from my mother, because he was fond of her and wouldn't want her to go into cardiac arrest.

Yes, that's the ticket, I thought as I dialed his number, crossing my fingers that he was not spending the night at my mother's, which he wasn't, luckily. After I laid out my story, he agreed not to tell Mom where I was going and he volunteered to sleep at the cottage for as long as I was away. I thanked him over and over and said I owed him one.

"Just put in a good word for me with your mother," he said. "Then we'll wipe the slate clean."

I said I would, hung up, and called Helen.

"It's Deborah," I said when she answered. "I need help."

"Oh, God. Don't tell me the police arrested you and this is the one phone call you're allowed from jail."

"No, I'm at the cottage, Helen. You were right about the murderer. He turned out to be the wronged business associate."

"No kidding."

"Unfortunately, this wronged business associate has flown off to his house in the Bahamas with my sister. She thinks he's in love with her. I think he's using her."

"For sex?"

"No, as a hostage. He's probably got her bound and gagged by now."

"So he *is* using her for sex."

"No, Helen. I meant that he's taken Sharon to the Bahamas as sort of an insurance policy. When the police come after him, he can pull one of those 'If I go, she goes with me' numbers."

"Oh, like that scene we did on the show a couple of years ago."

"Which one?"

"The one where Dirk Campbell, the bank president, fled to St. Barts to escape being charged with the murder of Hector Diaz, his personal trainer, and dragged Hector's sister, Carmen, to the island with him. Remember?"

"Not really. What happened to Carmen? Did she make it back to the States alive?"

"Carmen? She was a tough broad. She broke free from her handcuffs, surprised Dirk on the deck of his house and pushed him off, into the sea. He was still holding his martini glass when they found him bobbing in the water." Helen sighed. "We beat *The Young and the Restless* that day. Woody was ecstatic. How could you have forgotten?"

"It's all coming back to me now," I said. "Listen, Helen, I'm planning to fly over to Nassau to get my sister out of there. You're more plugged into things than I am. Do you know any hotels where I could stay?"

"No, but even if I did, they'd probably be booked up. It's spring break."

"Great."

"Cheer up. I bet you could spend the night in one of those little guest houses they have down there. They're usually kind of funky, but they'd suit your purpose, wouldn't they?"

I thanked Helen and told her I'd call her when I got back.

Next up: BahamasAir. I got a seat on the 9:00 A.M. to Nassau out of Ft. Lauderdale. Of course, the airport limo I also had to book, thanks to the dead Pontiac, cost more than the plane fare, but what was I supposed to do? Swim to the Bahamas?

My final call of the night was to my mother. I hated to lie to her, but that's exactly what I did. I told her that Ray and I had discovered that we were in love (she squealed with delight) and that I would be spending the next few days at his house because I couldn't bear to be apart from him (she squealed again). I suggested that if she needed to reach me, she should leave a message on my answering machine and I'd be sure to call her back (she said she was thrilled that both her girls had finally found happiness). Yeah, right.

I threw some clothes into a suitcase, scarfed down a frozen yogurt, and went to bed. The second my head hit the pillow the phone rang. I decided to let the machine take the call. The volume was way up on the incoming message, so I could hear Ray's voice telling me he wanted to explain.

What's to explain? I thought as I yanked the phone cord out of the jack. He had a date with Holly while he had his hands all over me.

Men.

The BahamasAir 737 was crowded, but there were empty seats, I noticed as I boarded the plane. I was exhausted and had hoped to doze, but the flight only took forty-five minutes. Before I knew it, we were up, we were down, we were there.

I was standing at the exit to Nassau International Airport, about to hail a cab, when I spotted a familiar face rushing toward me.

"If you hadn't been so unreasonable, we could have sat together on the plane," said Ray, flushed and out of breath. "Not to mention, shared the cost of the limo to the airport."

"What are you doing here?" I said, feigning anger but secretly pleased that he had followed me all the way to a foreign country. Very dramatic. I was especially pleased that Ray's circles under his eyes were even darker than mine.

"I found out which flight you were on and packed my bag. I told you I was coming with you."

He kissed me.

"Stop that," I said.

He kissed me again.

"You heard me," I said, trying to sound menacing.

He kissed me a third time.

I put my hands on my hips, exasperated, exhilarated. "In case you're not aware of it, there's such a thing as political correctness. In other words, when a woman says no she means no."

"Fine. Say no and I'll take the next flight home."

"No."

"No, as in, Don't take the next flight home? Or no, as in, Don't kiss me?"

"Oh, give me a break. You're making me the villain here when you're the one who's been playing games. First you're Mr. Platonic, the pal, the guy who's afraid to share his innermost feelings, remember? Then you're telling me I'm much more than a friend to you and coming onto me like some sex-starved prison inmate. And just when I'm falling for it, you've got another woman waiting on your doorstep. Why don't you go play your games with Holly while I go save my sister."

I started to walk away, but Ray grabbed the strap of my bag and pulled me back.

"Not so fast," he said. "You led me to believe you didn't want a relationship. All you talked about was Hirshon and what a two-timing jerk he was. I figured you weren't interested in starting anything after that experience, so I didn't push it. But then you told me about your plan to fly down here and I couldn't let you do it alone. I knew you were special to me, right from the beginning, but I didn't know how special until I realized I could lose you. That's when it changed between us, when it got *great* between us. The only problem was, I forgot to cancel dinner with Holly. Is that a crime?"

"Not a crime, exactly, although Holly did look a little under-nourished, like she could use a good meal. Did you ever feed her, by the way?"

"Yes, I fed her. And while we were eating, I explained about you. About you and me."

"What about you and me?"

"That we're going steady."

"Please."

"I'm serious, Deborah. I want us to take our friendship to the next level. I think I'm in love with you."

"But you're not sure."

"I didn't mean it that way. I just meant—God, you're tough."

"Why shouldn't I be? I've been through this before. I'm not the innocent lamb I once was."

"And I'm not the big bad wolf."

"No? There was a time in the not-too-distant past when I thought maybe *you* killed Jeffrey. Joan too."

Ray let go of my bag. "What did you just say to me?"

"I said there was a time when I wondered if you did it. Did them. The murders."

His expression changed, his smiling face becoming one of anger and disbelief.

"If that's what you *really* think of me, you're on your own, hot shot."

He started to walk away in a rage. I grabbed the strap of *his* bag and pulled him back.

"Wait," I said, wishing I hadn't opened my mouth. "Try to see this from my point of view. I came to Stuart and everyone was a stranger to me except my mother. All of a sudden, you show up at my door every other day, claiming to be my friend, inviting me places, being the supportive sidekick."

"Is that out of the realm of possibility? For a man to be nice?"

"No, but you were a man who hated Jeffrey."

"I had dinner with Gillby's niece the night Hirshon was killed."

"Yes, but I didn't know where you were before you picked up Laurel."

"Willow."

"Right. Not only that, how was I supposed to know if you did, in fact, go to Daytona Beach the weekend Joan was killed?"

"Because I told you I did!" He was yelling now. People in the airport were staring at us. "So you're admitting you didn't trust me?"

"No. I'm admitting I was confused. Two minutes after I moved to town, my mother's cardiologist, who seemed to be an honest person, lied to my sister and me. Then he was shot to death and we were standing over his body when the cops found him. Then, in order to remove the suspicion from us, I went around hoping I'd be able to figure out who was telling the truth and who wasn't. But it was hard, because no matter how much everybody blabbed about their stale marriages or their torrid affairs, they weren't *saying* anything; they weren't telling me who they were. The thing about people in Florida is that most of them are originally from someplace else, and when they get here it's easy for them to reinvent themselves. So you think, should I trust them or not?"

"But I'm not from someplace else, and I've told you who I am, shown you who I am. How can you even doubt that I'm crazy about you. I—" He stopped. His feelings were hurt. I wanted to slit my wrists.

"Look, Ray. Obviously, I was wrong not to trust you. Terribly wrong. But that was then. This is now."

"Yeah, and now you don't trust me because I made a date with Holly."

"For the same night you were so hot to get in my pants!"

Ray threw up his hands in frustration. "You're still mad about that?"

"Sort of."

He glanced at his watch. "Do you really want to stand here and do couples therapy or do you want to go to Lyford Cay and save your sister's life?"

"The latter."

"Okay. Then why don't we do that."

"Why don't we."

I wanted Ray to kiss me then, to prove that we were all better, but he didn't. I could have kissed him, of course, but I was still too riled up about Holly.

"I thought I'd ask a cab driver for suggestions of places to stay here in Nassau," I said. "The big hotels are probably booked, but he might know of some smaller inns or guest houses that have vacancies. Once we're settled, we can plot our strategy for getting into Lyford Cay."

"I'm here to serve," he said dryly. "Lead the way."

We hailed a cab and got in.

"Where may I take you, please?" asked our driver, a young man with a lilting Bahamian accent.

"We were hoping you could help us with that," said Ray. "Do you know of any inns or guest houses where we could spend a couple of nights? Someplace clean, not too expensive, not far from Lyford Cay?"

"Lyford's on the western side of the island," said the driver. "About a fifteen minute ride from here. I know a place where you could stay that's pretty close to the club."

"What's it called?" I asked.

"Reggie's," he said. "Very clean. Not expensive."

"And you think this Reggie's has rooms available?" I said.

"I'm sure of it," said the driver. "Reggie is my uncle. He'll take good care of you."

Small islands are a lot like small towns, I guess. No matter where you are, you're likely to run into somebody's relative.

———

Reggie's Bahamian Inn, as it was formally known, was basically a rooming house for eccentrics—a two-story, white shingled building that reeked of curry. Our room (Ray and I were forced to bunk together, given that the other rooms were occupied) was up the creaky flight of stairs and down the hall, sandwiched between the English couple who were hard of hearing and the German couple who hardly got along. If we experienced any peace and quiet during our stay, I certainly don't remember it.

"Enjoy yourselves," said Reggie himself as he showed us our room— a tiny, unairconditioned space taken up by a king-sized bed.

"Is there a bathroom?" I asked, my spirits sagging, along with the bed's mattress.

"Yes, my lady," he said. "One for you. One for the gentleman. Both outside your door, in the hall."

"Great. We'll be sharing with our neighbors, the major combatants of World War Two," I said to Ray after Reggie left us alone.

"Want to try someplace else?" he asked as he opened the window, to try to air out the curry, a fruitless endeavor since the smell was coming from outside.

I shook my head. "We're not here for a vacation. We're on a mission. We're not supposed to enjoy ourselves."

He stifled a smile. "Not even a little?"

I shook my head. "We've got to come up with a plan to rescue Sharon. Something really ingenious."

"Well, there are two obstacles we need to overcome right off the bat. The first is getting inside the gate at Lyford Cay. The second is finding out which house is Shiller's."

Just then, there was a knock on the door.

"Yes?" I called out, hoping either the Germans or the Brits hadn't mistaken our room for the bathroom.

"Housekeeping," came a pretty little voice.

Ray opened the door.

"May I bring you some fresh towels?" asked a native woman who identified herself as Sabrina, Reggie's wife.

"Thank you," I said, taking the towels from her. They were as soft as sandpaper.

"If you're hungry for lunch, there's a restaurant right next door," she said, smiling sweetly. "Their conch fritters are very nice. Lots of curry."

Why wasn't I surprised. "Sabrina, I wonder if I could ask you a question. Do you know anything about Lyford Cay?"

She giggled. "Oh yes, my lady. My husband and I both worked there, before we opened our own establishment. We were the cook and butler in the house of Baron and Baroness Pendleton."

"Really?" I said with interest. "Then you must be familiar with every nook and cranny of the place."

"Quite familiar, yes," she said.

I glanced at Ray. Was Sabrina someone we could trust? I wondered, trying to read his impression of her. Would she be compassionate if we told her why we'd come to Nassau and, perhaps, aid and abet us? Or would she think we were crazy American tourists and call the constable?

I went with my instincts—and with everything I'd learned from watching soap opera actors over the years.

I took a deep breath and fell onto the bed in a swoon. When Ray and Sabrina rushed over to see if I was all right, I launched into a "pretend" crying jag—the same sort of distraught posture that had worked so well on the Sirens of Stuart.

"What can I do for you, my lady?" Sabrina asked, hovering over me, her brow furrowed with concern.

"I'm sorry to break down in front of you, Sabrina," I said, sniffling. "But I'm overcome with worry over my beloved sister, who is being held against her will at Lyford Cay."

Sabrina's eyes widened. "Against her will?"

"Yes," I said. "She's in grave danger."

"Have you contacted the police in Nassau?" she asked.

"No," I said, "because the man who is holding her is a madman. There's no telling what he'll do to my sister if the police come charging in. I'd rather handle the situation more discreetly."

"Are you sure this man lives at Lyford?"

"Yes. His name is Barry Shiller, and he's a lawyer from Florida."

She nodded with recognition. "I believe his house is the third one down from the yacht club, on the water. My cousin, Serena, used to be his housekeeper."

"But she isn't anymore?" I said.

"No, my lady. She works for one of the other owners now. The gentleman you speak of has had several housekeepers over the past few years; there is a high turnover among the members of his staff. I don't like to speak harshly of anybody at Lyford, but people say this man, Mr. Shiller, is difficult to please."

"Is that so?" I remarked, as I lit on an idea. A harebrained idea, but an idea nonetheless. "You know, Sabrina, since Mr. Shiller has such a revolving door when it comes to his staff, I bet nobody would be suspicious if two new members of his staff show up this afternoon."

"I don't understand," she said.

"What if Mr. Scalley and I were to pose as his new housekeeper and butler, just to get us past the security guards at Lyford? Would you and Reggie help us do this? Dress us in the appropriate uniforms? Drive us there and drop us off? *To save my poor sister?*" I threw in a few sobs, a few wipes of the eyes, a few pleading looks.

"Of course, my lady. Of course," said Sabrina as she patted my hand. "My husband and I will do whatever we can for your sister. Serena will help too."

"That's very kind of you," I said, glancing at Ray who was, at that moment, either marveling at my performance or wishing he were back in Stuart. "Isn't it kind of her, *darling?*"

Chapter Twenty-eight

By later that day, Ray seemed to have forgiven me for the incident in the airport, for which I was very grateful. I, of course, was slower to come around.

"How do I look, my lady?" he asked as he stood by the door of our little room, modeling the butler outfit Reggie had lent him.

"Great," I said, "if the butlers at Lyford Cay wear clamdiggers."

Ray, you see, was tall. Reggie, on the other hand, was not. As a result, the cuffs of the black pants Ray now had on came up to the middle of his calves.

"How about the shirt?" he said.

It was pretty skimpy too, but it was white, it didn't have any rips or stains or buttons missing, and it got the job done. "It's beautiful," I said. "What about my get-up?"

Ray whistled. "Damn, you're a fox."

"I'm serious. Do you think it's okay?" I was decked out in a white polyester maid's uniform. *Stuffed into* a white polyester maid's uniform, to be frank.

Sabrina, you see, was small. I, on the other hand, was not. As a result, I was busting out all over, just like the month of June.

"It's mahvelous," said Ray with a gleam in his eye. "And the hair is a nice touch."

Sabrina had advised me to pull my unruly mop back, in a bun. The "help" at Lyford, she explained, were expected to appear neat and well-groomed. Of course, neither Ray nor I could fit into Sabrina or Reggie's shoes, so we wore our own—sneakers—and hoped nobody would notice.

"When is Cousin Serena taking us over to Lyford?" asked Ray.

"Around seven-thirty," I replied. "She'll be off from work by then. The plan is that she'll pick us up, hide us in the trunk of her car, drive back to Lyford because she forgot something—that's what she'll tell the guards—and drop us off inside the gates."

"I hope she has a big trunk."

"We'll only be in it for ten minutes. We'll survive. She thinks the timing will be perfect, because we'll be showing up when everybody's finished with the beach and the golf course and having cocktails. She said they'll be so blitzed they won't recognize each other, let alone a couple of strangers."

"Yeah, but I'm Barry's new butler. Aren't I supposed to *serve* the cocktails?"

"You're not really his butler, Ray, any more than I'm his housekeeper. We're just assuming the identity of his new butler and housekeeper in case anybody asks. The last thing I'm interested in is scrubbing that lowlife's floors." I stopped. Ray's head was cocked and he had a silly grin on his face. "What?"

"Come here," he said, waving me over with his finger.

"Why?"

"Because you look adorable in that dress. Like a maid in a porno flick."

"I'm staying right where I am. I'm still angry at you."

"That's too bad, because I'm still crazy about you, even after the things you said in the airport. You see, my sweet, I understand why you were suspicious of everybody. I probably would have been too."

"You're only saying that so I'll have sex with you later."

"Will you have sex with me later?"

"No."

"Will you have sex with me now?"

"Ray. I'm preparing for the role I'll be playing tonight. I'm trying to get in character."

He laughed. "You're already a character."

"*In character.* It's an acting term."

Ray came across the room (which took about three steps, since the room was the size of a closet) and put his arms around me. I did not resist. "You're gonna be terrific. We're both gonna be terrific," he said, nuzzling me. "And if we aren't, at least we'll die with our best duds on."

I smiled. "I feel better now. Thanks."

At seven-thirty, Sabrina's cousin Serena took us to the famed Lyford Cay in her Buick, which was as beat-up as my Pontiac but didn't stall or knock or overheat, and had a trunk large enough to hold Ray and me without causing us serious bodily harm. I'm not saying it was the smoothest ride of my life—I *still* have black-and-blue marks on my butt—but it got us where we needed to go.

During the trip, I mulled over everything Reggie and Sabrina had told us about the exclusive enclave where they had worked for so many years.

A lush eleven-hundred-acre community on a small peninsula at the western end of the island, Lyford was the setting for the old James Bond film *Thunderball*. Legend has it that the film's star, Sean Connery, was so captivated by the place that he purchased a house there. But Connery is only one of a number of international luminaries who belong to the club (Prince Ranier of Monaco is another). Over thirteen hundred members hail from thirty-two countries, the common denominator being money—lots of it. Sabrina giggled when she told us that the couple she and Reggie worked for, the Baron and Baroness, thought nothing of spending $20 million to buy their house but complained bitterly when they were forced to pay $14 for a club sandwich. She also got a kick out of the way the members dressed: faded and tattered clothing during the week; tuxedos and ball gowns on Saturday nights. I tried to imagine Barry Shiller in anything other than his Armani suits and gold jewelry, and wondered how he fit in with this crowd.

At some point in my musings, Serena's Buick came to an abrupt halt, and I heard her roll down her window and speak to someone.

"We must be at the gate house," Ray whispered. "She's talking to the guard."

I closed my eyes and thought of Sharon then.

We're coming, I said silently. We're going to save you. Hang on.

The car jerked forward. I squeezed Ray's hand. "We're in."

We kept moving for another few minutes, then Serena stopped the car and shut the engine off. She got out of the Buick, scurried to the back of the car, and opened the trunk.

"Are you both all right?" she asked.

"Fine, thanks," I said, my white uniform soaked with sweat, as were Ray's shirt and pants.

She helped us out of the trunk and explained that we were standing in front of the entrance to the Yacht Club and that Barry's house was just down the road.

"That one?" I said, motioning toward an enormous pink structure the size of a hotel. It was, by far, the most ostentatious house on the block. Very Barry.

"Yes, my lady," said Serena. "But I'd better leave you now. The security guards patrol every street. If they find out I let strangers inside, I might lose my job."

"Yes. Yes. You go," I said. "We'll take it from here, Serena."

"What about later?" she said. "How will you get back to Reggie's?"

I glanced at Ray, flummoxed. I'd overlooked that minor detail, hoping we'd have gotten Sharon out of Lyford by the end of the evening and would be on a plane back to Florida.

"Is there any way you could swing by and pick us up at a specific time, Serena?" said Ray, who was wearing a watch, along with his butler's outfit.

She shook her head. "It would arouse suspicion for me to return, Mr. Scalley, but Reggie could come for you. He still has friends on the security force."

"Perfect," said Ray. "Tell him to meet us here, in front of the Yacht Club, at ten o'clock. If, for some reason, we're not here at ten, he should call the police."

"The police?" I jumped in. "Ray, we decided we weren't—"

"What if Barry gives us more than we can handle?" he cut me off. "He may not be thrilled that we've flown in for a little visit. Personally, I wouldn't mind knowing the police are on their way if something goes wrong."

"Mr. Scalley is right, my lady," said Serena. "I worked for Mr. Shiller. When he gets angry, he isn't a gentleman."

I nodded, realizing they were both right. "When my sister gets angry, she's no picnic, either."

After Serena took off, Ray and I stood there, planning our next move. I said that we ought to sneak over to Barry's house, find Sharon, and, when he wasn't looking, drag her out of there. Ray, on the other hand, brought up what Serena had told us—that Sunday nights at Lyford are cook's night off and that everyone (even cold-blooded killers, presumably) goes to the seafood buffet at the Yacht Club. His theory was that we should wait for Sharon and Barry to leave the house, because it would be far easier to kidnap Sharon while Barry was helping himself to a Bahamian lobster.

I was about to concede that his strategy sounded more reasonable than mine when we were nearly run down by a procession of golf carts, all carrying hungry members en route to the seafood buffet.

"God, these people are dangerous after a few cocktails," I said, remembering something else Serena had told us: that golf carts were *the* mode of transportation around the club.

"Watch out. Here comes another one," Ray warned, pulling me out of the way. "And another."

"I guess we're in the flight path," I said. "Why don't we step—"

"I say there! You two!" a woman called out to us, waving her floppy straw hat in our direction.

We froze.

"You there!" she said, striding toward us. She had stringy blond hair with gray roots, tanned and freckled skin which she didn't bother to even out with makeup, and a lockjaw that suggested Locust Valley or, perhaps, Darien. Aside from the pearls around her neck, she was dressed like a bag lady. What's more, she was redolent with Tanqueray. "I'm Mrs. Croft, the chairwoman of the dining committee, and you must be the two they sent to help serve tonight."

She did not wait for a reply. She simply assumed we would follow her inside the Yacht Club, and toddled off. When she turned around, to see if we were behind her and discovered we weren't, she clapped her hands and said, "Come, come. People are arriving."

Ray and I looked at each other and shrugged. "After you," he said. We hurried to catch up with Mrs. Croft.

"There you are," she said, weaving a little as we continued toward the club. "You're both rather light-skinned, I see. Not natives, are you?"

"No, my lady," I said. "We're part of a cultural exchange program between the Bahamas and the United States."

"Ah, a sort of Peace Corps, is it?"

"Yes, my lady."

"Enchanting," she said and kept weaving.

By the time we made it to the buffet, the calypso trio was already belting out "Matilda," and a few hundred people in rumpled clothing were polishing off their umpteenth drink.

"All the men look like George Plimpton," I whispered to Ray.

"All the women look like him too," he whispered back.

"Here we are," said Mrs. Croft, steering us behind the mile-long buffet table. "Do try not to pile a lot of food on each plate, will you? It isn't gracious. Besides, the shrimp are awfully expensive this year."

We nodded and started serving. At first, I was worried that one of the members might be sober enough to question what our lily white asses were doing behind that table, but none did. And the other servers were too busy dishing out clams and mussels and crabcakes to pay any attention to us.

"Hey, sweetheart. What do you think of my red pants?" boomed the loud drunk to whom I was serving peas and rice.

"They're real snappy, sir," I said. "The same color as your eyes."

Ray elbowed me.

"Do you see Sharon anywhere?" he asked.

"Not yet," I said. "I don't see Barry, either."

"Then keep shoveling the grub," he said. "The night's still young."

I kept shoveling the grub—until I did see Sharon and Barry, sitting down at a table for two. My pulse raced as I observed them. Barry, in an effort to look nautical for the occasion, was wearing white slacks, white patent-leather shoes, and a blue-and-red-striped shirt with a large gold anchor on it. Sharon, well, never mind what she was wearing. The important thing was that she was alive, with no apparent bruises or cuts or post-traumatic tics that I could detect without my distance glasses.

"Ray," I said.

He didn't answer. He was chatting up Sean Connery.

"Ray," I hissed, amazed that he could be starstruck at a time like this.

When he didn't answer yet again, I pinched his arm.

"Ouch," he yelped. "What's the—"

"Over there," I said, nodding at Sharon and Barry, neither of whom Ray had ever met. "They're the ones who look way overdressed."

Ray took care of Mr. Connery and his wife and turned his attention to Sharon and Barry. "Do you want to just go to their table and grab her? Sort of like a hit and run?"

"No. Yes. I don't know." I popped a shrimp into my mouth and hoped Mrs. Croft wasn't watching.

"I'll do whatever you say, Deborah," Ray offered.

"I'm still thinking. Have a shrimp while I decide. They're delicious." I handed him one and treated myself to another. "Oh my God. Look, Ray. Sharon's getting up. She's walking this way. She's moving onto the buffet line."

"And Barry's staying put for some reason. Maybe he's allergic to seafood."

"No. Sharon's probably making up a plate for him. She's so servile when it comes to men."

"Come on. Let's go for it." Ray took my hand and led me around to the front of the buffet table, where Sharon was picking up a napkin and a set of utensils and humming along with the calypso trio.

Ray hooked one of her arms, while I hooked the other. "If you follow us, my lady, we'll give you a peek at the desserts," I said, attempting a Bahamian accent and keeping my head down.

"My sister's the dessert freak in the family," she said, struggling to wriggle out of our grasp. "With a waistline to prove it."

I tightened my grip on Sharon's arm. "Then your sister would surely enjoy the Concorde chocolate meringue cake," I replied, recalling that the confection was Lyford's specialty, according to Sabrina—its recipe straight from Maxim's in Paris. "We'll show you where you can taste it."

"But I haven't even had dinner yet," she protested as we marched her farther and farther away from the crowd, until we reached a private area, behind a cluster of palm trees.

"Dinner is the least of your problems, Sis," I said in my own voice. She stared at me. "Deborah?"

"Yes, and don't scream. They don't care for scenes at Lyford."

She continued to stare, her mouth hanging open in an entirely unflattering manner. "Why are you dressed like that?" she asked, after deciding that I really was me. She pointed at Ray. "And who's he?"

"His name is Ray Scalley and he's a friend of mine from Stuart," I said. "He came here to help me persuade you that the man you think is going to propose marriage to you is a murderer who is going to kill you the minute you're no longer useful to him. As I *tried* to tell you the other day, Sharon, Barry's already killed Jeffrey and his nurse. What's more, he's in up to his eyeballs in money laundering."

"I don't believe this," she said, tossing her head with disdain. "I simply do not believe this. If you flew all the way to Nassau to ruin my happiness, then you're more pathetic than I imagined, Deborah. You'll obviously stop at nothing to—"

"Your sister came here to save your *life,* damn it," Ray fumed. "She risked her own safety to protect yours. In my book, that's about as loving and unselfish as a person's capable of. So if I were you, I'd listen up. I'd pay attention to every single piece of advice she's giving you. And while I was at it, I'd thank my lucky stars that somebody in this world cares enough to keep you from getting yourself killed. Do you read me, Sharon?"

She looked stunned, as if she'd been slapped.

"Ray's big on lectures when he first meets people," I explained, hoping to smooth things over. I had enough to deal with without those two going at it. "You should have heard the one he gave me about my toilet. But he's right, Sharon. I did come here to save you from Barry. I did it because I love you—and because your son asked me to."

"Norman?" she squeaked, her lower lip quivering.

"Yes. He said he was suspicious of Barry, and, according to the evidence Detective Gillby is gathering, he had good reason to be. He made me promise that I'd watch out for you. I gave him my word that I would."

Sharon's heavily foundationed face cracked then, her tears staining her little Versace number.

"What have I done?" she sobbed, falling into my arms. "How could I have given my heart to a murderer?"

"Because you're a romantic," I said, patting her sympathetically. "You've given your heart freely over the years. Too freely."

"I didn't give it to you," she said wistfully. "I hated you."

"I hated you too," I reassured her. "More than I can express."

"I'm sure you did, although I probably hated you more than you hated me," she said. "I can't begin to describe how much I hated you."

"You don't have to," I said, "because I hated you with every—"

"Cool it, both of you," said Ray. "Barry's getting up from his table and he's not heading for the seafood buffet."

Sharon and I wheeled around.

"Where's he—"

I stopped when I realized that Barry must have spotted us, figured out we were on to him, and decided to beat it.

"He's running toward the marina," Sharon said, wiping away her tears and her drippy black mascara. "To his yacht."

"I'll tell security," said Ray. "They'll send the police after him."

"That's the ticket," I said. "Let them deal with Barry. The important thing is that *you're* safe, Sharon. Sharon?"

Her eyes had a glazed look, as if she'd finally snapped. Shaking her head, she yanked off her stiletto heels and flung them across the ground. "Can't run in these fucking things," she muttered.

"Sharon," I said, concerned about her mental state. More concerned that usual. "What are you doing?"

"Going after that asshole," she said. "I've had it with men taking advantage of me, promising me the moon and leaving me with zippo. *I've had it!*"

I grabbed her. "You can't—"

"Oh, yes I can!" she said, prying herself loose. "You two sit back and wait for the police to catch him if that's what you want to do. But not me. No way. Bye-bye."

In her bare feet and skin-tight dress, Sharon took off in hot pursuit of Barry.

Obviously, Ray and I couldn't let her chase a murderer by herself. As we made a mad dash after both of them, I wondered how it was possible that we had come to Nassau to rescue my sister, and yet she had now put us in danger.

Chapter Twenty-nine

Fortunately, the marina was lit up like a proverbial Christmas tree, the maze of docks relatively easy to navigate. As we were tearing after Barry, I couldn't help but notice how turquoise the water was, even at night, and how clear.

There was, of course, a bit of consternation among the diners at the seafood buffet as the three of us raced between the tables, en route to the marina, knocking over plates, glasses, a Baroness or two. As we zoomed past Mrs. Croft, she waved her straw hat at us, shouted "God bless America!" and passed out.

And then there was the tiny problem with the limbo. The leader of the calypso trio had just lowered the bar and sung the refrain of the ever-popular limbo song ("How *low* can you *go!*"), while a crowd of people had lined up to take their turn. The only way for us to get around them was to get ahead of them. Ray went first, slithering under the bar like a contortionist. I went second, crawling on all fours, which everyone thought was hilarious. And Sharon, complaining that her back was bothering her, simply removed the bar, which everyone thought was cheating.

Still, we managed to keep Barry in sight, although he was definitely gaining on us.

"His yacht is over there!" Sharon said breathlessly, pointing at the enormous phallic symbol called "Blue Waters," which also happened to be the name of the corporation that owned Heartily Hirshon, the Laundromat in Riviera Beach, and Barry's Boca manse.

We watched in frustration as he charged ahead and ultimately made it to his yacht. He climbed aboard the hundred-plus-foot vessel and untied the dock lines, then disappeared inside.

"If you're really determined to confront this guy," Ray told Sharon, "we've got to get onto that boat before he leaves the marina."

"Oh, I'm determined. Trust me," she said. "But he's not leaving so fast. He gave the captain the night off."

"Yeah, but he obviously has the keys with him," said Ray. "He must be planning to skipper the boat himself."

We hustled as fast as we could and had just gotten to the slip when we heard Barry power up the engines.

"No! He's going!" I said, as determined as Sharon was to make life miserable for the weasel, now that the adrenaline was pumping.

"Not without us," Ray vowed, clinging to the yacht's boarding ladders. "I'll climb up first, then pull you two up."

"I don't do ladders," Sharon insisted. "I have a thing."

"What 'thing'?" I demanded. *She* was the reason we were even contemplating this foolishness.

"A phobia," she said. "I'd take a Xanax, but my medications are back at Barry's."

"Then how do you expect us to get on this *Titanic*?" I shouted.

"No problem," said Ray as he grabbed Sharon's hands and lifted her petite body up onto the deck of the yacht. "Next." He reached for me. As my body is not petite like my sister's, it took him three tries before he managed to pull me up.

"Now what?" I said as I felt the yacht begin to move.

"I guess we're taking a little cruise," said Ray.

"Which means we're stuck on a boat with a killer," I said.

"Yeah, and he's stuck on a boat with us," said Ray. "It'll be three-against-one. I like the odds."

"What if he's got a gun?" said Sharon, reality sinking in. "He *has* been known to shoot people."

"No point in worrying about that now," said Ray. "We're under-way."

Sure enough, the gleaming white yacht was motoring out of the marina, into the harbor, out to sea.

"I can't believe we're doing this," Sharon moaned, as Ray opened the door to the main salon and waved us in.

"We're doing it all right," I muttered.

We stepped inside what was truly the most opulent, over-decorated room I'd ever seen, even for someone from Boca. The walls, the ceiling, the furnishings, the floor were all done in shades of bur-gundy—more bordello than boat—with enough gold accessories to rival the U.S. Mint. There were other grandiose touches as well—expensive artwork, sculptures, a gas-burning fireplace and, yes, a baby grand piano. Next door was a large formal dining room with seating for ten, and adjacent to it, a "galley" complete with granite counter-tops, a Sub-Zero refrigerator, and a butler's pantry. If there's one thing Barry Shiller isn't, it's quiet money, I thought.

"I bet he's up there," Ray whispered, after we'd spent too much time gawking and not enough time strategizing. We were now stand-ing at the base of a plushly carpeted spiral staircase, which appeared to connect the yacht's three interior levels.

"Or maybe he's down there," I suggested, pointing below to the staterooms.

"No, he's got to be on the upper deck if there's nobody else steer-ing the boat," Ray argued.

"Good guess," boomed a voice, causing us all to jump. It belonged to Barry, of course. "I wasn't really in the mood for company, but you might as well come up and make yourselves comfortable."

Like timid children, we mounted the stairs. When we reached the yacht's third level, Barry was there waiting for us, a glass of amber-colored liquid in one hand, a snappy little revolver in the other. There were still traces of scratch marks on his face, I noticed, courtesy of Sheldon. "Welcome to the sky lounge," he greeted us.

The aforementioned "sky lounge" was yet another adventure in excess, with unspeakably gorgeous views. Fitted with an auxiliary steering wheel, Barry could pilot the boat in complete luxury.

He told us to sit down. He had the gun at our noses, so we sat down.

"Well, Sharon, honey. Your sister decided to pay us a visit, huh?" he said, running his eyes over my body. "She doesn't have your fashion sense, but she's nothing to sneeze at."

Ray clenched his fist, testosterone coursing through his veins. "You'd better take a good look at her, buddy, because they don't have women we're you're going."

"Yeah? Where's that, Mr—"

"Scalley. Ray Scalley. You're going to prison, Shiller." He glanced at his watch. "The police are due at Lyford any minute."

"Too bad we'll miss 'em," said Barry, not heartbroken. "We're on our way to the Abacos. This baby can do forty knots, so we'll be there in no time."

"They'll find us wherever we are," I said as if I meant it. "They know what you did. Everybody knows what you did, you disgusting—"

"Hey, don't get your tits in an uproar, Deborah," said Barry, the essence of class. "We can talk about the unpleasant stuff later. Now I wanna brag about my yacht." He caressed the steering wheel. "I bought her a couple of years ago. Had her custom built in Lauderdale. She's loaded, naturally. She's even got a helicopter landing pad."

"As if any of this is yours," said Sharon. "You paid for it with funny money."

"Not true," he protested. "I earned every penny."

"Sure, you just forgot to pay taxes on those pennies," I said.

"Oh, grow up, all of you," said Barry. "A lot of people put their money in offshore bank accounts."

"Really? Do they kill their business partners too?" I said.

"I told you I didn't want to talk about that." He thought for a minute. "Since nobody's impressed by my yacht, let's talk about the Bahamas. Have you ever seen water like this? It's the prettiest blue water there is, so clear and clean you can look down and watch the sharks swimming around. Can't beat that, huh?"

"You're sick," Ray said. "You commit two murders and you act like you don't have a care in the world."

"He must be in denial," Sharon whispered to me. "Thank God I never had sex with him."

"That *is* lucky," I whispered in response.

"Who wants a drink?" Barry asked, continuing to play the host.

"I'll have a Perrier," said Sharon.

"The bar is over there. Help yourself," he said.

Sharon poured herself some fizzy water and returned to her chair.

"So tell us why you killed Hirshon and his nurse," Ray tried again. "You're planning to shoot us eventually. Why not entertain us in the meantime?"

"You're not gonna let up on me, are you?" Barry sighed. "How far back do you want me to go with the story?"

"To the day you and Jeffrey decided to sell vitamins," I said. "We're not interested in the slimy deals that went before."

He laughed. "Slimy to you, maybe, but your sister didn't seem to mind the kind of life I've been leading. Did you, Sharon, honey?"

"Shut up," she said.

"No, *you* shut up." He took a sip of his drink, then belched. Nice. "Hirshon and I went to college together, as Deborah discovered without much effort. We knew each other, but we weren't close friends, so we didn't stay in touch after graduation. About ten years ago, we ran into each other in the Abacos, where we're heading now. I used to make side trips from Nassau every once in awhile, and he used to take his boat over from Stuart for long weekends."

"So you did hatch the plan while you were throwing back a couple of Goombay Smashes," I said, recalling my earlier theory.

"They were Yellow Birds, but you're close enough," Barry conceded. "Hirshon told me he was a cardiologist in Stuart. I told him I was a lawyer in Boca. He mentioned that some of the doctors in town were selling private-label vitamins to their patients. I suggested he do it too. He said he didn't have the money to make vitamins. I said, why don't we go in on the deal as fifty-fifty partners? I was willing to put up the cash, oversee the manufacturing, and funnel the business through my corporation, if he would be the front man, hype the product through his medical practice, and handle sales of the pills to his patients. He loved the idea."

"I bet he especially loved the fact that the profits would go straight into a Bahamian bank account, where the IRS couldn't touch them," said Ray.

"Yeah. That part was key," said Barry. "He didn't really want to be bothered with the product unless he could make a killing on it."

"*You* ought to know about making a killing," Sharon hissed.

"How did Joan Sheldon get in on the act?" I asked.

Barry shrugged. "She was a pain in the ass, always sucking up to Hirshon. But he liked her, said we could trust her, and offered to cut her a piece of his share. I didn't mind as long as she kept her mouth shut."

"So what went wrong?" Ray said.

"Nothing. Not for years," said Barry. "Then all of a sudden, Hirshon came to me and tried to muscle me into changing the deal. The guy had balls, I'll give him that."

"How did he want to change the deal?" I said.

"He thought we should go sixty-forty, since *his* name was on the vitamins and people only bought them because of *him*. Greedy bastard. He said if I didn't go along with him, he'd tell the FDA that the vitamins were bogus, that I was behind the scam, and that he only found out about it by accident. I couldn't let that happen, so I killed him. And when Joan started putting the squeeze on me, I killed her too."

"Wait," Ray said. "Go back a second. Hirshon was going to tell the FDA he found out about *what* by accident?"

"Yeah. And what do you mean the vitamins were bogus?" said Sharon. She, like my mother, had been a heavy user.

"Just what I said. The vitamins were bogus. Vitamin E is an oil and is usually sold in transparent softgels. But we sold ours in capsules, as a powder. Bet you can't guess why."

"Joan claimed it was because some of Jeffrey's elderly patients were oil-intolerant and he wanted what was best for them," I said.

"Joan was a good liar. We sold our vitamins as a powder so we could fill the capsules with sand."

"Sand?" said all three of us at once.

"Sand. Vitamins are expensive, kids. You put sand in the capsules, you can mark 'em up like crazy and make a hefty profit, buy a yacht, a house at Lyford, whatever."

"You're telling me that my mother and I have been swallowing *sand?"* said Sharon, whose complexion was turning an odd color.

"It's harmless," said Barry. "Comes right out in the bowl with everything else you eat."

"You gross pig," Sharon said angrily, then tossed the contents of her drink at him.

The Perrier landed in his eyes, and the surprise of the gesture distracted him, allowing the gun to slip out of his hand, onto the floor.

Ray scrambled for it while Barry was still trying to clear his vision.

"Whoops. Looks like you lost something," said Ray as he held the revolver against Barry's temple. "Now, how about turning this tugboat around and taking us back to Lyford?"

Barry laughed mockingly. "I don't think so, pal. This is *my* tugboat and I'm taking her to the Abacos."

Ray pressed the gun deeper into the side of Barry's head. "Not if I shoot you first."

"Go ahead," Barry goaded him. "Then the three of you will be up a creek without a paddle. You don't know the waters of the Bahamas, do you, sport?"

"What's there to know?" said Ray. "Your yacht has more electronics than Radio Shack. I'm sure I can figure out how to get us back to the marina."

Barry moved away from the steering wheel. "Here. Have at it."

"Sit down," Ray ordered, tightening his grip around the handle of the gun.

"Can't. Gotta stretch my legs."

Before Ray could stop him, Barry bolted up from his seat and lunged for the gun. They wrestled over it, while Sharon and I stood by helplessly.

And then a shot was fired.

I held my breath, waiting for one of them to get up, waiting to see which *one* of them would get up. When it was Barry who emerged with the weapon, I rushed over to Ray.

"My God! Your leg!" I screamed. "He shot you in the leg!"

"I'll be okay," he said, grimacing in pain. "I'm just disabled, for the moment."

Sharon knelt beside Ray too. "I brought some Advil, but it's at Barry's house, with the Xanax," she said apologetically.

"Women," Barry mused. "They're useless creatures, huh?"

"You're a truly evil man," I said, shaking with rage. I was about to throw myself on him, pound him with my fists, gun or no gun, when I was nearly blinded by an intensely bright light coming off the water.

"What the fuck's that?" said Barry, shielding his eyes.

"It's the police!" Ray said, weary but jubilant, having spotted the official-looking boat motoring toward us.

"It must be ten o'clock!" I exhulted. "Reggie, bless his heart, must have sent them!"

"Which means that Deborah and Sharon and I are safe," Ray glared at Barry. "And *you're* history, buddy."

"Wrong." Barry jabbed the gun into Sharon's back and said, "You came to Nassau to rescue your precious sister, right, Deborah?"

"Damn right," I answered defiantly.

"Then do as I tell you or she gets a bullet through her flat-as-a-board chest."

Sharon flinched, either at his remark concerning an aspect of her anatomy about which she was extremely sensitive, or because he was stabbing her with the gun. The really awful part was that the scene I had conjured up in my imagination was coming true, I realized— that with the police's arrival, Barry had become desperate, he no longer had anything to lose, and he intended to take Sharon down with him.

"I want both women on the upper deck with me. Now!" he commanded. "Scalley stays here. To bleed to death, with any luck."

"I'm not leaving him," I said, clutching his hand.

"Oh, yes you are." Barry jammed the gun into one of Sharon's kidneys.

"Go with him," Ray urged, his voice growing faint.

"I don't want to," I said, my eyes pricking with tears. "You risked your life for me. There's no way I can—"

"Go with him, Deborah," he said hoarsely. "Please."

With the police boat drawing closer, Barry was frantic, out of control. He pulled me away from Ray, onto my feet, and threatened to kill Sharon on the spot if I didn't follow his orders.

I was paralyzed with conflict—should I go with my sister or stay with Ray?—and was, therefore, no help to either of them. Sensing my anguish, Ray nodded at me, once again reassuring me that he would be all right, that the three of us would be all right. "Go," he whispered.

"I'm not mad at you anymore," I said. "About Holly."

"Go, Deborah."

"I'm going, I'm going," I said reluctantly.

I took a final look back at Ray as Barry shoved Sharon and me out the door of the sky lounge, up onto what was a spectacular sundeck and entertaining area at the stern of the yacht.

"Now what, you dirtbag?" I challenged Barry, my fury overriding my terror.

"We're gonna stand right over here, where the cops can get a good view of us." He pushed us up against the yacht's shiny brass railing, high above the swirling sea. I suspected that Sharon's fear of ladders was nothing compared to what she was experiencing at that moment. "You. Stand on this side of me," he shouted, waving me to his left. "You. Stand on my right side. My better side." He laughed demoniacally as he pulled Sharon to him and moved the gun to the front of her body, the barrel targeted at her heart.

"Police!" came a voice over a loud speaker. "The owner of this vessel is under arrest!"

"If you arrest me, one of these bitches dies and her sister gets to watch!" Barry yelled back.

"Lay the weapon down!" the policeman warned. "I repeat: Lay the weapon down!"

"Up your ass!" was Barry's pithy retort.

"Again, you are under arrest!" said the policeman.

"Again, up your ass!" said Barry. "I'm holding these women hostage, do you understand what that means? Unless I get a helicopter, a pilot, and a couple of cases of scotch, they're dead!"

"You are under arrrest, Mr. Shiller!" was the cop's response.

God, this could go on for hours, I thought. One of those ridiculous standoffs. I had to do something. Sharon and I had to do something. We had to act, had to take charge of our own lives. After years of estrangements, we were finally in the same boat—literally. If we couldn't work together as a team at a time like this, we never would. The question was: What could we do as a team? We'd never been a team. We'd been enemies. That's all we knew how to be.

I felt utterly powerless until my words triggered an idea.

Enemies! I thought. Bingo!

I quickly began crafting a plot, a script, a *breakdown*—a scene for which Sharon and I would need no rehearsal.

Yes, I decided. Yes. I will provoke her into a big fight, the battle of the century, the spat to end all spats. Our bickering will turn violent. Well, not horribly violent, only a little slap, a little hair-pulling, something along those lines. And then Barry will just happen to get caught in our crossfire, taking a punch that will send him hurtling over the railing.

It was worth a try, wasn't it?

"Sharon," I said while Barry was bartering with the cops. "This whole situation is your fault. If you weren't such a ditz about men, so desperate to get married, so obsessed with snagging another husband, Ray wouldn't have gotten shot."

"A 'ditz,' you called me?"

"A ditz. A bubble-head. A dim bulb. Take your pick."

I waited. She didn't say anything. If we'd been on the phone, she would have hung up on me.

"Actually, I have been overly focused on getting married," she conceded, "and I swear I'm going to change if we escape this nightmare. I'm so grateful to you and to your friend Ray, so ashamed that I put you both in jeopardy. I can't tell you how sorry I am, Deborah."

Huh? Who wanted to be told how *sorry* she was? I wanted her to have a hissy fit, to be the witchy Sharon I'd always known and hated!

Okay, I told myself. Calm down. Just think of something else that'll push her buttons.

"Of course, men aren't your only problem," I said. "Your most unattractive quality is your petty resentment of me and my accomplishments. When I was working in daytime television, you made nothing but snide remarks about *From This Day Forward,* even though I was proud of it, even though I gave a hundred percent to it, even though the show enriches the lives of millions of viewers, as opposed to *your* business, which enriches no one but *you.*"

"You're criticizing my wedding business?"

"Yes, if you can *call* it a business." I was being cruel, sure, but I had to get a rise out of her. The trouble was, she wasn't rising.

"I'm sorry if I wasn't supportive of your career, Deborah," she said. "As your older sister, I should have been."

"Sorry? What is all this *sorry?*" Obviously, I wasn't being cruel enough. "And then there's poor Norman," I said. "Look what a mess you've made of his life."

"Poor Norman?" Her nostrils flared. There was fire in the old girl yet.

"Yes, Sharon. You haven't exactly been a model mother."

"What?" She looked horrified. "Don't you ever talk to me about being a mother."

"What's the matter? Does the truth hurt?" I said, egging her on. "You know damn well that your dead-end relationships have been devastating to his emotional health."

"How dare *you* tell *me* how to raise my son!" she said indignantly. "You're a lonely spinster who couldn't produce a child unless you went to one of those sperm banks and had them inject you with a turkey baster."

"Is that so?" I said. "Well, I'd take a turkey baster over any of *your* ex-husbands, speaking of turkeys."

That did it. She batted Barry's arm away and slapped me across the face.

On cue, *I* hauled off and slapped *her* across the face.

Then she slapped me.

Then I slapped her.

Then she slapped me.

Then I slapped her.

Then we got more inventive.

She pulled my hair. "You jealous, pathetic—"

I kicked her in the shins. "You controlling, whining—"

Barry, meanwhile, was waving his gun wildly, hurling obscenities at us, and bobbing and weaving to stay out of our way.

He did not succeed.

"Why you—" Sharon reared back to sock me in the jaw but she swung high, I ducked, and the punch landed squarely and forcefully on Barry's Adam's apple (Sharon was short, remember), sending him sailing over the railing.

"Oh my God!" she cried as we leaned over the side of the yacht, in time to watch the body hit the water. "I killed him!"

"No, you didn't," I said. "He'll float around for a few minutes and then the police will fish him out."

"So I didn't commit a crime or anything?"

"No. You defended us, Sharon. That must be very empowering for you." I figured I'd let her take the credit. *I* knew who had saved whom.

She fluffed her hair. "Yes, it is empowering, now that you mention it. I got to *feel* like I killed him, even though I didn't kill him. Of course, he deserves to die. I certainly wouldn't be *crushed* if he died."

"Neither would I. By the way, I didn't mean to insult you before. I hope you won't hold a grudge."

"*Insult* me? How about the slapping and kicking and hair-pulling?"

"I didn't mean to hurt you, period. I was just pretending—trying to get you mad, so you'd knock Barry—" I stopped, exhaustion setting in when I imagined the long explanation that was necessary. "The important thing is, I think you're a terrific businesswoman and a wonderful mother."

"You do?"

"Absolutely."

"I appreciate that, Deborah. But how about when you called me a ditz? Were you pretending then too?"

"You know, we should talk about that some other time," I suggested. "Now, we should congratulate ourselves for surviving this ordeal. Let's wave goodbye to Barry and go tell Ray what's happened."

Sharon and I peered over the railing. Barry was making a big splash, his arms and legs flailing in all directions.

"Boy, he wasn't kidding about the water here. It really is gorgeous," she remarked.

"As clear as glass," I commented. "I can see the sharks swimming around, just the way he said. As a matter of fact, they're swimming around *him*."

"So much for Barry then," she replied.

"So much for Barry," I agreed. "Pass the tartar sauce."

Chapter Thirty

Ray was transported by helicopter to Princess Margaret Hospital in downtown Nassau. The bullet from Barry's gun had only grazed his upper thigh and the wound required stitches, not surgery, thank God, but he was advised to remain in the hospital overnight, where he was being given fluids, antibiotics, and painkillers, intravenously.

"It finally dawned on me that you're Deborah's carpenter," Sharon said as the two of us sat on either side of Ray's bed, taking turns fussing over him.

"I'm Deborah's carpenter, all right," he said, gazing at me with tender, loving eyes. Groggy, Demerol-induced eyes.

"My sister's a lucky girl," said Sharon. "She's actually found a man who isn't a shit."

Ray smiled. "No, *I'm* the lucky one," he said, then conked out, not to be heard from again for the rest of the night.

Not that his heavy slumber kept me from talking to him, from pouring out my heart to him. Soon after he had fallen asleep, after Sharon had tiptoed out of the room to let us have some privacy, I told him how much he meant to me. It was easy to say "I love you," knowing he couldn't hear me, knowing he couldn't tease me, knowing he couldn't say or do anything that would cause me to doubt my feelings for him. We had been through a lot together during the course of our brief friendship, and while I had fantasies of moving into his house on Seminole Street and settling into a life of domestic bliss with him, I was fully aware that I should practice what I'd preached to Sharon; that jumping into a new relationship may be romantic, exciting, dramatic, but it isn't always smart.

At some point, while I was sitting at Ray's bedside, contemplating my future, I fell asleep. Sharon woke me, gently shaking my shoulder, and suggested that we go back to Reggie's. (By this time, she had heard all about Reggie and Sabrina and Serena and the role they had played in her rescue, and was eager to meet them.)

"Ray wants you to get some rest," she said, attempting to coax me out of his room.

"How can you tell?" I said. "He's out cold."

"I can tell from the way he looks at you when he *isn't* out cold," she said. "He's got it bad, Deborah."

"You think so?"

She nodded. "I've been married three times with a dozen more near-misses. None of them ever looked at me like he looks at you. Does that answer your question?"

I rose from my chair and hugged her. "Thanks for the vote of confidence. I'm kind of crazy about Ray myself, but I'm not rushing into anything."

"Neither am I," she said. "Ever again."

I smiled. "Can I have that in writing?"

Before we left the hospital, the policeman who had interviewed us after coming aboard the yacht updated us on Barry's condition. (He, too, was in the hospital, recovering from a couple of shark bites and an irregular heartbeat.) The officer also filled us in on Barry's arrest.

It turned out that while Reggie had, indeed, summoned the police when Ray and I hadn't shown up at the entrance to the Yacht Club at ten o'clock, Detective Gillby had summoned them too and asked them to issue what's called a provisional arrest warrant.

"The U.S. has an extradition treaty with the Bahamas," he explained, his manner formal but not unfriendly. "Which means that your law enforcement officers contact us if someone living or staying in our country is under arrest in the States, and we incarcerate the person here. Four to six weeks later, after the papers have been filed with the embassy and the International Extradition Department of Justice, both in Washington, D.C., a U.S. marshal flies down to get the prisoner and brings him back to the U.S., in this case, to Miami. He is then transferred to your local district to await trial."

"So Barry will be licking his wounds in your jail for a while," Sharon mused. "He should enjoy that."

"Did Detective Gillby indicate what prompted the warrant for Mr. Shiller?" I asked, still puzzled by the timing of Gillby's decision to move forward with an arrest.

"What I have been told is that Mr. Shiller is wanted for the murders of two Florida residents, a doctor and a nurse, and that it was a letter found in the nurse's bank—in a safety deposit box—that implicated Mr. Shiller in the two homicides."

"A letter," I repeated.

"It must have been one of those 'If something happens to me, the person responsible is . . . blah blah blah,'" said Sharon.

"Must have been," I agreed.

"Now, I'd be happy to escort you both to your lodgings," said the policeman. "And if there's anything else I can do—"

"There is," Sharon interrupted. "All my luggage is at Mr. Shiller's house in Lyford Cay."

"I will see that it is delivered to you by noon tomorrow," he said agreeably.

"By noon?" Sharon said, incredulous. "I've got three Louis Vuitton bags sitting in that place. I need my clothes, not to mention my jewelry, my medications, and, most importantly, my makeup. I can't go out in public without foundation."

"You can wear a veil," I said, then told the policeman to take us away.

Reggie and Sabrina and Serena were up waiting for us when we arrived at Reggie's Bahamian Inn at close to midnight. Sharon extended her hand to each of them, as if she were the queen and they her loyal subjects, and thanked them for their part in the rescue operation.

"It was your sister's idea, my lady," said Sabrina. "We just helped."

"My sister is very creative," said Sharon. "She used to write for a soap opera."

I smiled at her, at the pride in her voice when she spoke of me, at the lack of an edge in her voice. Maybe good things really do come out of every evil, I thought.

"You must be hungry as well as tired," Reggie said to us.

"Famished," said Sharon.

"Starving," I said, remembering with longing the two shrimp I'd swiped at the seafood buffet.

"We'll bring you some dinner from the restaurant next door," Sabrina offered. "They're closed, but we know the owners. They'll make up something for you."

"That would be divine, Sabrina," said Sharon. "Perhaps you could deliver the dinners to our rooms. If I don't lie down soon, I'm going to fall down."

"What *rooms* are you talking about, Sharon?" I said. "They only had one room available when Ray and I checked in, and he and I were planning to share it. I guess you and I will be sharing it now."

"One room?" she said, looking put out.

"One bed," I said and marched her up the stairs.

"This is it?" she said when I opened the door.

"Yup. There's a king-sized bed, see? Plenty of room for the two of us."

"Yes, but where's the bathroom? And what's with the curry?" She wrinkled her nose.

"The bathroom is in the hall. The curry is from the restaurant down the street. Look, this isn't Lyford, Sharon, but it's going to have to do."

She nodded. "You're right. I'm acting like a princess. I should be grateful that I'm still breathing, although I'm not thrilled about having to wear an expensive Versace dress to sleep."

"I'll lend you a T-shirt."

After we had changed our clothes, there was a knock on the door. Serena was standing there with a tray on which she had placed napkins, utensils, bottled water and two glasses, and two dinner plates covered with aluminum foil.

"Oh, Serena. You're so thoughtful to bring us these," I said. "I can't thank you enough for what you and your family have done."

"Yes, you can, my lady," she said. "You can tip us very generously upon your check-out."

I said I would and closed the door. Sharon and I sat at the foot of the bed and devoured our curried chicken with rice and peas in five minutes flat.

"That wasn't bad," she said. "Or am I so tired I wouldn't be able to tell?"

"It wasn't bad. *And* you're so tired you wouldn't be able to tell." I laughed.

After we visited the bathroom (Sharon wasn't crazy about touching the community bar of soap, let alone using it, and she was "positively lost," she said, without her unwaxed dental floss), we got into bed and turned out the lights.

Naturally, the second we closed our eyes, the British couple started yammering and the German couple started arguing, and the walls were so thin between the rooms that sleep was out of the question. As a result, we lay there wide awake in the dark, back to back under the covers, as far apart as we could get without falling off the bed.

"Deborah?" said Sharon.

"Yes?"

"Do you ever think about Daddy?"

"Sure. Do you?"

"All the time. I miss him. But then I missed him even when he was alive."

"I know. He was a great guy, but he was a little distant."

"He acted less distant with you."

"Only because I turned myself inside out to make him laugh. When he laughed, he was *there,* if you see what I mean."

"Yes, but he never laughed at *my* jokes. I once asked him why, and he said it was because my personality was different than yours, that I was more serious. He said we were both special children, but I was convinced he loved you more."

"Sharon." I flipped over in the bed. I was now staring at the back of her head. "I was just as hungry for his love as you were."

"You were?"

"Of course. Even Mom wished he were more demonstrative."

"How do you know?"

"She always had that look, as if she yearned for more but would rather die than ask for it. I suppose that's why she feels so liberated since the heart attack. She almost did die. Now she seems to have decided that she'd better grab someone who *is* demonstrative, before it's too late."

"You're referring to this Fred person she's dating."

"He's a sweetheart, Sharon. Not a matinee idol, but a kind, decent, *accessible* man."

"Good. She deserves to be happy."

"We all do."

"That's true. After this thing with Barry, I see that I let my relationship with Daddy turn me into a needy, desperate woman. I'm through with that, Deborah. I'm not chasing men anymore. I'm going to concentrate on my family and my work—and my clothes and hair."

I laughed.

She shushed me.

"What?"

"Listen."

"I don't hear anything."

"Exactly. Our neighbors have finally taken a break."

"Hallelujah! Maybe we can actually get some sleep."

I rolled over to my original position in my corner of the mattress and closed my eyes. But Sharon wasn't finished.

"I'm really excited for you, Deborah. About Ray, I mean."

"Thanks. I know you'll find someone too, Sharon. When the time comes."

"When do you think the time will come?"

I couldn't believe my ears. "Soon, Sharon. Soon. Let's go to sleep, okay?"

She yawned. "Goodnight, Deborah."

"Goodnight."

I reached my arm out across the bed and made contact with her bony little hip. I let my hand rest there.

"Lovyu," she mumbled, her face in the pillow.

"What was that?" I asked.

"Love you," she said only slightly more audibly.

"Love you too," I said and drifted off.

Chapter Thirty-one

By one o'clock on Monday afternoon, Sharon had gotten her luggage, Reggie, Sabrina, and Serena had gotten their tips, and Ray had gotten sprung from the hospital. He was told to stay off his feet for a week or so, until his stitches were removed, but, with the aid of a cane and his two extremely solicitous traveling companions, he managed to make it on and off the plane without great difficulty.

After the Lincoln Town Car picked us up at the airport in Fort Lauderdale, we headed straight for Boca, to drop Sharon off at her house. As the limo was pulling up to the gate, Ray remarked that Broken Sound, her upscale golf community, reminded him of BallenIsles, his brother's upscale golf community.

"I should fix you and Doug up," he said offhandedly. "You'd probably get along great."

Before I could muzzle him—hadn't Sharon pledged to go manless, at least for a little while?—she leaned over me in the backseat of the car, grabbed his hand, and, unable to keep herself from drooling, said, "You have a brother?"

"Sure, didn't Deborah tell you?" said Ray as we wound our way to Sharon's driveway. "His name's Doug. He's the 'Douglas' in Douglas's Menswear. You've probably seen his stores."

"Seen them? My ex-husband Lester used to shop in them. Before he switched to women's clothes, that is."

Ray glanced at me.

"Don't ask," I said.

"So *that* Douglas is your brother?" Sharon persisted.

"One and the same," said Ray. "You and he have a lot in common, now that I think about it."

I buried my head in my hands.

"Like what?" asked Sharon. We had already arrived at her house, and the driver was in the process of unloading the trunk and depositing her luggage on her front steps, but she wasn't going anywhere. Not now.

"Well, you both live in fancy golf communities," said Ray. "You both run your own businesses. You're both divorced with teenaged sons."

"Douglas has a son Norman's age?" she said, fluffing her hair.

Ray nodded proudly. "Phil's a freshman at Duke. Good school. Good kid."

"My, isn't that nice," Sharon mused. "Does your brother look like you, Ray?"

"No, he looks like *me*," I said impatiently. "Look, Sharon, I really want to get Ray back to Stuart. He should be in bed. You understand, don't you?"

"Oh, absolutely," she said, gathering her handbag and sweater. "I know I've thanked you two a million times for everything you did, but here comes a million-and-one: Thank you, from the bottom of my heart." She kissed me, then Ray, and exited the car. "Goodbye!" she called out through our open window, blowing us more kisses.

"Good-bye!" I said. "Good luck with the Glasserstein wedding!"
And then I told the driver to step on it.

When we finally reached Ray's house, he was fast asleep with his
head on my shoulder. I roused him, and the driver helped me get
him inside the house. I asked the man to wait while I undressed Ray
and put him to bed.

"You're not staying?" he said, his lids so heavy he could barely see
me.

"I can't," I said, stroking his arm. "I've got to go back to the
cottage and relieve Fred. It was sweet of him to stay there while I
was away, but I don't want to take advantage of his generosity—or
incur Melinda's wrath. Besides, I'm hoping he'll zip me over to my
mother's, so I can tell her what happened before she reads about it
in the newspaper."

"Have you made up your mind?" he said.

"About what, Ray?"

"About you and me."

I smiled. "You mean about our going steady?"

He nodded. "I want us to be a couple. I want us to go out every
Saturday night, automatically."

"Sort of like a standing appointment with the manicurist."

"Exactly. The rest of the week we can stay here."

"Ray. I'm not moving into your house. Not so soon. We need to
take this slowly. We only had our first kiss a couple of days ago. I've
never even met your friends, your boss, your brother."

"But you love me."

"And what makes you so sure, wise guy?"

"You admitted it last night in the hospital. I heard you. It was
quite a speech."

"Ray Scalley! You let me think you were asleep!"

"Sorry, but I did squeeze the *L* word out of you, didn't I? The
point is, you love me and I love you, so why should we live apart?"

I bent down and placed my cheek against his. He hadn't shaven
in days—we were way beyond a five o'clock shadow here—but it
didn't matter in the least. "Because it will be wonderful between us,
whether we live apart or not," I said. "Wonderful getting to know
each other. Wonderful sharing experiences. Wonderful building a

history together. And someday, if we still feel the way we do now, I *will* move in and we'll get married and spend the rest of our lives riding around on your motorcycle. Okay?"

There was no response.

I picked my head up and looked at him. His eyes were closed and his mouth was hanging open.

"Oh, I get it." I laughed. "You're playing your little game again, just so I'll make all kinds of incriminating declarations about—"

I was interrupted by—drowned out by—his snoring.

"See you tomorrow," I whispered, kissed his forehead, and slipped out of the room.

Fred was sitting on my bed playing solitaire when I staggered wearily into the cottage at nearly ten-thirty.

"Who's winning?" I asked.

"Debbie! You're back!" he said, jumping up to give me a hug. "How was the trip?"

"Well, there were a few glitches, but basically I accomplished what I set out to accomplish. Sharon's safe and sound in Boca; Ray is bruised but alive in Stuart; and Barry's shark-bitten and laid up in a hospital in Nassau, soon to be moved to a local jail cell."

"Doesn't sound like much of a vacation."

"It wasn't, although I did get to do the limbo. How was everything here? Any problems?"

"Just one: I hated lying to your mother while you were gone."

"Then let's stop the lying right now. If you don't mind running me over to her house—my car's dead—I'll break the news of 'Sharon and Deborah's Excellent Adventure' in person, and that will be that."

"What if she hates me?"

"She won't. I'm willing to bet that once she gets over the shock of it all and realizes how instrumental you were in helping her daughters, she'll be very grateful."

"From your mouth to God's ears. Are you aware that your mother has eyes the color of the—"

"—Florida Marlins' uniforms, yes, and what a beautiful analogy you've come up with, Fred, but it's late and she goes to bed at eleven, so I suggest we get going."

D eborah! Fred! What in the world are you two doing here at this time of night?" said my mother, looking pleased but a little bewildered by our appearance.

"Can we come in?" I said tentatively.

"Of course." She ushered us into the living room and offered us some tea, which I refused but Fred did not. He did not refuse the cholesterol-free macaroons she offered him either.

"Well, I'm back at the cottage," I began. "And since the Pontiac is out of commission again, Fred was kind enough to drive me over here. So I could have a visit with you."

"Deborah, dear. I can see that you're upset. You and Ray had an argument and you left his house in a huff, is that it?"

"No. Ray and I are very happy, Mom. Happier than I imagined. The truth is, I wasn't staying at his—"

"This is so exciting, having both my daughters in the throes of passion at the same time. Which reminds me: I haven't heard a peep from Sharon since she and Barry flew to the Bahamas. I wonder if he's gotten down on his hands and knees and proposed to her yet."

"Oh, he's gotten down on his hands and knees all right," I said, envisioning the police's strip search after they fished him out of the water. "But the marriage plans are definitely off."

"Off? Did you talk to your sister?"

"Yes." I took a deep breath. It was now or never. "Do you, by any chance, have your nitroglycerin handy, Mom?"

She arched an eyebrow. "Why are you asking me that? What's really going on, Deborah? Give it to me straight."

I gave it to her straight, minus the part where Sharon and I slapped each other. When I had finished, she was speechless.

"Mom? Say something. Please."

"Yes, Lenore. Say something," Fred urged, fanning her with his paper napkin.

"I can't. I'm still taking this in," she replied, her face becoming flushed and blotchy. I prayed her blood pressure wasn't going through the roof.

"You're telling me that Sharon wanted to marry a man who *murdered* two people?" she said finally, trying to make sense of what I'd recounted.

"Yes, Mom. That's what I'm telling you."

"And that Dr. Hirshon, my cardiologist, was prescribing vitamins that were *sand?*"

"Yes, Mom. But Barry said—and I quote—'It's harmless. Comes right out in the bowl with everything else you eat.' Such a charmer."

"And that nobody in this town—a town where everyone knows everything about everybody—suspected the doctor of being a *con man?*"

"I'm afraid he fooled a lot of people, Mom. He and Barry."

She retreated into her speechless mode. Fred asked her if she wanted him to call 911. She said, "Not yet."

"Look, Mom. The great thing is that the bad guys got theirs and Sharon and I are safe," I said in an effort to calm her. "What's more, after surviving such a traumatic experience, she and I are close now, closer than we've ever been. That's what you wanted, isn't it? For the two of us to end our bickering and forge a real bond? Well, that's what we've done."

"And nearly got yourselves killed in the process."

"True, but maybe we needed more than a lecture from you to get our act together. Maybe we needed a brush with death to make us realize how much we care about each other. Boy, you would have been proud of us out there on Barry's yacht, Mom. When push came to shove—and I do mean *shove*—we stuck together."

She sighed. "So there won't be any more silly spats between you?"

"Nope. We're through with that kind of childish behavior."

"No more nonsense about *her* men and *your* career and whatever else you fought over?"

"No more. We've achieved closure on our issues."

"No more lying to me?" She glared at Fred.

"Not unless Debbie authorizes it," he replied, winking at me.

She reached for the tissue tucked inside the sleeve of her blouse and blew her nose.

"Are you crying, Mom?"

"Yes," she said, dabbing at her eyes. "I was thinking ahead to Thanksgiving."

"Why? It's eight months away."

"I know, but it's my favorite holiday. I was picturing the whole family sitting together, enjoying the turkey and the stuffing and the gravy and the mashed potatoes and the creamed onions and the—"

"I'm up on the menu, Mom," I said, so exhausted at that moment that I wasn't sure I could wait for her to get to the string beans, the biscuits, and the apple pie with vanilla ice cream. "Where are you going with this?"

"Where I'm *going*, as you put it, is that if you and Sharon really have kissed and made up, this will be the first Thanksgiving in memory that my girls will be on speaking terms. That's reason enough to look forward to it, isn't it?"

"Yes, it is," I agreed. "I'm looking forward to it too."

"So am I," Fred chimed in. "You both will love my daughters and their families, and vice versa. If not, we'll all make the best of an awkward situation."

I slept until noon. I might have slept longer had I not heard the commotion outside my door. I peeked out the window and saw a handful of reporters and photographers and TV satellite trucks camped outside. Obviously, the sheriff's office had gone public with the story of Barry's capture.

I crept into the kitchen, not wanting the media to see me in my ratty nightgown, and called Ray.

"How's the leg?" I said when he answered.

"I miss you," he said nonresponsively. "When are you coming over to babysit me? I've already been on the phone to the office, to tell them I'm taking the rest of the week off, so I'm free to just lie here and have you wait on me."

"Which I'll do with pleasure. But first, there's the matter of these people who are hanging around the cottage. Would you happen to have heard if there's an article about our escapades in the paper to-day?"

"Front page in the *Stuart News* and the *Palm Beach Post*. My neighbor brought both papers to show me. You're famous."

"Not again."

"Yeah, but this time you're the hero. Both Frank Gillby and Avery Armstrong are quoted in the articles as saying how you helped break the case. Gillby credits you with tipping them off to the link between Hirshon and Shiller. 'A courageous woman,' he calls you in the *Post* piece. 'With an inquiring mind.' "

I laughed. "I'll have to thank him, thank everybody involved in the investigation. Did the articles mention you, I hope?"

"Yup. They both misspelled my name though. One called me Roy, and the other dropped the *e* in Scalley."

"Some nerve. Any other juicy tidbits in the articles?"

"There's the stuff about Joan Sheldon; how she left a long letter in a safety deposit box with chapter and verse about the vitamin scam, the Bahamian connection, the works."

"Poor Joan. Nursing is such an admirable profession. Why did she have to get greedy?"

"Who knows. Speaking of nurses, there's a great quote in the *Stuart News* from a nurse at Martin Memorial. She wouldn't let them use her name, naturally, but when she was asked if she was surprised that Jeffrey Hirshon had been leading a double life, she said: 'Not really. He *was* a cardiologist, after all.' "

"I guess she's had a few run-ins with cardiologists."

"No kidding. So am I going to see you today?"

"Absolutely. I do have to get my car serviced though. Yours is still here too, don't forget. Maybe I can have them towed on the same flatbed truck, right next to each other. How's that for togetherness?"

"Not bad. But I'd rather you were here right next to me on *my* flat bed."

"Then how about this: if my mother's not using the Delta 88, I'll borrow it and stop by later."

"Great. Hey, before you hang up, I want to tell you something."

"What?"

"My leg hurts like a son-of-a-bitch. I'm missing a whole week of work during our busiest season. And whatever's wrong with my car will probably cost me a healthy chunk of my salary to fix. But—and here's the important part—I'm so happy I don't know what to do with myself."

"Must be those drugs they gave you in the hospital," I teased.

"I'm serious, Deborah. All of a sudden, I'm waking up in the morning with a ridiculous grin on my face and a sort of gut feeling that, after the long, tough stretch I've had, it's finally gonna be *my* time."

I smiled, knowing just what he was talking about.

Epilogue

We were expecting twenty-two people for Thanksgiving—a big crowd compared to our usual holiday gatherings. Sharon wasn't the least bit stressed out about it though, as her dining room table comfortably accommodated twenty-six, and her party-planning skills were well-honed, thanks to the hundreds of weddings she'd coordinated over the years.

In fact, it was as a result of one of her weddings—the Teitelbaum wedding, to be specific—that she met Doug Scalley, Ray's older brother, a scant ten days after our return from Nassau. As chance would have it, she had accompanied the groom to Doug's Boca store in Mizner Park, in search of suitable attire for the forthcoming nuptials. While the groom was in the dressing room, trying on tuxedos, and she was at the counter, checking out cummerbunds, Doug, himself, put in an appearance at the store. Noticing his physical resemblance to Ray, she asked if he was, indeed, Ray Scalley's brother. When he said yes, she pounced. They'd been hot and heavy ever since.

At first, Ray and I were a little queasy about their relationship, given Sharon's previous fiascos. But as the weeks wore on, we resigned ourselves to it, decided to take the position that she and Doug were adults and that whatever happened between them was *their* problem.

Besides, Ray and I were so much in love, so consumed with each other, that it wasn't hard to lighten up and let our siblings run their own lives. I was still living in the cottage on Hutchinson Island and Ray was still living in his house in downtown Stuart, but we were beginning to discuss marriage, so certain were we that we had a future together, so certain was I that I had found my partner.

On the professional front, I no longer needed the keeper's job with the Historical Society and was free to move out of the cottage whenever I chose. You see, I had gone back into the biz, back into the wacky world of daytime drama.

It was Helen who had set things in motion, naturally.

"It's Woody," she said when she called one night. "Our old boss has just signed on as the head writer of *Santa Monica,* a new soap produced out of L.A. Rumor has it, there's a huge budget for the show. They're launching in September. Interested?"

Interested? How could I not be? I'd assumed that Woody would resurface; it had just been a question of when. But to hear that he was on top again, heading up a new soap, a big-budget soap at that, was better than I'd hoped for. On the other hand, *Ray* was better than I'd hoped for, and there was no way I was trading my happiness with him for another crack at an Emmy. "I'm interested in the show and it would be fun working for Woody again, but my home is in Florida now, Helen. I'm not going back to New York."

"Who asked you to? Tell Woody you want to be a script writer instead of a breakdown writer. Script writers live everywhere. We never laid eyes on ours, remember?"

"Yes, but I don't have any experience writing scripts."

"Please. You could write them in your sleep. And another thing to keep in mind: script writers make more money than breakdown writers. Look, here's Woody's number at the studio, Deborah. You can do what you want, but I'm calling him the second we hang up."

I called him the next day. I had the job the day after that. I sold the Pontiac the day after that and bought a Lexus the day after that.

My mother was enjoying equally good fortune. She felt well enough to resume her work as a mediator, and returned to small claims court with renewed vigor. Her friendship with Fred continued to surprise and delight her. He had become such a devoted companion to her that she invited his four daughters to fly down from Michigan and join us for Thanksgiving, along with their husbands and children.

Even Norman was bringing a guest—a fellow cadet whose parents were both in rehab and, consequently, not up to cooking a turkey with all the trimmings.

Yes, we were going to be twenty-two for dinner on Thanksgiving. We were going to eat ourselves sick and laugh at each other's jokes and watch entirely too much football. I had every reason to approach the occasion with genuine optimism for a change.

Ray and I were the last ones to arrive at Sharon's McMansion that fateful Thursday afternoon. She greeted us at the door with hugs and kisses, and told me she adored my dress. (It was the same *shmatte* I'd worn to my mother's birthday party back in February, the one she'd likened to a tablecloth.)

Doug came up right behind her and gave Ray and me a rousing hello. He was a taller, thinner, more animated version of his younger brother, as lively as Ray was laconic—a sort of Ray on amphetamines. I was very fond of him, but he was a bit of a provocateur and a tad smug—the kind of person best taken in small doses.

"Everything looks lovely, Sharon," I said. She had decorated the house with Pilgrim memorabilia as well as Horns of Plenty.

She thanked me, asked me how the job was working out, and hurried off to the kitchen to check on the food.

Ray and I joined the others in Sharon's family room, where my mother introduced us to Fred's relatives. His daughters seemed pleasant enough, although one of them whispered to me that Fred's will was uncontestable, and that neither my sister nor I would get a dime in the event that he married my mother and then kicked the bucket. I nodded and moved on to Fred's sons-in-law, each of whom was engrossed in the football game on Sharon's big-screen TV and rather apathetic about our getting acquainted. As for Fred's grandchildren, they were outside swimming in the pool, with Norman and his friend serving as lifeguards.

"Who's playing?" I asked Ray. "Is it your Gators, honey?"

"No." He smiled tolerantly. "Florida's a college team. The pros are the ones that play on Thanksgiving Day. This is the Dolphins-Patriots game."

Just then, Doug bounced into the room, picked up the remote control from the coffee table, and started channel surfing.

"Hey!" said Ray, looking irritated. "We're watching the game."

Doug winked at me. "My brother and his football."

" 'My brother' nothing. I'm not the only one who's into it." Ray glanced at the others, but they were remaining neutral. "We all want to see the game, Doug."

Doug ignored Ray and kept hitting the clicker, eventually landing on the Golf Channel, where a tournament was in progress.

I felt hungry, suddenly. I wondered how the turkey was coming along.

The instant that Doug placed the remote control down on the coffee table, Ray swiped it and put the football game back on.

Doug smirked. "In case you're not aware of it, bro, golf is the fastest-growing sport in the country. You ought to pick up a club and learn how to play, do some networking. Be good for your career."

As Ray's jaw clenched, I fantasized about the rest of the meal. Was Sharon going with a basic bread stuffing for the turkey or something a bit showier? Chestnut, for instance? Or polenta?

"My career's fine," Ray said tightly. "I'm doing exactly what *I* want to do, not what my *father* told me I should do."

"Ouch," Doug said mockingly. "I guess that was supposed to be a putdown. Well, excuse me if I don't think it's a sin to follow in Dad's footsteps. I'm proud I'm a moneymaker like he was. *I* don't have to stay awake at night wondering how I'm going to pay my bills."

"Neither do I," said Ray. "Because *I* don't live beyond my means."

Perhaps Sharon is putting garlic in the mashed potatoes this year, I thought. Or maybe she's doing her sweet potato puree.

"Listen, Ray boy," said Doug, his tone laden with condescension. "You're embarrassing yourself in front of all these nice people."

"Really?" Ray replied, *his* tone dripping with sarcasm. "My impression is that all these nice people are wishing you'd take a hike and let us watch the game in peace."

The truth was, all the nice people were talking among themselves and completely oblivious to the tiff *and* the game. All but me, of course. I knew what was coming. I *dreaded* what was coming. After I had finally made up with Sharon, after she and I had finally settled our differences, after we had finally become the loving sisters our mother had implored us to become, our men were about to allow their own sibling rivalry to boil over. The irony was breathtaking.

"You want me to leave, is that it?" said Doug.

"If you put that lame golf tournament on again, *I'll* leave," said Ray.

They were both on their feet by this point, fulminating over which of them would be the one to walk out, when Sharon appeared.

"Dinner is served," she trilled.

And a Happy Thanksgiving to you, too.